I0679175

Also by

DAVID ABIS

CALAMITY IN SWEET SPOT:
A POLITICALLY UNCORRECT WHIRLWIND
REDNECK ROMANCE

THOUGH I WALK THROUGH THE VALLEY

LAST GIRL STANDING

VOICES IN MY HEAD

PURE CANE

VILLAGE IDIOTS

DAVID ABIS

Sweet Spot Publishing

Village Idiots

Sweet Spot Publishing

Paperback Edition

Copyright 2015 David Abis

All rights reserved.

This is a work of fiction. Names, character, places, and incidents either are the product of the author's imagination or are used fictitiously. Any resemblance to actual persons, living or dead, event, or locales is entirely coincidental.

Cover images courtesy of 4x6, Apaxvn, & istock.
Cover by Joleene Naylor.

ISBN 978-0-9907739-1-7
eBook ISBN 978-0-9907739-0

Chapter 1

"Dumb animals," muttered Benjamin Walker to his limousine driver, musing over the story in his New York Times about a manatee found swimming up the Hudson River. "I've never heard anything so pathetic in my life," he continued.

The driver eyed Ben through his rear view mirror and took the bait. "What is it? What's so funny?"

"Get a load of this, Roland," Ben began, sliding forward and shoving the section of his newspaper over the front seat. "Bessie the Manatee Spotted Off Manhattan." He had to stop and chuckle, "Bessie the manatee. Can you believe that? They've given it a name. It's like a pet now. New York's got a pet manatee." Then, resuming the article, "Bessie the manatee continues to baffle scientists as she is spotted swimming past the Statue of Liberty headed up the west side of Manhattan."

Roland had to interrupt. "What the hell is a manatee?"

"Here, it tells all about them. It's like National Geographic. Listen. These gentle creatures, now an endangered species, are native to the warm waters off the coast of Florida but have been known on occasion to wander north, rarely past the Carolinas. This particular twelve hundred-pound sea cow is making history as the first ever to take in the sights of the Big Apple."

Roland had to stop him again. "Wait. Twelve hundred pounds? It's a whale. Right? It's some kind of whale."

Ben had to laugh. "No. No, it's more like—"

"Do they bite?"

"Don't be ridiculous. Here, let me finish." Ben returned to the article. "With the approach of autumn, however, there's been growing concern for Bessie's health, and as the waters of the Hudson River begin to chill, marine biologists have begun to consider a possible rescue attempt, according to Bill Jensen of the Department of Environmental Protection, who says—"

Ben couldn't resist editorializing one last time. "Here. Here's the best part," he interjected, grabbing Roland by the shoulder. "Time may be running out for Bessie. She just doesn't belong here." With that, Ben fell back in his seat, crumpling the newspaper in laughter. "Did you hear that? Time may be running out for Bessie. She just doesn't belong here. You switched my New York Times for your Post, didn't you, Roland?" he joked, making a show of checking the front page to be sure his driver hadn't played a trick on him.

Roland just eyed him through the rear view.

Ben shook his head and rolled his eyes. "Just like those whales in California that beach themselves or head up some small river," moaned Ben. "A bunch of nuts always try to roll them back in the water or turn them around. They're probably just sick and looking for a place to die. Why else would they go where they do?"

"I don't know," Roland began. "I kind of feel sorry for the poor things. Maybe they're just lost and need a little help finding their way, you know, a little nudge in the right direction."

Ben looked out his window at the polluted Hudson River half hoping to get a glimpse of the pathetic creature as his father's limousine wandered north along Riverside Drive entering Spanish Harlem. Raised on the Upper East Side of Manhattan, never straying north of 86th Street, it didn't occur to Ben that Bessie might have been out there bobbing in the Hudson River watching the long black limousine, itself a native of midtown, straying dangerously north. Maybe Bessie was out there frantically waving her flippers trying to warn the shiny black creature to turn around and head south back home. It just didn't belong there.

For a second, Ben actually thought he saw something in the water as the limousine turned right, leaving the river and disappearing among the soot-covered tenements. More likely just the body of a victim of some gang related killing or drug deal gone bad, he thought to himself.

The car continued east, passing into the shadows of towering Columbia-Presbyterian Medical Center. Ben always hated that ride up to Columbia medical school, whether it was just after a three-day weekend at home or after summer break. It wasn't medical school he hated. Frankly, it was the neighborhood. And it was more fear than hate. One hundred Sixty-eighth Street, just off Broadway. Spanish Harlem, where haute cuisine was served up among the mutant cockroaches at a fine eatery known as Chinos y Latinos. He couldn't help chuckling to himself each time he recalled his first day at Columbia. The other students all presumed he knew his way around the neighborhood because he was born and raised in Manhattan. They thought he was kidding when he said he'd never been that far north, only 4 miles away from where he'd grown up. To Ben, however, the question wasn't why he'd never been there. The question was why *would* he have been that far north. There'd just never been any reason to do so. After all, civilization as Ben knew it, ceased to exist north of 86th.

Why is it the best medical schools are always in the worst neighborhoods? Ben wondered to himself. Surely they weren't that way at the time the schools and hospitals were built. Maybe it was the hospitals in fact that brought down the neighborhood. Had anyone ever considered that? Well, in any case, it was bad now. This is what Ben pondered in the summer of 1990 as his dad's limousine stopped for a red light within a block of the hospital.

"I can't believe the blood stain where that pediatric intern was murdered last week is still there on the sidewalk?" Ben said rhetorically to his driver, pressing his cheek to the window for a better look. "It was over a week ago. Killed for eight dollars and a subway token." Then adding with a groan, "What am I doing here?"

At the next corner, they came to another red light. This time, a staggering black gentleman approached the front of the car. All men, no matter how tattered, are referred to as gentlemen among the medical profession. This particular citizen was wearing a carefully chosen ensemble of rags, the only purpose of which appeared to be to keep the body lice warm. The man started washing the windshield of Ben's limo in hopes of garnishing a tip from the well-to-do visitors. There was no question in Ben's mind that the man's washrag was indeed a pair of torn Fruit of the Looms. What he couldn't quite discern was what he was using for washing solution. There was a certain yellow tinge to it, but even Ben's opinion of the neighborhood couldn't quite convince him that bodily fluids were involved.

As the limousine drove on, ignoring the windshield washer's outheld palm, Ben couldn't help wondering how much better the man's tips might have been if only his reluctant customers could have paid him *not* to wash their windshields.

Turning onto 168th Street, the driver stopped in front of the homeless shelter across from the hospital emergency room. The main hospital entrance was a little further down the block, but the driver was reluctant to let his recently waxed limousine pass too closely to the car engulfed in flames just past the ER.

No, this wasn't the result of a horrible traffic accident. It was, instead, simply a poor choice for a parking space. It was no excuse that the man drove up to the ER in pain and practically crawled inside clutching his chest. It was no excuse that he was promptly admitted to the cardiac care unit with a probable myocardial infarction. He should have known better. The medical residents routinely passing the ER would bet among themselves how many days it would take for the local scavengers to strip a car down to its frame. The obvious goes in the first few hours, possessions within the passenger compartment, and stereo equipment, followed quickly by the contents of the trunk. The wheels and tires go next. By nightfall, the hood is open and various elements of the engine compartment begin to disappear. By the next morning, all mechanical components, including the motor, are gone. Between twenty-four and thirty-six hours after the time the car was parked, the body panels have been stripped and only the well-picked steel skeleton remains. It is at any point during the dismantling process that one or more of the scavengers will, for reasons not yet understood, set the car on fire. No one seemed disturbed by the impromptu cremations. It was just business as usual across the street from the entrance to the emergency room.

Another bit of local color included a wiry Jamaican six-footer affectionately referred to as Buck the Preacher, usually seen bounding down the street in a jerky sort of hop, skip, and jump, yelling at the top of his lungs.

"The Lord shall *strike* thee down, oh Satan! I am the *Lord's* hammer and I shall do the Lord's bidding!"

Unlike a blazing automotive inferno, however, Buck could not be ignored. He'd been known to act out occasionally, involving random passers-by in his version of the Lord's justice. A completely unexpected round house right to the jaw involving anyone within Buck's striking distance had brought many a new customer into the Presbyterian ER.

"I hear thy call, oh Lord, and Satan cannot hide! The *hammer* shall not forsake thee!"

Most people familiar with Buck knew the warning signs of an impending strike. One particular two-word phrase would send them running for cover.

"*Hammer time!*" roared Buck suddenly veering from the middle of the street toward the curb.

The meter maid never saw it coming. Fortunately, Buck's aim had no more control than did his id. The blow was only a glancing one, and as a couple of nursing students helped the dazed woman up, Buck vanished down the steps descending into the dark caverns of the 168th Street subway terminal.

Buck had made several cameo appearances at the neighboring Psychiatric Institute, Ben's very destination on his first day of clinical rounds. He was beginning his third year of medical school, the day they finally let the eager young doctors-to-be out of the lecture halls and laboratories and into the hospital, trading their slow-witted but docile cadavers for the somewhat more animated but vastly less cooperative live patients. While the Psych Institute did maintain a locked ward, it was not equipped to handle violent patients. And so, as many times as Buck had made an appearance there, so was he promptly deposited back on the street after abruptly striking a nurse without warning.

It wasn't just the Psych Institute that harbored patients with ill will toward their caregivers. With a significant proportion afflicted by either drug/alcohol addiction or violence-related trauma, doctor-patient encounters at Presbyterian Hospital were more like hand-to-hand combat. Marcus Welby never had patients like this. Students were routinely robbed by patients and accosted by their families.

His cloistered prep-school upbringing in the posh Walker flat on the Upper East Side and his four years as an undergraduate at exclusive Harvard University had hardly prepared him for his adventures in Spanish Harlem at Columbia University's College of Physicians & Surgeons. He'd tried to understand the cultural flavor and nuances of the indigenous population. He just didn't get it. According to Ben's father, a successful surgeon on the Upper East Side, Ben was there to learn a trade, and the local hospital clientele were merely lab rats on whom Ben could hone his skills. When he finished medical school, he would leave, setting up a comfortable practice back in civilization.

But Ben hadn't learned to despise his patients just yet. He hadn't actually heard very many of his father's opinions, seeing as his father was never around. And he was just starting his clinical rotations, still very much bright-eyed and bushy-tailed. He wouldn't have known an Uzi-carrying gang member from a boy scout. They both wore uniforms after all.

For now, anyway, the coast was clear. Buck was gone. All appeared relatively safe to cross 168th Street into the hospital. Ben leaned over the front seat of the limousine to address his driver.

"Well, here goes, Roland. Thanks for the lift."

"No problem, Ben. You be careful out there. Keep your eyes open. This neighborhood really sucks."

"Come on, Roland. These are my patients you're talking about. They're just a little different," Ben joked. He opened the door, tentatively placing one foot onto the sidewalk.

"You just watch your step around here, Ben."

Ben stepped out of the car with his duffle bag and closed the door. He waved as the limousine pulled away, already missing the soothing smell of the fine leather upholstery.

Hoisting the bag to his shoulder he stepped off the curb, only to stumble face first onto the street as his right shoe came off, seemingly glued to the sidewalk.

"What the hell?" Ben righted himself and went to retrieve his shoe. The heel was stuck to the pavement. As Ben tugged, the soiled condom stuck to the sole stretched a good twelve inches before relinquishing Ben's shoe with a snap.

"Toto, we're not in Kansas anymore," he muttered to himself, sitting down on the curb to put his shoe back on. He'd hardly noticed the frail old Asian gentleman approaching as he slipped his foot into the shoe. It was only when the shuffling old man was within two feet of him that Ben looked up. That's when the man's coughing began, a deep, wet, gurgling cough, bringing forth all matter of aerosolized secretions directly into Ben's face.

Chapter 2

Looking skyward as he approached the revolving door that was the entrance to Presbyterian Hospital, Ben tried to imagine what the gargoyle-trimmed building would look like without the construction scaffolding temporarily masking its true facade. The temporary scaffolding had been there since Ben could remember, now entering his third year of medical school. He'd never seen anyone actually working on the building nor had he ever been able to decipher what was wrong with it. Yet there it was, a never-ending work in progress.

Ben knew his calling the first time he walked through those doors two years ago. There'd never been any question that he was to become a surgeon. His father was a surgeon on staff for many years at Presbyterian, well known and respected. Now in private practice, there was no longer any reason for the house staff to fear Harrison Walker. Fear could now be replaced by respect. Most of the surgeons currently on staff had trained under Ben's father at one time or another. The days of the giants, they would say. In the operating room, Dr. Walker would grill the students and residents unmercifully with various questions of minutia. Preparing to assist in something as mundane as a hemorrhoidectomy was like preparing to go to war. Be prepared for anything.

Name eight causes of hemorrhoids. Why do fighter pilots have a higher incidence of them? What G-forces do they routinely experience? Is it greater than or less than the force exerted by a woman's Valsalva during childbirth? In what year was sterile suture first used? Why is suture the color it is? What country is it made in?

While one might reasonably have prepared oneself to answer a few of these questions, most of them seemed to come from well beyond left field. Some were not even in the stadium. There were three possible explanations posed for the nature of Dr. Walker's quizzing. The first, and most subscribed to, was that Dr. Walker knew the answers to every question and enjoyed watching the clueless students and residents squirm. A second explanation, favored among the hard drinkers, was that Dr. Walker knew none of the answers and was only asking the questions out of honest curiosity, hoping some third year student might enlighten him. The last explanation, favored among the paranoid, was that no one knew the answers to the questions and the great doctor only wanted to see how his disciples performed under pressure, enjoying an occasional chuckle at the students expense over ridiculous responses offered for fear of saying the dreaded "I don't know."

Dr. Harrison Walker no longer darkened the corridors of Presbyterian Hospital in body, but his legend lived on, haunting the memories of those now on staff.

The team of surgeons now calling the shots at Presbyterian were not the only ones whose lives had been affected by Dr. Walker. Benjamin Walker had, after all, grown up in his father's home. True, the elder Walker was seldom present, instead choosing the life of the academic deity to walk among his worshipping minions. Although Benjamin seldom saw him, he knew who his father was. "So what kind of surgeon are you going to be?" visitors would ask little Ben. It was never a question of whether Ben would become a doctor. And it was always to be a surgeon. The only options available were what kind of surgeon.

Yes, Harrison had an influence on little Ben, even in absentia. Ben's childhood fear of swimming pools was famous. You see, Ben knew all about Pasteur's germ theory, even as a child. He would analyze the pool water through his microscope for hours. He was convinced then that only no good could come from placing one's body in it. The bacterial counts were simply too high. He routinely carried a spray can of Lysol to school in his lunch box.

Growing up, his studies occupied his formative school years. His only relationships were formed on the debate team and quiz bowl. While other teenage boys ogled their dads' Playboy magazines by flashlight under the covers, Ben learned about sex from his father's Gray's Anatomy.

There was one girl, however, that made her mark on Ben. Jill Sterling was on the swim team. No, Ben hadn't quite gotten over the germ thing. But beautiful Jill Sterling in her tight blue and gold swim suit had a powerful effect on him. Alas, puberty had not been completely snuffed out by studies and phobias. Ben worshipped Jill. She was the one he dreamed of all through his dateless pre-med college years, endless reruns of his relatively carefree high school days with Jill. Ben was sure she must have been over the prom night incident by now. Studying for his college entrance exams clearly took precedence. She'd understand that eventually. Nevertheless, Ben harbored a certain guilt over not taking Jill to the prom. It all turned out for the best anyway. He'd aced the exams after all, gotten into Harvard, and then to his father's alma mater for medical school. There'd be other Jills. And surely someone as great as she would find someone else. Ben often wondered what became of her.

Ben entered the hospital and approached the security desk manned by a rotund black man whose uniform appeared several sizes too small. Even his policeman-like cap looked tiny atop his big round head. "Which elevator to the Psych Institute?" Ben inquired.

"You crazy?"

"No, why?"

"Den whatchou want wit da nut house?"

"I'm a med student and I'm starting a rotation there today."

"How you gonna fix dem nut cakes?"

"Well, I don't know yet."

"Shit. Ain't nothin you gonna do fo dem folks."

Ben couldn't disagree. In his heart he too felt this psychiatry rotation was a waste of time. Medicine and surgery each had something to offer. Medicine had things like antibiotics. Surgery used scalpels and sutures. What did psychiatry have? Just sedatives and theories. While medicine was less direct, you could actually see the problem and physically fix it in surgery. Students interested in internal medicine looked forward to talking to patients, holding their hands, and doling out pills, while Ben dreamt of removing tumors, bullets, and silicone breast implants.

Work rounds in surgery began at 5 AM, drawing blood, measuring urine output, collecting labs, eyeballing the patients with a quick note in the chart. Rounds with the chief resident followed, then off to surgery. The patients had no names. They were their procedures. Hernia repair in room 602. Colectomy in 618. It was all so efficient. No rambling notes in the chart about the patients' social situation or mental status. One or two words would suffice. There were only three options. Improving, no change, or deteriorating. Procedures were where it was at. How many different procedures could you master during your three-month rotation?

Ben tried to imagine what procedures he'd be learning in psychiatry. Too bad lobotomies were currently out of vogue.

"Well, I guess I'd better get up there and see what I can do," said Ben.

"You just wastin' yo' time." Pointing to the right," Third elevator. Tenth floor. Then walk down one flight to eleven."

Ben looked confused. "Walk *down* from the tenth to the eleventh? Don't you mean *up*?"

The guard was offended. "Do I look crazy to you? You think I don't know up from down?" He then started mumbling to himself. "Damn students. Can't follow simple directions."

Ben sensed his irritation. "I'm sorry. So, it's the elevator to the tenth floor. Then one flight *down* to the eleventh."

"Now you got it."

"Thanks," said Ben as he turned to head toward the elevators.

The guard continued to mumble under his breath. "Damn kids nowadays. No respect." Then, seeing Ben heading toward the wrong set of elevators, "Hey kid! Not those. The other ones. There."

Ben shifted to the correct set of elevators.

"Poor kid," continued the guard. Then with one last word of advice for Ben. "Hey! You watch your back. Dey crazy up dare."

"Thanks."

Ben was surprised to see how full the elevator was when it opened in front of him on the first floor. Only one person got out. Those familiar with the hospital knew the only sure way to get on the elevator to go up was to walk up one flight and board on the way down from the second floor. That's right. Grab the down elevator to go up. Ben had a lot to learn. Fortunately, there was now one vacancy.

As the elevator climbed, the net flow of passengers on and off was zero, scarce openings rapidly filled. At the eighth floor, when Ben was shoved out to allow those behind him to exit, the doors suddenly closed behind him.

"Hey, Virginia, the student's here for the blood," the blood bank technologist yelled over her shoulder.

Turning away from the elevator, Ben began, "No, I'm just—"

"Don't worry about it kid. Better late than never. Here," she said, handing three bags of blood to Ben through the Blood Bank window.

"But I'm not—"

"Go on. They're waiting on that blood. Patient's in the OR bleeding from everywhere. Go on! Move!" She shooed him away toward the now open elevator door behind him, arms stacked with blood products.

"But I have to go to—"

The elevator doors closed as the word psychiatry left his lips. The other passengers all stepped back from the man carrying bags of blood in need of a psychiatrist.

The elevator doors opened in front of the operating rooms. As Ben stepped through the doors marked "authorized personnel only" and approached the nursing station, he was immediately aware of the no nonsense atmosphere where life and death decisions were made without hesitation. No talk of pills or therapies. Instead, scalpels and sutures were used for immediate cures with visible results.

A nurse showed Ben where the scrubs were, and throwing on a pair, he entered the sterile white corridor with his plastic bags of blood headed to OR 4. The antiseptic smell in the air and the fast pace of the masked OR personnel had Ben's adrenaline pumping.

"Blood here," said Ben approaching the anesthesiologist at the patient's head.

"Who's that?" asked Dr. Henderson without looking up from his patient's open abdomen where he was rapidly tying off bleeders.

"Ben Walker, sir. Third year medical student."

"Benjamin Walker? You're not Harrison Walker's boy, are you?"

"That's me, sir," replied Ben, handing off the blood and moving behind the surgeon for a better look at the open abdomen. "What do you have here?" asked Ben, whose curiosity got the better of him.

"What do I have here? A train wreck. Motorcycle versus bus. Who do you think wins that one?"

"Bus every time," replied Ben.

"And you guys thought they didn't learn anything the first two years," kidded Dr. Henderson to his chief resident.

"Hey, Ben," said Dr. Henderson. "Why don't you scrub in and join us. Grab a retractor. We could use a hand."

"I'd love to, but I can't," said Ben. I'm already late for my first day on psychiatry."

"Psychiatry? No."

"Yeah, I know. Don't rub it in," said Ben.

"Hey, enjoy it while you can. Good hours, call's a joke, and a bunch of nuts to entertain you all day. It's like going to the circus."

"Yeah, but will I learn anything useful? Do they ever cure anyone?"

"No on both accounts," said the chief resident. "But, you know, I've dated some of those twisted women residents. They're really in touch with some warped sexual fantasies. It helps the time pass anyway. And then before you know it, your three-month rotation is over and you're back to the real world of general surgery. Hey, Dr. Henderson. You know, I don't think this bowel looks too good," he said looking at the angry violaceous color of the blood-deprived intestines. "Too much blood loss?"

"His torn spleen and kidney are already in the bucket over there. We've sewn up all the bowel lacerations. The problem here is that this train wreck is going into D.I.C., disseminated intravascular coagulation. Due to overwhelming shock, his blood clotting system is shot. We could pour blood into this guy all day and he won't stop bleeding. We're wasting our time. Let's close up. He just isn't cooperating and we don't want him to die on the table. That'd be an intraoperative death and there'd be all kinds of paperwork to fill out."

"Right you are," said the chief resident. "Let's not waste any more time here. Let's find a more salvageable patient, more worthy of our time and effort. Nurse, can you call preop and tell them to prep John Doe II."

"Doctor, our instrument count is off," said the circulating nurse. "There's a clamp missing. Is anything left in the abdomen?"

"No time to worry about that," replied Dr. Henderson. "This guy isn't dying in *my* OR. Let's close him up."

"Well, I gotta go. The nuts are waiting," said Ben heading for the door. "Sorry this guy didn't work out."

"Wait. Ben," called Dr. Henderson. "This guy will be gone before they get him to recovery. Could you make sure he gets to the morgue. I'm afraid if he lingers up here, the paperwork will haunt us."

"I'm really going to be late for rounds," Ben protested half-heartedly.

"Come on. It's only psychiatry, for God's sake. They probably spend the whole first day discussing the doctor patient relationship or medical ethics or some other crap like that anyway."

"Or Freud's theory of scalpel envy, where all psychiatrists secretly wish they were surgeons," added the chief resident with a chuckle.

"Well, I guess a few minutes won't matter," allowed Ben.

He followed the entourage escorting the patient out of the room to recovery. Blood and fluids were being pumped in as the dying patient's belly began to swell from continued bleeding into the abdomen. A nurse continued artificially aerating his lungs with an ambu bag as his monitor showed an agonal heart rhythm. Ben had to agree that he'd be surprised if John Doe made it to recovery. Too bad. Ben truly did feel bad. But he didn't kid himself to think that caring mattered. If anything, it would only get in your way, cloud your judgment. You had to treat the body, not the patient. For surgeons, the patients had no names, no stories, just diseases or mechanical breakdowns in need of correction.

Well Johnny Doe's warrantee had run out. The nurses in recovery were debating whether his heart would hold out long enough to hook him up to the respirator.

Sure enough, no sooner than they'd plugged in the respirator, John Doe went flat line.

Ben was late for rounds.

Chapter 3

Why was the morgue always located in the basement? Ben wondered as he pushed the gurney carrying pulseless John Doe toward the back service elevator. Perhaps there, patients' families wandering the upper floors would be less likely to run into one of their dearly departed en route to their new accommodations. At least Ben wouldn't have to deal with the patient's family in Mr. Doe's case, if he had one. He was merely transporting the body to the morgue. Ben dreaded the thought of talking to the patients' families, especially if the news was bad, almost as much as talking to the patients themselves. And it wasn't that he'd learned to be that way in school. He'd never been good at dealing with people. All that had been taken care of by Ben's father or the family servants.

The elevator stopped at the basement. The doors didn't open. Ben suffered a sudden sense of dread that he might be stuck in an elevator with a dead person. Well this was one way to get close to your patients. Not the way Ben would have chosen. Ben pressed the open door button. He let his breath audibly escape as the doors miraculously opened.

"Let's get out of here, John." Ben wheeled the gurney down the hall to the morgue. He rang the bell. He'd observed a couple of autopsies as a student and knew the purpose of the bell was to avoid visitors or queasy hospital workers from walking into the middle of a full-blown autopsy in progress.

One could envision Aunt Ethel getting lost on her way to visit Uncle George. Imagine her reaction entering what she thought was her husband's hospital room only to find a dead body on a table, entrails exposed, not to mention that tell-tale autopsy stench. Students usually found the stench to be the most objectionable aspect of the autopsy. After all, there wasn't anything about the body or its parts that they hadn't experienced in medical school anatomy class. But the odor was an entirely different story. Anatomy class was known for the strong scent of formaldehyde, used to preserve the body, not a pleasant perfume itself. Autopsies, on the other hand, were fresh. In most situations, fresh is a good thing. The autopsy is not one of those situations. Even in the absence of some kind of festering abscess or gangrenous stench, one mustn't forget the liters of gastrointestinal contents confronted during your average autopsy, substances varying from something vaguely resembling breakfast to something similar to that which is found in a soiled baby's diaper, only in much greater quantities, literally, buckets full. And while some might reminisce fondly of days on the farm inhaling the sweet smell of horse manure, no one would even remotely attempt to associate a pleasant memory with the smell of ripe human excrement.

There was a muffled shout from the back of the morgue. "Autopsy in progress. Enter at your own risk. For the squeamish at heart, *go away!*"

Ben reached for the doorknob, then remembered what a pathology resident had told him on a previous mission to the morgue. He quickly pulled the sleeve of his white lab coat down over his hand before grabbing the knob. He'd been guaranteed that someone at some point in the day would be too lazy or stupid to remove their bloody, soiled, possibly infectious autopsy gloves before opening that door for one reason or another. And although Ben supposed this was more of a problem concerning the knob on the other side of the door, he had no intention of letting logic get in the way of perfectly justified paranoia.

There it was. The smell. Ben brought in Mr. Doe.

"Got another customer," announced Ben.

"Oh yeah? People are just dying to get in here," said the pathology resident, up to his elbows in another visitor's internal organs. "Could you just slide him into the fridge with the other guests?"

"No problem." Ben wheeled John over to the wall of small stainless steel doors with slide-out drawers. As he opened one door after another looking for a vacancy, he was startled at the sight of John Doe's new roommates. It wasn't as if Ben had expected to see something else. They just seemed so cold and lifeless that he had a hard time imagining they'd ever been breathing human beings. He'd always tried to think of patients simply as the sum of their parts without accounting for the intangible personality factor, the part that makes them human. Ben had to turn away from the wall of refrigerated drawers as he felt a chill run through his boxer shorts. Whatever it was they'd died from wouldn't bother them anymore. At least all their problems were over. Ben suddenly felt a twinge of guilt as it occurred to him that the relief he felt was more for him than the deceased patients, relief that they could no longer be *his* problem. He'd never have to get to know them. He'd never have to worry about the sum of their parts.

Ben was backing away from the refrigerator, unconsciously afraid to turn his back on the wall of dead, when he heard a sloshing splat sound at his feet.

"Damn!" shouted the pathology resident. Ben found him on his hands and knees under the stainless steel table that carried the half-dissected remains of his very quiet patient.

"I hate when this happens. How do you lose a brain?" The pathology resident stood up, staring at the open very empty skull. It was here a minute ago. I cut the spinal cord and it flopped out. It's gotta be right here," he said gesturing at the floor.

"Looking for this?" asked Ben staring at his feet. He'd nearly slipped on the now somewhat flattened brain as gravity attempted to shape the Jell-O-like white matter to the floor beneath it.

"Hey! There you are," said the pathology resident as if locating a lost puppy. "I can't believe it could slide that distance. Like it had a mind of its own. Hey, that's a good one. Get it? A mind of its own?"

Ben did get it. He wasn't laughing though. Pathologist humor was an acquired taste. It takes a certain amount of daily exposure to grow accustomed to things most people only see in bad horror movies. But once acquainted with the little things that make pathology the butt of much humor, the opportunities for jokes abound. And like the class clown who learns to burp on demand or turn his eyelids inside out, they present themselves in a relentless fashion like a bad case of the runs.

"Listen, I've got to go. You take care of Johnny now," said Ben.

"Wait," answered the pathology resident, happy to have someone to speak to, at least someone who was still breathing. "How'd they kill this one?"

"Who?"

"The surgeons. How'd they kill this guy?"

"They didn't kill him," replied Ben. "A truck killed him."

"Oh. Well don't take it personally. You may not believe this, but I've actually seen surgeons close a patient up with a clamp still in the belly just so they could get him out of the OR before he died, just to avoid the added paper work."

Ben felt a pang of guilt by association. "You're kidding."

"No, it's true. They treat their patients like pieces of meat," he said, scooping the gelatinous brain up off the floor with his gloved hands. "Could you hand me that bucket?" Ben grabbed the bucket of formaldehyde. The fumes made his eyes tear. "They don't really care about their patients. They're just temporary projects for them on which to learn some new procedure."

"You're one to say they treat their patients like meat," protested Ben, watching the pathology resident neatly carve his subject's liver into slices like a loaf of bread.

The pathology resident picked up a heart and paused. "Have you ever noticed the number of pathology terms that refer to food? Just in the liver alone, congestion is described as nutmeg liver, and an amoebic abscess classically has the appearance of anchovy paste. Honeycomb lung is seen with emphysema, and sarcomatous tumors are described as having the appearance of fish flesh, which even through the microscope displays a herringbone pattern.

But you're right. It's true. I don't have to talk to my patients, or their families for that matter. If something bad happens to a patient, it's usually too late by the time I discover it. Even then, I report my findings to the patient's physician and he then has the pleasure of telling the grief-stricken family. That's why I'm here. When it finally occurred to me in medical school that a lot of patients just didn't get better, I realized I wasn't up to telling them how much longer they had to live, watching them die, handing out tissues to crying family members. But there's a difference between me and the surgeons I've known here. Maybe I can't handle it and would rather hide down here instead. But I care. If surgeons can't afford the time to comfort their patients or simply can't handle it, well then, they ought to get out of the kitchen. Do the whole job or find another one.

Hey look," he remarked, holding the sliced heart under Ben's nose, "a broken heart."

Ben gave him a disgusted look, pulling his head back.

"No really," continued the pathology resident. "This is what killed him. Looks like he had an MI about a week ago. Just when they thought he would pull through, he unexpectedly ruptured a ventricular wall aneurysm, where the wall weakened by the MI had ballooned out. A classic post-MI complication resulting in death. I'm telling you. He died of a broken heart. Get it?"

"I get it. I get it. Hey, I'm late for rounds," said Ben turning to leave.

"Don't get a lot of clients from psych," mused the pathology resident. "Probably because they don't have any surgeons up there."

"Don't worry. I won't kill anyone."

"I hope not, cause like I said, they're just dying to get in here. Ha ha! Gotcha again. I'm tellin' ya. You could bust a gut in here. Hey look. Here's one now."

"One what?"

"A busted gut." As the pathology resident held up a segment of torn large intestine for Ben's viewing pleasure, Ben reached for the doorknob with his sleeve-covered hand.

If that was sanity, Ben began to wonder what the psych ward would be like. He took the service elevator up to the tenth floor and walked down the hall where the old building connected with the new one, walked down a flight and ended up on the eleventh floor. It was one of those things that always fascinated the new students, how one could go down a flight of steps and end up on a higher floor. Of course, it had something to do with the fact that the height of the floors, or the space between them, of the two originally separate, now joined buildings, differed, resulting in the eleventh floor of one being lower than the tenth of the other. Soon enough, however, as most things in life tend to do, they balanced out. That's because, for superstitious reasons, the building with the taller floors had no thirteenth floor. That's where the shorter floored building caught up to the floor numbers of the taller. By the end of one's first couple of months on the wards, it all became rather natural, like the imperfections of a genuine pearl necklace. Of course, neither the patients nor their visitors ever had sufficient exposure to fully comprehend the situation, and instead, usually presumed they'd suffered a momentary loss of concentration, ending up on the unintended floor.

Ben approached the door to the ward. Over a small window in the door, a sign read "Authorized Personnel Only." On the wall, next to the doorknob, another sign read "Door to remain locked at all times. Visitors and other unauthorized personnel must ring doorbell for admittance." Ben rang the bell. He was startled when a face immediately filled the small window of the door. Ben reflexively stepped back from the door. When a buzzer sounded and the door opened, he didn't know what to expect.

The face at the window belonged to a plump bearded gentleman in a brown corduroy suit. A smile appeared on his face as he gestured with joviality for Ben to enter.

"Velcome, velcome, Dr. Valker. Come in. Come in. Ve've been expecting you. I'm Dr. Brunning."

Ben almost choked on the thick German accent.

"Sorry I'm late. I was detoured by a surgical emergency," said Ben, somewhat relieved by the warm welcome received despite his tardiness.

"Oh, perfectly understandable," said the doctor, taking Ben by the arm. "Ve all realize our patients' maladies don't always adhere to our schedules. Come right zis vay. Ve've already started rounds." Ben followed Dr. Brunning to the meeting room at the back of the nursing station. Entering the small room, Ben saw two residents, an intern, and another student seated at a table. Dr. Gelner, the chief resident stood up.

"Ah, Dr. Brunning, I see you've found our stray Dr. Walker. Thank you ever so much."

"My pleasure, Dr. Gelner," replied Dr. Brunning. "Benjamin, let me introduce you to my esteemed colleagues. Dr. Gelner is my chief resident, Drs. Golding and Morales, second and third year residents, and our soon to be doctor, Ms. Chin, our other student, you already know."

A nurse opened the door a crack and motioned to Dr. Brunning. "Doctor, you're needed in the recreation room."

Dr. Brunning had already taken a seat at the table. "Is it urgent nurse? You can see ve're right in zee middle of rounds."

"I'm afraid it is, Doctor. The oatmeal raisin cookies are running low, and I know how particular you are." A panicked expression came over Dr. Brunning's face and he turned to Ben.

"Vell, Benjamin, I apologize for zis untimely interruption, but you see, here in psychiatry, ve too have emergencies. I'd better get over zere before ze lunatics get all ze oatmeal raisin cookies. I detest Oreos, you know. Good luck here. I know Dr. Gelner vill take good care of you." The doctor left the room.

"Sorry, Dr. Gelner," said the nurse, closing the door behind her.

Ben turned to the chief resident. "Sweet tooth?" he said referring to Dr. Brunning. The others laughed.

Dr. Gelner began, "Had you been here anywhere near on time, you'd have already heard all about Dr. Brunning's sweet tooth, as well as his psychotic delusions of being a colleague of Sigmund Freud's."

Ben felt like a fool. "You meaning Dr. Brunning is a…"

"…patient," finished Dr. Gelner. "Congratulations Dr. Walker. Your first diagnosis. And you've only been here three minutes."

"Oops," responded Ben.

"I take it psychiatry will not be your chosen field."

"Actually, no," said Ben. "I'll be going into surgery. General surgery, to be exact."

"Didn't anyone ever tell you you're supposed to say your going into whatever specialty you happen to be on at the moment. That way the chief resident, that would be me, gives you a better grade thinking you're one of his kind."

"Wouldn't that be dishonest?" asked Ben.

"No, that would be brown-nosing, which is perfectly acceptable behavior during medical training. In fact, I think it was probably covered in your orientation packet the day you arrived at Columbia. Didn't you read it?"

"Well, I—"

"Where did you go to college anyway, Dr. Walker?"

"Harvard," replied Ben a little too eagerly, unable to hide a slight air of superiority.

"Oh, not another one. Are you some kind of gifted individual, or just a regular Hah-vud guy?" jabbed Dr. Gelner, emphasis on the Boston accent.

"Regular, I guess."

"Good choice. Well, Hah-vud, let's get to work."

Dr. Gelner stood up, a signal that they were about to go on rounds. The rest of the group did the same, following him out the door. Amy Chin followed, pushing the cart carrying the patients' charts. Ben fell in step behind her.

"Ben," called Dr. Gelner, "since you were the last to honor us with your presence this morning, being from Hah-vud and all, I will return the favor by honoring you with today's first admission after rounds."

Heading down the hallway, Ben couldn't help but stare at the assorted misfits residing on the ward. They seemed to Ben to represent a TV sitcom writer's gold mine.

There was Anastasia, the little old lady who claimed to be the missing daughter of Russian Czar Nicholas II, the remainder of the family having been wiped out by the Bolsheviks. Her accent was thick, and when they finally figured out the language she spoke wasn't Russian, it was enlightening to discover it was Yiddish. While that certainly did not exclude Russia as her birthplace, it absolutely ruled it out as her birthright, unless the czar was a closet Jew.

Her moth-eaten black fur coat never left her back. The lining was rumored to be stuffed with over $100,000. She wouldn't let anyone close enough to confirm or deny those rumors. Even if she had, the smell of the coat would have repelled all but the most desperate of thieves.

Anastasia was a "traveler." She lived with her daughter's family in San Jose, California. But a couple of times a year she got the traveling bug. Without a word to the family or any semblance of a plan, she'd grab her fur coat, head out the front door, and board the first bus she saw. A few transfers later and she'd be somewhere at the other end of the country. She generally reached a psychiatric facility after being found wandering the bus station, the street, or the men's room at an upscale restaurant.

Then there was Frankie Ventano, whose day was not complete until he'd convinced someone to give him a rectal exam. A teaching hospital is crawling with eager young medical students, all too quick to fall for his delusional fear of harboring a malignant rectal tumor somehow missed on yesterday's three rectal exams.

On the other hand, one mustn't forget Mrs. Mintz, the thin nervous wreck on the ward the previous year who was admitted by her family physician after insisting for two years that she'd had a brain tumor. All nature of scans and blood tests revealed no such tumor. After a week on the ward, when a new student asked her where her tumor was, and she pointed to her head, he was literal enough to ask his resident if it wasn't the mole on her temple she was pointing at and not her brain. A resident's ridicule on rounds, a dermatology consult, and a biopsy later, Mrs. Mintz's malignant melanoma was finally a reality. She'd proved the expression, "Just because you're paranoid, doesn't mean they're not out to get you." Of course, the confirmation that she actually did have cancer didn't improve the situation, sending her immediately into a catatonic state, where she remained, calmly reassured, awaiting her inevitable demise from metastatic melanoma.

There was Erik Robinson, a.k.a. Erika, a thin black man who may have experienced some psychological distress during his teenage years due to his homosexuality, but certainly seemed at home with it in his thirties. He enjoyed modeling his latest outfits for the other inhabitants of the ward. He would paint the fingernails of anyone that would let him. Erika simply seemed to enjoy the ambiance of the ward and had to continually stretch his imagination to keep finding ways of getting readmitted.

The nurses referred to him as the den mother. He took care of all the newcomers to the ward, virgins as he called them. And that included the new medical students.

"Well, show's over," said Dr. Gelner, concluding rounds. "Those of you with patients can chart a short note based upon this morning's tour. Those fortunate enough to have no patients, might as well take advantage of that rare pleasure to get some more coffee or do some laundry, or do *my* laundry maybe. Oh, and Ben, don't forget. You're up for today's first admission. So be back within the hour. It shouldn't take longer than that for New York City to regurgitate some kind of mental misfit into our ER."

The group began to disperse. Erika, the den mother, knew this was the first day of a new student rotation. He carefully scanned the group and spied the new face.

"Hey, Amy girl!" Erika called to the other medical student with Ben. "Who's your new boyfriend?" he flirted.

"He's not my boyfriend. He's the new student."

"Oh, a new stud," said Erika batting his eyelashes and smoothing his hair. "And he's available. Hey, what's your name, baby?"

Rounds were over but Ben couldn't get away before Erika spotted him. "Benjamin Walker. Just started today," replied Ben.

Erika shamelessly sashayed over to Ben and took him by the elbow, strolling down the hall.

"Well, Benjamin, you can just call me Mrs. Robinson. Coo-coo-cachoo."

"Uh, Dr. Gelner?" Ben called out, looking for an escape.

Erika persisted.

"I think I'm having a heart flutter. Or maybe it's just hot flashes." He pulled Ben closer. "Anyway, I think I need a complete physical, stat."

"Uh, Dr. Gelner?" Ben felt the perspiration forcing itself from the pores in his forehead. "Amy? Anyone? Help."

"Or maybe just a pelvic exam." Erika was incorrigible.

Ben managed to make it to the ward exit. He tugged on the doorknob as Erika tugged on his elbow. No luck. The door was locked. Ben couldn't escape the locked ward. He whirled around looking for a button of some kind or someone to assist him. He saw a box on the wall nearby with a slot for a card.

"Your ID card. That's your ticket out of here." Erika flicked at the ID clipped to Ben's lapel, and snuggled closer. "Or you could spend a little time at my place," he said looking deeply into Ben's eyes.

Ben turned, grabbing the card from his lapel. He slid it through the slot on the wall box and yanked on the doorknob. It wouldn't budge. He turned and ran the card through again. Again, no movement from the door. He ran the card through again, three times, in rapid succession, and shook the door attempting to force it open.

Erika sighed. He walked past Ben, shaking his head in disappointment, and approached the wall box.

"Poor boy. You don't know what you're missing." He reached into his pocket and pulled out an ID card. He slid it through the slot and the door clicked. "I guess your card isn't activated yet."

"Hey, where did you get—"

"Now just you hush and never mind about that," said Erika, holding his finger to his lips.

"But—"

"I suggest you make your move," said Erika holding the door open, then eying Ben up and down, "before I do."

Ben leaped through the open exit and scurried down the hall, dropping first his clipboard, then his backpack while bending over to retrieve the clipboard.

"Cute buns!" called Erika. He watched Ben turn the corner, stepped back into the ward, and shut the door. He leaned back against the door and placed a hand over one breast.

"Just look at me, acting like a lovesick school girl. I should be ashamed of myself."

Ben's hands were still shaking as he tried to sip his hot coffee in the cafeteria. And as he remembered that he was first up for new admissions, the extra pounding of his heart made the tremors uncontrollable, sending a good portion of his hot coffee spilling onto his shoes.

Chapter 4

Angel McGovern was a genius with a long history of hypersexual manic depression.

It was apparent to anyone who knew her history that Angel had acquired her disorder at a very early age. Many suspected it might be reportable as the first documented case of manic depression having a congenital onset.

Early on, it was evident that she seemed to be ahead of the other children in all areas of cognitive development. No one could recall teaching Angel to read. But by the time she'd begun kindergarten, her teacher would find copies of her mother's Cosmopolitan magazines in Angel's cubby. While the other kids would look at the pretty ladies in the fashion section, Angel would read the articles to them. "Ten Ways to Keep Your Extramarital Affair Alive." "Women Who Sometimes Prefer Women."

And while the other children didn't really understand them, Angel comprehended every word.

But it wasn't just sex. She read scientific textbooks as well, though anything remotely related to sex drew the most attention. Biology and anatomy books were particular favorites.

Of course it wasn't until her infamous little science experiment in second grade that she was finally shipped off to Catholic boarding school. She was fascinated by the idea that sperm had motility, that they could swim. And after finally getting her first real microscope at the age of seven, she was intent on seeing for herself.

Thus began Angel's quest to find a semen donor. She'd studied well and knew exactly where to get it. Most of the boys in her class didn't mind playing Angel's game, but some had grown quite sore by the time Angel did some additional research only to discover that boys didn't actually start producing sperm until puberty.

"Maybe I'm not doing it right," she'd say.

"I don't know about that, but don't stop," they'd reply.

"Well my hand's tired. You do it yourself for a while."

And sure enough, Angel was relieved to see the problem wasn't in her technique when she procured her first adequate specimen from an all too cooperative 13-year-old subject.

Her parents were pleased to see Angel finally using that microscope she'd wanted so badly.

It wasn't until the boy had enlisted several volunteer subjects from among his friends to nobly assist in Angel's research that the trouble began.

Long after she'd been packed off to Our Lady of the Blessed Virgin Catholic Boarding School, carvings and drawings on the walls of the junior high school's boys' bathrooms continued to pay tribute to Angel's epic study of the human condition.

The nuns thought they were prepared. They knew why Angel was with them. True, she was younger than most of their students, but one was never too young to learn the proper way for a young lady to behave.

For a while, Angel only encouraged them. She dazzled them with her appetite for learning. Angel eagerly absorbed everything from science to art to philosophy, even religion. Within two years, she'd mastered three languages, not counting Latin, as well as physics and calculus, piano and violin. They'd never seen anything like Angel. And without the distraction of boys, the nuns saw no reason to expect any trouble.

They'd seriously underestimated Angel. They didn't understand her condition. They should have realized the breadth of her appetites. Just as Angel's interests weren't only limited to sex, but included science, art, and philosophy, they might have suspected that she wasn't necessarily committed to just boys either.

By the age of 14, Angel had managed to be involved with most of the students at the small girls' school in one form of sex play or another. For some of the students, it was simply a matter of innocent curiosity. For others, it quickly evolved into more.

But it wasn't until one of the younger nuns found herself both physically and emotionally infatuated by Angel that Angel's troubles resumed.

When the nun realized she alone could not satisfy Angel's boundless sexual energy, she turned from lovesick to jealous to suicidal.

And while Angel's insatiable appetite for learning had grown to legendary status among the school's teaching staff, the note found by the body of the suicidal young nun exposed Angel's other appetite, also legendary, but until that point, closeted only among the students.

Expelled from Catholic boarding school by 15 years of age, Angel's parents quickly realized they were no match for Angel. It was evident that no variety or amount of parenting could bring Angel under control.

Angel never meant to be difficult. In fact, she was fully aware of her condition, having researched and made her own diagnosis at the age of 12 at the medical library. Just being aware, however, was not enough. Classically, manic-depressives lack the ability to deal with their condition. In a manic phase, they are on top of the world with no intention of coming down. Nothing is impossible, physically or mentally. Weeks of sleepless nights by manic-depressive personalities resulting in great works of literature, art, or scientific breakthroughs are well known. Immersed within this manic phase of expanded consciousness, productivity, and artistic expression, the patient cannot comprehend the concept that one would want to curb it all with medication, replacing the euphoric state of well being with the humdrum existence of the average human being.

Not entirely aware of Angel's academic achievements, her parents were surprised to find out that she had taken it upon herself at the age of 15 to apply to college. They were in fact relieved to learn she would be moving out of the house when Angel showed them her acceptance letter with full scholarship to Columbia University.

The initial twinge of guilt they felt for exposing a prestigious but unsuspecting university to the force that was their Angel was just that, a mere twinge, and rapidly faded with the knowledge that they had survived a kind of right of passage raising Angel and now they might have their own lives back.

They wished Columbia the best of luck with a wink to each other as they dropped Angel off at the dorm and drove off to reclaim their home.

By her second year at Columbia, Angel was taking more than double the average course load, easily excelling in every class. Her learning speed was only limited by how fast she could obtain and read the related textbooks or literature. She only had to read them once and they were automatically absorbed. Rereading or studying was foreign to Angel, as was sleep. She seemed to require less and less sleep, soon averaging only two hours per night.

By her fourth year at Columbia, she had long graduated and was working on her third PhD at the age of 19. The first two were in Literature and Molecular Biology. Her third field of endeavor, Psychology, seemed overly simplistic and naive, and she soon planned to switch to something more useful.

Anyone who met her could see there was something exceptional about Angel. Her razor sharp intellect was legendary among the student body. And Angel's body was itself legendary among the many fraternities at Columbia.

It was not uncommon for Angel to happily find herself the only guest invited to a frat party. And after the last of her many hosts were spent and fast asleep, Angel would often head for the all night dance clubs.

She seemed to have conquered all aspects of college life when, once again, scandal interrupted Angel's world.

She saw nothing wrong with the age difference between herself and her psychology professor, with whom she was working closely on her third PhD. After all, sex was sex. And he did keep it interesting. It didn't take Angel long to learn that people in the field of psychology had more sexual kinks than most. She never believed that they picked this up over time from analyzing their patients' sexual habits and fantasies. It was apparent to Angel that it was their own sexual appetites that in fact drew them to psychology in the first place. This was no chicken or egg mystery to Angel.

The professor himself picked out which of her underthings he was wearing that day, complimented by a few of his own personal accessories including the red garter belts and size 12 stiletto pumps. The leather handcuffs were Angel's idea.

And while they had discussed in graphic detail his many bizarre and intricate fantasies, including the one du jour involving the cruel female warden at the prison for male sex offenders, he never once mentioned his heart condition.

The paramedics were quite amused by the scene when they arrived. In all the excitement, Angel couldn't find the key to the handcuffs. And so as not to mar the entire effect before presenting their patient to the crowd at the hospital emergency room, the paramedics neglected to cut them off.

The professor's life was saved. His career, however, as well as Angel's studies at Columbia, were not.

After being asked to leave Columbia, Angel had no intention of going home, but instead she thought she would take her two and a half PhD's and find a job.

Somehow, the people who knew her from school were not surprised when they learned her chosen profession would be that of a stripper down at Club Platinum, two and a half PhD's and all.

The club was open nearly 24 hours a day from 10AM to 5AM. Angel was sleeping less and less those days and the five hours downtime was plenty for her to eat and sleep. The rest of the day, she stripped.

Like everything else in her life, she seemed to be a natural. Her energy was boundless. She radiated sexuality. And her natural 38D's didn't hurt either.

But it was as much mental as it was physical. There was a science to stripping. Angel often mused that there should have been a course at Columbia called, How to Get All of a Man's Money Without Actually Removing His Pants 101. The course would include lessons on Removing Your Clothes to Gain a Man's Undivided Attention, and Maintaining the Bulge in his Pants until the Bulge in his Wallet is Gone. And for the advanced students, perhaps lessons called, Take Nothing Less than $20 Bills, and Friction Dancing for Fun and Profit. It didn't take Angel long to master these skills. And at $20 per three-minute song, it didn't take long to empty wallets. The other girls only dreamed of earning Angel's $2,000 per night. It would have been more, but Angel often became so turned on by her own performance that she'd forget to collect money from her customers.

Having mastered the strip club gig, Angel soon grew bored and kept her eyes open for new more challenging facets to stripping. That's when a young best man approached her about performing at a pre-wedding bachelor's party.

At the club, they had their own version of a bachelor party. It usually involved some form of crude, but pleasurable, humiliation of the drunken groom on stage by several of the dancers.

After announcing the presence of the groom with all the appropriate denouncements of the institution of marriage, and mustering the crowd to cheer him on in his final night of unbridled freedom, the beer-sodden semiconscious groom is pulled onto the stage by several of the strippers. There he is stripped to his underwear and tied to a chair in the middle of the stage. With three of the dancers in his face, chest, and lap for the first song, it isn't long before his shorts are saluting his supporters in the audience. Only after the mandatory drinking of champagne poured through the G-string of the girl standing over his face is the wet and staggering groom untied to find his clothes and follow his pointer off the stage back to the comfort of his comrades.

But a private party in a hotel room, just Angel, the groom, best man and four ushers sounded like a new challenge to her. The ushers were concerned that the best man was being cheap in hiring only one girl, fearing they might wear her out. The poor wedding party didn't know what they were up against.

It didn't take Angel long to strip their wallets empty, well-versed as she was at extracting tips from her admirers. But by that time, Angel was on a roll. She'd started to get horny herself, and the poor unsuspecting wedding party didn't even notice that the show was still going on long after the tip money was spent.

Angel wore only a thong at that point. The young men were down to their boxer shorts. All eyes were on Angel's undulating breasts as she rocked to the music in the groom's lap. Their shorts were at attention long before they'd had their own turns.

Angel instinctively knew just when to stand up and switch laps before resulting in a mess in the front of someone's boxers. And after a couple of hours of that, even the massive amount of beer consumed couldn't numb the aching congestion developing in their groins, blue balls, the best compliment you could express to a professional stripper. Yes, blue balls and empty wallets. A job well done.

But Angel wasn't ready to stop. She'd turned herself on as much as her admirers and wasn't going home until her own itch had been scratched. It was going to be a long night for the boys.

Angel knew from experience that in their current state of excitement, even the six of them strung end-to-end wouldn't last long enough to meet her requirements. But they'd certainly last longer on the second and third go round.

The boys thought it was quitting time after the first round, Angel efficiently relieving them three at a time using her mouth and two hands simultaneously. They didn't realize that that was just the appetizer.

They were just reaching for their clothes when Angel slipped off her thong and threw a dozen condoms on the bed. All six of them stopped as their genitals rose to the occasion. The clothes could wait.

As the boys took turns napping between rounds, Angel just seemed to get more and more turned on. Each time they thought the condoms had run out, Angel almost magically produced another box. Night soon turned to morning. The pizza they'd ordered was gone, as was the young man who'd delivered it, appreciative of the unusual form of tip he'd received from Angel.

It was the bride's mother, consoling the impatient wedding guests at the church, who panicked and called the police. While others assumed the boys were simply running late, struggling through their post-bachelor party hangovers, she instead assumed the worse, perhaps they were in a car accident.

In a way, they were. At the hotel room, they were in a head on collision with Angel. And unable to muster the will to leave, one could say they'd been paralyzed from the waist down.

Although this wasn't the type of case that policemen fear, it was a good thing, nevertheless, that there were two of them. If not, no one would have believed what they'd found when they opened the door to the hotel room using the security key.

The bodies of the six young men were naked and scattered about the room. It wasn't until the first snore was appreciated that the cops realized it wasn't the scene of some horrific mass murder. The room was littered with condoms, clothes, and pizza boxes. Angel alone showed signs of movement, frantically fingering herself after abandoning any further attempts to rouse one of the boys.

They looked at each other. They looked at Angel. One finally nudged the other to speak.

"Hey, uh, what's going on here?"

Angel didn't hear them as another orgasm racked her body.

"Hey you! I said what's going on here?"

As her cloud cleared and Angel's sight returned, she saw the two policemen, quite handsome in their uniforms.

"Thank God you're here," she breathed.

The cops again looked at each other, surprised by Angel's statement. It certainly didn't seem as though she'd been held against her will. She wasn't restrained and all the men were asleep.

"Quick," she urged, "get out of those uniforms."

They looked at each other again, confused and speechless. It wasn't until Angel was already upon them, tugging at their clothes, that they began to sense the situation.

Backing off, rebuckling his belt, one of them spoke. "Now just a minute there, miss. What's your name?"

"Angel," she replied, reaching for the other officer's belt buckle.

"OK, Angel. What's wrong with these guys?

"They're just tired," she said.

"Were they using any drugs?"

"No, just me."

"Just you were using drugs?"

"No. They were just using me."

"And that knocked out six men?"

"They're not knocked out. The poor babies are just worn out."

The cops looked at each other. "And how did you do that?"

"I'm trying to show you," said Angel simultaneously unzipping both their flies, placing a hand in each of their pants.

Their report would not describe the slight but definite delay between the time Angel's hands went in their pants to the time they stepped back, protesting, "Whoa there! What do you think you're doing?"

"If you'd just stand still for second, I'd show you," she said, unconsciously rubbing herself.

The officers tried to rouse some of the young men, prodding them with their feet and nightsticks.

"No more. Please stop," they groaned, half asleep, clutching their groins.

"What the hell happened here?" muttered one of the cops to the other. Poking one of the ushers again, "Hey, did you pay her for this?"

"Only to strip," he answered. "She'd already gotten all our money before the other stuff started." The boy sat up, beginning to realize he was speaking to a police officer.

"Are you trying to tell me that this girl isn't a prostitute?" asked the cop, incredulously.

"Well, not with us she wasn't. Stripper yes. Prostitute no."

"And you expect me to believe she screwed the six of you silly just because she was horny?"

"She's crazy. Look!" he said pointing at Angel kneeling next to the other officer deep throating his nightstick.

"He may have something there," said one officer to the other. "Hey, miss, you on anything? Any drugs?"

"No, don't need 'em," said Angel removing the nightstick from her throat and wiping the saliva from her chin with the back of her hand. "At least this guy won't wear out on me," she said rubbing the nightstick between her legs.

As she changed her grip and the angle of the nightstick preparing to get more intimate with it, the policeman grabbed it back. "That'll be enough of that," he said. "We'd better get her to the ER. She's either on something or she's crazy. Let them sort it out."

The boys gathered their clothes and went on to the wedding. The bride was not happy.

The officers attempted to get Angel dressed. But for each article of clothing they struggled to get on her, she removed two of theirs. At one point, she'd actually managed to get one of their guns. She said she found the metal barrel erotic and asked if she could play with it in the back of the squad car.

Finally, they just wrapped her in a bed sheet, grabbed her clothes, made it to the car, and headed uptown to the Columbia-Presbyterian emergency room.

Angel's visit to the emergency room was a brief one. She was immediately diagnosed with a manic disorder manifesting as hypersexual behavior and sent up to the ward.

The police escort up in the elevator was not uneventful. As the doors to the elevator opened at the ward, the buttons on both policemen's shirts had been ripped open. Angel sat on the floor of the elevator, down to her G-string again, wearing a cop's hat, and playing with one of their whistles. The two cops were zipping up their flies.

Dr. Gelner, the chief resident, was waiting for them at the elevator door.

"Nurse!" he yelled. "Where's the student? I believe Hah-vud's up first. Let's hold off on the heavy medication until after the student's interviewed her. He ought to kiss my feet for this one. I know guys that would give their right testicle to get assigned a case like this.

Chapter 5

Ben couldn't keep his eyes off her crotch. It was the way she sat, not five feet away, knees wide apart, exposing that soft, worn out area between the legs of her pants. She'd chosen just the right clothes to be brought from her home. The holes in the jeans seemed almost strategically placed to draw one's attention. Ben found himself wondering whether she was wearing any panties as he contemplated two particular holes around her fly. He tried to stop staring, thinking he'd kill himself if she ever noticed.

Angel spread her knees a little wider for Ben's benefit, thinking she'd actually seen a drop of drool forming at the corner of his mouth. She slowly arched her back as if stretching, deliberately pushing out her chest. Her braless 38D's strained at the thin white tank top T-shirt she wore, following the lead of her semi-erect nipples.

Ben thought he could see a small rim of areola, through her T-shirt, surrounding each straining nipple.

Angel smiled to herself over her small victory when Ben unconsciously raised his sleeve to wipe the drop of saliva that somehow started running down the side of his chin.

The six foot square interview room seemed rather warm to Ben. It contained only two chairs, an end table holding a lamp and an ashtray, Ben, and his first patient, Angel McGovern.

The ashtray was quickly filling up with Angel's spent cigarette butts. Between all the chain-smoking residents and their patients, Ben no longer wondered where all the cigarettes were going in this time of increased public awareness about the dangers of smoking. It seemed to live on undaunted behind the doors of psychiatric wards all over the land.

"Have you had any suicidal thoughts?" asked Ben, tearing his eyes away from her chest just long enough to read the next question from the mental status exam on his clipboard.

"You're kidding right?" replied Angel, tapping the ashes from her cigarette. "Of course not. I live in a perpetual manic euphoria. I make more money than most of the doctors in this place. And I have sex several times a day. Look at you. You're depressed about having to study all the time. You don't get paid at all. And my guess is you've never had sex in your life." She leaned forward, granting Ben one more look down her T-shirt, then raised his chin with her finger so that his eyes came back up to hers, and blowing just a bit of smoke in his face, asked, "Have *you* had any suicidal thoughts?'

After an uncomfortable pause, Ben replied, "No, I haven't."

"Not until now, you mean," added Angel.

"No. I meant I never have," insisted Ben.

"Well maybe not yet anyway," allowed Angel.

Ben was a little shaken by the matter-of-fact way in which Angel responded, so sure of her opinions. Ben was never so sure of himself.

"So why do you think you're here?" Ben asked, trying to resume the interview.

"I'm here because two gay cops handcuffed me and brought me here. What's you're excuse?"

Ben was about to reply, but caught himself, and again, tried to resume control of the interview. "Why do you think the police brought you here?"

"Because I like to have fun," Angel replied, slowly slipping a hand down inside the front of her jeans.

"What kind of fun?" continued Ben, not entirely comfortable with the question.

"I like to fuck," answered Angel, adding after a pause, "a lot." She had slowly started rubbing herself with her hand inside her pants. "You should try it some time."

Ben checked his watch as he wiped a few drops of perspiration from his brow. The interview seemed to be taking an awfully long time. He looked back at Angel as he noticed her breathing becoming heavier and slightly irregular. If he'd had any doubts before, they were gone now. She was definitely masturbating right in front of him.

"What makes you think I haven't had sex before?" asked Ben, thus taking the bait and effectively relinquishing control of the interview.

Angel's eyelids were half closed, concentrating on the task at hand, but she now opened them sensing the game was afoot. Without interrupting the motion in her pants, she took over the questioning.

"Do you have a girlfriend?"

"You mean now?"

Angel smiled, amused by his response. "I mean *ever*," she responded.

"Sure I have," said Ben.

"When? Back in high school?"

"That's right," said Ben, wondering how Angel knew that.

"Did you fuck her?"

Ben thought of lying.

"Now don't lie," added Angel, noticing his hesitation at a simple question. "It's not a trick question."

"No," said Ben.

"No, what?" added Angel.

"No, I didn't fuck her. How did you know?"

"This isn't my first visit here, you know. And you're not my first medical student. They all suffer from a certain lack of life experience, particularly in the area of sex. I've been able to help most of them."

"Help them? How did you help them?" asked Ben, taking the bait.

"I fucked them."

Ben thought the hand in her pants was moving more rapidly now. "You mean you dated them when you were released from the hospital?"

"No. I fucked them, right here, in this room, at least once a day for their entire six week rotation on the ward."

Ben had to put his clipboard down on his lap to hide his rapidly rising erection.

"I cleared up a lot of bad skin in my day," she joked.

"How many students does that include?" inquired Ben.

"Including the women?'

"The women!?"

"Actually the women seemed even more frustrated. And while the guys generally gave out after one interview, the girls would keep coming back throughout the day."

"The girls?" asked Ben, swallowing hard.

"Oh definitely," answered Angel.

"You're bisexual?" followed Ben.

"You're not?" asked Angel.

"Of course not."

"Oh, I see," said Angel. "You're gay."

"What? No!" Ben was in full retreat.

"Oh, so you do like girls?"

"Well, sure," replied Ben.

"Well then, why shouldn't *I*?" followed Angel. "I'm really getting turned on just talking about it," said Angel, picking up the pace of her hand in her pants. "Doesn't the thought of that sweet musk between their legs give you a hard-on?"

Ben quickly readjusted the clipboard in his lap, hiding the affirmative reply to Angel's question.

"Doesn't the thought of tasting it make you want to jerk off?" continued Angel, raising the ante.

"I don't think we should be—"

Angel cut him off. "You do jerk off, don't you?"

"Well, I—"

"Why don't you do it now, here, with me?" she added, reaching to undo Ben's belt.

"We can't do that," protested Ben.

"Then let's fuck," decided Angel, standing up. "My pussy's dripping." She unsnapped her jeans and lowered her zipper six inches from Ben's watering eyes. Turning around, she slowly peeled her jeans down her hips, bent slightly at the waist, head arched backward so that her long blonde curls framed her emerging buttocks. It was apparent she knew how to play to the audience.

Ben had lost the ability to form words. But he was relieved to see that Angel did indeed have at least a thong on under her jeans.

Angel turned her head back to look at him. "Come on."

Ben shook his head no.

"Please," she begged.

Ben swallowed and shook his head no again.

"OK," said Angel, giving up. "Have it your way." She turned around again, her crotch eye level with Ben, six inches away, and resumed masturbating in earnest, the hand inside her panties a blur of movement. Ben found he couldn't turn away as Angel's breathing became labored. She seemed to alternate between short rapid hand movements and slow deep motions. With one motion of his coat sleeve, Ben was able to catch both a drop of perspiration from his forehead and another drop of saliva from the corner of his mouth.

Angel's breathing became more irregular with throaty moans punctuated by short gasps.

Ben couldn't keep his clipboard flat on his lap anymore. It seemed to defy gravity like the table at a cheap séance. He looked up past Angel's chest, heaving with every breath now, only to find her eyes tightly shut, her eyebrows taut in concentration, lips slightly parted.

Ben noticed her face suddenly change, more relaxed. When he looked down, he saw her hand had stopped moving. Just as he felt Angel's knee involuntarily shutter against his, he looked up again to see her eyes roll up into her head and a slight smile form at the corner of her mouth.

Ben came in his pants. He couldn't help it. His hands were clutched to his clipboard the entire time. But the touch of her knee and the whites of her eyes sent him over the edge.

He hadn't caught his breath before Angel could notice.

"I hope it was as good for you too," she said, looking down at him, slowly removing her hand from her thong. Raising her hand up past his face in deliberate slow motion, she noticed Ben respond as if to smelling salts.

Ben shook his head to clear the fog, checked his watch, and replied, "I, uh, guess, we're, uh, about out of time for today."

Chapter 6

Rounds in the conference room with Dr. Gelner began in the usual fashion.

"Yes, thank you so very much, Dr. Brunning, for reporting back to us with the findings from your study comparing the therapeutic efficacy of oatmeal cookies versus Oreos on the delusional patient. Now, nurse McGuire will escort you back to your office."

Dr. Brunning tensed up a bit as nurse McGuire gently helped him up from the chair by his arm. He became visibly more cooperative after she made the customary offering. "Will it be oatmeal or Oreo this morning?" she inquired with a gentle smile.

"I believe today's randomized trial calls for oatmeal cookies," he replied.

Nurse McGuire shut the door behind her.

Dr. Gelner took the floor. "So, Dr. Walker, how is our dancer doing?"

"Oh, just fine," answered Ben, swallowing hard.

"You know she's a genius, don't you?" Dr. Gelner continued.

"No, I didn't realize that, but it doesn't surprise me."

"She ran circles around you, didn't she?"

"Well, you see, she—"

"You didn't learn very much from your first session, did you? She told me all about it. Who was interviewing who anyway? Well, I hope you get something out of your future sessions with her."

"Something tells me I'll be getting all I can handle," answered Ben.

Dr. Gelner turned to the other student. "OK, Amy will be taking over Dr. Goldstein's new admission from yesterday."

"Why is that?" asked Amy. "Am I that good? Or is the patient that bad?"

"No big deal really," replied Dr. Gelner. "It's just that the patient wants to kill Dr. Goldstein."

"Excuse me?" choked Amy.

Dr. Goldstein explained. "Well, I was taking an initial history when the patient immediately felt compelled to delve into his neo-Nazi tendencies."

"And then?" led Amy.

"So I gave him plenty of line and off he went, ultimately relating his all-consuming hatred of Jews, describing in intricate and vivid detail what he would personally like to do to each and every one of them."

"And you let that get to you?" asked Amy.

"No, it wasn't that so much as his direct threat of physical harm. He is 6' 4", 340 pounds after all."

"He threatened you?" asked Amy, looking about the room wondering why she should be next.

"Well, he had cause. After all, he could see my name tag. And my Jewish ancestry is as plain as the nose on my face, literally. I asked him if he intended to actually inflict harm on Jews, to which he replied, any that he could get his hands on. Luther's a large man, with large hands. Shaved head and swastika tattoos aside, he's an impressive figure. I proceeded to ask the next logical question, whether he felt any uncontrollable compulsion to hurt *me*, personally."

"And?" followed Amy.

"He just smiled his wide, toothless smile."

Amy just stared, speechless, then turned to Dr. Gelner, who responded, "He likes girls."

"And why doesn't that comfort me?" asked Amy rhetorically.

"Oh, don't worry about Luther. It seems our next admission *really* likes girls. Juan Martinez is a *large* 17-year-old Hispanic male with a problem. It seems Juan raped a 15-year-old girl and murdered her father. He's here for evaluation on a plea of insanity, after which he'll go back to prison pending further action."

He turned to Amy. "Luther's looking pretty good now, isn't he?"

"A real alter boy," conceded Amy.

"And since Amy's already been assigned to take on the third Reich, it looks like you're up again, Hah-vud."

Ben choked on his coffee. After clearing his airway, "No, really?"

"Hey, you still owe me for Angel," Dr. Gelner reminded him. "Besides, you're developing a niche in sexual deviates. You just can't expect them all to be beautiful and affectionate, can you?"

Ben responded, "Sure, but I wasn't expecting homicidal either."

"Well, let's get to work," said Dr. Gelner, distributing patient charts. "Ben, Mr. Martinez awaits."

Had there been more time, Ben would at least have gotten his personal effects in order and consulted his family attorney concerning his will. Even now, walking toward the room to interview Juan Martinez, Ben imagined he wouldn't have to search too far in this neighborhood to acquire some form of handgun with which to defend himself.

The presence of the burly uniformed security guard outside the door to the interview room was somewhat reassuring. Ben stopped in front of him.

"I hear this guy is pretty big," said Ben. "Is that gun you're wearing loaded?"

"You bet your life it is," replied the security guard, affectionately patting the pistol at his side with a grin.

"Precisely," said Ben. "But between you and me, I'm not exactly the gambling type. You have enough bullets in there?"

The guard sucked in his somewhat protuberant gut and spread his feet a bit as if to give his reply more credence. "This baby's prepared to take down a wild elephant if need be."

"It's not Dumbo that concerns me. It's Mr. Martinez, the mountain behind that door, that I'm worried about," said Ben.

"Don't you worry, Doc. I hear any kind o' commotion while you're in there, it'll all be over 'fore two shakes of a lamb's tail."

"Just how fast exactly does a lamb's tail shake, Mr. Fife?" countered Ben.

The security guard's gut jiggled as he laughed at Ben's question. When he saw Ben wasn't laughing, he composed himself and straightened up. "Uh, pretty fast, sir," he replied.

Ben turned to the door, took a deep breath, glanced once toward heaven, knocked, and entered the small cubicle that served as a place to interview patients, many of whom were psychotic, and some, apparently, homicidal.

As Ben closed the door to the dimly lit room behind him, the fluorescent overhead light fixture began to flicker momentarily, adding a strobe light effect to the already tense atmosphere.

Ben looked across the small room, through the flickering light, to see a huge form filling his view. Ben's heart pounded in his throat as he realized he could see nothing but the large body across from him. The muscular body seemed a couple of sizes larger than the clothes trying to confine it. The unkempt shoulder length hair surrounded an unshaven face which sprouted small tufts of hair alluding to the patient's young age. His size, poorly-fitted clothing, and unkempt hair all contributed to the serial killer look he was sporting.

Ben managed somehow to make his vocal cords move and asked, "Juan Martinez?"

"Is Bessie OK?" responded the massive creature across from him.

"Bessie?" asked Ben, confused.

Again, it spoke. "Bessie. The manatee. Did she go home? Did she get home OK?"

Ben detected a thick Spanish accent. Then, as if on cue, the light suddenly stopped flickering, and Ben's eyes were suddenly able to focus on the massive form of Juan Martinez, slouched in the chair in front of him, quietly humming to himself as he nervously sucked his thumb.

Chapter 7

Juan Martinez was a village idiot. He was raised on a tiny island called Isla de los Locos, just off the coast of Cuba, which, if it were known for anything, would have been known only for the fine mangos that grew there. Island lore maintains that the first mango tree on the island was a gift from Muchas Frutas, their ancient god of fruits, who thousands of years ago descended from heaven, bearing a great supply of mangos. After consuming all the mangos, the very source of his great powers, he was forced to return to heaven for more, but not before leaving the island littered with mango pits and promising to return someday to share the fruits which would eventually populate Isla de los Locos with its only natural resource.

There were, of course, other theories to explain the heavenly nature of the island's mangos. But it seemed unlikely that the quality of the fruit was attributable simply to some rare rootstock upon which the trees grew, indigenous only to that island. That would be too simple. Perhaps it was a combination of rootstock and unusually favorable climate conditions. But if that were the case, one would expect a similar product from Cuba, not five miles away, under whose jurisdiction the island loosely fell, loosely, because of Cuba's profound lack of interest.

Isla de los Locos was considerably less than five miles across at its widest. Mangos were its only natural resource, for which Cuba was its only market. Cuba bartered all other bare essentials for living to the people of Isla de los Locos in exchange for the mangos. The island had never really been part of Cuba, because, well frankly, Cuba didn't want it. True, the mangos were particularly delicious, with smooth, sweet, juicy flesh, completely lacking in those stringy fibers with which lesser mangos seem to be burdened. But Cuba already consumed all the island could grow for next to nothing. No, there was no question they didn't *need* Isla de los Locos. But there was another reason Cuba kept the island at arms length.

It was the village idiots, more specifically the number of them, too many, it seemed, for an island so small. This, in fact, was the only thing, other than mangos, for which the island was referred to in Cuba, and only then as the butt of much humor.

"How many Isla de los Locos does it take to screw in a light bulb?"

"All of them. One to hold the bulb. The rest to turn the island."

An equally acceptable response would be, "Light bulb? When did they get electricity on Isla de los Locos?"

The people of Isla de los Locos were, in fact, permitted by Cuba to emigrate to the United States. Some saw this as akin to the Mariel boat lift, a ploy to unload certain undesirables. Those with a greater sense of melodrama suspected Castro of something vastly more sinister, a plot to pollute the vast American gene pool with the island's pedigree of stupidity. This was to be Castro's new secret weapon. The Cuban missile crises would someday be looked upon as merely a decoy for Castro's new secret weapon, Isla de los Locos. Of course, most of the people subscribing to this conspiracy theory could also be found in heated conversation with inanimate objects.

Nevertheless, it was this policy of open and free emigration that allowed Rosalita Martinez, Juan's mother, to come to the United States, more specifically, New York City.

No, she didn't bring Juan. Juan was born when Rosalita was only 14. When his father saw the other children his age starting school while Juan was still trying to master the mobile over his crib, he knew that his boy was more than one mango short of a bushel. He quietly fled to New York one night to hide, leaving behind a teenage mother to care for a less than perfect five-year-old Juan and his genius, by comparison, two-year-old sister, Innocencia.

Rosalita was not far behind. With Innocencia in tow, she too headed for New York. As Juan would have been too much of a burden, he was left behind to stay with his grandmother on Isla de los Locos.

For the next twelve years, all was fine on Isla de los Locos. Juan grew to a height of 6'10" by the age of 17, as if shoulder height could somehow make up for his shortcomings above the shoulder.

He wasn't allowed to go to school. But on the island, he and the many other lentos, or slow ones, as they were called, were well accepted among the rest of the villagers. One trait all the lentos seemed to possess was an extremely good natured, almost docile, disposition. And while some could only manage to stand in the middle of town singing nursery rhymes as they methodically removed all their clothing before jumping into the fountain in the town square, others managed to lead productive lives.

Juan's height was a real asset, enabling him to pick more bushels of mangos per day than anyone on the island. Although he missed his mother at first, his grandmother quickly became the one he called Mama. Life with her was loving, peaceful, and stable. On an island with so many lentos, and so many mangos to harvest, Juan fit right in and was well accepted by everyone.

He had friends there, most smarter than he, but true friends nevertheless, friends that saw and appreciated his gentle innocence. One such friend was a girl Juan grew up with named Christina.

She was two years younger than Juan. Because of this age difference, they were very compatible as toddlers. Although it was apparent to observers early on that three-year-old Christina was as smart as her five-year-old friend was dumb, and was in fact the leader of the duo in all their activities, it wasn't for another couple of years that Christina caught on. But no matter, for Christina and Juan were equals in their kind and gentle dispositions. They were the perfect playmates. They were inseparable, that is until Juan turned 17, when his grandmother became too ill to care for him.

With no family left able to watch over Juan, he was sent to New York to live with his mother and sister. Christina begged her parents to take him in, but the elders of the island felt he should be with his family. So Juan got to ride in a big boat to a big plane which flew him to the biggest village he ever saw, New York City.

Rosalita never found Juan's father. What she did find, however, was vastly different from the orchards of Isla de los Locos, where food and shelter were never concerns. There was always more food than the islanders could eat and the tropical climate required only minimal shelter from the elements. Everyone had these essentials and they couldn't be bought.

Things were different in the giant village of New York City. Rosalita quickly learned the importance of money and the myriad of ways by which it could be acquired in New York. Although she naturally settled in the Hispanic neighborhood known as Spanish Harlem, Rosalita soon realized the importance of learning English, for it was only then that she could make the American dream a reality for her. Rosalita had a plan.

Of course, running a phone sex operation wasn't her first choice. But it *was* the one that worked. It put a roof over their heads and food on the table. Rosalita could work at home and still be able to care for her daughter, Innocencia. As her friends took her advice and learned English, Rosalita hired them, expanding the business until she had five lines operating out of her apartment.

No longer tending the mango orchards of her native land, Rosalita gained quite a few pounds over the years, and she and her rotund friends manning the phones made for quite a sight, filling her living room with moans of ecstasy and orgasmic expletives between mouthfuls of Dunkin donuts.

Innocencia had grown into a precocious 14-year-old girl, raised amid the flurry of phone sex that had become her living room. Preoccupied with their own telephone relationships, over the years, none of the ladies noticed the unique tone of the conversations moderated by young Innocencia on the floor of the living room between her Barbie and Ken dolls. It seems Barbie had become quite the slut. And by the time she was 14, Innocencia not only knew the words, but she also knew what they meant.

It wasn't long before Innocencia was, herself, manning the phones after school to earn some spending money. She got a big kick out of relating her phone experiences to some of the girls at school, and before long, two of her friends, Maria and Carmen, had come aboard, joining Rosalita's team. The giggling teenage girls found the whole thing quite entertaining. They had T-shirts made for themselves which said "We Give Good Phone," and soon convinced Rosalita to branch out and offer a separate line featuring themselves, called, "Teenage Girls After School."

"Hey Carmen, this guy wants two of us on the phone together," called Innocencia down the row of phones to her friend, her hand over the mouthpiece of her headset. "Are you free now?"

"I'm available. Not free," Carmen replied, feigning indignation. "Does he know the charge is double? I don't do this for my health, you know," added the 14-year-old.

"Yea. Yea. I told him. He's really into it. Come on. Line three. OK?"

Carmen picked up on line three. "Hello? Can I come over and play?" she began, trying to sound as young and innocent as possible, which wasn't hard.

Responding to the caller, Innocencia said, "Yes sir, that's my friend I told you about. The one I met in church at Sunday school. The priests taught us how to play so nicely together while they watched over us. We'll let you take confession from us if you like. Remember though, you'll have to buy us twice as much candy, right?"

After a brief pause, "Yes sir, I already have your credit card number. Do you want to hear what we're wearing?"

The giggling girls described in detail their Catholic schoolgirls' uniforms, including the plaid skirts they'd shortened so much they made the priests stutter. Even the nuns seemed to perspire excessively when their skirts rode up revealing their white-laced panties during their frequent spankings.

Juan Martinez had never seen a telephone before, and he certainly didn't understand what his sister and her friends were talking about on the calls. But at least until Rosalita could find something her slow-witted son could do to contribute to the rent, he would have to hang around the apartment while the women attended to the telephones.

His favorite time of day was when Innocencia and her friends came to work after school. He may have been too slow and naive to understand the telephone conversations going on around him, but he wasn't blind. The girls were usually barely dressed as if to fit their phone personas, the short plaid skirts of their school uniforms not much less revealing than the way they described themselves for their customers drooling on the other end of the telephone. And while Juan may have been a little slow from the neck up, he was, nevertheless, a 17-year-old boy with the full compliment of associated hormones.

The girls certainly noticed the household's new addition and found the 6' 10" tropical native quite distracting. Their afternoons filled with telephone fantasies only tended to peak their interest in areas where Juan's intellectual shortcoming was not a factor.

One afternoon, it was just Innocencia, her two girlfriends, and Juan, alone in the apartment. The telephones were momentarily silent.

"Does your brother like girls?" Maria asked Innocencia.

"I don't know. Ask him. His English is getting pretty good."

"Hey Juan. Do you like girls?"

"Or do you like boys?" Carmen joked.

Juan had been immersed in the English language since taking up residence in his mother's place of business. Even though all the girls spoke Spanish, it was not the first language for all of them, and certainly English was spoken with the telephone clients.

"Yeah," replied Juan.

"Yeah what. You like girls or boys?" pressed Carmen.

"I like both."

"Oh man! He's bisexual!"

"That's OK with me," said Maria. "Don't be so picky. As long as he likes girls."

"Hey Innocencia, your brother's bisexual!" they joked.

Innocencia turned to Juan. "What do you mean you like girls *and* boys? You have sex with both?"

"I like to do everything," he replied. "I can play soccer with the boys. I can play house with the girls."

"You can play house with me anytime," joked Maria. "Yeah, I'd like to show him my bedroom."

"But wait. You have sex with both?"

Juan thought for a couple of moments. "What's sex?"

Carmen and Maria looked at each other. "Oh my god! He doesn't—"

"You mean, he's never—"

"He's a virgin!"

"Oh my god."

"I'll teach him what sex is."

They turned to Innocencia. "Can we? Do you mind if we have some fun?"

"I don't care. I mean I barely know him myself. What did you have in mind?"

The two girls turned to Juan. Carmen stood up and walked over to where he was sitting. The hemline of her short skirt was at his eye level.

She looked down into his eyes and slowly raised her skirt to the top of her thighs, black bikini panties just out of view. "Like what you see?" she asked in a soft husky voice.

A silly smile came over Juan's face and he started to nervously bounce one knee up and down.

"Hey, I think he likes it," said Maria. "Give him some more."

It didn't take much goading for her to raise her skirt to her waist. She slipped one hand inside her panties and slowly rubbed her crotch.

Juan's smile had faded, replaced by a concentrated stare, eyes fixed on the movement of her hand. It wasn't until she slowly removed her hand, brought it up to her mouth and started slowly sucking her middle finger, that Maria noticed Juan's erection forming a tent in his pants.

"Well, I guess he likes girls," she said, pointing at his pants. "Hey, it's my turn now."

Shoving the first girl aside, Maria took her spot in front of Juan and unbuttoned her blouse. Juan stared at her white lace bra and giggled.

"Wanna touch?" she said, bending forward.

Juan reached out one hand, but she stood up straight again. "Wait. Wait. Let's do it right." She quickly unfastened her bra and removed it. "There. Now," she said squatting slightly in front of him.

The other girls stared with undivided attention as Juan slowly raised one hand and poked at a breast with his finger. They all giggled then.

"No, not like that," said Maria, naked above the waist. "Like this." She grabbed both of Juan's hands, cupping them around her firm breasts and rubbing them in circles.

"You're crazy!" shouted the other girls, laughing.

Juan laughed too, bouncing both knees up and down in nervous excitement.

The bare-chested girl backed up and pointed at Juan's crotch. "Look at his hard-on. I think it's getting bigger."

Maria turned to Innocencia and coyly dared her. "It's your turn, Innocent. Show him what you got."

"Yeah, Miss Innocent. Your turn," agreed Carmen.

Innocencia frowned at them. "Don't be gross. He's my brother."

"But you said yourself you hardly know him."

"Hey, this is your chance to get to know each other better," joked Maria, both of them breaking out in laughter.

Juan laughed too, and pointing at his sister, agreed excitedly. "Your turn! Your turn!"

"See," said the girls. "He wants you to play too. Come on. Don't be a prude."

Innocencia looked at them, contemplating the dare.

Then Juan broke the silence in his excitement. "Please, Innocencia. You play with us too."

At that, Innocencia broke down and jumped up from her chair giggling excitedly. "OK!"

The other girls backed away, giving her room as she approached Juan. Rolling her hips exaggeratedly, she walked up to Juan, and bent down, her face was inches from his. She slowly licked her lips, then brought her middle finger up to her mouth and began sliding it wetly in and out.

The other girls cheered her on.

Innocencia stood up and turned her back to Juan. She tipped her head back and shook it so that her long dark hair spread over her rump. Then bending at the waist, she reached back and slowly began to raise her skirt. As it cleared above her hips, she turned her head back to look at Juan.

Juan's eyes did not meet hers as they were mesmerized by the view directly in front of him.

Looking back at Juan, Innocencia didn't see the other girls rush up to push her backward onto Juan's lap. Juan caught his surprised sister and gave her a hug around the waist.

"Ow. Hey!" said Innocencia removing his arms and jumping up.

After she stood up, Juan grabbed his crotch and smiled excitedly, rocking back and forth.

The other girls laughed and asked Innocencia, "Well, tell us. How did it feel?"

Innocencia looked back at her behind, rubbing a sore spot. "Big and hard," she answered. They all laughed.

Juan laughed too, now holding his throbbing member.

"I want to touch it," said Maria to the others.

"Yeah," said Carmen. "Me too."

"Go ahead," said Innocencia, feigning disinterest.

The two girls approached Juan, each kneeling down on one side of his chair. They tentatively reached up to survey the tent formed by Juan's pants.

Juan nervously covered his erection with both hands.

The girls laughed. "We're not going to hurt you," said Carmen.

"No, I bet this will feel real good," added Maria smiling.

Feeling reassured, Juan slowly removed his hands from his lap.

As the girls' hands settled around Juan's erection, a smile came over his face and Innocencia said, "This is even better than working the phones."

"Yeah, this way we get to see and touch everything too," said Carmen marveling at Juan's firmness.

"Yeah, this is so cool," said the Maria, unzipping Juan's pants and reaching inside.

"Cool," said Juan, coming in his pants before Maria could even pull it out.

Chapter 8

Everyone seemed to be having such a good time, that is, until Maria got pregnant. Even then, the only one who really seemed upset about the whole thing was Maria's father. Or maybe it was all relative and it was just in comparison to him that no one else seemed too upset. He was pretty upset.

It was only when he showed up at the apartment with two friends and a knife that it became apparent how upset he was. He'd already threatened Maria with the same knife when he forced her to falsely claim the pregnancy was a result of rape. And now he'd come to kill the animal that raped his sweet young daughter. He'd come to kill Juan.

His death was too sudden for the coroner's report to show any evidence of a heart attack. All it showed was the knife in his chest. It was apparent to the phone ladies that Maria's father had a heart attack when he saw just how large Juan was. Bad luck for him that he fell squarely on his own knife.

But his friends wouldn't see it that way. They claimed that he died a hero, struggling with the much larger and younger man in defense of his daughter's virtue. And they threatened the ladies to remember it that way too. The rapist became a murderer when he brutally attacked and killed the girl's father.

The trial verdict was straightforward. The only question remaining was whether Juan would spend the rest of his life in prison or in a mental institution.

Now, Ben Walker never claimed to be Sigmund Freud, but even *he* could tell Juan wasn't crazy. And after deciphering what really happened, despite Juan's limited verbal skills, Ben felt bad for the poor young man. Weighing the choices in his own mind, comparing life in prison with life in a mental institution, Ben looked up at Juan.

"Juan, do you understand what's going to happen to you?" he asked quietly.

Juan looked down at Ben and asked softly, "Can I ask you something, Dr. Walker?"

"Sure, Juan. What is it?"

"Is Bessie going to be OK?" asked Juan.

Ben looked quizzically at Juan, "Bessie?" he asked.

"You know. The manatee."

Ben stared at him blankly until he put two and two together and remembered Juan's preoccupation with New York's only manatee. When it finally registered, he responded, "Oh, the manatee! Bessie the manatee! That's that crazy animal from Florida that got lost, took a wrong turn, and ended up in the Hudson River. Right?"

"She's not crazy!" insisted Juan.

"I'm sorry, I didn't mean—"

Juan cut him off. "How will she get home? She doesn't belong in this place," he added, on the verge of tears.

Seeing his concern, Ben tried to console him. "I'm sure she'll be alright."

Juan wasn't so sure. "But how? She's so far from home. And she's all alone. Pretty soon the snow's going to come and—"

Ben couldn't take it anymore. "I'm sure she'll be OK. Trust me."

"But I think she's going to need help," Juan continued.

Ben paused thoughtfully. "Then someone will help."

"Really?"

"Trust me."

Chapter 9

Angel and Juan hit it off from the start. All it took was a haircut and a shave to make Juan quite the young Latin heart throb. And although Angel's medication had calmed her down enough to keep her clothes on, she still had an eye for the young men. Having heard Juan's story and gotten to know him, Angel knew the boy could never have done the things he'd been accused of. If anything, he seemed a bit undersexed to her. She took Juan under her wing when she saw the orderlies chastising him for his rape conviction. In his defense, she toyed with the orderlies, sometimes teasing them into a sexual frenzy, and other times quizzing them on quantum physics. It helped her pass the time anyway. And Juan appreciated her companionship.

Angel kept trying to teach him to play Chopin on the piano in the recreation room, but Juan was so happy the first day he'd mastered chop sticks that he played it continuously. Before the end of the day, the orderlies were threatening to have the piano removed. Only when Angel hopped up on top of the piano and started a striptease accompanied by Juan's chopsticks did the orderlies back off.

As much as Ben was enjoying the show provided by his new patients, he was just counting the days, waiting to get back to real medicine, that is, surgery. He was actually looking forward to his first night of being on call in the emergency room, even it was just for psychiatry. He thought that while he was there, maybe he'd get to see some real action, maybe even trauma.

Besides, if he didn't get off of the ward pretty soon, he thought he'd go crazy. He was well aware that medical students often began to think they were coming down with the particular disease they were studying. On neurosurgery, minor headaches were interpreted as brain tumors, and on dermatology, freckles become melanomas. Ben knew it was only a matter of time before he'd begin to notice subtle signs of schizophrenia in himself, a little paranoia here, a few delusions there. Just a matter of time.

Ben's ruminations were interrupted by the sound of his beeper going off. It was the ER. Finally, a chance to get out of the loony bin. He lingered just a moment longer because he'd become so familiar with Angel's performances that he knew the removal of her top was imminent. And sure enough, just like clockwork, Ben watched as she turned toward the drooling orderlies, smiled, made an obscene gesture with her tongue, and slowly began unbuttoning her top. Only after the top was completely removed did Ben feel obliged to make his way down to the ER to see what was up.

* * * *

Arriving in the ER, Ben was finally back on familiar turf. He could sense illness in the air, real and not imagined. He could see blood-soaked dressings, surgical gloves and scalpels. He could hear cardiac monitors and moans of pain. He could smell the gangrenous leg of a diabetic yearning to be amputated. This was what medicine was about.

Ben immediately observed an eclectic mix of patients. There were the essentially healthy ones dropping in for the occasional sore throat or sprained ankle. There were the visibly ill but reasonably serviceable ones young and strong enough to make it. And then there were the living dead, the ones in multisystem failure, gurgling on or lying in various bodily excretions, that no tune-up or tweaking of medications could cure. The cirrhotic alcoholics, the elderly, the cancer-ridden, and the end-stage AIDS patients. They often didn't know where they were or why they were there. Their productive years behind them, it seemed to Ben that their only purpose was to continue, to persist, to fester, like boils on the lives of their families and the interns whose job it was to prolong the whole thing. Ben didn't blame them. It wasn't their fault. It was all part of life, or to be more exact, death. But it wasn't Ben's fault either. And they disgusted him. They all disgusted him as unsalvageable blemishes on the image that was Ben's version of what the medical field was about, a Marcus Welbyan image where every problem had a solution, all ills could be cured within the network-allotted thirty minutes. They were as foreign to that image as a junky would be in a Norman Rockwell painting. Ben wished they would just go away.

Ben's utopian ruminations were suddenly disturbed when the emergency room triage nurse sent him to see a patient complaining of lower abdominal pain. Ben thought that was great, that he would get to see real patients while on his ER call, maybe even someone he could help, unlike the assorted nuts up on the ward. He took the patient's chart and walked toward room three to see him.

Mr. Phillips was a thin, nervous looking 27-year-old male. He was currently lying quietly on a gurney, a thin hospital blanket pulled up under his chin, reading his personal copy of the Merck Medical Manual. He had six bottles of various prescription medications lined up on the stainless steel tray next to the gurney. As Ben entered the room, Mr. Phillips began to moan, and rather loudly.

Ben was taken aback at the apparent gravity of the situation. "Mr. Phillips," he began, "what's wrong?"

With a grimace of pain, doubling over on his side, he managed to answer the question through clenched jaws. "Either I'm dying or I have appendicitis."

"Well let's hope it's the latter," said Ben, approaching his patient. "Let's have a look."

Mr. Phillips lowered the blanket and lifted his hospital gown, exposing his belly for examination.

As Ben reached over to palpate his abdomen, he was startled to see the number of scars of various length scattered about the patient's midsection.

"What happened here?" inquired Ben.

"War injury over in Vietnam," Mr. Phillips replied matter-of-factly.

"Wow," said Ben reaching over to press on his belly. "I bet that hurt."

Mr. Phillips watched Ben's hands apprehensively as Ben gently assessed the situation. Mr. Phillips was obviously in severe distress as evidenced by the screaming and writhing in pain elicited by the lightest of touches from Ben. During the brief exam, perspiration had started to bead on Ben's forehead as he imagined rupturing Mr. Phillip's tense swollen appendix by one overly aggressive prod with his index finger.

"Please! No more!" moaned Mr. Phillips. "I'm begging you!"

Ben gladly accepted the opportunity to allow an end to the screaming. "All done, Mr. Phillips. I'm sorry that hurt you."

Mr. Phillips pulled his hospital gown down over his belly again and pulled the blanket back up to his chin. "What are you trying to do, kill me?" he pouted.

"No, of course not, but I have to do a thorough exam to be able to entertain all possible diagnoses."

"All possible diagnoses? You're looking for a brain tumor? I've got appendicitis. Haven't you ever seen a case of appendicitis before?"

"Well, I—" started Ben.

"You haven't, have you? You're not a real doctor are you? You're a student right?" he said, pulling the blanket up tighter under his chin while sliding backward on the gurney away from Ben.

"Well, yes, I'm a student. But—"

"Oh, my God! I was right! I could tell. Only a student could miss such a classic case of appendicitis."

"Hey, I didn't miss anything," Ben replied defensively.

"You didn't? Oh. So you agree I've got appendicitis?"

"Well, of course I do. Do you think I'm an idiot?"

"So you'd better get me to surgery right away, huh?"

"Well, I—"

"Ohhhhhh," Mr. Phillips began moaning again. "I think it's rupturing! Help! Somebody! Help!"

Ben whirled about and leaped for the door. "Don't worry, Mr. Phillips. I'll get a surgeon immediately." He bolted through the door and frantically looked about the ER for a resident.

Seeing the triage nurse, he ran up to her and grabbing her by the shoulders, began shouting. "Nurse, where are the residents?"

"The who?" She stepped back from Ben's grip. "What's wrong?'

"I need one of the doctors."

"You don't look sick to me. A little out of control, maybe."

"No, not me. I need to speak to one of them about my patient. Where are they?"

"Where do you think they are? Sleeping, like normal people."

"Well, we'd better wake one up. Now!"

"You're serious, aren't you? Your first hour in the ER and you want me to wake someone up? This better be good. Who's dying?" she inquired, glancing about the ER.

"My patient. He's got appendicitis. I think it's about to rupture."

"*Your* patient? I thought you were on psych?"

"I am. But—"

"Who *is* your patient?" she asked looking at her clipboard.

"I really think we ought to wake the resident and get a surgical consult, stat," pressed Ben.

The nurse calmly looked Ben up and down, then went back to her clipboard. "Let's see here. You've got Mr.—"

She cut off mid-sentence consumed by uncontrollable laughter, interrupted only by an occasional gasp for air. The occasional gasps, judging by the crimson hue the skin of her face had taken, were apparently insufficient. As tears began to roll down each cheek, the laughter changed to coughing interrupted only by wheezing as she clutched a nearby counter for support.

Ben's initial surprise at her sudden laughter turned to irritation when he assumed she was laughing at him, and ultimately to concern that the ER triage nurse was going to code right in front of him, as her coughing turned to choking and her skin tone turned to blue.

He quickly scanned the ER for signs of a crash cart as vague recollections of last year's CPR course ran through his mind. Was it five compressions to one breath or was it 15 compressions to two breaths?

When the nurse stopped making noise and seemed to be having a seizure, Ben became frantic and grabbing her by the shoulders shouted, "What should I do? What should I do?"

The nurse placed one hand on Ben's, slowly looked up at him, and as Ben leaned closer to hear, she managed a faint whisper.

"Cigarette."

It didn't seem to register with Ben who looked at her with a confused expression.

The nurse placed a hand behind Ben's head and pulled him closer with surprising force.

"A cigarette," she repeated between gritted teeth. "Get me a goddamned cigarette," she growled, launching into another coughing attack.

Ben was too frightened to object and turned to scan the ER for signs of some source of cigarettes. He spied a thin cachectic (which is medicalese for near death's door) old man in a hospital gown, IV pole in tow, shuffling back to his gurney with a brand new cigarette he'd just bummed off another patient. As he climbed back onto the gurney, his gown opened in back providing the obligatory droopy old butt mooning so characteristic of hospital life. He didn't actually light up his newly acquired treasure until he'd picked up and repositioned his nasal oxygen line.

That's when Ben dashed over and yanked it from his lips. After all, this was an emergency.

After a few drags, the triage nurse seemed rejuvenated and Ben mustered up the courage to ask, "What was so funny?"

The nurse put one hand over her mouth to stifle the return of laughter that could prove fatal.

As Ben began to repeat his question, she put her other hand over his mouth and said, "Don't get me started. You trying to kill me?"

Putting both hands on Ben's shoulders, she continued. "Let's play a little game of logic for a change. What kind of nurse am I?"

Without waiting for an answer she proceeded with her lecture. "A triage nurse. What does triage mean?"

Again no answer was required. She resumed the lesson. "The sorting of and allocation of treatment to patients according to a system of priorities designed to maximize the number of survivors. Now tell me what kind of rotation are you on this month Dr. Walker?"

Ben stood silently waiting for her to continue answering her own questions.

The nurse leaned into him. "Hello? Anybody home?"

"Oh!" said Ben, surprised by the request for a response. "Uh, ER."

"Aaaannnnhhhh!" replied the nurse, imitating a game show buzzer indicating an incorrect response. "You're not on an ER rotation, are you? No, I don't think so. You, my young doctor to be, are on a psych rotation. You just happen to be on psych in the ER this evening."

"Oh, right," recalled Ben.

"Now, in review, I'm a triage nurse. You are playing psychiatrist today. Agreed?"

Ben began to open his mouth but was cut off again.

"Now, what kind of patients would a triage nurse assign to a psychiatrist?"

Ben awaited her answer.

"Well?" she pressed impatiently. "This isn't rocket science."

Ben came back to life. "Oh! Uh, psychiatric patients?"

"Nuts! That's right! You're catching on."

"But what about Mr. Phillips?" asked Ben.

"What *about* Mr. Phillips?" she replied.

"He's a surgical patient. He's got appendicitis. You assigned me a surgical patient."

The triage nurse turned to a Hispanic gentlemen with blood oozing around the ice pick still lodged in his knee. He was barking to his brother in Spanish about who they would now have to kill.

"Hey! Am I not speaking English?" she asked them.

The man stopped talking, looked at his brother with a blank expression, and holding up his impaled knee said, "No comprendo inglés."

The nurse turned back to Ben. "Good. Just checking. Now, I've confirmed the fact that I've been speaking English. You seemed to have more than a rudimentary grasp of the language. So, tell me, what part of what I've been saying didn't you understand?"

Ben looked lost. "Uh, what do you mean?"

The nurse grit her teeth and moved her hands as if to strangle Ben. Then calming herself down, "OK, class. In summary. What kind of patient would a triage nurse assign to a psychiatrist?"

"Well, normally—" began Ben.

"Nuts!" shouted the nurse. "Say it! Nuts!"

"Nuts," said Ben out of fear.

"Good," said the nurse, beginning to relax. "Now, just to check your deductive reasoning. Ergo, Mr. Phillips is a..." She left the sentence dangling, her brow lifted in anticipation that Ben could fill in the missing word.

Ben scratched his head. Then slowly, not wanting to let the word go, he said, "Nut? A nut?"

"By George, I think he's got it!" she said in her best Pygmalion. "Your first diagnosis in the ER. A case of nuts." She shook his hand in congratulation. "Now, lesson number two. What kind of nut is he?"

"But what about his appendicitis?" asked Ben, not yet sure of lesson number one.

"Oh, no. We're regressing. Come on now. Try to keep up. Mr. Phillips does not have appendicitis."

"He doesn't?"

Taking Ben by the shoulders, "He's already had his appendix out eight times."

Ben may have felt confused, but he was still pretty sure from anatomy class that humans only had one appendix. "What do you mean? How can someone have their appendix out more than once?"

"Did you see those scars all over his belly?"

"You mean his war injuries? Sure."

The nurse began chuckling again. "War injuries? Which war is he talking about?"

"He said he was in Vietnam."

"Vietnam? Really? Mr. Phillips is 27 years old. He must have been, what, no more than ten years old at the time?"

"Then what are all those scars from?" asked Ben.

"There's one for each time he's convinced some green intern or student that he's had appendicitis, gallstones, bleeding gastric ulcer, or some other form of surgical abdomen."

"You mean he intentionally tricks people into performing unnecessary surgery on himself? That doesn't make any sense."

"Now, in review. Mr. Phillips is a what?"

"A nut?"

"Good. And nuts don't have to make sense, do they?" She continued without waiting for a reply. "So, getting back to lesson two, what kind of nut is he?"

"A crazy one?"

"More specific please."

"Uhhmmm…"

"Sorry. Time's up. You've never heard of Munchausen's Syndrome?"

"Well, uh—"

"What are they teaching in medical school these days? Don't answer that. Probably wasting a lot of time on ethics, how to empathize with your patients, and all that touchy feely stuff. Tell me. What genius came up with the idea that you could teach ethics to someone over 21 years old anyway? If you're over 21 and you haven't already acquired a set of ethics, then you're in the wrong field. Maybe you should consider being a car salesman, a politician, or better yet, a lawyer."

"But, I—"

"Anyway, Munchausen's Syndrome is when nuts get off on the attention they receive by faking illnesses. They love having surgery and they will go from one ER to the next until they can convince some idiot to cut them up."

"You're making this up, right?"

"No, fiction was never this good. They've been known to swallow metal nails to cause bleeding. They've injected themselves with feces to spike a fever. You name it, they've tried it."

"But how did you know right off?"

"That's easy. This isn't Mr. Phillips's first visit."

She marched confidently over to Mr. Phillips's room with Ben tagging along behind her. She flung the curtain to the room open finding a surprised Mr. Phillips amusing himself by building a small house out of tongue depressors surrounded by cotton ball landscaping. When he saw them, he dropped everything and began moaning again.

"Mr. Phillips," she began, "I guess you don't remember me, do you?"

Mr. Phillips stopped moaning only long enough to take a good look at her.

The nurse continued. "Oh, I thought for sure you'd remember our session the last time you were here with appendicitis. Don't you remember how I called Roosevelt Hospital down the road and they informed me that you'd been there with the same problem many times and were officially banned from their ER."

"Banned from their ER?" repeated Ben incredulously.

"That's right, banned. But seeing as you've come all this way, I've decided to have that rigid proctoscope shoved up your butt just to make sure nothing's wrong?"

Mr. Phillips didn't look up, but started to moan louder.

"I see," she said. "So I was right. I tried to tell your doctor you were only getting off on it."

At that, Mr. Phillips, still moaning, rolled onto his stomach and raised his rump into the air.

Unfortunately the mood was broken when paramedics stormed into the ER, one of them doing standup on the way to the trauma crash room. "Hey everybody, what's black and white and red all over? Give up?"

As the gurney in tow made it through the doorway, the still body of a fully robed nun was revealed. "Would you believe a 68-year-old penguin with an eight-inch switchblade in her gut?"

Chapter 10

Ben watched as the black and white robed nun rolled past him with a bloody knife handle protruding from her belly like something from a Monty Python comedy sketch.

"Well, Mr. Phillips," the nurse began, "as much as I'd like to accommodate you, I'm afraid we're not going to have time for your little session today. It looks like you're going to have to drag your loony butt home."

Mr. Phillips stopped moaning and turned to Ben for a more sympathetic face.

"Let's go, you sick bastard!" shouted the nurse throwing Mr. Phillips's clothes at him. "Mother Theresa's waiting!"

With that, she turned, grabbing Ben by the sleeve, and left the room, adding from the hallway, "Come on, Dr. Walker, enough pretend medicine for tonight. Our bleeding angel of mercy is going to need some bloods drawn. Get to it!"

Surprised at the force with which the big nurse shoved Ben toward the trauma crash room, he dropped his clipboard, and bending to pick that up, dropped the stethoscope from around his neck, sending the assorted supplies in his breast pocket scattering about the floor, including pens, penlight, ruler, and reflex hammer. Scraping his possessions together on his hands and knees, he quickly scurried off to the crash room, dropping the reflex hammer one last time, pinning the bouncing instrument under his foot.

"Finally, real medicine," thought Ben as he raced to the crash room, lightheaded with excitement. "Trauma! Something rational. Not a bunch of sexually confused, delusional, nuts."

In the crash room, the chief resident was barking orders. Ben was assigned to draw blood for various tests including hematocrit, electrolytes, and blood gases. But Ben didn't know the nun was still conscious, and when, for the purpose of obtaining the specimen for blood gases, he inserted the needle into her right radial artery, a particularly sensitive spot, he didn't notice her left arm coming across the table.

The power behind the frail old nun's left hook surprised all the medical personnel attending to her. But none more than Ben who was hurled over a stainless steel instrument tray against the wall, ultimately slumping to the floor as he watched the crash room lights spinning along with the rest of his world.

As the room began to come into focus amid the sounds of doctors and nurses complimenting the nun on her agility and strength, Ben felt a painful twinge in his left buttock. Standing up and looking over his shoulder, he spied the very needle and syringe he had just poked into the nun's wrist bobbing up and down as it hung from his rear end.

One of the nurses noticed as well, commenting, "Hey guys, the stud's taken a dart in the butt."

"I can see that," said the chief resident, "but did he get the blood gas?"

Pulling the syringe from Ben's rump, the nurse held it up, and seeing 4cc of blood in the syringe, said, "Yea, well, assuming this is her blood, he got it."

Ben was rubbing his throbbing buttock.

"Hey, great job," said the chief resident to Ben. "Now, when you bring it to the lab, be sure they also run a hepatitis profile and HIV. Then have your own blood drawn as well for a baseline hepatitis and HIV."

Finally distracted from his sore bottom, Ben looked up. "My blood?"

"That's right," replied the chief resident as he probed the nun's knife wound to help determine the depth of penetration.

"Why should I have *my* blood drawn?" asked Ben.

"You just suffered a needlestick with a contaminated syringe. It's standard policy."

"Contaminated!?" asked Ben suddenly gripped with terror. "Contaminated with what?" shouted Ben, his mind conjuring up sinister secret government plots exploiting nuns as guinea pigs to test some new form of germ warfare.

"Take it easy," said the chief resident calmly as his finger suddenly entered the nun's abdominal cavity and blood began gushing from the wound. "Oops."

As Ben looked down at the blood from the nun's belly flowing freely over his bleached white shoes, he feebly repeated his question, "Contaminated with what?"

"Nothing… you hope," said the chief resident. "Uh, nurse. I guess we'll need surgery after all," he added, as the nun's heart monitor went flat line.

Ben persisted. "Are you saying she could have hepatitis… or AIDS?"

"Well, sure."

"But she's a nun, for Christ's sake! What risk factors could she possibly have?" asked Ben. "Intravenous drug abuse? Promiscuous sex?"

"Hey now, you can go to hell for saying less than that. Besides, there are other risk factors. Maybe she's received transfusions in the past. Maybe she's been stabbed before and received a tainted unit of blood." The chief resident now straddled the nun's midsection, beginning chest compressions as the team went to a full code.

The triage nurse, now squeezing the ambu bag which pumped air into the dying nun's lungs, spun around to glare at Ben. "Dr. Walker! It is hospital policy to draw hepatitis and HIV serology on anyone suffering a needlestick. In order to determine if a healthcare provider contracts either hepatitis or AIDS from a needle used on a patient, it must first be documented that the healthcare provider is not already positive for the virus."

Ben began to panic. "Already positive!?"

As the cardioversion paddles were applied to the nun's chest the resident shouted, "Clear!" The nun's body convulsed. Still flat line.

The triage nurse glared at Ben again. "If you don't stop whining and get your ass down to the lab right now, we're not going to need those results!"

"Clear!" shouted the resident.

Ben turned tail and ran for the lab. His mind raced with thoughts of contaminated blood, AIDS, death. He imagined viral particles creeping into his blood stream from the needle track in his hind quarters, insidiously infecting his defenseless T-lymphocytes, and beginning to multiply. He ran past the elevator, no time to wait, and raced down the stairs, four at a time. What did she mean, already positive? How could he be already positive? He didn't have any risk factors. He was still a goddamned virgin for Christ's sake, though he couldn't vouch for the nun. Maybe she slept around with the altar boys. Maybe she was a closet heroin addict and shared needles with the rest of the clergy. Maybe... maybe... maybe Ben was losing his mind.

* * * *

Ben burst through the door to the laboratory, the nun's specimens in hand. Crashing into the front desk, he held out the tubes of blood and shouted to the bald rolly-polly man in front of him, "Quick, these are STAT from the ER!"

The front of the desk was covered with a collage of test tubes full of blood, patient paperwork, and a computer printer spitting out endless ribbons of patient identification labels. The rotund gentleman manning the desk had both hands full of specimens in plastic bags. Rubber bands hung from his wrists. He had a telephone handset wedged between his ear and right shoulder while three other phone lines continued to ring unanswered. As he rubbed a bead of sweat from his brow with the back of his hand, a specimen biohazard sticker accidentally stuck to his forehead.

He didn't so much as look up when Ben slammed into his desk shouting.

Ben tried again. "Hey, these are STAT from the ER!" he repeated, shaking the bag.

The man spoke into the headset.

"We didn't *lose* your specimen."

"…"

"No, I don't know where it is."

"…"

"No, that's not the same as it being lost. If you sent it, it's here. Hang on."

Pressing the flashing line on the phone, "Lab, hold." He repeated the same phrase over and over as he went down the line of flashing lights.

Ben interrupted, "Hey!"

The man looked up perturbed, "What!"

"STAT from the ER!"

"So!"

"So where should I put them?"

"You don't really want me to answer that, do you?"

"I'm serious."

Pointing to a wire bin overflowing with specimens, "Just put them with all the other STATS."

"But this is priority," emphasized Ben.

"Wait. Which is it STAT or Priority?"

"What?"

"Make up your mind." Pointing to a larger overflowing wire bin, "Priority goes over there."

Ben looked back and forth between the baskets. "Well, which is fastest?"

"Neither."

"Neither?"

"Right. Super STAT is fastest."

Eyeing a third bin, Ben pointed to it. "Is that for Super STAT?"

"You kidding? That's just Expedite."

"Well, how do I get Super STAT?"

"You can't."

"I can't?"

"No."

"Why?"

"She's not here."

"Who's not here?"

"The Super STAT tech."

"Well where is the Super STAT tech?"

"She quit last week."

Ben shook his head in exasperation. "Well just get this done ASAP."

The man raised an eyebrow. "Well, alright, but ASAP's won't be done until tomorrow day shift.

"Never mind," said Ben, in defeat. He looked over at the three wire bins, glanced from one to the next, and then, taking the three tubes of blood out of the bag, placed one in each bin.

Turning back to the chubby clerk, "Where can I get my blood drawn?"

The clerk continued tossing specimens into bins without looking up. "Jabbed yourself?"

"Lucky me."

"Have a seat over there." The clerk pointed to two chairs outside the phlebotomy room.

Ben walked over and sat on one of the cracked plastic orange chairs outside the phlebotomy room. He soon started thinking once again about the possibility that he might actually have contracted the AIDS virus only minutes ago from a blood-tinged needle in his left buttock. And just as quickly he began to comfort himself with the notion that things like AIDS only happened to people like all those poor slobs in the ER as if their lowly station in life had all but assured them of contracting some horrible illness.

His rationalizing acrobatics were interrupted when a thin sickly looking young man sat down next to him. At first Ben thought the man was just wearing baggy clothing. But when he noticed the gaunt look of the man's face with the prominent cheek bones, Ben recognized the signs of a gravely ill man. Judging from his age, roughly thirty, AIDS was more likely the cause than some form of cancer. When the man looked up, Ben saw the purple plaques so characteristic of Kaposi's Sarcoma, an AIDS-associated malignancy.

Then he spoke to Ben. "I'm going to be negative this time."

"What do you mean? Negative for what?" asked Ben pretending not to understand.

The man saw through Ben's charade. He knew the look all too well. That look that says oh, not another AIDS victim. Look what he's done to himself.

But he was happy to let it slide. After all, he was virus-free now. "The virus," he said. "HIV."

It didn't really make much sense to Ben. The man looked like he was at death's door. But Ben had his own problems to worry about. "That's great. Congratulations," he said.

The bony gentleman persisted. "It's those pills from Mexico, you know. A friend of mine knows a guy who gets them for me. It takes most of my disability check to pay for them, but apparently they eradicate the virus completely, and within six months your HIV test converts back to negative."

Ben looked up, eyes narrowed. "Your friend has a cure for AIDS?"

"Well, no. But this guy he knows—"

"And it's only available in Mexico?" Ben began to nod his head.

"Right."

"So now you're cured?" asked Ben eyeing the emaciated man skeptically.

"Well, it's been six months as of yesterday. I told my doctor, but he suggested I come down and get tested just to make sure.

"I think that's a good idea," said Ben, checking his watch.

"Next!" came a shout from inside the phlebotomy room.

Ben jumped, startled by the sudden call.

"Hey, well, uh, good luck," Ben said to his thin friend as he entered the phlebotomy room.

The phlebotomist wore a short pink coat, his back to Ben. Turning around, he saw Ben's white student's coat and stethoscope.

"Needlestick?"

Ben looked up. His jaw dropped. The phlebotomist wore no shirt under his coat. There was a tattoo of a syringe on his chest, flanked on each side by a nipple ring. A cigarette dangled from the pale young man's lips, the smoke rising past his bleached white hair.

"Hey, give me a break. I'm between gigs," said the phlebotomist, noting Ben's surprise at his appearance.

"The hospital permits you to go shirtless and smoke on hospital grounds?" asked Ben in disbelief.

"Hey man. It's 2 AM in the morning, graveyard shift, I handle blood and tainted needles from people with all sorts of deadly diseases, and I'm paid minimum wage. What did you expect? Black tie and tails?"

"Well, no, I just—"

"Hey, I speak English and I don't have any open sores... today. Consider this the VIP treatment. Now, show me some veins. I don't have all night."

Ben closed his jaw, which seemed to be stuck in the down position, and rolled up his right sleeve.

"Oh man. Look at those pipes," remarked the phlebotomist eyeing Ben's healthy large caliber veins. "You don't shoot up, do you?"

"Shoot up?"

"Yeah man. Most of the clientele in this place have destroyed every available vein shooting heroin. The challenge of finding one to draw blood from is the only thing that keeps this job interesting."

"Sorry," said Ben.

"I bet I could do you with my eyes closed."

"No need for the blindfold today, thanks," said Ben declining the circus act.

Turning to his supplies, the man with the bleached white hair and pink lab coat asked Ben, "So you'll be wanting a fresh needle?"

Ben jumped to his feet in shock. "You reuse needles?"

"Just kidding. Calm down," said the phlebotomist turning to Ben again armed with a fresh needle. "A little uptight, sort of type A personality, are we?"

"I guess so," said Ben taking his seat again. "Just like my blood type. A."

As the needle entered a vein in Ben's arm, the chubby man from the front desk poked his head in. "Hey Danté, you're going to have to pick up the pace. They've got a bus load of teenage revelers coming to the ER directly from a rock concert in Central Park. Apparently some bad booze laced with something was passed around, and now they're all puking their guts out. You've got to get down to the ER right away to draw blood for all sorts of toxicology studies. ETA three minutes."

"Oh great." The phlebotomist abruptly snapped the rubber tourniquet off of Ben's arm as the tube of blood finished filling. "Now I know what they mean when they say don't give up your day job." Then, poking his head out into the waiting area, "Next!"

As Ben left the room rubbing his sore arm, the thin sickly gentlemen with the Mexican cure struggled to get his frail body up from his chair and slowly shuffled in to have his blood drawn.

The phlebotomist looked him over impatiently and said, "You're not a type A kind of guy are you?"

"My blood type? No, I'm type O," he replied.

"Never mind," said the phlebotomist reaching for a new needle as he rushed to finish up and get to the ER.

It only took a couple of seconds and the blood was in the tube. The phlebotomist grabbed his tray of blood drawing implements, threw the two tubes of blood from Ben and his thin partner on the front desk, and raced to the ER mumbling something about vampires and the living dead.

Before Ben could make his way out of the laboratory, his beeper sounded, calling for him to come to the ER, STAT. Ben could only imagine they were calling for help with the bus load of teenagers coming from Central Park. Once again, Ben had forgotten he was on ER call for psychiatry, and nothing so mundane as a busload of stoned teenagers having a bad trip would be waiting for him upon his return to the ER. No, Ben hadn't met the Rocket Man yet.

And as Ben jogged past the lab front desk on his way to the ER, he never noticed the perturbed look on the chubby clerk's face when he discovered the two tubes of blood haphazardly tossed on his desk void of any patient identification labels. Nor did he see the look of relief on the man's face when he found the two requisitions for HIV testing, one in Ben's name and one for a Kevin Love. Ben was long gone when the overworked clerk, isolated from any sense of the consequences all the little specimens strewn about the room had for their respective human sources, randomly assigned one of the nameless tubes to Kevin Love's requisition and the other to Ben's.

Chapter 11

"Has the bus arrived?" asked Ben, arriving in the ER.

His old pal, the triage nurse was there to meet him. "Why? Does this look like a bus depot to you?"

"Well, I heard there was a busload of—"

The nurse cut him off mid-sentence. "Have you already forgotten all I've taught you? You're covering psychiatry. The only bus load you'll be dealing with is a busload of lunatics."

"But what about—" started Ben as he saw stretcher after stretcher of teenagers being transported into the ER?

"I'm afraid those kids are here to see *real* doctors. Your patient is in—"

Another nurse, frantic, on the verge of tears came running up to them, interrupting the triage nurse. "Help! He's got some kind of knife!" she shouted gesturing toward one of the exam rooms, pulling Ben by the sleeve.

"Who's got a what?" asked Ben, resisting.

"The patient in room three! He's got some kind of knife! Someone's going to get hurt!" she explained.

"I can see that. But why should it be me? Whose patient is he?" asked Ben looking at both nurses.

The triage nurse couldn't resist smiling. "I believe that would be *your* patient, Dr. Walker," she said calmly.

The nurse began tugging at his sleeve again.

"*My* patient?" asked Ben, incredulous. Then seeing no way out, "It figures. Well, where's security?"

"He needs a psychiatrist, doctor. I think you'd better come quick," urged the frantic nurse.

"But he's got a knife!" Ben pleaded.

"Oh, he's perfectly harmless," said the triage nurse.

"Harmless? How do you know?" asked Ben.

"It's my job, remember?" said the triage nurse. "Now why don't you go do yours?" she added.

Ben took one more look at the triage nurse, hoping for a last-minute reprieve from the governor. The warden stood firm however.

Ben slowly turned toward room three, resigned to his fate. Still, were it not for the nurse alternately pulling him by his sleeve and pushing him from behind, Ben would never have reached the room on his own.

As the curtain to room three and the machete-wielding maniac behind it approached, once again Ben found his life passing before his eyes. But just as he was beginning to think the life he'd lived seemed quite the adventure, Ben recognized the lagoon from Gilligan's Island and realized it wasn't even his own pitiful life he was reliving. Ben's life to this point, in fact, had been a bleak collage of endless school exams punctuated by television sit-coms, half of those in black and white.

The nurse finally pushed Ben into room three, his arms raised over his head to ward off any impending knife attack. When he heard a loud thud, he dove to the floor and everything went black.

That's when Ben realized his eyes were closed. Lying prone on the floor in self-imposed darkness, all Ben could hear was rapid heavy breathing, punctuated by an occasional rustle of paper, as if there were a wild animal in the room with him.

When the anticipated death blow never materialized, Ben ventured to peak between his arms which were folded protectively over his head.

He seemed bigger than he was simply because of Ben's perspective from the floor. But there was no question this was a wild man. He was thin but wiry, standing on top of the exam table, where he'd jumped when Ben entered, perched like a cat ready to pounce. The first thing Ben noticed were the wild eyes that wouldn't hide behind the wire-framed coke bottles the man wore. They seemed to glow like embers against his dark skinned complexion, obviously a product of India, framed by the tangled silver bush that was his hair and beard, long, wild, and unkempt, a cross somewhere between Einstein and Sasquatch. Over his head he held what appeared to be, yes, a can opener.

Noticing the slightest movement of Ben's arms, the man threateningly shook the can opener held tightly in his fist over his head and shouted, "Do not try to stop me!" Ben's initial impression of the man's Indian descent was confirmed by a thick accent, rather high-pitched and somewhat melodic.

With as little movement as possible, Ben scanned the room in hopes of finding the intended target of the can opener, a can of pork and beans perhaps.

"I won't stop you," said Ben, face pressed to the floor. "I promise." After a brief pause, "Just curious though. What is it you're planning to do?"

"Tell me. What would *you* do?" barked the man standing on the exam table. "They won't leave me alone. They follow me everywhere I go."

"Who's following you?" asked Ben without looking up.

"FBI. Thugs from the FBI. I told them I don't have their stinking plutonium. But they won't believe me. Damned transmitter!" he growled hitting himself on the head.

"What's that about a transmitter?" asked Ben, gathering the nerve to look up.

"They use it to track me. Like some kind of animal."

"What transmitter? Where is it?"

"You will see in one moment please," said the wild man, suddenly smashing the mirror over the sink with a kick. Then grabbing one of the larger mirror fragments and holding it up to see the side of his head, he placed the can opener to his scalp.

Chapter 12

Rocket Man. That was the nickname Makesh Guptah had picked up in college at MIT. But it all really started even as a child back in India. His thoughts were always in the stars, fascinated by anything even remotely related to outer space. While many children managed to convince their parents to buy telescopes for them, Makesh carried the idea one step further. He actually used his. By the time he was seven years old, he could identify all the major constellations, and many not so major ones.

He learned English from Flash Gordon comics and anything related to Buck Rogers. He was consumed by dreams of interplanetary travel and the possibility of extraterrestrial civilizations. And as a result, life here on earth for Makesh Guptah, had, in many respects, ceased to exist.

He often dreamed about men from outer space. Sometimes they were mean, especially after Makesh had eaten too much candy after dinner, but more often then not, he dreamed of friendly aliens. In any event, they had always assumed human form, pretty much as depicted in Flash Gordon or Buck Rogers, along with an occasional little green man.

One particular morning, however, he awoke in such a state of excitement that his parents were at a complete loss as to how to handle the situation. Makesh told his parents that spacemen had actually come to visit him that night. When his parents asked him to describe his dream he became furious, adamant that it was definitely not a dream. Not unfamiliar with a young boy's imagination, they asked him what the aliens looked like. They felt relieved when he couldn't describe them. They didn't have bodies, he told them. They were more like light and energy without form. But Makesh was so convinced they were real that his parents' concern was renewed. Their son's pretend aliens had always had bodies before and more importantly, their son always new the difference between a dream and reality.

To humor him, they asked what the aliens wanted. They were hungry, he told them. They wanted some fruit. This reply put his parents at ease again. Just a little boy's fantasy.

Makesh saw aliens every night that week. And just as Makesh's parents began to wonder what Makesh was doing with all the fruit, the visits ceased. Just as suddenly as they had started, they'd stopped. Makesh's parents felt relieved that they had their eight-year-old back.

A nerdy teenage bookworm with thick glasses rimmed by 1950's style black plastic frames, Makesh's life's ambition became shaped by the television series Star Trek. He decided to pursue a career in aerospace engineering with the intention of working on projects involving manned space missions. It became rapidly apparent that he could only pursue this dream by moving to the United States and seeking a position with NASA where the space program was in full swing.

Getting into MIT was a dream come true for Makesh. Once there, he found others with similar interests. No longer could he be singled out as the weirdo known for his ability to recite the dialogue, word for word, from every episode of Star Trek. It seemed, to the contrary, to be a form of prerequisite for admission to MIT.

There did remain one subtle difference, however. While, to most, the Star Trek infatuation was simply a hobby for the sake of distraction from their rigorous studies, it was different for Makesh. His studies were more the distraction, simply a means to reach his life's goal of interplanetary travel. The starship Enterprise was not simply a product of fiction. It was, in his mind, completely attainable.

"It's a dream come true," Makesh proudly wrote home to his family when he was recruited by Lawrence Livermore Laboratories in California to work on building rockets. He could then officially wear his college nickname with honor. He truly had become the Rocket Man.

He showed up at Lawrence Livermore for his first day of work, proudly displaying his shiny new security clearance ID, for which he'd had to pass all manner of investigations concerning possible ties to communism or unusual sexual practices with potential for exploitation by international spies. When investigators asked him whether he liked girls (as opposed to barnyard animals, he wondered?), he replied simply that he didn't know any.

Where are the spaceships, he thought, as he was shown to his very own personal 5'x5' office cubicle? Patience, he told himself, as he cheerfully went to work on his first assigned engineering project, a new more water-efficient flushing mechanism for the more than 500 toilets at the Lawrence Livermore complex.

Although no one ever spoke of spaceships at the lab, Makesh presumed that was simply due to tight security measures. He eagerly worked his way up the ladder winning increasingly prestigious assignments. By the end of his first year, he had designed a new system for transporting luggage at a nearby Air Force base. But still no sign of spaceships.

Over the years, Makesh eventually came to the realization that manned space flight was not on the menu at Lawrence Livermore. He did, nevertheless, ultimately get promoted to the rocket program. The rockets Makesh made, however, were not designed for space travel. They weren't even designed to carry people. They were designed to kill them. Though one could technically call them rockets, they were, in fact, more commonly referred to as missiles. And at the height of his career, what Makesh's missiles carried were nuclear warheads.

And so, childhood dreams of interplanetary travel and establishing relationships with extraterrestrial civilizations were tidily filed away somewhere deep in the back of Makesh Guptah's psyche and life went on, a life centered around the construction of weapons of mass destruction.

During that time, amid the daily drudgery of building bombs capable of wiping out entire countries, Makesh somehow managed to find a wife. And when they had a little girl, Makesh hauled out all his old childhood dreams and enthusiastically transplanted them to her. His beautiful little Leeza had become his life. But Makesh Guptah was not a lucky man.

It was during their usual bedtime game of fly to the moon where Makesh would swing the giggling four-year-old up over his head that she inadvertently bumped her leg on the edge of her bed frame. It was just a tap. She didn't even cry. It was only while getting dressed for nursery school the next morning that the bruise was even noticed. It didn't seem to bother her, so he and his wife let her go to school anyway.

Makesh's wife had to stop and take some deep breaths to calm herself when the call came from school that Leeza wasn't herself that day. Wasn't herself? What did that mean?

When she arrived to pick up her daughter, Mrs. Guptah was frightened by the look on the school nurses face. Leeza was resting on a cot in the nurse's office.

"Is it your leg, baby?" she asked, rushing into the room to see her little girl. She stopped in her tracks when she saw the pale white listless creature on the cot, a child resembling a photographic negative of her own olive-skinned baby.

"What's that about her leg you said?" inquired the nurse hovering behind the little girl's mother.

Mrs. Guptah rushed to the cot to hug the little girl. "She banged it on her bed last night. There was a little bruise this morning," she replied, tugging at the waist band of Leeza's pants to assess the bruised thigh.

"My God!" was the startled response upon viewing Leeza's left leg which had now ballooned to almost twice its girth from hip to toe. It would have been bigger, but in fact, it had been limited to that size by her pants leg which had contained its expansion. The skin was an angry purple.

"She's bleeding," was all the nurse said as she reached for the telephone to call an ambulance.

The hospital didn't find any of this mysterious. They'd seen it any number of times, and in fact, the case was quite classic. An innocent childhood bruise that wouldn't stop bleeding. The cute four-year-old child, ghost-white from blood loss and ensuing anemia. Her blood counts confirmed the suspected dangerously low platelet count which explained why her bleeding would not stop. The bone marrow biopsy documented the cause of her low platelet count. The hospital personnel made it all seem almost matter-of-fact, an obvious case even a medical student could have solved.

Leeza's diagnosis of leukemia devastated the Guptahs. This was the beginning of the end for Makesh.

They said today's chemotherapy regimens were so successful that they could cure greater than 90% of childhood leukemias.

They couldn't cure them all. They couldn't cure Leeza. Makesh Guptah was not a lucky man.

She died within the year, but she wasn't the only victim. The cancer also killed Makesh's marriage. It appeared to metastasize from Leeza to her parents, the strain of a chronically ill child eating away at their relationship. And running a parallel course, the day Leeza died, so did the Guptahs' marriage. Makesh's wife left him.

So did his missiles. The man who had dreamed of designing spaceships for interplanetary travel, but settled for building bombs, hadn't anticipated the end of the cold war. Just as the Berlin wall had fallen, so did the bottom fall out of the market for nuclear warheads.

His beloved child died. His wife left him. His job was threatened. No, Makesh Guptah was certainly not a lucky man.

And that's when he first started to receive the messages. Initially they appeared on his computer. He was at the terminal in his cubicle at work. He had a rather complicated graphic representation of a jet engine component on the screen. He had just reached for a sip of coffee when his screen went black. He calmly put the coffee down and reached for his computer keyboard. These network downtimes were all too common occurrences. He punched in a few commands. No response.

He tried again. Nothing. Even the commands he typed did not appear on his completely black screen. That was distinctly unusual.

He stood up and peaked over the partition into the next cubicle. "Hey Ron. Are you down?"

"No," replied his neighbor.

"Humph," he grunted. Why was his terminal the only one down? He checked his cable connections behind his computer. He crawled under his desk to check the rest of his lines and plugs. Everything seemed to be in order. He crawled back out to get into his chair and bumped his head on the underside of his desk. Holding back an expletive, he plopped back into the chair, rubbing his head. When he looked back at his computer screen, he stopped rubbing his head. There in the upper-left hand corner were three words.

"Are you there?"

At first, Makesh didn't know what to make of this, but quickly decided it was simply one of his colleagues just fooling around.

"Where else would I be?" he typed in response, adding, "Who are you?"

"A friend," was the reply.

Makesh stood up and looked about the large cubicle-filled room for signs of the prankster, perhaps someone looking his way, holding back a snicker. No one.

He sat down again and went back to his keyboard, repeating, "Who are you? And what happened to my project?"

"This is a friend. Your project was flawed."

Makesh was rather indignant that some unidentified coworker was critiquing his project, a project he'd been working on for months, a project that seemed to have disappeared. "What do you mean, flawed? And, I repeat, what happened to it?" Makesh started bouncing his knee in a nervous twitch.

"The design would not provide sufficient thrust for interplanetary travel. It's been discarded."

Makesh's knee stopped bouncing. His eyes widened and the hair on the back of his neck stood up. He tried to respond with shaking hands. "fodvstfrf?" Looking at his monitor, he realized he had inadvertently placed his hands on the wrong keys. "Discarded?" A bead of sweat rolled down his forehead to the tip of his nose and hung there in anticipation of the anonymous computer hacker's response.

"Discarded," was the reply in simple confirmation.

Makesh reflexively pounded the desk with his fist, then, realizing the noise he made, quickly peered over his cubicle wall to see if anybody had noticed.

His neighbor looked up at him. "Everything OK, Rocket?"

Makesh nervously apologized. "Oh, yes. Thank you. Uh, everything is just fine, thank you. Sorry for the noise."

Back at his keyboard again, Makesh typed, "I need my project back. I've worked a long time on it. If you've destroyed it, I'll lose my job."

"Your project was flawed. It's been discarded."

Makesh pulled his hands from the keyboard in frustration and started pulling at his hair. Then, back at the keyboard, "Who are you?"

"A friend."

"Why do you do this thing to me?"

"Do not worry about your project. I think you will agree this will be more satisfactory." Makesh's monitor went blank. But almost immediately thereafter, the screen became a whir of words, mathematical equations, and frankly unrecognizable symbols flashing by at speeds almost too fast to see, let alone digest. Makesh just stared wide-eyed, the endless stream of information on the screen reflected in his glasses. Suddenly the blur of data ceased, followed by three words, "Error: insufficient memory." Then, "One moment, please, Makesh. System upgrade in progress." After a pause of 20 seconds, the data started to flow again.

Makesh stood up again to look about the room to see if there were any suspicious characters looking his way, someone who might be behind this whole thing. But nothing appeared out of the ordinary. When he sat down again and looked at his monitor, he noticed the flood of data had finally halted. And in its place was a complex three-dimensional image. Makesh stared at it, blinked, rubbed his eyes, and looked again.

A spaceship.

It was a spaceship. No doubt about it. On the surface, it looked not unlike something from a Star Trek episode. But on closer inspection, Makesh could see that the three-dimensional blueprint on his screen detailed all the components to make the deceptively toy-like model a reality. Using a zoom function on his computer, Makesh was able to enlarge individual components for closer inspection. His mouth dropped open in awe as he stared from the edge of his seat in wide-eyed fascination. He'd become a child on his first-ever visit to the candy store.

For the next hour, Makesh forgot to blink as he examined in detail each of the spaceship's working systems, many using technology completely unfamiliar to him. Some of the basic components were nevertheless recognizable. The propulsion system, in fact, appeared to be powered in some manner by nuclear energy.

When Makesh finally collapsed back into his chair in exhaustion, he noticed one word at the bottom of his screen. It was a question.

"Well?" was all it said.

Makesh typed his response, also one word. "Wow!"

"I thought you'd like it," came the anonymous reply.

"Who are you?" typed Makesh, the fog in his mind starting to lift.

"You don't remember us? We remember you."

"No, I don't remember you. What do you want from me?"

"Many years ago, you were so kind to us. You said if we ever needed any more fruit, to just ask."

"You've come to me for fruit?" demanded Makesh, incredulous. "You've destroyed the project I was working on, and now you're hungry? What would you like? A banana?"

"No, thank you. Just some plutonium, please."

Makesh thought he misread the monitor. He looked again. Plutonium. Yes, that's what it said. "Plutonium?" inquired Makesh in disbelief.

"Yes, please. We're running rather low. A kilo would do for now."

"A kilo!? Of plutonium? I thought you wanted fruit."

"Fruit's good. But right now, our need is plutonium."

"You eat plutonium?"

"No, of course not. You must have seen in the design of our spacecraft that plutonium provides our source of energy. We are running low, and without it, we cannot get home."

"So you want me to steal plutonium for you?"

"It seems you hardly use yours. We just thought—"

The screen went blank. Makesh pounded a few keys with no response.

Two words appeared at the lower left hand corner of his screen. "Security violation." Immediately following that, the plans to the original project Makesh was working on reappeared. They hadn't been destroyed after all. All his hard work over the past several months was still intact. But what was all that nonsense about spaceships, fruit, and plutonium that had taken over his computer terminal for the last hour? It was as though nothing had happened. Makesh slumped back in his chair. Had it happened? Maybe he'd imagined it. Makesh quickly looked up at the clock on the wall. Yes, an hour had passed. He then compared the time on the clock to his wristwatch. The clock was right.

Makesh quickly copied the data from his project onto floppy disks to have a backup copy should something happen to his computer again. He then quickly closed that computer file, cleared his screen, and typed, "Hello?"

No response. He tried again. "Hello. Is anyone there?"

Nothing.

If he'd imagined the whole thing, where did the last hour go? What happened to the time? It didn't make any sense.

Makesh went back to work. He didn't have time to think much more about the unexplained encounter. The rest of the day was uneventful. No mysterious computer phenomena. He left work to head home to his empty apartment to try to put the whole thing out of his mind. He'd been under a lot of stress the past few months, considering his daughter's death, quickly followed by his divorce. He just needed a little rest.

Makesh was driving home through the rolling California countryside when his car radio began acting up. His usual easy-listening station suddenly developed static. As Makesh tried to adjust the dial, the radio went completely dead. He tried turning it off and on again, but when he turned it back on, a high-pitched frequency sounded with such force he thought he'd burst an eardrum. When he reached out in pain to turn it off again, sparks began to fly and the radio literally exploded. The force of the explosion knocked Makesh against the driver's door as he swerved off the road into a nearby field. Going down an embankment from the road, the car rolled over twice, coming to rest, nose buried in a hay stack. The car filled with black smoke that billowed from the dashboard. Makesh threw the door open and fell out of the car, clouds of black smoke rising behind him.

He crawled to safety, clutching a bruised shoulder. After accounting for all his limbs, he looked around and found himself in the middle of a field of high tech windmills used for generating electricity. The hundred or so giant propeller blades slowly revolving about the setting sun had Makesh mesmerized, almost hypnotized, until a sound from his car broke the spell. He looked over to the burning car but noticed that there didn't actually seem to be any flames, and, in fact, the smoke seemed to be clearing. When only occasional wisps of smoke could be seen escaping the passenger compartment, Makesh thought he heard something again. It was coming from the car. Maybe it was something melting. Maybe a rubber hose or tire was straining to burst in the heat.

Then he heard it again. It sounded like a voice. Was he losing his mind? Or was someone in the car? How could that be? The back seat? Makesh scrambled to his feet and raced to the car. Without regard for his own safety, he thrust his head through the open door to see who was in the back seat. Were they hurt in the explosion, the wreck, the fire?

The back seat was empty. The entire car was empty. There were no signs of a fire or explosion either, except for an occasional puff of smoke coming from the radio. Makesh thought it odd that the radio was still on, given the fact that it exploded only minutes ago. Maybe that was the source of the voices he'd heard. No sooner had the thought occurred to him than the radio began to speak. At first Makesh was relieved that there wasn't anyone in the car that might have been hurt. Then he immediately chuckled to himself just as relieved that he wasn't losing his mind. But then he began to listen to the voice on the radio.

"Are you there?" it said. The voice was rather monotone but calmly soothing in a way, certainly not the histrionics of a radio disc jockey. A pause followed the question and Makesh thought it funny that it almost sounded as though the radio were speaking to him. Then the voice on the radio repeated the question. "Are you there?"

Makesh felt a chill and a bead of perspiration form on his brow. Could the voice actually be speaking to him? Then he heard his name.

"Makesh, are you there?" the voice asked, confirming Makesh's fear.

Makesh, still leaning in the open door of the car, finally slumped into the driver's seat. He was losing his mind.

"Makesh." The voice again. "Are you injured?"

Makesh put his hands over his ears as if to keep the voice out of his head. He responded nevertheless. "Who are you?"

"You're there. Good," the voice answered.

"Who are you and what do you want?" shouted Makesh in frustration.

"A friend," came the reply. "Sorry to have startled you but we were interrupted earlier today."

Makesh suddenly made the connection. This was the voice behind the words that had taken over his computer that day. How was this possible? "Where are you?" he asked, speaking to his car radio, then quickly looking about to be sure no one was watching.

"Near."

"Where?"

After a pause, as if weighing whether to respond, the voice answered, "Above you."

Makesh shoved his head out the car window and looked to the sky. There was nothing to see. No helicopter. No plane. The sun had set and stars were beginning to appear. Back in the car, Makesh spoke again to the radio. "Where? I can't see you."

"Of course you can't see us. We're beyond your atmosphere."

Makesh was dumbstruck. "Beyond my...?" Then he picked up on something else the voice said. "We?"

"Of course. My craft requires a crew of 593."

Makesh instantly shoved his head out the window again unable to accept that a ship of that size couldn't be seen. Then he saw some flashing lights in the sky but quickly realized it was just a passenger jet.

"So you are trying to make me believe that you are creatures from outer space?" asked Makesh, turning back to the radio.

"Well, I think the word creatures is a little harsh, don't you?" the voice answered. "I'm surprised you don't remember us. It was only forty years ago."

"Forty years ago?" thought Makesh. Then aloud, "I was only seven years old 40 years ago."

"The fruit was delicious. It was the highlight of our visit."

Suddenly it all came back to Makesh. The dreams. He was seven years old. They particularly enjoyed the pears.

"You're real," he mumbled, as if hearing it would make it more believable. The idea that his childhood dreams were real, that he had actually met, and was now at this very moment communicating with, an alien life form left Makesh dumbfounded. His mind reeled at the thought and almost seemed to fly from his body, no longer bound by this planet alone.

"Now, about that plutonium..." the radio said, interrupting Makesh's trance.

Chapter 13

Makesh never knew how he ended up aboard the alien spaceship. Perhaps that was one of the reasons he had such a hard time convincing others of his experience. Maybe he was so overwhelmed by the very existence of alien life forms that the small details were lost. Maybe they forced him to take a pill that would sanitize his memory of particular facts, facts that might represent a security risk to the visitors should their hosts on earth learn too much. Or maybe it never happened at all.

But Makesh preferred to believe that had someone else been out in the rolling California hills that night, they would have seen the wreckage of his car with him aboard slowly rising heavenward in the green fluorescent tractor beam emanating from the mother ship overhead. They would have seen Makesh's hands shake as he dutifully fastened his seat belt. And if they'd been just outside the earth's atmosphere, the Great Wall of China just a hair on the smooth blue orb that was earth, they'd have seen the gargantuan mass of the alien ship. They'd have seen a port, a mere pinhole in comparison to the rest of the craft, open to accept Makesh's space-born Ford Taurus.

But that's neither here nor there, only conjecture, as Mr. Guptah was the first to admit he had no recollection of those events. There were certain things, however, he did remember. He couldn't explain why he remembered these particular things but had no recollection of others. It was probably all part of some alien master plan. They'd probably chosen just what they wanted him to remember and erased the rest. Those things he did remember, however, were permanently chiseled into his psyche, and no one would convince him that they never happened. The memory of those events were as clear to Makesh as the face on his four-year-old daughter.

Little green men? He couldn't remember. Did they have huge heads to enclose their massive cerebral cortices? He couldn't remember. But they definitely had heads… at least one anyway, and hands. The reason Makesh knew this was because he recalled a peculiar sign they made with their hands against their heads. It seems that when Makesh was aboard the spaceship, his hosts noticed an almost imperceptible skin cancer on the tip of his nose. It was small and superficial, relatively harmless. Makesh's doctor had offered to simply shave it off. But Makesh kept procrastinating.

When the aliens noticed it, they appeared concerned and huddled together in consultation, muttering in a language unfamiliar to Makesh. After conferring with one another, they appeared to summon one of their own, but a smaller version, perhaps a child. The small one approached Makesh, who was startled when it reached up with both hands and placed the index and middle fingers of each hand on Makesh's temples. Makesh, wide-eyed and apprehensive, tried to keep still. With its hands on his temples the little alien began to slowly oscillate its head right and left as if shaking its head no. After what seemed to be a long time, but was actually only about one minute, the motion of head shaking changed as if now to indicate yes, instead of no.

When the alien removed its hands, it first looked very closely at Makesh's nose, then seemed to smile in satisfaction.

Makesh didn't recall whether English is what came from their lips, but English is certainly what he heard when the little one looked at him and said, "Good as new."

Not until they brought over some sort of huge crystal, in which Makesh was able to see his reflection, did he understand.

The cancer was gone.

"Oh, very nice. Thank you," was all Makesh could think of at first. But then, as he rubbed the tip of his nose with his fingers, feeling the smoothness it was originally intended to have, the huge significance of what had just transpired became evident and Makesh began to see the big picture.

He slowly lowered his hands, then pointing at the aliens before him, plainly said, "You can cure cancer."

The aliens looked at each other, then shook their heads no.

"But you did. Didn't you? You cured my skin cancer," insisted Makesh, pointing to his nose, practically accusing them of a crime.

"We cannot," they replied.

Makesh was getting flustered. "Then it's not gone?" he asked. "I still have my cancer?"

"No. It's gone," said one.

"Good as new," added another.

"Then you *can* cure cancer! I was right!"

"No. We cannot."

Makesh was stumped.

Then turning and pointing to the smaller alien that had touched Makesh, the group of full-sized aliens in unison said, "It is the children. Only the children can."

The little one giggled at all the attention and said once again, "Good as new." And they all laughed.

Makesh was given a tour of the ship. They indulged his particular interest in their propulsion system and took the opportunity at that point to reiterate their request for plutonium. Makesh tried to explain to them the security issues involved and the trouble he could get into, but they wouldn't hear of it. They required plutonium, and they would have plutonium... one way or another, even if the Lawrence Livermore complex had to be destroyed.

Makesh saw that he had no choice. Besides, it was only a kilo. Maybe they wouldn't notice it was missing, Makesh thought to himself, with a resigned chuckle.

The aliens were beginning to show him to the door, assuming there was a door, so that he might go home and get their plutonium, when, as an afterthought, Makesh remembered to ask, "What about the cancer?"

"What about it?" was the alien reply.

"Can you cure it all?"

"I told you we cannot."

"But I saw you. You cured *mine*," insisted Makesh, pointing at his nose again.

"I cannot. Only the child can."

Makesh's eyes widened. It was too late for his daughter Leeza. But what about all the others? The new cases of cancer. The cases that didn't happen yet. He didn't remember if they had shoulders. But if they had, he was sure he would have grabbed them at that point and shook them. "Your children then! Can your children cure it all?"

"We only have the one," the alien replied, pointing to the small one. It was not customary for children to accompany the adults on interplanetary voyages, but it seems this child had somehow won the privilege in this case. Makesh couldn't recall the reason, whether the child showed some special promise by winning their planet's science fair, or whether it was just the offspring of some well-connected politician. "It could not possibly cure your whole planet. Too much for just one."

"Besides," the alien continued, "why go through all the trouble for a planet scheduled for conclusion?"

Makesh wasn't paying attention, still reeling from the possibilities, the realization of a cure for cancer. But the alien's remark kept coming back, like a fly at a spring picnic, until he couldn't ignore it anymore.

"Conclusion?" asked Makesh.

"Yes. Conclusion."

"What do you mean by that?"

"Conclude. To end," stated the alien, plainly.

"The earth is scheduled to… end?" asked Makesh, becoming concerned.

"Oh yes. This experiment has concluded. This coordinate in your solar system must be recycled."

"Recycled? The Earth isn't an aluminum can!"

"You are correct. Its major elements include iron, oxygen, silicon, and magnesium."

"Whatever. But what do you mean by recycle? You're replacing Earth with something else?"

"Oh yes. This is a very strategic coordinate. You know what they say, location, location, location."

"Strategic how? In a military sense?"

The alien looked puzzled. "Military? Oh, we have no military. Our last enemies were destroyed centuries ago."

"Then how is this location strategic? What would you put here?"

The alien looked about to make sure no one was within earshot, leaned toward Makesh, and whispered just two words into his ear, "Fast food."

Makesh raised one eyebrow as the alien stepped back with a look of enlightenment. "Fast food?" asked a confused Makesh.

The alien nodded with a smile and a wink of one eye. Makesh didn't remember how many eyes the alien had, but he definitely winked one of them.

Makesh closed his eyes and stepped back. "OK. So you're replacing the Earth with a fast food restaurant," he said, just to see if it sounded as ridiculous as he thought it would. And it did.

The alien leaned in a bit again and whispered, "Let's keep this between the two of us, OK?"

Makesh froze in disbelief, staring blank-faced back at the alien. "Keep what between us? The fast food restaurant or the end of the Earth?"

The alien began to answer, "The restaur—"

Makesh snapped out of his daze and interrupted, "You can't do that."

"Oh, on the contrary, a planet the size of yours would actually be no trouble at all. We could probably finish up before breakfast," countered the alien. And then, a bit confused, "You have a better plan for this coordinate? Fast food seemed like a sure thing. Do you realize how far it is from here to—"

"No I don't have a better plan. I don't have any plan," Makesh admitted.

The alien looked confused. "Then what's wrong with fast food?"

"Nothing's wrong with fast food," replied Makesh. "I just can't see destroying the Earth for a Big Mac."

"Big Mac?" The alien looked confused.

"Please don't do it. Don't destroy the Earth."

"Why not? I told you. This experiment has been concluded."

"What about all the people?" pleaded Makesh.

"We are not a mushy race," responded the alien.

Makesh saw that emotions would get him nowhere. He had to think fast. "Is there nothing of value to you on this planet?"

"Nothing."

"What about plutonium? You need our plutonium," offered Makesh, thinking he'd come up with something.

"Oh, we can get plutonium anywhere. But right now, we are here. So we will take yours."

Makesh felt as though he were trying to sell sand to an Arab.

"Give me some time. I'm sure I can find something you value. Just give me some time," pleaded Makesh.

"Tell you what," offered the alien, "this project isn't going to happen over night. It's going to take us a while to get all the necessary permits through planning and zoning anyway. Why don't you go home and think about it. We'll give you three of your months. If there's any reason at all to spare this planet, it shouldn't take longer than that to think of it."

"Three months?" asked Makesh incredulously. "Three months to save the Earth?"

"Too long? I understand. Three hours then."

Makesh almost choked. "No, no. Three months is fine."

"OK then," agreed the alien, "but if it's not too much trouble, we'd like you to get us the plutonium right away."

"Oh, no problem," assured Makesh.

Before he knew what was happening, Makesh felt himself dematerialize only to rematerialize inside his undamaged Ford

Taurus heading down a California highway at exactly 55 mph. Even the radio worked fine. The only suggestion of anything out of the ordinary was that the car's odometer had reset to zero.

Chapter 14

The kilo of plutonium was surprisingly light. Makesh imagined it would feel heavier. He thought of the old riddle, what's heavier, a pound of plutonium or a pound of feathers? And with the high level of security clearance he'd managed to earn over the years, it only took a few flashes of his identification badge to perform the heist.

The aliens were very appreciative.

Makesh's employers were not.

At least that's what he thought when he showed up for work the next day and his security badge wouldn't function. When he asked security what the problem was, he was told only that apparently his position had been terminated. No details were provided.

The rest of the day, Makesh packed his bags and sat at home waiting for the authorities to handcuff him and take him away.

But no one came.

After waiting what he thought was more than enough time for the police to come, he began to feel hungry. His bachelor's refrigerator was characteristically barren, so he set off for the neighborhood 7-Eleven for a microwaved burrito.

Seeing he was out of cash, he first stopped at an automatic teller machine at the corner. However, when he entered his PIN, the screen read "Improper authorization number. Please try again." The second attempt was also unsuccessful.

After checking the number he'd used hundreds of times against a little slip of paper he kept hidden in his wallet, Makesh tried a third time. Again, the same result, but this time it was followed by a grinding sound. Standing patiently in front of the ATM, Makesh soon realized he'd never see his beloved ATM card again. He felt a bead of perspiration forming over his brow.

He inquired within the bank and when the teller he'd known for years claimed he had no account there, Makesh's fears began to take shape. They were definitely on to him. And as what he assumed to be hunger pains in his stomach began to crescendo, his wallet just as empty as his stomach, Makesh began to wish they would come get him already, better sooner than later.

Passing the 7-Eleven again on his way home, Makesh noted the "Help Wanted" sign in the window. Feeling a new kinship to the homeless carrying signs "Will Work For Food," he entered the store.

"Excuse me, sir," began Makesh, "I am hungry and I saw the sign."

The store's owner, also of Indian descent, took an immediate liking to Makesh. "Welcome! Welcome! You seek employment?" he asked smiling widely.

"Well, I don't know how long I'll be able to stay," began Makesh, peering back over his shoulder out at the street as though he were waiting for a ride, "but I am certainly hungry."

"Welcome! Welcome! Tell me, what is your experience?"

"Well, primarily nuclear engineering, but—"

"Ha ha! That is very good, Mr. Nuclear Engineer," the owner chuckled.

"As a matter-of-fact—"

"Ha ha! You are a very funny man. Very funny. Tell me, Mr. Funny Man, can you start today?"

"I do not see the humor, but I am most certainly very hungry." replied Makesh.

"Very good then, you start today, OK?"

"But I don't know anything about—"

"No, no. Don't be so negative. No worry. This isn't rocket science after all."

"And that is precisely what bothers me," began Makesh. "You see, if this were rocket science—"

"Here," said the store owner, opening the cash register. Grabbing a handful of twenty-dollar bills, "I have not had a day off in a year. I'll pay you in advance for the week. Here's $300." He stuffed the bills into Makesh's shirt pocket. "Well?"

Makesh was speechless.

"Well?" repeated the owner.

Makesh thought for a moment, then smiled. "May I have one of your frozen burritos?"

"Excellent!" said the owner, consummating the deal with a pat on the back for Makesh. "Here are the keys to the register. I'll be back later." The owner headed for the door.

Makesh stared at the keys in his hand. "But I don't know anything about…" Looking up, he saw the owner'd already gone.

Immediately taking charge, Makesh went right to the freezer and found the burrito he'd so desired. Banging it on the counter, he confirmed it would be too difficult to ingest in its current physical state. He read the directions on the package for microwave heating. Spying the microwave behind the sales counter, Makesh tentatively approached the apparatus. He'd had plenty of experience in the operation of jet turbines and nuclear warheads, but a microwave oven was whole different ballgame. Makesh proceeded cautiously but saw no reason he couldn't figure it out. He could read directions after all.

And if not for the tin foil he wrapped it in before placing it in the microwave, he'd have pulled it off. Once the fire extinguisher was depleted and the smoke had cleared, Makesh decided to settle for a couple of chocolate bars.

The whole afternoon turned out to be a less than stellar performance for Makesh at his new vocation. After the lottery tickets turned confetti trick and the projectile slurpy incident, the armed robbery seemed almost anticlimactic. At least Makesh new what to do. When the big man put a gun in Makesh's face and ordered him to turn over all the money in the register, Makesh was somewhat relieved to finally receive an order he thought he could follow. Of course he hadn't anticipated having trouble getting the cash register to open, but the robber was extremely understanding and quite helpful in that respect.

It wasn't long after the robbery when two men in dark three-piece suits and sunglasses entered the store and purchased what seemed to be an excessive quantity of Slim Jims. Makesh had to apologize to them when he realized he had no change for their twenty-dollar bill in the recently emptied register.

"Oh, you just keep it, Mr. Guptah," insisted one of the men as the other eyed the overhead camera monitoring the immediate area.

"Excuse me, sir," began Makesh, "but how did you know my n…?" Makesh fell silent when he noticed both men suddenly turn to face him, each with a hand reaching inside their coats as if to retrieve weapons.

Makesh felt suddenly calm. "You're here about the plutonium, aren't you?" It seemed like a simple question at the time. In fact, he had every intention of cooperating with them. Unfortunately, things don't always go as planned.

I guess this is what it feels like to get roughed up, thought Makesh as he came to, alone, next to the dumpster behind the 7-Eleven. He slowly uncurled from a fetal position, consciously checking to see that all systems were functioning. Everything seemed to be in working order except for an aching head, most painful behind the right ear. He reached behind that ear to find a sizeable lump. He didn't know what to make of it at the time. But he knew they were on to him.

The men in dark suits had come for the plutonium. First they asked him nicely. Makesh told them he didn't have it. Then they got a little rough. Makesh told them he gave it to aliens. That's when one of the men pinned him to the ground while the other calmly filled a syringe with a clear solution from a small glass vile and said, "OK then. We're good at playing games. If you don't want to bring the plutonium to us, then you'll just have to bring us to the plutonium." He then jabbed the needle into Makesh's shoulder and unloaded the syringe.

The last thing Makesh remembered was the man with the syringe opening a little black briefcase lined with shiny stainless surgical instruments. Assuming Makesh was already knocked out by the drug, the man pulled on a pair of latex gloves and, reaching for a scalpel, said to the other, "Once this baby's installed, he'll be our very own plutonium homing pigeon. All we have to do is follow this transmitter and he'll lead us right to it. Either that or he'll take us to his leader."

"His alien leader," added the other assailant. The two men laughed loudly at the thought.

Now alone behind the dumpster, Makesh rubbed the bump protruding from behind his right ear and repeated the word to himself. "Transmitter." Then he noticed the money the 7-Eleven owner had stuffed in his shirt pocket was still there. He never even went back into the store.

They seemed to be everywhere. Men in black suits and dark sunglasses, behind every tree, loitering in phone booths, ducking into alleyways. Makesh spent the next week trying to lose the two goons following him while simultaneously doing his best to think of a way to save the Earth from destruction.

After a week, however, the men in black suits ran out of patience. And when they tried to throw Makesh into the trunk of their car, he knew it was time to run.

The ticketing agent at the airport didn't know what to make of Makesh when he inquired, "How far will $200 take me?"

But checking her rates she noted a fare to New York for $159. "Is New York far enough?" she asked.

"New York! Very good. Yes, thank you," answered Makesh. "Tell me, when does the next flight leave?" he asked, checking behind him to see if he'd been followed.

* * * *

The flight seemed to go uneventfully except for a minor delay at the airport metal detector. His head, it seemed, kept setting off the alarm.

"You got some kinda metal plate in your head, sir?" inquired the security guard.

Makesh couldn't let it go. "It's a transmitter."

"A transmitter? What for?" asked the guard, just making conversation.

"The FBI wants the plutonium I gave to the aliens," replied Makesh.

The security guard thought he seemed harmless enough as he disappeared down the tunnel boarding the plane. Thinking the whole story rather humorous, he retold it to a supervisor in the break room a few minutes after the plane departed.

Makesh wondered who the VIP was that no less than ten security guards were waiting for at the gate when his plane unloaded in New York."

"Please come with us, Mr. Guptah."

Makesh's first instinct was to run for it, but when he saw the way the guards were fondling their pistols, he thought otherwise.

"Where are you taking me?" he asked.

"To get you some help," was the reply.

Makesh's eyes lit up. "Help? Great! We've only got about two months left, you know."

"What happens in two months?"

"In two months, aliens will replace Earth with a Taco Bell."

Makesh couldn't reach the itch behind his ear until the handcuffs were removed in the Presbyterian emergency room. And knowing it could be his last chance to escape, Makesh decided he had first better remove the transmitter or it would be only a matter of time until the men in black suits caught up to him. And that's how Benjamin Walker met The Rocket Man, a can opener pointing at his head.

Chapter 15

Angel and The Rocket Man hit it off. Angel enjoyed discussing nuclear physics with Makesh, and Makesh enjoyed looking at Angel.

Angel was busy painting a rectangular rendition of Michelangelo's Sistine Chapel on the ceiling of the recreation room when she noticed Ben walk by with a five-year-old little girl.

"Psst. Hey Rocket, what's Hah-vud doing with the cute kid?" she asked Makesh, who was holding her ladder steady while contemplating the perfect shape of her behind.

Makesh looked at the girl and was immediately struck by her resemblance to his own daughter that died years before. "I don't know but she doesn't look crazy to me."

"I love a good mystery," said Angel, climbing down the ladder. "Come on. Let's investigate."

Angel and Makesh practically tiptoed down the hallway to where they saw Ben take the little girl into a patient's room. Angel peaked through the doorway to see Ben and the girl with their backs to the door facing a bedridden woman. The first thing that occurred to Angel was that the woman seemed too ill to be on a psychiatric ward. She was extremely thin, probably less than eighty pounds, pale as death, with an intravenous line and oxygen hookup. Angel had seen some very serious cases of anorexia come to this, but they were usually removed to a medical ward under these conditions.

Ben sat down in a chair next to the little girl who clutched her stuffed bear and stared at the woman in the bed.

"Why are her arms tied to the bed?" asked the little girl, touching her mother's wrist restraints.

"She's been trying to hurt herself. That's why she's in this part of the hospital."

The little girl just stared at the gaunt figure in the bed, counting the attached plastic tubes and taking in the smell, that terminal patient smell.

"Your mother is dying," Ben said flatly.

The little girl raised the thread-worn bear to her mouth, only her eyes visible peaking over the bear's head, and continued to stare at the woman.

"Lucy, did you hear me?" asked Ben.

The little girl slowly nodded her head, never removing the toy from her face.

"Do you know what that means?" continued Ben.

After a pause, "Mama's going away…" she began, then added, "…and never coming back."

"We thought you should know that," said Ben.

Starting to shake all over, "It's all my fault," she said sobbing into her bear.

Oh, why me, thought Ben, checking his watch. This isn't what I signed on for. "Don't be silly," he said.

The little girl turned to him in anger. "Don't call me silly! I heard you. You said it was my fault. I heard you tell the other doctors that she would have been OK if she hadn't waited until I was born. They said she needed a his-her-enemy to get all the cancer out, but she didn't have it because I was still in her tummy.

"Oh, good one, Benjamin," Angel whispered to Makesh at the doorway.

"It's not your fault," argued Ben.

"Then why is God punishing me?" asked the little girl, tears trickling down her cheeks.

Ben checked his watch again, then answered in the only way he knew how. "It has nothing to do with you. While she was pregnant with you, your mother was diagnosed with cervical dysplasia. She chose to wait until you were born to start treatment. By then it had become cancer and spread to her lymph nodes. Now she's dying."

The little girl looked at him and asked, "What's a lymph node?"

Ben started to answer, "Well it's a gland that filters out—," but then caught himself, "That doesn't matter." Then, starting to get up, "Where's your dad?"

"I don't have one."

"What do you mean?"

"He died when I was still a baby."

Ben rolled his eyes as if the little girl were out to get him. *Why is she torturing me?* he thought.

"The government lady that brings me here said I'm going to be an orphan."

Ben thought quickly and replied. "Well, Bambi was an orphan and everything turned out OK for him."

The little girl picked up her mother's hand and held it to her cheek. "Bambi was not an orphan. His father wasn't dead."

"Well what about Dumbo or Simba?"

"They had mothers. You don't know anything, do you?"

"Oh," said Ben, tiring of this game. "Well, let's go," said Ben, taking the child by the hand.

"No! Wait!" she insisted pulling her hand away. "I have to pray for Mommy."

As the little girl knelt at her mother's bedside with her teddy bear, Ben looked about uneasily, not knowing what to do with himself. That's when he spied Angel and Makesh, tears running down their cheeks. When she saw him looking, Angel gave him a menacing look and pointed to the bedside, indicating for Ben to pray alongside the child. When Ben silently balked at the idea, Makesh had to hold Angel back before she could storm into the room to give Ben a piece of her mind.

She sufficiently frightened Ben enough for him to turn and kneel with the little girl.

After a brief while, the girl got up to leave. Ben saw she'd left her bear behind in the bed. "What about this?" he asked her, pointing to the stuffed animal.

"Bear's going to stay here to take care of Mommy," she said. "That's OK, isn't it?"

Ben started to shake his head no when he saw Angel giving him the evil eye. "Oh, what a good idea," he said. "I bet your mom would like that."

As they approached the door, Angel knelt down to talk to the girl. I'm Angel. Mr. Makesh and I will help Bear. Why don't you go wait in the rec. room over there for a minute while I talk to Dr. Walker?"

"Are you really an Angel?" asked the little girl.

"Oh, no," chuckled Angel. "Believe me. I'm no angel."

"Well, you sure look like one," said the child heading down the hall.

Once she turned the corner, Makesh had to grab Angel again before she could attack Ben.

Then, in Ben's face, "Great job, Dr. Welby," she exploded. "Where were you the day they handed out the bedside manners?"

"What do you mean?"

"What kind of a jerk are you?" Then imitating Ben, "What about Dumbo?"

"Yeah, well—" started Ben before getting cut off.

"I'm sure that lymph node story cleared everything up for her."

"Yeah, but—"

Angel cut him off again. "I can't believe you weren't going to pray with her." She then just stared at him as Ben felt himself grow smaller and smaller. He had no answer for her. At least not one that sounded right anymore.

Finally, Makesh spoke. "You know. The little alien could cure this woman."

Chapter 16

The chief resident in the ER took the call from the lab concerning the nun they treated for trauma, a stabbing to be more specific.

"Yeah? What about the nun? She didn't make it."

"You recall that needlestick incident? The student got stuck with a syringe containing her blood? Well, we've got some bad news," reported the lab supervisor.

"What now?" joked the resident. "Don't tell me the nun was HIV positive."

"No, no. The nun was negative."

"Good," said the ER resident. "So, what's the problem?"

"It's the student," replied the lab.

"What about the student?"

"He's positive."

The resident was momentarily silent. "The student? The student is HIV positive?" he asked incredulously.

"Benjamin Walker. Yes."

"Say again. The whole thing," requested the resident.

"Benjamin Walker is HIV positive," came the lab supervisor's voice through the telephone.

The resident just stared at the telephone.

The lab persisted. "Hello? Hello? Are you there?"

Chapter 17

Ben Walker was growing concerned over a nagging cough he'd developed, when he got the call from the ER resident.

"What did I do now?" asked Ben when he recognized the resident's voice.

Ben listened to the resident, then said, "No, you can tell me over the phone. No point in me coming down. I know how busy things are there."

"..."

"I must have killed someone if you're asking me to sit down."

"..."

"Well, I've been coughing a bit. I'm sure it's nothing."

"..."

"Why do you ask? Why are you suddenly so interested in my health? Is the ER shorthanded?"

"..."

"I *am* sitting!"

"..."

"The nun? Oh, what happened? I guess she didn't make it, huh?"

"..."

"Yeah, I brought her blood to the lab. Don't tell me those buffoons lost the specimen. Well, if she died anyway, what's the difference? No harm done."

"…"

Something in the way the resident said "It's about your blood," emphasizing the "your," made the hair on the back of Ben's neck stand.

"*My* blood? What about my blood?" Ben could sense the storm clouds gathering.

"…"

"What kind of abnormality?" Through nervous laughter, "What? Are you're going to tell me the *nun* was HIV positive? After all, she had so many risk factors. Was she a closet heroine addict? A nun with a bad habit? Get it? Habit? Or was she actually some gay guy on his way to Mardi Gras?"

"…"

"I didn't think so. Why doesn't that surprise me that a nun would be HIV negative?" Finally, the resident ran out of patience.

"…"

Ben dropped the telephone. He couldn't hear the small voice coming from the floor talking about waiting for confirmatory testing. His cough had suddenly grown worse.

Chapter 18

There was bedlam in AIDS clinic that day. It came as no surprise to Kevin Love when his latest HIV test came back negative. He had no doubt that his Mexican miracle drug would work. His dancing and singing peaked the curiosity of the other AIDS patients. Kevin's announcement of a cure for AIDS sent everyone into mass hysteria.

The clinic attending, however, all too familiar with the shoddy work coming out of the hospital lab since the administrative bean counters' irresponsible staffing cuts, was already ordering a new blood sample be drawn from Mr. Love to confirm a laboratory screw up. At the same time, he insisted that the other half of the screw up be identified and tracked down. Experience dictates that specimen mix-ups come in pairs, as it takes two, two patients' specimens, for a mix-up to occur.

Chapter 19

Angel couldn't quite put her finger on what was different about Ben that next day during their usual session as she eyed him across the confinement of the interview room, or closet, as she called it. He looked the same, that same pathetic medical student look. But something was definitely different.

"What's with you?" she said, firing the first shot.

Ben hesitated, as if about to answer, but then quickly put his game face back on. "Let's not worry about me. You're the patient, remember?"

Angel pulled the cigarette from her mouth and vigorously tapped the ashes into the ashtray on her lap.

"OK. You want to talk business? Let's talk business." Placing the cigarette back between her lips, she stood up and made quite a show of slowly pulling her sweater off over her head, making sure the bottoms of her breasts just revealed themselves as her now famous T-shirt clung to her sweater. Before reaching up to straighten her T-shirt, she looked at Ben to gauge his reaction but was disappointed to see none. Nothing. He wasn't sweating. He wasn't drooling. Certainly no salute from his pants. Angel pulled the shirt into place and sat down. Something was wrong. He wasn't even staring.

Angel proceeded, undaunted. "My father started fucking me when I was 12."

Ben was all business. "Your father used to molest you?"

"Twice a day, like clockwork. More often when my mother was horny."

"Your mother? What do you mean?"

Angel deliberately spread her legs and pushed out her chest. "Well, when Mom was horny, she liked the way Dad got all excited around me. So she'd give me some extra allowance if I'd promise to give Dad a boner for her." She studied Ben for any signs of reaction.

"Really," asked Ben almost matter-of-factly.

"Oh yeah. Eventually she'd just have me reach in his pants and suck him till he got hard," she said licking her lips. Ben hardly noticed. But Angel rose to the challenge. She stood up, walked over to Ben, kicked his legs apart, and squatted between them. With her hands on his upper thighs, she looked up into his eyes and asked, "Want me to show you how Daddy liked it?"

Ben took her hands and gently led her back to her seat. Angel noted that his hands weren't even shaking. She was getting pissed off.

Ben slowly sat down and placed his clipboard on the table with the ashtray. "I'm an only child too," he began. "My mother died when I was young. And my father cared more about surgery than he cared about me. I was planning to follow in his footsteps. I'm glad that's apparently no longer the plan."

Angel wasn't sure where this was going but she figured she'd go along for the ride. "Having second thoughts about your chosen profession?"

"Well, I guess it's out of my hands now," Ben replied.

"Just as well, you know," Angel added, throwing salt on the wound. "After that pitiful scene with the little girl and her dying mother, I wanted to report you to the Board of Medicine myself."

Ben looked her in the eyes. "You're right you know. I never would have been any good to anyone." At that, his cough started acting up.

Angel thought it was just for added effect. It did play well, she had to admit. But she wasn't ready to fall for whatever game he was playing.

"You sure weren't much good to that high school girlfriend of yours, were you?" she said, raising the ante. And then, with another turn of the screw, "You never even got the thing out of your pants." Angel's eyes were riveted on Ben, looking for the anticipated response. But, to her disappointment, again, nothing. Instead, Ben's monotone self-mutilation continued.

"I stood her up at the prom you know. Just to study for some exams. To get... here."

"And where's that?" asked Angel.

"Nowhere. That's where." After a pause, "Boy, I'd sure do things differently given a second chance."

"Next time you'd fuck her, right?" Angel didn't give up easy.

Ben continued, quietly, looking off into space, as if he were with her, with Jill Sterling, at that moment. "No. I'd just love her. That's all."

Angel slumped back in her chair, defeated.

Ben continued. "She was my soul mate. And I could have had it all. But I let her get away. God, I practically threw her away."

Angel couldn't take it anymore. "I don't know what's wrong with you, but why don't you do everyone a favor and just kill yourself." As soon as Angel saw the pitiful look on Ben's face, she wished she could take it back. "Hey. I was only kidding. What is *with* you anyway?"

"Oh, uh, something's come up. That's all," answered Ben.

"Something's come up?" countered Angel. "You're acting like your dying. Snap out of it, would you!?" she shouted reaching for another cigarette.

Ben just smiled.

"What!?" Angel was beginning to feel uneasy, a feeling Angel McGovern was not accustomed to.

"May I have one of those?" asked Ben gesturing toward her box of Marlboros.

Angel did a double take at the box of cigarettes. "One of what? One of these? You want a cigarette?" she asked, incredulous.

"Yeah. Why not?"

"OK. Sure. Here ya go." Angel tapped the box on her wrist allowing one cigarette to appear. She then held it out for Ben.

Ben took the cigarette and placed it between his lips. An uneasy silence hung in the air until Ben held out his hand again.

"What now?" asked Angel.

"Are you going to loan me your lighter or do I have to rub two sticks together?" asked Ben, pointing at her lighter on the table.

"What? You're going to light it?"

"Of course I'm going to light it. What did you think I was going to do?"

Angel squinted her eyes in confusion. Then, never completely without a comeback, "You do realize that if you light the cigarette, you might actually get some smoke in your lungs. That's a bad thing, remember, Doctor Walker? Besides, you've got the wrong end in your mouth," she added, reaching over to Ben's mouth and turning his cigarette around.

"Thank you for your concern, Doctor McGovern. Just give me a light, please. My health just doesn't seem so important anymore."

Angel lit Ben's cigarette as she studied his face, looking for answers. Before Ben's violent smoke-induced coughing episode could completely subside, Angel proceeded.

"So about a million years ago, you stood your girlfriend up at the prom. You've since decided you have no reason to live. And now you're killing yourself with one cigarette. And I'm the one under lock and key?"

Having regained the use of his airway, Ben confirmed Angel's account. "That about sums it up."

Angel refused to let Ben get the better of her. Standing up with indignation, "Listen Sigmund Freud. I don't know what's suddenly shattered your world, but you know, in my little world here on the eleventh floor, we've got a few folks depending on your sorry ass for some help. You might not be a real psychiatrist, but you get to play one in medical school."

"*You* need *my* help?" asked Ben in disbelief.

"Me? You think *I* need psychiatric help from *you*. What kind of kinky fantasy life are you living? No, I don't need your help."

"Then what are you talking about?" asked Ben.

"You do have other patients, don't you?"

"Oh, yeah, that's right. There's the guy with the can opener who speaks to little green men. And, let's see. Oh yeah, there's the rapist murderer. You're right. My life *does* have meaning." Ben rolled his eyes and chuckled as he took another drag on his cigarette followed by the obligatory choking fit.

"Give me that thing," demanded Angel, snatching the cigarette from Ben. "Now listen to me, you miserable excuse for a human being. You're talking about friends of mine. Whether Rocket speaks with little green men or not isn't the point. The point is that he's convinced people are after him, and he needs help. Your help. And Juan. Juan is neither a rapist nor a murderer. He's as gentle as a lamb. He just wants to go home. Home to the little island where he grew up."

"What makes you think I can do anything for these people? Maybe the next student after me can do something."

"The next student? There's no time for a next student. Rocket's climbing the walls and Juan's going to prison. What do you think'll happen to that poor kid in prison?"

Ben slumped back in his chair with a sigh. "And what about you?"

"Me?" Angel sat up, methodically lit up another Marlboro, and leaned back in her chair with her feet up on the table. "Oh, I'll be just fine. Nothing a little lithium can't handle. Any shrink worth a damn knows the routine. Just when it seems life is getting to be a little too much fun, you guys drag me in here to correct a slight chemical imbalance. Then I take just enough of your pills to gather my wits, just enough wits, to elope."

"Elope? You're going to marry someone?"

Angel spit out her cigarette laughing. "You're so funny. Marry someone. No, I'm not going to marry someone. This isn't Cinderella. This is a psychiatric ward for Christ's sake. And on a psychiatric ward, elope means fly the coop, you know, escape."

"Escape? How can you escape?" Ben's interest was peaked.

Angel took a drag on her cigarette and blew smoke rings over Ben's head. "You just leave that to me." After an uncomfortable silence. "Besides, it seems you have some of your own demons to wrestle with."

Ben slowly nodded his head in agreement and reached for his clipboard on the table next to them. "You might say that." Then, standing up, "Well, I guess that's enough for one day."

Again, playing on Ben's suicidal demeanor, "I *will* be seeing you again, won't I?" asked Angel, still seated in her chair, legs comfortably crossed.

Ben looked back over his shoulder. "Why? Would you miss me?"

Angel hesitated teasingly, as if contemplating Ben's question. "You know all that stuff I said about being abused by my parents and blowing my Dad?"

"Yeah. What about it?"

"Never happened. I made it all up." Then, uncrossing her legs, spreading them wide, and pushing out her chest, "I just thought it might turn you on a little. You looked like you needed a little excitement."

She was still licking her lips as Ben left the room.

Chapter 20

He was screaming with all his might, but there was no sound to be heard. The pain was excruciating. But as untold volts of electricity were repeatedly sent from the electrodes at his temples through his brain, Makesh's throat would spasm and the only sound emitted from his clenched jaw was the sound of saliva spurting between teeth to join the rest of the drool pooling in his right ear. If he'd been able to form conscious thought, he'd have wondered what the effect of electric shocks on brain tissue was, and whether it was being turned to Jell-O or more of a cottage cheese-like consistency.

Instead, all Makesh could do was gasp for air between the jolts of electricity engulfing his head, his mind, his entire being. When the torture paused long enough for them to continue the questioning, he was only able to weep, a hollow, high pitched, yet nearly silent weeping. Even if he could stop, he wouldn't have been able to appease them. He'd already told them everything. He'd admitted stealing the plutonium. He told them all about the aliens. But that only seemed to infuriate them and intensify the voltage.

Almost from the moment he'd arrived, the two new orderlies now carrying out his torture had it in for Makesh. Initially, they'd upset his belongings searching for something. Soon they were cornering him alone at night with threats of physical harm if he didn't cooperate. Only after they'd directly questioned him concerning the plutonium did Makesh place their faces back to the 7-

Eleven in California. These were the same men in black. The ones he'd run from, run all the way across the country. How did they find him? How far could the transmitter be tracked? Makesh presumed they were from the government. Now he was on a locked ward and his captors were in charge. He was a caged animal, cornered and helpless.

Just as in California, they wouldn't buy the alien story. Never mind that it was the truth as far as Makesh was concerned. They weren't going to let him rest until they found the plutonium. Makesh didn't know what else to tell them. The aliens came from outer space. They demanded plutonium or they would destroy the Earth. Makesh gave it to them. End of story.

The orderlies must have really turned up the juice one last time, because when Makesh woke up, he was alone in his room. He couldn't tell how long he'd been unconscious. Minutes, hours, or days. Nevertheless, it was morning now. Maybe the whole thing was just a dream. Maybe it was all his imagination. Maybe it didn't matter. Because, imagination or not, Makesh knew he couldn't take it anymore. He couldn't survive another torture session. He had to escape.

* * * *

When they told Juan Martinez he'd be leaving, he presumed they meant he'd be going home, home to his mother and sister, maybe even back to his grandmother on Isla de los Locos. They must have decided he wasn't crazy after all. Maybe a little slow or lento as they'd told him. But certainly not crazy. Wonderful. Juan presumed this was a good thing, not to be crazy. Unfortunately, Juan had never been more wrong about anything in his life. For if Juan Martinez was sane enough to leave the ward, then he was sane enough to stand trial for rape and murder. Sane enough to be found guilty. And sane enough to be put to death.

Makesh was just telling Angel about his latest run-in with the orderlies when Juan came bounding up to his friends.

"Angel. Rocket. I get to go home," bragged Juan, grinning from ear to ear.

Angel couldn't help smiling at Juan's happiness. "That's great, Juan." Then adding in a skeptical tone, "How come?"

"I'm not crazy. That's how come." Then realizing how that sounded, "Not that you guys are crazy. I mean, it's just—"

"No offense taken," interrupted Makesh.

"I don't like it. Something's fishy," mused Angel. "What about those bad things they said you did? Did they say anything about that?"

"No." Then brightening, "But they said I'd be able to tell the judge all about it."

Makesh looked at Angel. "At a trial, no doubt."

"They've pronounced him sane to stand trial," added Angel, putting two and two together.

"The girl's family will make her stick to her story. The prosecutor will eat him alive," pronounced Makesh.

"Who's going to eat me," asked Juan, looking concerned.

Makesh slapped the big man's shoulder laughing.

Angel, smiling, kissed Juan on the cheek. "No one's going to eat you, Baby." Then, turning to Makesh, "Time for a road trip."

Makesh looked confused. "Road trip?"

"I've got to get both of you out of this place. We haven't much time."

"But how can we get out of here," asked Makesh.

Angel's wheels were already turning. "You just leave that to Angel," she replied.

* * * *

Erika Robinson had on his favorite cocktail dress that night in anticipation of his blind date. His make-up was perfectly applied. Not too much to appear slutty, yet, just enough to be sure his date knew he meant business. It wasn't uncommon for Erika to use his black market ID card to have an evening out every once in a while. But he hadn't planned on having chaperones. It would have been hard to say no to Angel, whom he looked upon as a fellow party girl. But when he saw the giant and the nerd with her, he had to put his foot down.

"Ya'll must be joking," he said to Angel, shaking his finger. "What do I look like? Some kind of underground railroad for crazy folk? Nuh uh. I don't think so. Ya'll take your crazy asses back to bed."

Angel stepped forward. "It's an emergency, Honey. Juan and Rocket are in trouble."

"Of course dey in trouble. Ya'll on a psych ward, remember."

"No. Not that kind of trouble. People are out to get them."

Erika put his hands on his hips with a look of disappointment. "Why doesn't that surprise me coming from a bunch of psychos?"

Angel persisted. "No. This is for real."

"What makes you think so?" asked Erika.

Angel saw time was wasting. She had to clinch the deal and get on with the plan. Then she saw it. Erika's weakness. "Woman's intuition. *You* understand, Erika."

Erika couldn't help smiling a little, but looking at Angel from the corner of his eyes, "I see right through you, girl. What, do I look easy or something?"

"Like an escort at a political convention," Angel quipped.

Erika let out a giggle. Then fixing her hair, "Don't you know it."

"Well, what do you say," begged Angel?

Erika looked at the three stooges in front of him, then pulled out his ID card. "Ya'll pathetic, you know."

Angel, Makesh, and Juan looked at each other. Angel, the spokesperson, replied. "We know."

The bright lights of the hospital corridor outside the locked ward felt strange to the three elopers. Like cockroaches caught in the brightness of a kitchen light, they hugged the walls as they crept down the corridor toward the elevator looking for cover. Fortunately, hospital gowns were not standard issue on the ward. Angel and Juan wore jeans while Makesh wore khaki trousers below his 7-Eleven T-shirt. It was, nevertheless, the middle of the night, and they had no visitor passes. Even that would not have been noticed in the big inner city hospital with its less than enthusiastic security force, had it not been for Makesh's reflex response at seeing two orderlies in white approaching as the elevator doors opened in the hospital lobby.

Quite to the orderlies' surprise, as well as the lobby security guard asleep at his desk, Makesh screamed, knocked them to the ground, and started frantically pounding simultaneously on the up and close door elevator buttons. Juan became frightened. As the elevator doors closed, Angel tried to keep calm, thinking of a way to iron out the first wrinkle in her plan.

"Oh Rocket, why would you go and do a thing like that?"

"They were coming to get me," he replied.

"Who was? The orderlies?" she asked.

Makesh couldn't gather enough wits to reply as he was literally climbing the walls of the elevator, his eyes wide in panic. Angel calmly pressed the button for the 14th floor, the roof, as she heard security alarms sounding from outside the elevator.

"Were those the men you said tortured you?" she continued.

"No, they were not," Makesh replied.

"You're sure?" asked Angel as the elevator slowed down at the eleventh floor.

"Oh yes. I am sure."

"Then why did you panic?"

"Because they dressed like them."

"You knew it wasn't them, but you panicked just because they dressed the same?"

Makesh looked at Angel indignantly. "You've heard of Pavlov's dogs, haven't you?"

When the elevator door opened, a smile came to Juan's face. "Look. It's the ward. We're home." He started toward the open door to the ward, security alarm ablaze, until Angel grabbed him by the back of his belt, pulling him back into the elevator.

"Shit," was all she could say as she hit the close door button on the elevator and it continued up to the roof.

Makesh turned to Angel. "Did you notice the door to the ward?"

"What about it?" she replied.

"Why was it open?"

Angel understood the question, but as the elevator door opened to the roof, the urgency to proceed with the escape seemed more pressing than pondering who left the door to the ward open and which of the other loony tunes might have wandered out into the world besides themselves.

Juan and Makesh followed Angel out of the elevator, through the exterior door, and onto the flat tar roof. Juan marveled at the beauty of the twinkling city lights over the Manhattan skyline, only to be interrupted by Makesh who was peering back at the elevator.

"They follow. Look," he said, pointing at the floor indicator over the elevator door. The elevator was on its way back up to the roof.

"Let's go," said Angel, matter-of-factly, starting toward the edge of the roof.

"Let's go? Where?" asked Makesh.

Juan's interest was peaked. Peering over the edge of the roof, "We're going to fly?"

Angel was kneeling at the corner of the roof, looking over the edge. "Those wires," she said, pointing at a set of wires connected to the side of the rooftop.

"What about them?" asked Makesh, beginning to fear the worst as he visually followed the wires spanning the street between theirs and the other hospital building.

"That's our escape," replied Angel.

Makesh stared back at Angel. "*This* was your plan?"

Juan was looking over the edge of the roof at the moving cars 14 floors below. "I don't think I like your plan either."

Angel turned to Makesh. "No, Einstein, this wasn't my plan. *My* plan was to walk out the front door. At least that was my plan until Pavlov's dog screamed, assaulted some orderlies, and alerted security."

Makesh's tail was between his legs when he nodded back toward the elevator. "Well why don't we just go back down and try again?"

Pointing at the floor indicator over the elevator, Angel replied, "Because your friends in white are making their way up to the roof as we speak. Angel reached over the edge of the roof to grab one of the wires preparing to shimmy across to the other hospital building across the street.

Makesh looked down at the street below them, the cars the size of small toys. Then he glanced back at the elevator. It was passing the sixth floor. "Look out," he said, pulling Angel away from the wires. "You'll get electrocuted if you grab the wrong wire. Makesh looked back at the elevator one last time as it approached the eighth floor, thought back to the painful interrogation sessions at the hands of his friends in white, then quickly grabbed one of the wires in both hands.

"They'll never take me alive," he added, as his feet left the edge of the roof and he straddled the wire.

Juan looked at Angel. "How did he know which was the right wire?"

"He *is* a rocket scientist, after all," replied Angel. Then calling out to Makesh, already a third of the way across the street, "How did you know which wire was safe?"

"Simple," he replied, without looking back. "After I grabbed it, I was still alive. That is how."

Angel looked at Juan.

Juan smiled, and added, "Rocket scientists sure are smart."

After glancing back at the elevator, now three floors away, Angel turned to Juan. "Be careful," indicating which wire he should grab.

"Oh, but ladies first," smiled Juan, bowing to Angel.

"Alright Romeo. But you follow right behind." Angel started out across the canyon between the two buildings, arms and legs wrapped around the wire. She stopped half way across to rest, but yelled back for Juan to start across. Makesh was just clambering over the wall to the neighboring rooftop.

"Are you sure it's strong enough to hold both of us?" yelled Juan.

"No, I'm not," replied Angel, out of breath. "But there's no time to wait." Having said that, she could hear the ding of the elevator approaching its destination.

"Ready or not. Here I come," shouted Juan as he started across, hand over hand.

Angel was in trouble. Her upper body strength was giving out about ten feet short of the other building. Makesh saw her arms start to tremble as the muscles began to spasm.

"Hold on," he shouted. "I'm coming."

But as he was about to add a third bodyweight to the already straining life line, Angel saw the bolts anchoring the wire to the new building begin to bend. "No. Don't," she shouted, eyeing the tenuous connection.

Makesh saw what she was looking at and backed off. By that time, Juan was only a couple of feet away from Angel anyway. "Hurry," he pleaded to Juan as he heard the elevator doors opening.

"Juan. Please," whimpered Angel. She couldn't hold on any longer. Her fingers were beginning to slip from the wire. Angel's "help" was barely audible as she strained to hang on. As her hands inevitably slipped from the wire, Angel didn't hear Juan's shouts to grab onto his shoulders.

Fortunately, she didn't need to, as Juan caught her around the waist, anchoring them both to the wire with one hand. Taking her hands from her eyes, she wished she hadn't, dangling from Juan's arm, 14 stories above the pavement.

"Grab my shoulders," repeated Juan, hoisting Angel upward. Angel wrapped her arms around Juan's neck. "That'll work, I guess," choked Juan, finally able to get both hands onto the wire.

In all the commotion, none of them had noticed that the elevator door they'd been fleeing had opened. And as Makesh scrambled to help them both onto the roof with him, they could feel the weight of another body mounting the wire. Only when they were all safely on the new rooftop did they look back to see who was stalking them. Their jaws dropped in unison as they saw something resembling a sasquatch shimmying along the wire toward them. It was black and furry, like a bear. And it looked as though it was shedding green feathers as it struggled to move its mass along the thin wire toward them. Only as the thing turned its head toward them did they realize the true nature of the beast, what, or who, it was.

"Anastasia!" all three yelled in unison as they recognized the little old Russian woman with the smelly fur coat from the ward. So it was true then. As she randomly crisscrossed the country by greyhound bus, she did indeed keep her life's savings stuffed into the lining of her fur coat. Having snagged the lining on the roof flashing, various denominations of paper U.S. currency were escaping and falling to Earth like feathers from a molting bird.

"Anastasia! What are you doing!? Go back, honey!" shouted Angel. The weight of the fur coat was clearly stressing the escape wire, let alone poor Anastasia's heart. She grunted with each pull of her arms as she inched her way across the span separating the two buildings. Glistening perspiration was clearly visible on the struggling old woman's face. "Go back!" pleaded Angel for a second time.

"Go back?" replied Anastasia. "Never. I escaped Rasputin when I was a little girl. I can escape from here. Compared to the Russian revolution, this is a walk in the park." Her face was the color of borscht, as she struggled to pull herself under the weight of her coat and its contents.

"She must have followed us out the ward door before it closed behind us," Makesh said to Angel. "That's why I saw the open door from the elevator. I bet the whole ward is on the loose by now."

"Crazy," smiled Juan.

Anastasia was in trouble. She was carrying too much weight. Angel called to her. "Honey, drop the coat. It's too heavy for you."

The old woman couldn't pull herself another inch, stranded midway between the two rooftops. When she hooked her knee high stockinged legs and one arm around the wire, placing the other arm in her coat, Angel thought she was preparing to remove it. Instead, to everyone's amazement, she pulled out a portable television set and sent it careening 14 stories to the street below. The reduction in weight was just enough to let her resume her trans-rooftop journey. Unfortunately, the crash from the shattered TV set frightened a flock of pigeons roosting nearby. They immediately took flight, battering Anastasia about the head with innumerable flapping wings.

"Anastasia!" shouted a panicked Angel. "Hold on!"

The old Russian carefully reached into her coat again. "A walk in the park, I'm telling you."

Makesh turned to Angel. "Don't tell me she's got a sawed-off shotgun full of birdshot in there." Angel hit him on the head with one hand, the other one nervously cupped over her mouth.

Anastasia pulled her hand out of her coat clutching a handful of bread crumbs. She placed it on her upturned belly like a feeding sea otter and began throwing it, sending the pigeons in pursuit. Once again, she began inching toward her destination, only slightly heavier from the two pigeons fighting over the remaining crumbs on her belly.

Angel was quite relieved to see Juan and Makesh pulling the sweet old woman over the ledge onto the roof with them. Her relief was short lived, however, as they all heard the ding of the elevator from where they'd left returning once again to the roof. The doors of the elevator seemed to open in slow motion in contrast to the flood of uniformed security officers that flowed from them onto the roof the escapees had left behind. Juan watched them fan out across the roof, quickly conclude it was deserted, and start filing back into the elevator. The other fugitives were already looking for access from the roof into their new building so they could descend to the street unnoticed, when they heard Juan call out.

"Over here! We're over here!" he called to the last security guard leaving the roof.

"Shit!" added Angel, glancing back to see Juan waving to the security guards now looking their way.

Even Anastasia couldn't help adding, "Mashugana," as she slapped her forehead in disbelief. Angel thought she recognized the Yiddish word for crazy, but imagined Russian might sound similar.

Makesh looked back from the door he'd just found to see the last man, now pointing at them, call the rest of his team back onto the roof. "Angel. Over here," he shouted.

Juan was gesturing to the security officers to come on over to his side when Angel grabbed him by the back of his belt, pulling him to the door Makesh had found, where all three of them stood looking at a heavily chained and padlocked metal door.

"Now what?" said Makesh, yanking at the chain.

Juan grabbed the padlock and tried fruitlessly to break it from the chain.

Anastasia then stepped forward, and reaching into her fur coat, stated, "Strength may be your strong suit, but this is going to take a little more umph." With that, she produced from her coat four sticks of dynamite.

Makesh's eyes widened. Angel yanked the dynamite from Anastasia's hand. "Give me that," she ordered, confiscating the explosives. "Don't you think this is overdoing it a little?"

Juan was impressed. "Do you have anything else in that coat?"

"Like a helicopter, maybe?" added Makesh.

Angel couldn't help stepping back as Anastasia reached back into her coat.

"How about this?" asked Anastasia, pulling out a three foot long pair of bolt cutters. Angel broke into a smile and looked over at Makesh who took the bolt cutters from the old woman's hands. The chain jumped as Makesh easily cut it with the tool.

"You'd better get that one too," suggested Angel, indicating for Makesh to cut the wire they'd used to cross to their building, the same wire now being eyed by the team of security guards across the way.

Before they left the edge of the roof for the door, Juan noticed a commotion starting down in the street. Several police cars had gathered in front of both hospital buildings, sirens ablaze. Some of the officers were looking up from the street holding walkie talkies where they could see the rooftop security pointing at the three fugitives on the next building. As the police began streaming into the building beneath them, Makesh turned to Angel. "All of that for a little plutonium?"

"I don't think they give a damn about your plutonium," answered Angel. Then, nodding toward Juan, she added quietly for

Makesh alone, "I suspect they're more interested in an escaped homicidal sexual predator."

"Why are there so many policemen?" asked Juan, innocently. "There must be bad people here?"

"No, Honey," answered Angel, herding the rest of them through the open rooftop door. "Just us."

Chapter 21

They kept to the stairs, for fear of getting caught in the elevator, until they heard policemen climbing the steps toward them. In order to avoid them, they detoured out of the stairwell onto the sixth floor. Once out of the stairwell and onto a patient care floor, Angel and Makesh decided they'd better blend in. Apparently Anastasia had already done so as she was nowhere to be seen. She'd probably get away easier on her own anyway, thought Angel.

Angel, on the other hand, felt responsible for the other two with her. She quickly found a small locker room near the nursing station where she found a nurse's uniform hanging. Trying on the uniform, it was clearly a couple of sizes too small, but Angel, being Angel, actually enjoyed showing a little extra leg and cleavage.

Makesh and Juan found only one uniform in their locker room. Makesh tried it on, but decided it was Juan's size when he kept tripping over the ends of the pants covering his feet. The outfit made Juan, however, look like the perfect orderly. Makesh would have to content himself with wearing a patient gown. The draft from the opening in the back would take some getting used to.

No sooner had they made their way back out onto the patient floor than they saw the police headed their way checking room to room. Angel quickly pulled the other two into what appeared to be an empty room.

"Quick," she said to Makesh, "in the bed."

Makesh looked at the bed and stated, "This is hardly the time for a nap."

"It's not for a nap," she replied.

Makesh couldn't help but notice Angel's too small skirt riding up her behind as she bent at the waist to pull the covers back, and that reminded him of the reason Angel was on the ward in the first place. "This is certainly not the time for that either."

Without straightening up, Angel looked back at the two men staring at her behind. It's a curse, she thought to herself, letting a small smile return to her face. "Just get in. You're supposed to be a patient. Patients belong in beds."

As Makesh got into the bed, Juan started to get in the other side. "Where are you going?" Makesh asked him, pulling the covers all to himself.

"Angel says we are patients and should be in the bed."

"Me," replied Makesh, grabbing the front of his gown. "I'm the patient." Then, pointing at Juan, "You. You are the, uh... the... uh..."

"What do I get to be?" asked Juan to Angel.

"You get to be an orderly," announced Angel.

"Yay," cheered Juan. "I get to be an orderly." Then, after a pause, "Angel?"

"Yes."

"What's an orderly?"

"An orderly... uh... an orderly... uh... takes orders. That's right. You can do that, can't you?"

"Oh, yes," answered Juan. "That's my favorite thing."

No sooner had they been assigned their respective roles when a team of residents, interns, and medical students started streaming in. Not knowing what to do, Makesh quickly pulled the sheets up to his chin and thought it best to pretend he was asleep.

"Mr. Phillips," began the chief resident, to Makesh, "how are you today?"

Trying to cover for Makesh who was frozen with fear, Angel replied, "He's been rather tired lately."

By then, the entire team of 12 had squeezed into the room. The chief resident addressed Angel. "Well, Mr. Phillips seems to have taken a turn for the worse," he said, shaking Makesh, then running his knuckles forcibly down Makesh's sternum trying to evoke a response. Makesh, however, had been through much worse than some knuckles down the sternum, and held fast to his feigned sleep.

Checking the front pages of a chart, "His admitting physician states that Mr. Phillips has been alert and oriented to date and his brain tumor has had no effect on his mental status. Well, sadly, he appears to be unresponsive this morning. How are his vital signs, nurse?"

"I'm sure they're just fine," replied Angel, nudging the bed with her knee, muttering under her breath for Makesh to wake up.

"Fortunately," continued the chief resident, "Mr. Phillips has the honor of being the subject of our grand rounds this morning. And, as luck would have it, we have a visiting director of Neurosurgery from Austria today."

Angel was barely able to muffle her scream when she looked up to see a familiar face from the ward strut through the door.

"Please welcome the renowned Dr. Brunning."

Angel had to grab Juan by the wrist to keep him from bounding across the room to hug the physician impersonator, one of Juan's many friends from the eleventh floor.

After several good mornings and welcomes all around, Mr. Phillips's history was presented to Dr. Brunning by one of the interns, the unfortunate story of a man who presented with signs and symptoms felt to be related to a solitary mass occupying the right parietal lobe.

Dr. Brunning approached the patient. "I vill first demonstrate for all of you zee proper vay to examine a patient for evaluation of zee central nervous system." But when Dr. Brunning attempted to pull the bed sheet down from Makesh's chin, Makesh kept pulling it back up. "Zis vould appear to zee untrained eye to be an unusual response coming from an apparently comatose individual. However, I vould beg to differ. In fact, vhat you are observing is a classic presentation of vhat I have termed Brunning's Sign. Note zee clenching of zee fists vich just happened to have closed around zee top edge of zee bed sheets, and zee bilateral upward motion of zee arms in response to a tug in zee opposite direction." The motion was demonstrated each time Dr. Brunning attempted to pull the sheets off of Makesh. "Zis particular sign, in my vast experience, indicates involvement of zee pineal gland."

"The pineal gland?" asked one of the residents, incredulously.

"Indeed," responded Dr. Brunning. "Zee pineal gland. Known to many as zee seat of zee soul."

The interns and students all looked at each other and began taking notes. In the crowded room, no one noticed the face peering from behind the curtain dividing the room between them and a second patient bed. The face couldn't help but notice Angel's figure standing out from the crowd in its short tight nurse's uniform.

Angel was startled when the face tried to get her attention. "Pssst." She whirled around to find the face staring around the curtain. "Nurse," it continued, "may I have a word?"

"Shhh," whispered Angel politely, "we're in the middle of grand rounds this morning." She was afraid to leave Makesh and Juan alone.

"But it's important," continued the face.

"What's so important?" whispered Angel without turning away from rounds.

"That's not Phillips."

Angel stiffened, then slowly turned to the face at the curtain. "Wh… What do you mean?" asked Angel, trying to hide the fact that she already knew the patient's true identity.

"That's not Phillips."

"Shhhh," repeated Angel, now turning toward the face. "How do you know that?" she added, fearing they'd been discovered.

"Because *I'm* Phillips."

Angel quickly tiptoed around the curtain to see the small, nervous man in a hospital gown seated in the next bed.

"I'm Phillips," repeated the little man. "I'm the one with the brain tumor."

Angel held her finger to her lips as a sign to be quiet while making sure the curtain behind her was drawn closed. "We don't want to disturb the doctors."

"But—"

Angel cut him off. "Now, tell me, sir, what makes you think you have a brain tumor?"

"Well," continued the patient, "this CAT scan, for one." He pulled a jacket of x-rays off the night table at the head of his bed and handed it to Angel.

Now Angel hadn't had the pleasure, as Ben had, of meeting Mr. Phillips, known throughout the city as the Munchausen Syndrome poster child, famous for his ever more innovative attempts at convincing someone to inflict additional bodily harm upon his already scar-ridden person. But, on the other hand, being the proud owner of two and a half PhD's, she wasn't born yesterday either. Even if she hadn't noticed the fact that the patient name on the x-ray jacket had been tampered with, when she pulled out a chest x-ray instead of the CAT scan, by accident, and held it up to the light, she knew something was up, because if it's one thing Angel McGovern could recognize, it was female breasts. And as Mr. Phillips quickly snatched the film from her hands, replacing it with a CAT scan of the head, Angel was no longer worried that Mr. Phillips was going to be a problem.

"See," he added, pointing at the film, "a large left parietal brain tumor. Just like I said."

Angel was impressed. "Gosh. You poor thing. It's huge," she said, looking up at the scan.

"I told you," he said with self-satisfaction.

"You know, I would have expected a left-sided tumor that large to cause significant left-sided weakness," she continued, knowing full well that the left brain actually controls the *right* side of the body.

"It kind of comes and goes," covered Mr. Phillips, suddenly collapsing onto the bed grabbing his suddenly weak left leg.

Angel put her hand to her mouth trying to contain the laughter rising from her belly. Quickly regaining her composure, she stepped forward and slowly leaned over Mr. Phillips who was flat on his back. She wasn't through with him yet. Mr. Phillips pulled his hands up over his chest in a defensive manner as Angel's substantial cleavage came uncomfortably close.

"There's something else the left side of the brain controls," she lied, parting her lips and breathing heavy. "I expect with a tumor the size of yours, you'd lose all sensation in your..." grabbing him firmly by the balls, "...testicles."

The small peep from her victim's lips was more out of surprise than anything else. But as Angel began to tighten her grip, he began to gasp for air.

"It's a good thing you can't feel this," she proceeded, "because anyone without left-sided brain damage would be climbing the walls by now."

For someone with left-sided weakness, Mr. Phillips had quite a vise-like grip on both bed side rails.

Angel squeezed...

Mr. Phillips groaned.

...and squeezed.

His eyes turned up into his head.

Angel finally released him.

He began to breathe again.

"It's the most amazing thing I learned in nursing school," began Angel. "You didn't even know I had you by the balls, did you?" Her patient hadn't regained his ability to speak yet. "Mr. Phillips? Are you OK?"

He shook his head in the affirmative.

"Oh. Good. I guess we'd better get started."

"Started?" he asked, making his way back from the edge of unconsciousness. "Started with what?"

"Preparation for your surgery, of course."

Mr. Phillips could barely contain the ecstasy he felt at hearing those familiar words. "What's first?" he asked, nearly salivating.

Angel giggled, leaned over, and ruffled his hair with her hand.

"Silly boy. Your enema, of course. I'll be right back."

For a moment Mr. Phillips thought he'd gone to heaven.

Angel walked around the drawn curtain, back to where she'd left grand rounds in progress, which, to her surprise, had disappeared. Makesh, Juan, Dr. Brunning, all gone. Only two medical students were left, discussing Brunning's sign.

Angel approached the empty bed. "What happened? Where is everyone?"

The students turned to Angel, then one replied, "They're gone."

"I can see that. Gone where?"

"To the OR."

Angel's legs felt weak. "To the OR? Just like that?"

"He had a positive Brunning's sign, you know," replied one of the students.

"Yeah," added the other. "Dr. Brunning was adamant that the surgery couldn't wait a moment longer. He ordered him to the OR STAT."

"Dr. Brunning did that? And they took him to the OR?" Angel was in shock.

"That's right," continued the student. "And Dr. Brunning's going to perform the surgery himself. That's quite an honor."

Just the thought brought horror to Angel's face. "Dr. Brunning? Dr. Brunning's going to perform the surgery himself?"

"Quite an honor," the student repeated.

Angel raced from the room in search of the operating rooms.

Juan had no idea where he was pushing Makesh's gurney. He didn't know where the operating rooms were. But all he had to do was follow the Neurosurgery team from rounds, led by the chief resident, and at his side, Dr. Brunning. Once they reached the OR's, OR personnel pointed Juan to room eight, already set up for the surgery. Juan was about to turn and leave the room when Makesh grabbed him by the sleeve.

Juan looked down at the panicked face and responded in a reassuring tone. "Don't worry. Dr. Brunning will have that brain tumor out in no time."

"Dr. Brunning? Dr. Brunning's no brain surgeon."

"He's not?" asked Juan.

"Of course not. That quack isn't even a doctor."

"But you heard him," Juan continued. "What about Brunning's sign?"

"There's no such thing as Brunning's sign. Besides, you're forgetting one small detail."

"I am? What's that?"

Makesh practically sat up on the gurney. "I don't have a brain tumor."

At that moment, the anesthesiologist entered the room.

"Ah, Mr. Phillips, I'd heard you were in a coma," began the anesthesiologist. "You're looking much better."

"Uh, I feel much better," replied Makesh, balancing his desire not to blow his cover with his gut feeling that he had to get out of the operating room. "In fact, you know, I was just thinking. I don't think I need this surgery after all."

"Now now, Mr. Phillips, that's just last minute jitters. You have nothing to worry about. I hear you've got some world renowned hot shot doing your surgery." During their conversation, the doctor had already started an intravenous line and was preparing several syringes with anesthetic.

"Yes, well, uh," continued Makesh, "about my surgery, um, I don't actually have a brain tumor."

"I know. I know."

"You know?" barked Makesh, sitting up.

"Of course. This is a classic case of denial."

"Denial?"

"Sure. Happens all the time. You actually believe you no longer have your tumor. I see it all the time as the patient's surgery finally approaches."

"No. You don't understand. It's not that I no longer believe. I never believed. Because I never had." Makesh was getting upset, starting to get off the table.

The anesthesiologist took him by the shoulders. "Now calm down, sir. Believe me. I see it all the time." When Makesh began to struggle with him, the doctor called the orderly over to help restrain his patient. "Please, sir, you'll hurt yourself."

When Juan took Makesh by the shoulders and pushed him down onto the table, Makesh looked at him in disbelief. "What are you doing? Why are you helping him?"

"I don't want you to get hurt," replied Juan.

Makesh was beside himself with anger. "You don't want me to get hurt? They're going to take my brain out. Don't you think that's going to hurt?"

Juan looked to the anesthesiologist.

"Don't worry," said the doctor, taking one of the syringes of anesthetic. "He won't feel a thing."

That made Juan feel better. "See, the doctor says you won't feel anything."

Makesh was yelling, red in the face, struggling against Juan's strength. "No. But when I get my hands on you, you'll feel plenty."

As the contents of the syringe entered the intravenous line, the stress on Makesh's face instantly began to melt away. "There. This will relax you," assured the doctor.

No longer struggling, Makesh began to go limp. "Yes. I need… to… relax," he slurred, losing consciousness.

Juan released him. And seeing a smile come to Makesh's face, Juan, too, couldn't help but smile along.

The OR soon began to fill with nursing personnel and additional equipment. A nurse at Makesh's head had just pulled out a disposable razor when Juan was hustled out of the room.

At first, Angel felt a wave of relief when she burst into the pre-op area just outside the ORs and Makesh wasn't there. She thought, perhaps she'd gotten there first. But when Juan emerged alone from the double doors leading to the ORs, she knew she was mistaken.

"Where is he?" she half shouted, running up to Juan.

"Who?" asked Juan.

"What do you mean, who? Rocket Man. Where did you leave him?"

"He's in there," nodding back at the OR doors. "But don't worry. There are a lot of people taking care of him. He's taking a nap. And I think he's getting a shave."

"He's getting a shave?" snapped Angel, grabbing Juan by the shirt. "Which room is he in?"

"I don't know. But I think they were going to have something to eat because they brought in a table with all sorts of silverware on it."

Angel pushed him away in frustration and ran to the white marker board on the wall listing all the scheduled cases and their respective OR's by number. Then she saw it.

"Patient - Phillips. Surgeon - Brunning. Operation - Craniotomy. Room - 8. In Progress."

Angel whirled around toward Juan. "What are we going to do? We've got to stop them." Juan wasn't there. But when she looked around the corner, she found him playing with a toy train left behind in the pre-op area by a little boy having his tonsils removed. "What are you doing?"

Juan replied with choo choo noises.

But that gave Angel an idea. She ran to the front desk, momentarily abandoned while the clerk went to the restroom, to find a microphone for the OR intercom system. There were buttons for each OR number, and then a button that said "All". Angel pressed that button, then grabbed the microphone. "Attention all ORs! Attention all ORs!" she announced. "Disaster alert. Train versus school bus. ETA five minutes. This is not a drill. All cases that haven't been started are being bumped to clear all available ORs for incoming trauma. Repeat. This is not a drill. Clear all available ORs to trauma."

Massive confusion broke out as orderlies and nurses began running in all directions at once. Angel turned to Juan. "Come on, let's go," she shouted, dragging him through the doors to the ORs.

When they arrived in OR 8, the sterile drapes were just being removed from Makesh. Juan helped slide him onto a gurney. Not until Juan turned the gurney to head for the door did Angel notice Makesh's new hairdo. She almost screamed when, in stark contrast to the his trademark wild Einstein-like gray hair on the left side of his head, Angel saw that his right side was now cue-ball smooth. The right side of his head had been shaved.

"Well, this is going to make some fashion statement," she said to Juan.

Juan thought of collecting the shaved hair from the floor and bringing it along, but he didn't know where they kept the glue around there anyway.

Before they left, however, Angel noted the full syringes lined up on a stainless steel tray. "I wonder what's in these," she said to Juan.

"The doctor used that to help Makesh relax," answered Juan.

"Good," said Angel, grabbing one of the syringes and placing it in her pocket. "You never know when someone else might need some relaxing."

They were trying to plan their next move as they headed back to the pre-op area, pushing the now unconscious Makesh with his half-shaved head. But through all the commotion now engulfing the area in preparation for Angel's fabricated incoming trauma cases, Angel could see police officers now stationed just outside the pre-op area.

Gambling on their disguises, Angel pulled the sheet all the way up over Makesh's head and motioned to Juan to wheel the gurney right past them. Fortunately, the only thing the police noted were Angel's legs glaring from under her undersized nurse's uniform. Their eyes followed her all the way to the elevator, where Angel hoped to at least head back to Mr. Phillips's room until Makesh regained consciousness.

Unfortunately, when the elevator door opened to reveal two more police officers, Angel thought they were done for. And when the officer held the door opened and said, "Going down?" she was sure he meant to the lobby and into his waiting car.

Seeing her frozen in indecision, the officer made his intentions clear. "To the morgue?"

Angel was caught off guard. "The morgue?"

"Yeah. You know," he continued, indicating Makesh's motionless covered body, "where the dead people go."

"But he's not—" began Juan before Angel could kick him in the ankle.

"Yes, please. The morgue," smiled Angel with relief.

It seemed like it took forever to reach the basement. Angel thanked the officers for the personal escort, after they'd informed her of the incident at the ward including the escape of a dangerous rapist. She watched to make sure the policemen left in the elevator before heading to the morgue. Angel knew that there must be a way of getting out to the street from the morgue, a direct route used by funeral homes to export their customers.

After locking the entrance door, they wheeled Makesh's gurney right through the morgue, past the refrigerated wall with its individual two by two and a half foot stainless steel square doors, to the exit sign at the end of the room. But when they opened the door, they saw the street crawling with policemen. Angel didn't think they'd get very far pushing a gurney through the streets of New York.

"We'll have to hide out until things cool off," said Angel, closing the door. When she turned around, she saw Juan reaching for one of the doors to the cooler.

"Hey, what's in the refrigerator?" said Juan. "I'm starving."

Angel began to say, "I don't think it's that kind of refrigerator," but Juan was already screaming as he stared face to face with the dead body on the stainless steel tray he'd rolled out. It was an elderly 300 pound woman, only 5'2" in height. Her girth barely squeezed through the small door. Sparse plugs of gray hair sprouted from the top of her head, her ghost-white face covered with crusty skin lesions. And judging from the way her lips disappeared into her head, it was apparent that her teeth had been left behind and would not be accompanying her to the hereafter.

"Wh... What's that?" he gasped, clutching his chest.

"It's a dead person," Angel replied.

"No," said Juan, pointing at the cold lump of flesh. "I've seen dead. That's more than dead."

Angel walked over to the body on the tray in front of Juan. "OK. Dead, *and* ugly."

They suddenly heard the policemen speaking loudly outside the entrance door to the morgue. "Do we really have to check the morgue? I hate dead people," they heard one officer ask.

"We have to check everywhere," answered a second voice.

"Oh, look. Too bad. It's locked," continued the first voice with relief, jiggling the locked door knob.

"Let's go. We'd better find a key."

"Quick," said Angel, grabbing the gurney carrying Makesh, "we've got to hide." She dragged the gurney toward the wall of small stainless steel doors and began opening them one at a time, looking for an empty one. Each time she rolled out one of the stainless trays, she was greeted by another dead *and* ugly corpse. Juan was unconsciously backing further away with each unveiling. Finally, an empty tray emerged. "Come on," grunted Angel, yanking the gurney to the small opening. "Help me get him in."

"In there? You want to put him in there?" asked Juan, hoping he'd misunderstood.

"Hurry up," confirmed Angel. "Those cops will be back any minute."

With a look of disgust, Juan helped Angel stuff Makesh's anesthetized body into the empty drawer of the morgue refrigerator. "Won't he get cold in there?" asked Juan, as Angel slammed the door shut.

"Don't worry," replied Angel. Then continuing to open the small doors looking for another empty one, "We won't be in there for long."

Juan froze. "We?"

"What do you mean?" asked Angel continuing her search.

"We're going in there, too?" he clarified.

"It's that or go to prison."

"As long as they don't make you sleep in refrigerators full of dead people, I'll take prison, thank you."

Angel had come to the last door without finding an empty drawer. "Damn. Looks like a full house."

"Yeah. Too bad," added Juan, backing away.

Just then, they heard the voices of the police officers returning to the door to the morgue. There was a jingling of keys.

"We'll just have to double up," said Angel, hurrying back to a door behind which she'd noticed a particularly cute dead guy.

Juan watched in horror as Angel climbed aboard the tray with the body, snuggling close. Noticing how stiff rigor mortis had rendered the hunk's manhood, Angel felt more at home and eagerly slid the drawer with herself and her date back into the refrigerator.

"Quick," Angel ordered Juan in a forceful whisper as she heard the policemen trying different keys in the lock, "Get in one of these drawers."

"OK," answered Juan reluctantly.

Angel closed her door just short of catching the latch which would lock her in.

When the officers entered the morgue, they found it empty. "No one here. See? Dead silence. Let's go," pleaded the first one.

"Not so fast," said the second, pushing ahead. "What about all these doors?" indicating the refrigerator doors behind which Angel, Juan, and Makesh had taken refuge.

"Who would hide in drawers stuffed with dead people?" asked the first officer.

"Well, one's a rapist/murderer, and the others are just crazy." He began opening the doors, meeting the same dead *and* ugly people Angel and Juan had met only moments earlier. Makesh didn't look as clammy as the others, but his half-shaven head certainly made him look scary enough to appear dead. As the officers came to the final door, the one Angel had gone through, they noticed it wasn't completely closed. Looking at each other, they pulled their guns out of their holsters, and guns drawn, flung Angel's door open, yanking the drawer out.

The body didn't match any of the photos of the escaped loonies they'd been shown. And so, turning to leave, they made sure that this time all the doors to the morgue refrigerator were fully closed and locked. They passed one more door on the way out, a closet door with a sign on it, which read, "Limbs for Anatomy Class Dissection." Someone had scribbled underneath the sign in pen, "Parts is parts."

The first officer looked at the second. "Don't even think about it."

"Alright. Alright. Skip it. Let's go." The officers left the morgue. When the door closed behind them, the morgue was cold and silent, glaring lights against stainless steel.

Angel had crawled over to the corpse next to her just as the policemen were about to open her door. Behind the doors, there were no walls separating one drawer from the next. She now tried to push the door open. Then, pounding on it, she called out to Juan.

"Juan, we're locked in. Can you open yours?" There was no reply. "Juan, it's cold in here. Stop fooling around and answer me." Angel could tell by the girth and shape of the body under her that she'd managed to end up on top of a dead *and* ugly person. Still no reply from Juan. Angel had never panicked in her life. But she was beginning to feel that unfamiliar sensation grip her. And why wasn't Juan answering her?

Juan didn't care what Angel said. He never had any intention of getting into a drawer with a dead person. On the other hand, he hadn't read the sign on the closet he chose to hide in. Hearing Angel's calls, he found the pull string to turn the light on in the closet. He wished he hadn't. Jars crammed full of hands and feet greeted him. He couldn't find the breath to scream. But when he turned to run, things got worse. He met another wall full of jars. And each jar contained a severed head floating in it, assorted grimacing faces staring back at Juan. There really wasn't any reason to break down the door. After all, it wasn't locked. All Juan had to do was turn the knob. But that would have taken too much time. Without actually taking the time to weigh his options, Juan chose to simply smash the door off its hinges, sending it crashing to the floor. If not for the brief second of indecision as to which way to run, Juan wouldn't have heard Angel's muffled calls for assistance from behind the latched refrigerator doors.

Angel managed to calm him down once she'd crawled out from the land of the dead. Peaking out the exit door at the back of the morgue once again, it appeared the police had left for the time being. Unfortunately, they still had Makesh's sedated body to carry around. That's when Angel noticed the long hearse parked a few feet away. The driver, in his wrinkled black suit, was standing at the hot dog stand on the corner, apparently grabbing some lunch before grabbing his next customer from the morgue.

Angel quickly stepped outside to make sure the hearse was unlocked, then indicated to Juan to bring Makesh out. She hadn't expected to see a mahogany coffin inside the hearse when she opened the tailgate, but fortunately it was unoccupied. And when she noticed the undertaker beginning to head back toward them, she considered it an added bonus, helping Juan place Makesh inside the padded box.

The undertaker wasn't sure what to make of the large Hispanic man at the wheel of his hearse, but when the beautiful nurse, in her uniform a couple of sizes too small, started unbuttoning her blouse and beckoning for him to come around to the back of the vehicle, he was no longer thinking with his brain. The little head inside his pants was doing the thinking now.

Not a word was spoken as Angel slid backward into the hearse, hiking her short skirt up over her hips. Apparently not the first time the undertaker had used the company car for illicit purposes, he crawled right in after the bait. For him, the presence of the coffin was just icing on the cake, a sort of mood enhancer.

As the undertaker began ripping his clothes off in the back of the hearse, Angel noticed the policemen had returned to check the area again. She decided she'd better make this last, at least until the policemen had passed. Angel began to make a show of it, slowly removing her blouse, then even more slowly unzipping her skirt.

The undertaker was already naked, his little brain bobbing in front of him, when the lid to the coffin slowly started to open. Angel had never before seen a man's penis go from so large to so small so fast. It almost vanished completely when Makesh lifted his half-shaven head from the box.

Angel's fascination at the disappearing penis act was interrupted when she noticed the policemen heading her way in response to the undertaker's screams. When they arrived, she was still scrambling to get her uniform back on. Angel was pleasantly surprised at Juan's masterful handling of the situation.

Trotting up to the driver's window of the hearse, one of the two officers asked Juan, "We heard a scream over here. Did you see where it came from?"

Juan kept it simple. "It came from him," he replied, pointing toward the undertaker, running naked down the street."

"Yup. That's got to be one of 'em," remarked the second officer, as they both ran off in pursuit.

"Am I dead?" asked Makesh, slowly regaining his wits as the anesthesia finally began to wear off.

"No," answered Angel. "Not yet, anyway." She then ran around the car to get up front with Juan, still in the driver's seat. It looked as though they'd pulled it off. Sure, there were a few glitches, but here they were, about to head out on the open road. The threesome had eloped. "Start her up, Juan. Let's get out of here."

Juan was about to ask where the funeral was when two men in black suits, hats and sunglasses rapped on his window. He lowered the window and one of the men flashed an official looking identification badge.

"FBI," said the man. "Can I ask what you have in the back?"

Juan looked at Angel.

"It's a body. What do you think would be in the back of a hearse?" she replied. If they were eloping, it appeared the wedding was off again.

The second man in black was already running a Geiger counter down the side of the hearse. "We have reason to believe you may be harboring a fugitive."

"A fugitive?" asked Angel, innocently, watching the man with the Geiger counter heading toward the back of the hearse.

"Yes, ma'am. We believe you're familiar with a certain Makesh Guptah," he replied pulling out a photograph of Makesh.

"I'm sorry sir, but we're very late. We've really got to get going," she said nudging Juan with her elbow.

"I'm afraid I can't let you do that," stated the agent.

Angel reached across Juan, and, turning the key, started the car.

The man in black drew his gun, and pointing it at Angel and Juan, he shouted to his partner at the back of the hearse. "Go ahead. Open it up."

Angel slumped back in her seat, conceding defeat. After all they'd gone through, the acrobatics, the surgery, the morgue. Only to be nabbed at the brink of freedom by a pair of pesky FBI agents. It didn't seem fair.

Then again, it probably didn't seem fair to the man in black with the Geiger counter at the back of the hearse either, when he fell to the ground unconscious. As a matter-of-fact, it didn't seem fair to the one with the gun either, when he was struck in the head so quickly and with such force, he never knew what hit him.

As Angel leaned across Juan to look out his window at the fallen FBI agent, she was startled by the crazed face of Buck the Preacher, the deranged neighborhood servant of the Lord, as it suddenly filled the open window, staring back in at her and Juan.

Then, stepping back again, Buck stood over the fallen man in black, fist raised toward the heavens, and shouted, "*Hammer time!*"

Angel almost applauded. "Thanks Buck," she said with a smile.

And without any perceivable reply, Buck then bounded off across the street screaming something about Armageddon at the top of his lungs.

"Let's get out of here," Angel said to Juan.

"I don't know how to drive," he replied.

Angel reached across him and put the transmission into drive. Pointing to first the gas pedal, then the brake, she instructed, "That one makes you go, and that one makes you stop."

As the hearse pulled out of its parking spot, alternately jerking forward, then screeching to a stop, every 20 feet, Angel began thinking aloud, "We won't get far without any money."

Juan was so proud of himself as he eventually figured out what the steering wheel was for. Only one car had actually been forced off the road before Angel could explain the significance of red and green lights. Green was good. Red was bad.

What about Anastasia? She has lots of money in her furry coat," suggested Juan.

"Oh, she's probably on a bus headed cross-country by now. Besides, a credit card would be more convenient." Then, with a twinkle in her eye, she continued. "I do know of a little rich boy who might be persuaded to help us out."

Chapter 22

Ben was having trouble keeping up with the other medical students on their afternoon run to the George Washington Bridge. He normally ran at the front of the pack as it headed past the drug dealers inhabiting the park on the way. But he didn't seem to have the energy this time. Maybe he was just depressed. Or maybe it was that nagging cough he couldn't seem to kick. He couldn't seem to get quite enough air. Then the diagnosis hit him. PCP. Could he already have contracted Pneumocystis carinii, the AIDS associated pneumonia?

He pushed on, continuing to jog, as his classmates extended their lead, soon out of view. But his pace slowed even more as his mind strayed to his future, or lack thereof. Not much use for an HIV-positive surgeon. It was 1990 with no cure in sight. Not even any way to slow the progression of the disease. Thoughts of every known sequelae of AIDS raced through his mind. Thoughts of wasting away, bedridden, one complication after another. It was only a matter of time until he'd become one of those end-stage cases he'd always found so pathetic, lying in his own excrement on a gurney in the hallway of some emergency room waiting for someone to change his soiled hospital gown.

But all those pleasant thoughts were suddenly interrupted when the pavement came up and hit him in the face. Of course, the pavement wouldn't have hit him if he hadn't fallen on it, face first, which he wouldn't have done if he hadn't been hit in the back of the head by Dr. Goldstein's escaped 240-pound, skin-headed, swastika-tattooed, anti-Semitic, neo-nazi patient. Just before passing out, Ben remembered looking up at his assailant, recognizing the ward resident, and informing him he wasn't Jewish. He didn't find Luther's reply particularly comforting.

"Just practicing," was all he said, before flicking his cigarette butt at Ben on the ground, turning, and walking away.

Ben wasn't unconscious very long. He sat up, wiped the blood from his nose, then slowly got to his feet, still a bit shaky at the knees. It had grown dark during his rest on the hard New York pavement, but he could see the lights of the George Washington Bridge up ahead, spanning the Hudson River. He slowly walked the rest of the way.

As he walked out onto the massive suspension bridge, Ben's thoughts returned to his hopeless situation. His mother had died years ago. His father barely acknowledged his existence. He'd driven away the only love in his life so that he could pursue a career caring for people he loathed. Oh, yeah, and then there was this whole AIDS thing. Almost forgot about that.

Ben leaned against the rail at the center of the bridge, contemplating the choppy water of the Hudson River churning what seemed like a mile below. It wasn't a hard decision. No lengthy self-examination, balancing of pros and cons. It was very simple really. Ben had no reason to live. And even if he did, AIDS would prematurely cut it short, compounding his suffering daily, until he became some other medical student's headache. No. Better to finish it now.

The sky over Manhattan never had any stars, what with the pollution and all. Just the lights of skyscrapers illuminating the Manhattan skyline. There wasn't much of a breeze as Ben climbed the railing of the bridge, yet he could feel a gust of air each time a car sped by. The larger trucks really had quite an effect, like a group of hands pushing Ben, urging him over the edge. The water, hundreds of feet below, was quite rough. Ben was almost certain the impact of the fall would kill him. But even if it didn't, he'd certainly drown.

Teetering on top of the railing, each successive gust of wind nudging him on, Ben straightened up, ready to jump. No need for a count down, he simply stepped off the rail into the starless night that engulfed him.

Chapter 23

If not for the sudden vanishing lights of the city, Ben wouldn't have noticed the darkness that had overtaken him. The darkness, not of the cold polluted Hudson river, but instead, the confining darkness of a cloth sack thrown over his head, followed by numerous hands surrounding his body and pulling him from the bridge railing and back down to the hard sidewalk. It seemed he couldn't even kill himself without getting mugged one last time.

He didn't even bother to struggle as his entire body was being stuffed into what could only be described as a body bag. And he didn't even flinch as he felt that all too familiar sensation of a needle penetrating the skin of his right buttock. It didn't take long for the anesthesia to take effect.

Ben's head was still spinning as he later struggled to open his eyes. It was all still very blurry, but when he was just able to recognize that he was lying in an open casket, he was quite frightened at first. However, as the preceding events came back to him, including his intention to jump from the George Washington Bridge, Ben was relieved to conclude he was dead. Apparently he'd jumped from the bridge, drowned, and was now likely on the way to his own funeral. He took a certain pride in the fact that he'd finally done something right.

He began to wonder who would be attending his funeral. He wasn't really close to anyone at school. Oh there'd probably be some of his father's important friends and maybe some rich relatives. He wondered briefly if maybe Jill Sterling from high school might show up, but then he remembered hearing she'd moved to Miami. She wouldn't even know if he'd died. Would she even care? He regretted not taking the time to patch things up with her. He wished he could have had a second chance, a chance to tell her he was sorry, that he'd been a jerk, that she was the best thing that ever happened to him. But it was all too late now. No, apparently no one of any importance to Ben would be at his own funeral. He should have sent out invitations if he'd hoped to attract a better crowd. Oh well. Next time he'd think ahead.

As Ben rolled along with the soft suspension of the hearse, he began to hear voices, only faintly at first.

"Why was he standing on top of the bridge railing like that?"

"I don't know, but he sure seemed depressed during my last session with him."

"So what did you say to him?"

"Let's see. Oh yeah. I suggested he do us all a favor and kill himself."

"You said what?!"

"Well, he was getting on my nerves."

"Great. Just great."

"Well, it's just a good thing we came along when we did. He could've gotten hurt."

"First you tell him to kill himself. Then you're concerned that he might have gotten hurt?"

"Well, he is kind of cute, you know. I kind of feel sorry for the guy. He's so pathetic."

"How much anesthetic was in that syringe, anyway? You didn't kill him, did you?"

"I don't know. I snatched it when we pulled you out of brain surgery. It didn't kill *you*."

The voices were beginning to get clearer as Ben's drug-induced fog slowly began to lift. He struggled to focus on the two faces looking down at him.

"Look. I think he's waking up. I told you it wouldn't kill him." Angel began going through the wallet in Ben's fanny pack.

"What are you doing?" asked Makesh.

"Don't you remember why we brought him along?"

"Well, sure, but, it just seems so—"

"Got it!" Then holding up her prize catch, "Daddy's credit card."

Through squinted eyes, Ben was finally able to recognize his abductors. Even with Angel's nurse uniform and Makesh's new hairdo, there was no denying it. The crazies had taken over the asylum. There's no telling who was driving, he thought. It seemed the party was over. He wasn't dead after all.

"Where are you taking me?" asked Ben.

"See. It speaks," said Angel to Makesh.

"Where are you taking me?" repeated Ben.

"Let's see," Angel began, "we're taking the Rocket Man where he won't get tortured by people looking for plutonium. We're taking Mr. Martinez where he won't get executed for a crime he didn't commit. We're taking me where I can get laid."

"And what about me?" added Ben.

"We're taking you back to school," she replied. "We only needed to borrow something from you," she replied, quickly stuffing his credit card into a pocket.

The hearse had come to an intersection. And although they had a green light, "Green is good," remembered Juan, a steady stream of cars with their headlights on was crossing in front of them. Juan didn't notice the motorcycle cop directing traffic. And when Juan proceeded to cut through the line of cars, mass confusion broke out as the rest of the funeral procession began to follow the hearse in front of them, the hearse carrying Juan, Angel, Makesh, and Ben.

Makesh was the first to notice. "We're being followed," he said.

"You're always saying that," said Angel.

"No really. There's a long line of them. They all have their headlights on."

Ben was still groggy. But he was with it enough to throw in his interpretation. "Which is it? The mysterious men in black, or the little green men?" He and Angel chuckled.

"Laugh if you like," replied Makesh. Then continuing to stare out the rear of the hearse, "But they do follow. Of this I am certain."

Finally Angel and Ben conceded to take a look out the rear window. Unaware of Juan's confrontation at the intersection with the line of cars shining their headlights, it became nevertheless apparent to Angel and Ben, eyeing the 50 cars lined up behind them, that they'd somehow become the head of a funeral procession.

"Look," Angel said to Ben, pointing at the long line of cars, "at least you know you would have been missed."

Ben didn't appreciate the humor.

"We'd better lose them," suggested Makesh. "Juan, step on it."

As Juan searched the floor of the hearse for whatever insect Makesh wanted him to step on, the hearse bounced up onto the curb and proceeded down the sidewalk for nearly a block before Juan could get back on the road. Hesitant at first, the 50-car funeral procession rolled up over the curb and dutifully followed them down the sidewalk.

Angel began giving directions. "Quick, turn left. Hurry down the alley. Turn left again. Faster. Into the park again. The lawn. Cross the lawn."

As much as Juan tried, the funeral procession stuck like glue. Fifty-one cars rolled across the park lawn. A softball game in progress had to be halted while the funeral procession made its way across the outfield and out the other side of the park. Not until Juan took the hearse through an automatic car wash were they able to lose the other 50 cars, slowed down as they were during the wash cycle.

Angel finally admitted to Juan, "We'd better look for a new car. This hearse kind of stands out in a crowd." They had doubled back to only a block from Presbyterian Hospital.

Ben had no intention of spending his final days at school. He'd probably head right back to the George Washington Bridge in hopes of properly killing himself this time. But right now, he was losing the battle to just stay awake.

Juan stopped the hearse near the emergency room. As he got out of the car, Angel suggested he get a car that was fast, but one that wouldn't stand out in a crowd, something common. Juan nodded and left the hearse to find a new car.

Ben was still struggling to gather his semi-anesthetized wits when the hearse started violently rocking. The rear doors were flung open and the two men in black were upon them again without warning. Makesh was pulled from the hearse by an arm around his neck. Angel was kicking and screaming as the other one cornered her in the back of the hearse. They both ignored Ben, who, showing no signs of movement, appeared to be the only one truly deserving of his place in a hearse.

"Isn't this cozy," said the man in black, forcing Angel to the floor of the hearse with his weight. "Maybe we've got time to get to know each other a little better." With that, he started unzipping Angel's uniform.

"As appealing as that sounds, I'm afraid I'm going to have to decline," she replied, doubling her efforts to escape. As the struggle intensified, Ben drifted back into consciousness to find the man in black forcing himself upon Angel. Although her screams were muffled by the hand held over her mouth, Ben could still see her eyes imploring him for assistance.

When the corpse grabbed the man in black by the shoulder, the surprise distracted him from his captive just long enough for Angel to send a knee where he'd feel it.

To his partner outside the hearse, the sight of the man in black being rolled out the back of the hearse by the corpse who occupied it was enough to send him running. Makesh gasped for air once the arm around his neck was gone. Angel was about to thank Ben when a large box-shaped ambulance pulled up behind them, siren blasting.

"No, no, we're OK!" shouted Angel at the ambulance, hoping to avoid any additional attention. But when the driver yelled, "Come on you guys. Get in," the Spanish accent sounded familiar.

Makesh, still holding his bruised neck, peered up into the ambulance's driver seat. "Juan? Is that you?"

"You said to get something common that wouldn't stand out. Well, there were a whole bunch of these, and this one had the keys in it."

"At least turn off that siren," insisted Angel as she got in front with Juan, rolling her eyes at his choice of vehicles. Makesh was climbing into the back of the ambulance when Angel looked back at Ben, who had just saved her.

"Hey, Hah-vud, if you've got nothing better to do, why don't you come along?"

Ben was about to tell her why. All the reasons went through his mind in a flash. He hated the practice of medicine. He had no real friends to even notice he was missing. He had AIDS. He was dying. Why would a total failure at life want to get into a stolen ambulance headed who knows where with a bunch of escaped lunatics, including a murder/rapist, a man who believed little green men were preparing to destroy the planet, and a woman whose goal in life was not to destroy the planet but to have sex with it?

Why? Why the hell not? Ben took Makesh's hand in assistance and hopped into the back of the ambulance which headed off down the sidewalk, pedestrians jumping out of the way, until Angel could explain to Juan why the road would be a better choice.

Angel was trying to get them to Penn Station in hopes of slipping out of the city by train, but Juan's propensity for heading down one-way streets the wrong way was uncanny. Fortunately, most people seemed to give the southbound ambulance the right of way, leaving behind a wake of jumbled cars looking more like a bumper car arena than a city street. They'd managed to plow about 40 blocks to 120th street when their radio came to life.

"Motor vehicle crash with loss of consciousness, 118th & Broadway."

"That's just two blocks ahead of us," said Makesh, looking between the two front seats out the windshield.

"Hey, you're right," said Angel, checking the street signs. They were headed down Broadway. "Juan, stop ahead at 118th."

As the ambulance slowed at the site of a crowd gathered on the sidewalk, Ben had to speak up. "Don't you guys think you have enough on your plates right now? You're trying to escape and there are all kinds of people after you. Remember? Let's try to stay focused now."

"Someone may be dying," argued Angel. "We can't just drive by."

"Why not?" countered Ben. "It's none of your business."

Angel turned to look at Ben. "We saved your miserable life. Why wouldn't we save this one?"

Ben was caught off guard, a twinge of guilt rising within him.

"But we don't know if this one has a credit card," said Juan, stopping the ambulance by the crowd of people.

"What does he mean by that?" asked Ben, growing suspicious.

"Oh, uh, nothing I'm sure. He's just a little confused," covered Angel.

"No I'm not," countered Juan. "I thought we only took Dr. Ben because we needed his credit card." Angel tried to shush him as Ben grabbed for his wallet.

"Hey," he complained, confirming that his card was missing. "So that's it."

"It's not like that," said Angel.

"You didn't have to kidnap me, you know. You could have just asked for my credit card. I would have just given it to you, then gone back to killing myself."

"So you *were* trying to kill yourself," stated Makesh, as if he'd won a bet with Angel.

"You mean you didn't even know I was attempting suicide?" Ben was growing more and more depressed.

Angel looked Ben directly in the eyes and said gently, "I knew."

Ben looked back at her, registering her concern.

The crowd at the sidewalk parted as the ambulance pulled up. A frantic woman started pounding on the window of the ambulance. "Hurry. Hurry! He won't wake up," she shouted, pointing at the wreckage. "I think he's dead."

Angel threw her door open. "Come on, Doctor," she called to Ben.

"But I'm not—" started Ben.

"Not what?" interrupted Angel. "A doctor? Well I'm not a nurse. Juan's not an ambulance driver. And Makesh isn't... Well we don't know what Makesh isn't. But we're all these people have got. Don't you know anything about medicine?"

They all stared at Ben who stood frozen with indecision. Finally, the woman who'd been pounding on the ambulance window, now surrounded by her three small children clinging to her dress, grabbed Ben by the arm and dragged him over to the car-shaped accordion folded up against the concrete building. "Doctor," she pleaded, "my husband, please help him."

"But ma'am," Ben began, "I'm not really a—"

Ben was interrupted by the smallest of the woman's three children, a little boy with tears in his eyes. "Please, sir. My daddy's sleeping. Could you wake him up for me, please?"

Ben looked down at the little boy. He looked at the boy's mother. Then he looked back at Angel. She threw him a stern look, then gestured toward the wreckage with her chin. Ben knew when to concede defeat.

He poked his head through the window of the former automobile and began to access the situation. It almost seemed as though the child was right. He looked like he was asleep. The big man still wore his seatbelt and shoulder harness. He barely had a scratch. Apparently the deployed airbag had done its job.

What do I do first? Ben wondered. Then he recalled his CPR course. Check for airway. Ben looked at the man's chest moving with each breath and the near snore which accompanied. Well that was easy. He's breathing. Pulse! That's right, check for a pulse. Although, if the man were breathing, he more than likely had a pulse. Ben touched the man's neck anyway, feeling for a carotid pulse. There it was. If Ben could find it, he reasoned, it must be a pretty strong pulse. Now what?

"Sir? Sir, wake up." Well, what the hell, thought Ben. It happens. Ben gently shook the man's shoulder. "Sir, wake up." No, that would be too easy, wouldn't it? Yet the man wasn't even bleeding. Why was he unconscious? Ben looked closer at the man's head. No contusions. No broken windshield. What else do I do?

History! Take a history. History and physical. That's what doctors do. Well the limited physical wasn't offering much. The history starts with the "chief complaint." This guy's not doing much complaining. But if he could he would say, "My complaint is that this concrete wall got in the way of my car and I can't wake up. Oh, and one other thing. How come I can't even get a paramedic, let alone an actual doctor?" How was Ben going to get a history from an unconscious patient? Ben wished the man would stop being so difficult and start being more cooperative.

Ben turned to the gathered crowd. "Did anyone see the accident?"

No reply. Then, "We just heard the crash, the sound of the car hitting the wall."

Ben turned to the man's wife. "You weren't in the car with him?"

"No. We live one block over. The people here know us. They came to get us."

So much for history, thought Ben. But what about past medical history? "Ma'am?" began Ben. "Did your husband have any medical problems before the accident? Is he on any medications?"

"Just the usual stuff, I guess. He's got a bad back." After a pause, "Oh, and his sugar's bad."

"His sugar's bad?" asked Ben. "What does that mean?"

"He takes insulin."

"He's diabetic?"

"Yes."

"I see," said the blind man. Ben knew that that had to mean something. But what? Diabetic on insulin. Blood sugar too high? Nothing to do for that right now.

The crowd was onto him. "How come he's not doing anything?" they grumbled. "I don't think he knows what he's doing." "He looks kind of young." "Hey kid, you sure you're a doctor?" "Maybe give the gray-haired guy with the half-shaved head a shot at it." "Do something."

Ben felt the crowd closing in around him. He was losing his concentration. Now where was he? Diabetic on insulin. Blood sugar too high? No. Low. Blood sugar too low. Maybe. What the hell. Start an IV. I think I can do that. "Angel!" shouted Ben.

"Whoa. You don't have to yell." She was right behind him.

"Sorry. Angel, get me an IV setup from the ambulance. And a bag of saline with glucose."

Angel lingered, eyeing Ben. "Do you know what you're doing?" she whispered.

Ben looked back at her and gave a definitive, "Maybe."

Angel glared at him.

"Hey," began Ben. "I'm not the one who decided to accept this mission. I was kidnapped. Remember?"

"OK. OK. Don't get your panties in a wad." Angel went back to the ambulance to fetch the requested supplies.

It seemed to take forever, as Ben was left alone with his patient. He began to question his diagnosis. What other possibilities were there? A rare brain tumor? Meningitis? Polio? Bubonic plague? All right now. Calm down.

"Here you are, Master," said Angel upon returning, offering her best impersonation of Frankenstein's Igor. "One IV setup and saline with glucose. I hope it is to your liking."

Ben opened the IV tubing and momentarily didn't seem to know which end was which.

"The long needle part goes in the patient's arm," Angel suggested.

Ben threw her a look of contempt.

"Just trying to help," she added. Angel observed as Ben surveyed the man's arm for a good-sized vein. "Ooh, look at that one," pointed Angel, now sounding more like a vampire.

Ben had never actually started an IV before. He'd seen a resident do one, though. And as they say in medical school. See one. Do one. Teach one. Now it was Ben's turn to do one. If only he could hit the vein with the needle. The vein wouldn't cooperate and seemed to roll away from the needle every time Ben tried to poke it. At least his patient was unconscious, sparing Ben the usual critiques, such as, "Is this the first time you've done this?" or "You don't look old enough to be a doctor."

The patient was unconscious, but Angel wasn't. "You're turning him into a pin cushion. Why don't you let me try it? Is this the first time you've done this?"

Ben felt the perspiration beading on his forehead. One particularly large drop was finally dangling from the tip of his nose when he thought to pin the reluctant vein down with one hand while harpooning it with the other. He was in! He knew this because when he withdrew the stylus from the catheter, blood started pouring down the man's arm.

"Is that supposed to happen?" inquired Angel, watching a small pool of blood forming on the floor of the wrecked car.

Ben just gave her a nasty look as he connected the IV tubing to the bleeding catheter. Grabbing the attached bag of saline and glucose, Ben opened the valve wide open. As the fluid headed into the man's arm, the blood that had begun to fill the line retreated. He did it. It worked.

"What happened?" asked a voice from within the car.

Ben looked up to see who was speaking only to find his patient was awake. He quickly looked over at Angel.

"That's it?" she asked incredulously. "Just like that?"

Ben looked back at the man. He was definitely awake. "You take insulin?" asked Ben.

"For 20 years," replied the man.

"Did you have breakfast?" Ben continued.

"No time this morning," said the man.

Ben turned back to Angel. "Insulin and skipped meals don't go together."

"That's it? Just like that?" repeated Angel.

"That's it. He just needed a little sugar."

As the entire neighborhood of grateful family and friends descended upon Ben as though he'd just scored a winning touchdown, Makesh could hear the siren of another ambulance, one with real paramedics, finally approaching the scene. "Uh, guys," he shouted over the crowd, "we'd better get going."

After convincing his jubilant fans to place him back on the ground, Ben laid the saline bag on the roof of the man's car and made his way back to the ambulance, cheering children wrapped around his legs. When he and Angel finally succeeded in getting back to the ambulance, Juan had already started the engine.

A woman, the patient's wife, came running toward them and gave Ben a bear hug. "Thank you, Doctor," she started, kissing Ben's hand. "Thank you for saving my husband's life."

Ben broke free as the ambulance began to pull away. "He'll be just fine, ma'am."

As Juan proceeded the wrong way down a one-way street, Angel turned to Ben. "Pretty cool, huh?"

"What do you mean?" asked Ben, his eyes lingering on the crowd now dancing in the street.

"Saving a life. Making a difference."

"Oh, that," said Ben, eyes still lingering down the street. "Not bad."

"Not bad? What's wrong with you, asshole? You just saved a man's life. Doesn't that mean anything to you?"

Ben finally looked at Angel apologetically. "No. No. It's not that. It's just—"

Ben wanted to explain to Angel that due to his own terminal medical condition, his time as a superhero was limited. He wanted to tell her all about his diagnosis of AIDS. But instead, quite by coincidence, he was interrupted by one of his newly acquired coughing spells.

"You ought to get that checked," suggested Angel, "by a real doctor."

By the time he'd caught his breath, the subject had changed.

"Where are we going?" called Makesh from the front of the ambulance.

"Well, first, we'd better get out of town," Angel replied. "They've probably noticed the missing ambulance by now. I think a train ride would be fun. How about Penn station?"

Juan's interest was peaked. "A train!? We get to go on a train!?"

Angel smiled. "Yeah. Sounds like fun, huh?"

"But where will we get the money for train tickets?" asked Makesh.

"You forget," Angel began, "we have a benefactor." She nodded toward Ben, holding up his credit card.

"Oh, yes," said Makesh, turning toward Ben. "If that's OK with you, Dr. Walker, we would be most appreciative."

Ben's thoughts were elsewhere when he responded, "Sure, sure. No problem."

Makesh turned toward the front again to see car after car, at the last second, swerving out of their way. "Tell me, Juan. Why don't we try driving on the right side of the road for a while?"

"Which side is the right side?" Juan inquired.

"That way," said Makesh, pointing to the right. Following Makesh's finger, Juan pulled the ambulance all the way across the street and up onto the right sidewalk.

"No! No!" continued Makesh, watching horrified pedestrians leaping out of their path. "Back on the street!"

"Well make up your mind," protested Juan. "Do you want me *on* the street, or on the *right side* of the street?"

"Pardon me for being less than precise," Makesh calmly replied. "English is not my first language either. How about the right *half* of the street? Let's try driving on the right *half*."

Chapter 24

Life was such in midtown Manhattan that it could be days before anyone even noticed the abandoned ambulance outside Penn Station. In fact, by the second day, a homeless family of five had moved in, impressed as they were by the spacious living accommodations.

Most of the homeless in that area, however, preferred residing right inside Penn Station. Nice high ceilings, large benches, heat and indoor plumbing, and a constant source of sustenance provided by the never-ending stream of passengers headed to or from their trains, whether it be in the form of cash handouts or unfinished lunch from trash cans.

Benjamin Walker wouldn't normally have sat on the same bench with the homeless, as he waited for Angel to check out the train schedule. He was normally too afraid of them. However, the events of the day had taken a toll on him. In the past 18 hours, he'd tried to throw himself off the George Washington Bridge, he was drugged and kidnapped by three escapees from the insane asylum, he woke up in a coffin, drove in two stolen vehicles, and saved a man's life. Oh, and all that, with a fresh case of AIDS.

He'd begun to feel a certain kinship with his brethren on the bench, his life spinning out of control as his health deteriorated. He didn't even flinch when the creature wrapped in rags at the other end of the bench sidled up to him, sneezed on his neck, and asked if he had any spare change. Ben checked every pocket but had nothing to offer. It was the homeless man's response that affirmed Ben's sense that something had changed.

The man held his prized paper bag containing his bottle of spirits out to share with Ben. "Go on, brother. Looks like you've had quite a day."

That was certainly an understatement, thought Ben, as he found himself accepting the man's offer of the unidentified brown liquid. Ben couldn't be certain whether the burning sensation imparted to his esophageal mucosa by the potent elixir was the predictable response to cheap bourbon, or the heartwarming effect of sulfuric acid. Nevertheless, through the ceremonial drink, Ben had found a compatriot.

"So what's your thing?" the man asked.

Ben looked up, waiting until his liquor-induced coughing spell had passed. "My thing? What do you mean, my thing?"

"Your thing. You know. Your profession."

"Oh," began Ben. "I'm... Well, I was... sort of... a doctor."

"Oh yeah? Is that so? Me too."

"You're a doctor?" asked Ben.

Raggedy Man replied, "How about those HMOs, huh? Drove me over the edge. Spent all day on the phone trying to get preauthorization for treatment. Then they automatically deny your claim. And even when they actually pay a year later, it isn't even enough to cover your overhead." After a swig of magic potion, "Drove me to drink."

Ben was beginning to wonder if he'd eventually wake up in bed, head off to his first day of medical school, and soon forget the bizarre nightmare he was apparently experiencing.

His thoughts, though, were interrupted as Angel and company returned from the ticket counter. On the way, however, they'd apparently taken Ben's credit card on a shopping spree, replacing their hospital attire with clothes that wouldn't attract as much attention. That is except Angel, of course. She'd managed to find some microscopic spandex outfit sold in a tube, with matching six-inch high heels to complete the ensemble that would be the envy of any stripper.

"There's a train leaving any minute for Miami. Here's your ticket," said Angel, handing it to Ben, while stashing his credit card back into her own pocket.

"*My* ticket? Where do you think *I'm* going?"

"With us, of course," Angel replied.

"Why would you think I'd be going with you?"

"Look at you," she began, eyeing Ben and his new medical associate. "I think you could use a change of surroundings."

"Who's that?" interrupted Ben's new friend. "The old ball and chain? My ex and her vermin lawyer took me for everything I had. Tell her to take the credit card and get lost." Leaning in, he continued in a whisper, "As soon as she's gone, we'll call and get that card cancelled."

Ben ignored him and asked Angel, "Why Miami?"

"We're taking Juan home. Isla de los Locos, remember? Miami's as close as we can get by land. Then we'll need a plane or a boat."

"I don't know," began Ben. "This place kind of grows on you," he added as a bag lady wrapped in blankets, accompanied by the distinctive smell of urine, sat down next to Ben.

Then after a fresh coughing spell, "Besides, I might just slow you down. Why don't you guys go on without me." At that, Ben's new neighbor began her own coughing spell, during which she managed to summon a throat full of phlegm to spit onto the floor, only half of which landed on Ben's shoe. "I'll stay here."

"God," said Angel, "You make it sound as though you were dying."

Ben hesitated, wondering if he should share his big secret, but thought better of it. "And what if I was?"

"Was what?" Angel replied.

"Dying."

"Oh stop being ridiculous. Why would you be dying?"

"Doesn't matter why. Let's just say I was. Wouldn't be much point in going to Miami with you nuts, would there?"

Angel wasn't sure what it was, but something was going on with Ben. Something big. She growled at the bag lady next to Ben until she slid over and made room for Angel to sit down next to Ben.

"All the more reason," she began. There's nothing to keep you here. If your days were numbered, why would you spend them in a medical school library studying a craft you'll never get to use? I'm sure that somewhere in your application to medical school you wrote that you wanted to help people. Why not do something noble with your final days? Use what's left of your life to save another. Let's help Juan get home."

"But look at us," said Ben. "People are after us. We're driving stolen vehicles. Who knows what's going to happen next?"

"Precisely," Angel replied. "We're having an adventure. That's what adventures are about."

Ben looked at Angel. "Are you still taking your medication?"

Angel ignored the question. "Well? Are you with us?"

Ben didn't know if the AIDS virus was affecting his mind or whether it was just the brown fluid his benchmate was sharing with him, but for one reason or another, Angel was beginning to make sense. Why not? Why not have an adventure? And she was right about Juan also. Why not help the big idiot?

"I guess you're—" He was going to say "right," but was interrupted by Makesh who ran up to them with a frantic expression. Of course, his half-shaved head didn't help.

"They're here!" he said, half shouting and half whispering.

"Who? Who's here?" asked Angel.

"You know. Them. The men in black!"

Here we go again, thought Ben. First it was the little green men. Then it was the men in black. What was I thinking? Pass the medication please.

"Where are they?" asked Angel, giving Makesh her full attention.

"Down by the platforms. It looks like they're checking all the trains."

"But how did they know we were here?" wondered Angel.

Makesh pointed to his head. "It's the damned transmitter. They know my every move." Then, banging his head on the wall with surprising force, "Maybe I can deactivate it."

Angel grabbed him by the hair. "Whoa there. I don't think that's going to work. So before you deactivate your brain, let's think of another plan. Come on."

Angel headed toward the train platforms. "There's our train. Quick, let's get on the other one."

"Why are we getting on the wrong train?" asked Juan.

Angel was about to explain when she saw the two sunglassed men in black suits pointing at them. "No time to explain. Quick, on the train." Angel herded them all aboard.

Aboard the train, Juan jumped into the first seat. "I like these seats," he said, bouncing up and down. "They're nice and soft."

"No no no," said Angel, pulling him up by the collar as she spied the men in black through the window headed their way. "Not here. Come on."

They proceeded down the aisle toward the back of the train.

"How about these seats?" asked Juan every few aisles.

Ignoring him, Angel poked her head out a window, just to make sure the men in black were boarding the train. "They're on."

She didn't have to tell Makesh to keep heading toward the back of the train. He was already putting as much distance as possible between himself and his tormentors. The others followed his lead.

The train started to move as the fugitives reached the rear of the train. Ben looked over the rail at the tracks as the train pulled away.

"What? Now I'm jumping from moving trains? When did I turn into some kind of action figure?"

"Oh, stop whining," said Angel. "We're not moving that fast..." Then peering over the rail at the tracks pulling away from them at an ever faster pace. "...yet."

Makesh was already clambering over the rail.

They jumped in unison, the four of them rolling up into one big ball of arms and legs as they hit the moving tracks below. As they watched the train head into the tunnel leaving Penn Station, they were sure by that point it was moving too fast for anyone else to jump off.

The rats were kind enough to clear a path for their guests as the four headed back to the platform. Helping each other up out of the soot-filled ditch, they finally boarded the right train. And this time they stayed long enough for the conductor to check their tickets.

In fact, after a visit to the snack car and a few bags of potato chips later, the gentle rumbling of the train rocked them each off to sleep. Juan was first, followed by Makesh who had his first nightmare-free rest since he could remember. Even Ben, whose last sleep took place in the back of a hearse, seemed to relax at the thought of their newfound freedom. Only Angel didn't sleep. Of course, she rarely did when she was off her medication.

Chapter 25

The three guys in the passenger car next to theirs were a little sore by the time Angel decided to head back to her own seat just before dawn. The spent young men had already missed their intended stop, but then again, there are certain things in life you just don't pass up. A night with a fallen Angel was certainly one of those things. And several days off her medication, Angel was falling fast. She wasn't sleeping. And the more time she spent awake, the more time she spent thinking about sex. That old persistent hum between her legs was back.

Juan had already found some small children to play hide and seek with. His size, of course, put him at a distinct disadvantage, running up and down the length of the train, darting in and out of seats. Juan hadn't had that kind of fun for a long time, probably not since he left his beloved Isla de los Locos. Of course, it wasn't long before one of the six-year-olds started picking on him. After all, six is the age when children learn how to be mean. "Retard" was one of the first words of English Juan had learned upon his arrival in America. He used to think "stupid retard" was one word. But he soon learned that each word could be used independently.

Makesh was up early as well. After all, he only had about a week left in which to save the world.

He stared at the telephone poles flying past his window as he pondered the fate of his planet. How does one convince an alien wrecking crew that Earth was worth saving, that the spinning ball of mud had some intrinsic value, value above and beyond that of some intergalactic fast food court. He thought of the plutonium again, but remembered the alien's remark that they could get that anywhere. No, it would have to be something unique to Earth, something not sold in alien stores. Makesh hadn't a clue. And he had no plan on how to come up with one. There was no one to help him. The best response he could get from the others was chuckles of disbelief. No, he was on his own with this one. At least he wasn't locked up anymore. All he could do now was stay away from the men in black, help Juan get home, and keep his eyes open. Something would come to him.

Ben wasn't much different. He didn't know what he was looking for either. But just like Makesh, he was along for the ride, and when he saw whatever it was, he would know. That is if he lived that long. His cough persisted, and was worsening. In addition, he'd begun waking up at night, alternating between bouts of sweats and chills. His viral load must be growing, he thought, the nasty little buggers wreaking havoc on his immune system. Just his luck, too. Here he was, on the road with a beautiful nymphomaniac, finally of a mind to live a little, maybe spend some time scratching Angel's itch, and here he was HIV positive. No, he couldn't bare the thought of passing on that legacy.

It wasn't clear to them at what stop the men in black boarded the train. In fact, only Makesh seemed to know they were there. In some sort of dream, the little green men came to him in warning to say that the men in black had boarded the train. And for once, at least in the dream, they really did appear as cute little green men with round heads and bellies.

It shouldn't have surprised Makesh and the others that their tormentors would simply jump ahead to try and intercept them at the next scheduled stop. Nevertheless, Makesh awoke from his dream in terror, bolted upright, eyes wide, heart pounding out of his chest. They had to get off that train, and they had to do it fast.

While the rest of the escapees were willing to take Makesh's tale at face value, that the men in black were here to recover stolen plutonium, Ben thought it more likely they were FBI agents trailing Juan, an escaped murderer/rapist. Either way, they'd have to get off the train.

This time, however, the train was traveling much too fast for them to just jump off. But this was an emergency, after all. So no one should have been surprised when Makesh pulled the cord for the emergency brake. At least no one who knew about the little green men and the plutonium. And so it was fair to say that the entire train, save a handful of escapees from the funny farm, erupted in pandemonium, bodies falling all over each other when the train suddenly jerked and came to a screeching halt.

Amid the confusion, no one even noticed the gang of four tiptoeing off the stopped train in the early pre-dawn darkness. Even had someone looked outside the train, the starlit sky was not enough to illuminate the dark deserted landscape through which the train tracks ran. So when the train resumed its journey and the men in black finally made it through to the last car of the train, they had to wonder if they'd gotten on the wrong train. How had the homing transmitter failed them?

"Now what?" asked Ben over the deafening sound of crickets. There they were, still an hour or so before sunrise, standing alongside a set of railroad tracks somewhere in South Carolina.

"I'm hungry," said Juan, in what he thought was reply.

"Where do you expect to find something to eat? We could be hundreds of miles from civilization," noted Ben.

"Why can't we eat over there?" asked Juan, pointing behind Ben.

Sure enough, not 100 yards beyond the other side of the tracks, there was a shabby wooden shack bearing a flickering neon light. Ben was gripped with terror as he first made out the eerie blue lights which spelled out one ominous word. "DIE." Maybe he was still asleep and he was only dreaming along the lines of some cheap horror movie. Then, as he focused, he realized the sign didn't say "DIE" after all. What it actually said was "DI E." The N and the R had burnt out. The sign was meant to read "DINER."

"Well look at that," said Angel. "An oasis."

"Let's go," prodded Makesh, looking down the tracks to make sure the train had indeed disappeared into the night.

The four scrambled across the tracks, down a small embankment, then past the tractor trailer rigs and a 1968 lime green convertible Plymouth Road Runner occupying the dirt parking lot of the diner. The torn screen door slammed shut behind them as they entered the shack.

Looking about, it was clear to Ben that they were far from Manhattan. Johnny Cash was on the jukebox. Five flannel-shirted, John Deere-capped, good ole boys sat on stools flirting with the dentally impaired, bleached blonde waitress behind the counter proudly displaying her only asset, her ample cleavage. She skillfully leaned over the counter, placing a cup of coffee and a pickled egg in front of one of the truckers.

At one particularly long and loud zap from the bug zapper, the group at the counter turned amid the hiss and smoke emanating from the violet light to see who had let the now cooked pest in. Judging by the looks from the home team, the escapees from New York might just as well have been the zapper's next victims. Trying to ignore the stares coming from the counter, Ben sat down with the others in a booth, handing out the menus from the stand at one end of the table.

If they weren't as hungry as they were, their cosmopolitan low fat palates would have shut down in protest to the scent of lard and lipids with which they were soon confronted. Everything on the menu came dripping in butter and grease. Even the coffee looked oily. Despite the cholesterol challenge, they ordered everything in mass quantities including extra helpings of bacon and grits, even though none of them actually knew what grits were.

As they waited for their food to arrive, they noticed the juke box kept playing "A Boy Named Sue" over and over again. The scientist in him got the better of Makesh as he got up and walked over to investigate. Ben noticed all eyes were on Makesh as he approached the machine, and he wondered if the locals had in fact rigged it so it would keep playing that one song over and over. He wondered if Makesh should get the hell away from it and mind his own business. He wondered if they were all soon going to die.

The men at the counter had stopped eating as they watched the stranger closing in on their beloved juke box. Squeezing behind the big box, Makesh found the rear panel already removed as others had been fooling with it.

Ben held his breath at the sudden silence that resulted when Makesh pulled out the plug. The men at the counter all put their forks down and swiveled in their chairs to watch Makesh. Ben broke out in a cold sweat as he quietly, but with an edge of panic, ordered Makesh, through clenched teeth, to put the music back on. He even began to feebly mumble the words to the song that until recently had added so much to the place's ambiance.

Although initially relieved when the music came back on, Ben feared they'd jumped from the frying pan into the fire when he recognized the tune. It seemed to be a disco medley of The Village People. Ben felt his testicles reflexively retracting up into his body as if seeking refuge. It didn't seem to Ben that this would be the music of choice for this crowd, although it could have been worse. It could have been Broadway show tunes.

But when Ben looked over at the counter, he couldn't believe his eyes. Their heads were actually bouncing to the pounding disco beat. They were practically snapping their fingers. And when "In the Navy" came on, they were on their feet. Well, it wasn't dancing, but more of a military salute. Apparently, the jukebox, through no intent of their own, had been stuck on that one Johnny Cash song for the better part of a year now, and frankly, the boys had had enough.

Makesh received a hero's recognition as the men from the counter hoisted him above their heads, trotted once around the room with him, then deposited him, standing, upon the counter. Only after mastering the synchronized arm movements to the song YMCA did they finish by kneeling on the floor and bowing to their new god of the jukebox.

Ben slumped down in the booth wishing all the attention would go away. But it didn't. And when Makesh started talking about aliens, Ben wanted to disappear.

"Please, please," began Makesh, addressing his subjects. "It's only music. This isn't the cure for cancer. That, I'm afraid, lies with our friends up there," he said gesturing toward the heavens.

The men in the diner went silent.

"What's he doing?" whispered Ben to Angel, growing more nervous.

One of the truckers spoke up. "You mean Christ our lord?"

"Please agree with him," whispered Ben, not knowing if he actually said it, or just whispered it.

"No, sir, not God," began Makesh. "They come from other worlds far far away." He was looking upwards.

Ben closed his eyes, wishing none of this was happening.

Another trucker broke the silence. "You talkin' about aliens?" The other truckers just stared. Ben opened his eyes again, fearing they were about to be beaten to death.

"Yes, sir," said Makesh. "That's exactly what I'm talking about."

The crowd of truckers started grumbling among themselves. Ben knew they were done for now.

Again, one of the truckers stepped forward as spokesman. "You seen 'em?"

"Sort of," answered Makesh.

After an awkward silence, another trucker stepped forward, "Me, too."

All eyes turned to him.

"And me," added another trucker.

"Took me up there with 'em," added a third.

Ben finally opened his eyes.

"Did they do experiments on you too?" from another trucker. And so the conversation went, each trucker, in turn, telling his own woeful tale of alien abduction. "Don't you hate when they stick them computer probe doohickeys up your ass?"

During the impromptu group encounter session that ensued, Ben was able to get Makesh's attention, who quietly slipped down from the counter, and walked through the parting crowd of fellow abductees as they began clapping both for his success with the juke box as well as his ice-breaking alien revelation.

"No, please. It was nothing, really," he insisted, pulling them up from the kneeling position they'd assumed.

"Well you're all right, little guy," said one of them, slapping Makesh so hard on the back that he stumbled into the booth where Ben sat dumfounded.

"Have you lost your mind?" Ben said under his breath, grabbing Makesh by the arm. "They might have killed us all just for looking at their juke box, let alone all that alien nonsense."

"But I fixed it," replied Makesh. "It was malfunctioning."

Ben wasn't calmed. "Maybe they liked it that way."

"They seem to be happy with my work," said Makesh nodding to his burly fan club.

"We were just lucky this time. We should mind our own business."

Ben's voice had escalated to a point where his aggressive tone caught the ear of the truckers at the counter. One of them put down a half-eaten donut to turn to Makesh.

"Is he bothering you?" he asked, indicating Ben.

Ben turned white, frozen with fear.

Makesh looked at him and started, "Well I—"

Ben, sensing he was in danger of great bodily harm, again grabbed Makesh's arm, "What do you mean, well I?"

Ben's sudden physical contact with Makesh brought the self-proclaimed body guard another step closer.

"Well, if you must know," began Makesh, "I do feel your criticism of me is unjustified."

Ben dropped Makesh's arm in disbelief and pushed himself further back into the booth.

"Want me to hurt'm?" asked Makesh's protector.

Ben put his hands over his head in a defensive posture. "I was just kidding," he implored. "Angel. Angel tell him what a joker I am."

Angel looked at Ben and acknowledged sarcastically, "Oh yeah. You're quite the clown."

Ben had broken out in a sweat.

Makesh decided Ben had suffered enough. "No, no. Thank you very much, sir. But I don't think injury will be necessary."

Ben exhaled in relief as the flannel wall in front of him backed off.

Angel turned to Ben. "Well? Aren't you even going to thank Makesh?"

Ben appeared indignant. "Why? For almost getting me killed?"

"No. *You* almost got you killed. You should thank him for saving your life."

"But—" began Ben. Then seeing Angel's piercing glare, he reluctantly gave in. "Oh, alright already. Thank you Makesh."

Without missing a beat Angel shifted gears and got back to business. "Makesh, we need some transportation. Can you hotwire a car?"

Makesh looked confused. "What is the meaning? Hotwire?"

"You know. Start a car without its keys. Can you borrow a car for us from the parking lot outside?"

"Why not just ask for the keys from one of these gentlemen?" he continued, indicating the men at the counter.

"Because they won't do it, that's why," answered Ben. "Can you or can't you?"

Well of course I can start a motor vehicle without its keys. You're not talking rocket science after all. It's just that borrowing someone's car without their permission seems like it might be against the rules."

"Ya think so?" asked Angel innocently. "How could borrowing be against the law... uh, I mean, the rules?"

"Well, I guess, if you put it that way, it wouldn't be any harm," agreed Makesh.

"Good," said Angel. "Why don't you see if you can find a fast one out in the parking lot while we wait for our food?"

"OK." Makesh slid out of the booth and out the screen door to the parking lot.

Ben turned to Angel. "I can't believe you're going to steal a car from one of these brutes."

"Would you rather just live in this diner? Maybe get jobs here?" asked Angel.

Ben was about to reply when Juan announced, "I want candy."

Ben was taken aback by the change in subject, then annoyed by the request, "What do you mean, you want candy?"

Angel came to Juan's defense. "What part of I want candy don't you understand?"

"We ordered a big breakfast. And, anyway, I don't see candy on the menu," Ben replied.

"There's some on the counter," Juan continued, pointing toward a bowl by the cash register. He hadn't had candy since he'd left his grandmother on the island.

"That's for after we eat," said Ben, turning the menu over to read the back. "How about some pancakes?"

"Candy," was Juan's one word response.

"Eggs?" asked Ben.

"Candy."

"But that's for after you pay for your breakfast," continued Ben in explanation. "We don't get that until we're ready to leave."

"Then I'm ready to leave," responded Juan, standing up at the table.

"Sit down," said Ben in a loud whisper trying not to disturb the burly clientele at the counter as he grabbed Juan by the wrist.

Juan Martinez may not have been a child, at least not in size, but his mind didn't know that. And his mind remembered the sweet taste of candy. Many of the truckers at the counter had at one time or another somehow managed to have children. None of these men would ever understand their wives, but the one thing a man learns having had a child is not to get between one and its candy. Ain't no amount of logic that's going to convince a child why he shouldn't have candy once it's in eyesight. Just step back and get out of the way.

So when Juan's tantrum started, all eyes turned on Ben. "Candy! Now!" yelled Juan, pointing at the candy jar and banging his fist on the table.

Ben didn't know when to give in. "I told you. Not until—"

One particularly red neck turned toward them, cutting Ben off mid-sentence. "You'd best give the boy some candy, 'for I come over there and shove the whole jar up your ass."

"But—" started Ben, not having enough sense to know when his life was in danger.

"Really," cut in Angel. "You're such a meany. Why don't you let him have some candy?"

"Because that candy is for after your meal. It's not for sale."

"Oh, that's OK, honey," announced the waitress. And grabbing a handful of the candy and holding it under Juan's nose, "Here you go, sweetie. You just take as much as you want."

Juan emptied her hand with a "Thank you, ma'am."

The waitress gave him a mostly toothless smile and the men at the counter turned back to their food. "That's a good kid over there," said one to the other. "It's a shame his daddy's such an asshole."

Ben looked at Angel. "Daddy? They think I'm Juan's father?" Ben started to turn toward his fan club at the counter. "I'm not his fath—" he began, before Angel could cut him off.

"Shsh. Just let it go," she said.

"But how could they think—"

"You ain't his daddy?" from one of the flannel shirts, dropping a spoonful of grits. "Then where is he? A boy should be with his daddy. You ain't one o' them molesterers, are ya?" All heads at the counter turned.

Ben turned to Angel looking for support.

Angel just looked back at him. "Well?" she asked.

"Well, what?" replied Ben.

"Are you?"

"Am I what?"

"A child molester." Angel was enjoying this.

Ben looked back at the intent stares of the jury and felt a sweat breaking out. Then back to Angel, "How could you think I would—"

"You likes little boys over women, do ya?" asked the redneck with no neck.

"Little boys? He's over six feet tall!" began Ben in defense of himself on a technicality.

The no-neck redneck got off his stool, expanding to a height of 6' 5". "So you likes big boys, do ya?" he inquired.

"Of course not," said Ben, a pinch of panic in his tone. "Angel!" He turned to Angel for support.

Angel wasn't ready to let him off the hook yet. Turning toward the flannel-shirted wall standing at the counter, "You're not his type."

Ben grabbed her forcibly by the arm. "Not his type!? What do you mean?"

Angel pulled her arm back. "You're hurting me."

Realizing his faux pas, Ben turned back toward the counter. The entire jury was now on their feet.

"Take your molesterin' hands off the little lady," from a redneck spokesman.

"But I'm not—" began Ben. Then noticing his hand still gripping Angel's arm, he pulled away.

The large flannel shirt spoke. "So you like pickin' on little boys *and* pretty ladies, do ya?"

"Me? No, I... I... I..." stuttered Ben.

What ensued could not really be called a fight. It was more of a chase, as Ben managed to barely keep out of the hairy clutches of his assailants by leaping from tabletop to tabletop, over the counter, and about the kitchen.

At first he thought he was in a cartoon when he heard the familiar "beep beep" of the Road Runner coming from the front of the diner. It wasn't until he'd been caught by the flannel shirts, hoisted in the air, and thrown through the front window, that he saw the getaway car waiting for him.

Angel and Juan had already joined Makesh in the lime green convertible Road Runner he'd borrowed from the parking lot out back. Ben quickly scrambled to his feet and leaped head first into the rear seat of the car which revved its collectable 426 hemi motor sending over 400 horsepower to the rear wheels. The fuzzy dice hanging from the rearview mirror jerked backward as the car shot forward with a roar, leaving a cloud of dust completely whiting out the diner and its guests.

While Ben lay face down cowering in the back seat of the 1968 green rocket, Angel was having such a good time peeling out onto the road that she couldn't help standing up straight in the back seat, looking back with a big smile, and giving a friendly wave goodbye to the folks back at the diner.

Angel and Juan had also managed to bring along some of the food which the waitress had brought during the melee. Juan, of course, took the whole jar of candy from the counter. He almost took the jar of Slim Jims, thinking they were licorice. But seeing the bright candy jar next to it, he made the right choice. A good thing too, because, had he taken the Slim Jims, one of the men in black that entered the diner later that day would have been out of luck.

Chapter 26

Assuming the owner of the vehicle they'd borrowed might want it back, they kept to the back roads until they crossed over the border into Florida where they picked up Interstate 95.

The Florida sun was hot, beating down on the open convertible. Try as they might, even the rocket scientist couldn't get the convertible top to go up, which was just as well, since the car had no air conditioning. Of course, by noon, it also allowed them to do their laundry as there was no place to hide from the downpour of rain which soaked the humid Florida summer briefly each day like clockwork. If not for the rust holes in the Roadrunner's floorboards, they'd have needed a bilge pump. The rain was particularly blinding in the absence of functioning windshield wipers. But as quickly as the rain appeared, it was soon gone and replaced by the relentless southern sun again.

Juan had become quite the chauffeur over the past couple of days. Of course, it helped that all three lanes of traffic on their side of the interstate were headed in the same direction. Ben had dozed off between bouts of fever, separated by shaking chills and drenching sweats, while Angel, on her second day without any sleep at all, had unconsciously started rubbing herself again.

But it was Makesh who started becoming agitated, and not just because he couldn't get the old eight-track player to work. It was the billboards at the side of the highway. They were starting to get to him. No, it wasn't those annoying "South of the Border" signs every mile, or the ones selling pecans or fireworks. It was the ones with the motion video and sound, the ones that were talking to him.

At first, he thought it was quite ingenious, how far advertisers had come in their never-ending quest to grab the public's attention. He wasn't sure what they were selling, but that's often the case in cutting edge advertisements, style over substance.

They started with a count down from seven, then an image of Earth, slowly rotating in space. Soon some sort of laser beam strikes Earth, shattering it into millions of tiny particles. When the space dust clears, a futuristic McDonald's is left rotating in its place as all manner of spacecraft pull up to dock with it. Finally, large print appears over the image, "Coming to a galaxy near you in seven days!"

It was only when the billboards started using Makesh's name that he knew something was wrong. It read, "Makesh Guptah. Don't forget. Only seven days until demolition," then by the universally irritating, "Have a good day."

Seeing his name on the billboard, Makesh whirled about to confront his friends in the car. "Did you see that!? Did you see my name!?"

"See what?" responded Ben, still a little woozy since his redneck adventure.

"The billboard. The end of the earth," continued Makesh.

Ben looked up to see yet another South of the Border sign fly by. "Oh, is that where that place is? The end of the Earth? What do they sell there anyway?"

"No! No!" insisted Makesh. "The destruction of the Earth. The aliens are reminding us that we've only got seven days until the Earth is demolished to make room for an intergalactic fast food restaurant."

"Oh, right. Your aliens. And so what is it they want from us?" continued Ben.

"That's just it," replied Makesh. "There isn't anything here they want. If we could only find something they want, maybe they'd leave us alone."

"So in realtor's lingo, Earth is the equivalent of a tear-down," continued Ben. "Great location, but the ceilings aren't high enough." Makesh stared at Ben, trying to understand his little joke.

"Never mind," added Ben, recalling just exactly who his travel companions were. "Besides, I thought our mission was to get Juan home. Now we have to save the world as well?" He then started coughing so uncontrollably that his ribs hurt. "I don't know if I'm quite up to it these days."

Makesh responded. "One could argue that getting Juan home will not be possible if his home is vaporized by aliens."

Ben couldn't believe the conversation he was having. "Yes. I suppose that's so," he replied, beginning to wonder if his own failing health would allow him to see this mission to completion.

"There's some kind of roadblock up there," interrupted Juan, taking his foot off the gas. "Should I try to go around it."

All eyes turned to the road ahead, each one of them feeling a jolt of "what now?" grip them. The panic, however, was quickly replaced by relief as Juan's "roadblock" came into focus.

"That's not a roadblock," chuckled Angel. "That's a tollbooth. Any change in the ashtray?"

Makesh, forgetting where they'd gotten the car, opened the ashtray looking for coins, only to find, that's right, ashes. "Do they take credit cards?"

"Credit cards at a tollbooth?" began Ben. "Don't be ridiculous."

"Don't look now, Einstein," said Angel, pointing ahead to one of the tollbooths over which a big neon sign flashed, "credit, this lane only."

"I don't think I've ever seen that before."

Makesh directed Juan to the credit lane.

"I know *I've* never seen that before," confirmed Ben in amazement.

As the Roadrunner rumbled up to the tollbooth, Angel produced Ben's credit card, remarking, "I've never charged 75 cents before." Nevertheless, without thinking twice, she passed the card up to Juan who handed it over to the tollbooth attendant.

Only Makesh eyed the attendant suspiciously, who seemed rather on the short side. As the short attendant ran the card through the scanner, Makesh felt certain he winked at him. And something else seemed amiss. Could it have been that the little attendant had no nose? Or maybe it was the third arm that reached out to return the credit card. Ben signed the slip while Makesh observed a gob of green slime drip from the corner of the credit card. The attendant kept the white copy and returned the yellow receipt, making a point of handing it across to Makesh in the passenger seat with a wink. It seemed an awfully long third arm for such a short attendant.

Makesh's eyes widened as he read the receipt to himself. "Required Public Notification: Seven days to commencement of land improvements at this site, commonly known as Earth. Your signature below indicates that you have received the required notice. P.S. You're being followed."

Makesh looked behind them to see a black Lincoln Town car with darkly tinted windows. "The men in black," he said to himself.

Without thinking twice, he reached over to the driver's side and mashed the gas pedal to the floor with his left leg.

"Hey!" from a surprised Juan.

"Drive!" yelled Makesh, looking back.

"But I want to work the pedal too," whined Juan.

"Just drive," ordered Makesh.

"What's going on?" demanded Ben, noticing the sudden acceleration.

"They're after us," replied Makesh, eyes still riveted to the rapidly shrinking tollbooth behind them.

"Who?" asked Angel. "Who's after us?"

"The men in black," he replied.

"Wait," interrupted Ben. "I thought your aliens were after us."

"They're not *my* aliens. And no, the aliens are not after us. They're after our planet."

"Oh. They only want our planet. I see." Ben didn't see. "Then who are the men in black?" asked an amused Ben. "What do they want?"

"They want the plutonium."

"Oh. That's right," Ben agreed, recalling his early sessions with Makesh and the events at the Lawrence Livermore lab. Ben had never bought into that whole plutonium thing right from the beginning. After all, look at the source of the story; a paranoid schizophrenic whose head was now shaved on one side. He had, nevertheless, seen these men in black. And they were indeed after them. As Mrs. Mintz, the patient with melanoma, would tell you, just because you're paranoid doesn't mean they're not out to get you. It was just the plutonium part he didn't buy.

"You don't suppose they're simply after Juan, maybe the FBI after an escaped murderer/rapist? No offense, Juan," he added, reaching forward to pat Juan on the shoulder reassuringly.

"Does it matter?" interrupted Angel. "Either way, we've got to lose them."

They all looked back frantically as the Lincoln Town car continued to gain on them. The Roadrunner had plenty of torque for those rubber-burning quick starts, but it's gear ratio wasn't designed for a top speed much over 100 miles per hour. The Lincoln was closing the gap. The highway was becoming more crowded with the addition of turns and elevated overpasses as they approached Jacksonville. Juan weaved in and out of the slower traffic with surprising skill for a new driver without so much as a permit. And while the others maintained a white-knuckled grip on anything they could grab, Juan giggled giddily, thoroughly enjoying this new roller coaster ride.

Ben was feeling queasy. He was thinking of puking until one particular turn revealed a mass of stopped cars less than 100 feet ahead of them, a traffic jam filling all lanes. The thought of puking subsided when Ben realized there wouldn't be time. At greater than 100 miles per hour, without room to stop, they were going to smack into the mass of stopped cars and die.

The last thing Ben saw before the Roadrunner went airborne off the side of the highway overpass was a bumper sticker on one of the stopped cars ahead of them which read, "My kid got your honor student pregnant."

When Ben opened his eyes again, the clouds overhead were spinning as the Roadrunner went into midair three sixties. He was strangely relaxed, lying head back, observing the clouds as if in slow motion. Apparently this would be a better way to die than the slow drawn out torture of AIDS. He'd blocked out the screaming of the other passengers and only heard the wind blowing by his ears when a shadow passed over the car and the spinning clouds were momentarily upstaged by what appeared to be a muffler. And attached to the muffler was the rest of the undercarriage of a car, a Lincoln Town car to be exact. And in the Lincoln Town car were two men dressed in black suits with dark sunglasses. And they were screaming.

Soon the clouds reappeared as the Lincoln passed overhead and fell to the side. A second later, Ben heard the crash of the Lincoln hitting the pavement below followed by black smoke rising to mingle with Ben's white clouds. Growing bored, Ben peered over the side of the Roadrunner to see the fiery remains of the Lincoln smoldering on the highway below. The two men in black apparently were thrown to the grass at the side of the road. Ben thought he saw some movement. Indeed, Ben could make out the two tattered men in black crawling from the twisted wreckage.

And what of the Roadrunner, Ben began to wonder? When would he feel the impact of his own crash? When would the flying chariot introduce Ben and the others to its friend, Mother Earth? Ben suddenly had a flashback of a flight attendant providing instructions in the event of a crash. Skipping over the part about the oxygen mask automatically dropping from the overhead bin, Ben doubled over, putting his head between his knees (in anticipation of kissing his ass good-bye).

But it wasn't to be. Not yet. Juan observed the highway coming up to meet them, but it was a slow and deliberate approach, like an airport runway reaching out to welcome home one of its passenger planes. And as Makesh and Angel looked about in wide-eyed wonder, Juan executed a perfect four-point landing with barely a tapping of the wheels.

While the others cheered Juan, Ben pulled his head out of his ass in time to see a billboard for Disney World pass by.

Makesh seemed to be the only one to notice something funny about that billboard. He couldn't recall ever having seen a green Mickey Mouse before. And before he could even give it a second thought, Mickey was talking to him.

"Your vehicle was not intended for flight. Its design requires contact with Earth for proper functioning. Fortunately for you, we were able to momentarily remedy the situation in order that you and your friends not suffer any significant bodily injury. Oh, and by the way, you have only 6 days, 21 hours, 14 minutes, and 41 of your seconds to live."

And Mickey looked like he meant it.

Chapter 27

What better place to lick your wounds and regroup than at Disney World? With no direction from the others required, Juan followed the signs right to the ticket gate. And after their encounters at the diner and with the men in black, they all agreed a brief distraction was in order.

They parked the Roadrunner in the Tigger parking area and hopped the tram headed toward the entrance. Out came Ben's credit card for four tickets to the Magic Kingdom. It was unanimous. All four runaways seemed to have a sudden need to escape from their escape and all of its associated pressures. They needed a day off. Juan was a wide-eyed five-year-old again, wanting to go in every direction at the same time, to be on every ride, to get every character's autograph, and to devour every piece of junk food he encountered.

Makesh immediately found Tomorrowland on the map and was already planning on a way to steer Juan and the gang over to Space Mountain. Space travel hadn't always been a matter of nuclear missiles and connotations of Earth's destruction. It had been a wondrous thing for Makesh as a child, and that's how Disney made him feel again, a new frontier opening up endless possibilities for mankind.

Off her medication now for several days, Angel was already in a sort of Disney World, even before boarding the tram at the parking lot. Every Disney character and every Disney theme ignited within Angel her own out of control fantasies. She was Snow White with seven horny dwarves. She was Cinderella in bondage. Let's not mention Beauty and the Beast. And one look at the size of Goofy's hands had her wet between the legs.

Ben just wanted the great American escape. Even the others had begun to notice his coughing spells, and he didn't need a thermometer to know he was spiking fevers regularly. Once they'd left the Roadrunner and begun walking through the park again, Ben became acutely aware that he was short of breath. He couldn't keep up with Juan, and a flight of stairs was almost insurmountable. He'd become resigned to the fact that he was dying. And he was doing it sooner than later. But right now he was in Disney World, and what better place to spend your final days? Ben thought of it as his own sort of Make-A-Wish Foundation gift to himself.

As soon as they were handed the map of Magic Kingdom, the others were forced to hustle in a near run to keep up with Juan who'd bolted straight for the Dumbo ride. The line wasn't too long yet and Juan insisted that Makesh ride with him. So there stood Ben and Angel with the other beaming parents, watching their squealing children rise and fall in their flying elephants. Perhaps it was the combined weight of Juan and Makesh, or maybe just Ben's imagination, but their Dumbo seemed to have a little more trouble reaching full altitude than those of the other children.

Disposable camera in hand, Makesh insisted on taking everyone's photographs with the characters they found walking about the park. Angel couldn't keep her hands to herself and sent Tigger bounce bounce bouncing off after she groped him through his costume. Ben couldn't help pointing out to her that the person inside the costume could just as easily have been a woman as a man. The only question, though, was why he thought that would matter to Angel. Man, woman, tiger. It made no difference to Angel.

All the walking and standing on lines in the hot sun was taking its toll on Ben. Even the drenching water flume at Splash Mountain didn't relieve him. So as soon as they left Mickey's dressing room,

Juan beaming at the most prized autograph in his collection, they all agreed that a cool place to sit was in order.

Ben found the boat ride through the Pirates of the Caribbean quite relaxing, while Makesh tried to explain to a frightened Juan that the pirates weren't real, that they were just machines.

"They're not *all* machines," protested Juan pointing at the pirate village.

"What are you talking about? Of course they're…" began Ben as he turned only to find something different about the scene where the pirate chases the wench around the barrel of rum.

It didn't take long for Ben to discern what was wrong. There was an extra wench. And that wench was Angel. Apparently the bawdy atmosphere overcame what little control she'd been able to muster, compelling her to leave her friends and join the partying band of pirates. It took all three of them to wrestle her back into the boat. Yo ho ho ho, the pirate's life was for Angel.

At least on the Space Mountain ride, there were restraints to keep guests from falling out. It was a good thing too, because given the chance, Makesh surely would have set off on his own to other-worldly destinations.

The whole day really was quite a vacation for the four. Even Ben had a thoroughly good time, momentarily forgetting his own predicament. Their stay at the Contemporary Hotel went fairly smoothly. And it wasn't until the character breakfast the next morning that they discovered Ben's credit card was maxed out. Who would have thought that a breakfast buffet could cost so much?

And so they left Disney World continuing south, stuffed to the gills with waffles, unsure where their next meal might come from. One thing was for sure. They were going to need some money if they hoped to get Juan home.

It wasn't until they reached Palm Beach that Angel came up with a plan. It seemed Angel was the only one with a marketable talent.

Chapter 28

Angel could always manage to find strip clubs, just as sea turtles can always find the beach of their birth where they return each mating season. It was a truly amazing phenomenon. She could tell by the character of a street or neighborhood when a topless bar might be around the next corner. Sometimes it was the pawn shops or check cashing establishments. Sometimes it was the mirror-windowed massage parlors. But the clubs in these neighborhoods were usually somewhat short on class and heavy on the sleaze factor. The girls ranked three or below, the unemployed clients often smelled badly, and neither had any money, alcohol being the true commodity.

These, however, were not the lucrative sexual ATM's that Angel sought. She needed to locate the clubs where the girls ranked seven and above, and the working class clients came each week to exchange their hard-earned paychecks for a raucous evening of sexual abandon. There was only one place to find these clubs, at the back of the newspaper's sports section. And it was easy enough to tell from the ads which were the better clubs. They often had headliner acts, and the girls in the picture ads still had all their teeth. Angel's research and intuition led them to a club called Sapphire.

Just from the parking lot, Angel could tell it was the right place. The cars parked there represented a good cross-section of society, from the testosterone-driven Mustang/Corvette crowd to the yuppie BMW/Porsche owners. The cars were well-maintained with plenty of college window stickers in the rear. Testosterone, money, and youth, the perfect combination. And no stuffy valet parking or gaudy facade in faux Roman architecture. Just a black understated entrance with neon sign over a small door. All business. Yes, this was the one Angel was looking for, a gold mine, the holy grail of exotic dancers.

"But I don't want to wait in the car," protested Juan, hearing the pounding bass of the music coming from inside the club. "How come we don't get to come to the party?"

"It's not a party," answered Angel. "Besides, I'm sure there's a man inside the door that's going to want money, a cover charge, for each of you to come in, money we don't have."

"That's not fair," continued Juan. "Why doesn't he charge you?"

"In fact, he's going to charge me even more, if I want to work here," answered Angel.

Makesh joined the conversation. "He's going to charge you to work here? That doesn't sound right."

"Think of it as renting office space," said Angel. "I give him 20 bucks and he gives me a place to run my business."

"What does your business sell?" asked Juan innocently.

"You never mind," answered Angel as she stepped from the car.

"What about the $20? Where are you going to get that?" asked Ben.

"Never mind that either," she answered over the pounding of the music as she opened the door to the club and stepped inside.

The boys were just settling in the car for what they imagined to be a long evening when Angel popped her head out the front door again, motioning for them to come inside.

"But what about the cover charge?" started Makesh.

Juan was already heading through the door with Ben acting as chaperone, trying to keep up.

"It just took a little oral persuasion," answered Angel, wiping her lips as the others filed past the doorman still fumbling to zip his pants back up.

A fine blend of smoke and cheap perfume hung in the air, vibrating to the pounding beat of the music. Angel felt at home again making her way through the testosterone-saturated club. Juan fit right in with the youngish crowd. Makesh felt unnerved by the sensory overload. And Ben couldn't breath. He felt choked by the smoke. He knew he'd been having a real problem breathing back at Disney, but the smoke now seemed to suck away what little oxygen still managed to find its way to his lungs.

Small tables filled the room, separated down the middle by a raised runway leading to a central stage. On the stage, actually above it, a beautiful girl was spiraling back to earth from the top of a pole held only by her legs.

Juan wanted to take a closer look. He dragged Makesh with him to some stage-side seats. Ben found a seat back away from the action. And while some of the scantily clad dancers sat at the bar wasting their time playing video games, Angel was on a mission.

This was strictly business for her. And she went right to work. She'd already spoken to the DJ, finding her place in the stage rotation. But the real money wasn't on the stage. You had to work the crowd, up close, and very personal. She scanned the room, looking for the money. Money didn't wear sneakers or backward baseball caps. Money wore ties. Money was balding. Money wore wedding bands. Money also had too much to drink.

Then, at a corner table, almost at the back of the room, Angel found some money. Three men, two power ties, and one toupée. They tried to avert their eyes as Angel stalked them. But once she reached their table, she was in their faces, her legs, her hair, her cleavage. She pounced and they couldn't escape, like antelopes, their necks caught in the lion's jaws. It was only a matter of time until she'd drain enough blood to leave her prey dazed and involuntarily twitching.

She first had to divide her victims, separating the weakest from the rest of the herd. And so, when she found the balding chubby one with the stutter who couldn't look her in the eyes when she introduced herself, she could smell an easy kill. Angel circled behind the prey and pulled his chair from the table. She then, in one smooth motion, hiked her micro-skirt to her waist and straddled his lap, facing him. If she could lock eyes with him, like the cobra with the mouse, his will would be broken. But like the mouse scurrying about the cage, his eyes kept darting side to side, avoiding hers as if he knew the consequences. First looking to one side, then joking with his friend on the other, direct eye contact was not to be made. Angel would have to raise the ante.

She stood up slightly and trapped his face in her cleavage. She made sure he felt the softness and smelled her perfume before settling down again and not so subtly grinding into his crotch. She didn't stop until she got the required response. Even if she couldn't get the head on his shoulders to look straight forward, she certainly got the attention of the other head, the one between his legs. That one quickly straightened out as if to get a better look at who had disturbed its sleep. And so, having flipped on his switch, Angel stood up and looked down at her victim. And sure enough, like a deer caught in the headlights, his glassy-eyed stare was straight ahead now. She had his attention, and she could smell blood, blood engorging his loins, and straining at his zipper.

"Would you like a dance?" Angel offered.

Whether he wasn't sure of his response or whether the words were simply stuck in his throat wasn't clear. In any event the reply didn't come fast enough for Angel. She would have to extract it from him. And so she lowered her hips again, making contact with the decision maker between his legs, and slowly ground into his lap as if milking the required response from somewhere inside his trousers. She didn't have to repeat the question.

"H… H… How much?" he stuttered, forgetting to breath.

"Twenty," she answered.

"T… T… Twenty dollars?" came his reply, like an old man buying gas for his model T for the first time in 60 years. Sticker shock.

Angel knew a verbal reply wasn't necessary. Just a subtle twitch of her hips and…

"OK, OK, t… twenty dollars."

He'd swallowed the hook. Now she'd give him some line. It was too soon to start reeling him in. Angel stood up. She felt his lap bob up after her like a magnet trying to maintain contact. Un un unhhh, she thought. Not yet. That'll come later. For now, she would dance.

Kicking his legs wide apart, Angel stood between them and pulled her dress off over her head in one motion. She danced for him, topless, in her thong panties. Slowly, seductively, she danced for him, touching herself, undulating between his legs, letting her legs graze the inside of his thighs as if by accident, occasionally letting her full breasts touch his chest, backing into him, her hands on his thighs, as if to sit on his lap again, but pulling up just short, and most importantly, letting her hand unintentionally sweep over his bobbing joystick each time she turned to make eye contact.

Five songs and $100 later, it was time to reel in some line. Angel abruptly sat down in his lap, facing away from him, trapping the tent in his pants between her butt and his belly. She stopped moving and waited, waited for his move. It only took a few awkward seconds, but then, like clockwork, he reached around with his hands and cupped her breasts. Angel counted to three slowly, and after she was sure he'd remember what they felt like, after she was sure he'd unconsciously determined they were real, she took his hands and pulled them away.

Twisting back toward him with an extra grind of her hips, "You can't do that," she whispered, her warm breath caressing his ear. "I'll get in trouble."

He looked like a baby that just had its candy taken away. Then, almost whining, he pointed across the room. "Wh... wh... what about them?"

Across the room were the couches. And the couches were filled with topless dancers. They were moving, more like writhing. At first it seemed to be only women. Then one could make out sets of hands, as if many of the breasts had extra hands glued to them. Only with some concentration could one tell there were men on the couch as well, under the women, arms wrapped around them, hands glued to breasts.

"Oh, well, that's different," Angel replied. "Those are the couches. Did you want to go over to the couches?" she added, as if surprised by the suggestion.

"Sure," came his one word reply.

"It's $40," stated Angel.

"F… F… For how many dances?" he inquired.

"Each. Forty per dance," she answered. "But," she began, pointing toward the couches with one hand while pushing with her other directly on his manhood as if to prop herself up to get a better look, "how many dances do you think you'll need?"

His eyes had involuntarily rolled up into his head from the pressure of her hand on his shaft, but when he managed to direct them back toward the couches, he could make out the motion of the dancers rubbing their rumps back and forth to the music against their clients' crotches. It hadn't escaped his notice that Angel's hand remained on his controls. He couldn't imagine it would take more than one dance for the deliberate contact of the couch dance with the hair trigger now bobbing below his belt to produce the desired results. As the not so subtle pressure of Angel's hand between his legs seemed to grip his entire body, the pulse in his pants pounding all the way up between his ears, he couldn't imagine a whole song passing before he'd wet his pants. He'd tell the dry cleaner he'd spilt something at dinner. But at least then he could go home, spent, with money still in his wallet. It seemed like a plan. It was a bad plan. The bald chubby guy with the stutter didn't know Angel McGovern.

Angel took her prey by the hand and led him toward the wall of couches. With his other hand, he tucked his hard-on up behind his belt so it wouldn't knock anyone's drinks off their tables bobbing side to side as he walked past. Like parallel parking, squeezing a full size car into a spot for a subcompact, Angel expertly backed her ride into a small space still available on the couches. As chubby melted into the mushy couch, springs long ago worn out, he quickly saw just how tight his spot was. Even with his eyes straight ahead, his peripheral vision was filled by the dancers on either side of him trying not to be thrown by their own bucking broncos. Their long hair brushed his arms and legs and their smell filled the air, a fine blend, two parts perfume and one part sweat, all bound together by just a hint of female musk escaping the confines of the thongs undulating just inches from his nose.

His eyes snapped straight ahead again as Angel kicked his legs apart and sat down hard on his crotch. Angel had his full attention. He watched as she raised and adjusted her rump until her cheeks locked on his rod like a set of hands. And when she began to rock to the music, she held her grip. She gripped him with her perfect butt and rocked. Her thong slid up and down over his shaft, up and down. He felt the pressure building in his loins. He reached around and cupped her 38D's. They were soft and warm. They were real. He thought she would pull his hands away. She didn't.

She just kept grinding her behind into him, up and down. He felt her nipples harden under his fingers. She continued back and forth, up and down. His whole body was going numb, that is all but one part. His breathing was becoming erratic. He felt small explosions popping in his head. He ultimately felt his balls contract, followed by a surge rising from the base of his shaft. He was about to come. He was about to get the release he needed so badly, release he'd paid for, release from the torture he'd been enduring. Yes, finally, release, any second…

Angel abruptly stood up.

"Hey!" he protested, feeling his wad stall midshaft.

Angel looked down at his pants. Even in the dimly lit club, she could make out the involuntary twitching. In that way, like a nurse, she quickly checked his vital signs, measuring his pulse, pressure, and gasps for air. Perfect. Her evaluation of the patient confirmed he'd been less than a second from coming. She was so proud of herself. She hadn't lost her touch.

"W… W… Well?" came a small voice from the couch.

"Well what?" responded Angel.

"I was about to… c… come. W… w… why'd you s… s… stop?"

Angel acted surprised. "You were? Oh, I'm sorry," she apologized. "It was so fast. I didn't know. It was only the first song."

Bald and chubby threw his head on the back of the couch in frustration. Then Angel asked the obvious.

"Would you like another dance?"

The man nodded, his big head bobbing in rhythm with the small one below his waist.

Angel raised one knee, sliding her shiny black pump under his balls. She pulled her garter belt away from her thigh and waited.

"Wh... What?" from chubby.

"Forty dollars," from Angel, all business.

He fumbled for his wallet, producing $40 to add to the $100 already tucked under her garter belt. The formalities aside, Angel went back to work. No, not on his lap. Not yet, anyway. He was much too close to popping his cork. Instead, she danced for him, standing there between his legs, just inches away. She pushed her breasts together, rubbed her nipples, adding an occasional flick of her tongue. She moved her hand to her crotch, slowly slipping her hand down the front of her panties. Checking to make sure his eyes had locked on the movement of her hand, she slowly removed it, bringing it up to her lips which slowly parted, allowing one moist finger to enter. She made love to her finger, sucking it, licking it, in and out. Her other hand slowly snaked its way into her panties taking its turn to work. When she removed it, it didn't go to her lips as the first one did. No this one was for the hypnotized hulk on the couch. She knelt on the floor between his legs, bending forward until her breasts surrounded his twitching shaft. She then held her finger just under his nose. He couldn't help but inhale her musky scent. His eyes closed as he inhaled. He didn't know where he was for a second. Then Angel started to rock back and forth on her knees, her breasts gripping the hot iron between them. Again he felt his balls contract, followed by a surge involuntarily rising from the base of his shaft, making its way up, looking for escape. He was half a second from exploding, inches from Angel's mouth... when song number two ended.

Angel instantly stood up, casually adjusting her thong. Bald and chubby felt as though he would split as his ammunition got clogged half way up his barrel... again.

"H... h... hey!" he protested, now dripping in sweat.

"Oh, I'm sorry. The song's over," replied Angel cordially smiling. "That'll be $40 for another."

His brain had ceased functioning. He'd turned into Angel's ATM. He reached into his pocket and felt a dull ache coming from his groin. No, it wasn't his wallet aching. It was the first sign of blue balls. He was just too confused to realize it. He'd been near coming for almost an hour now. Angel knew it, though. She hadn't lost track of the time. Angel was right on schedule. She'd have to relieve the pressure in his wallet first, before the pressure in his balls. She noticed his hands shaking as he slipped the money under her garter belt. Angel didn't know how much cash he had. It didn't matter. He surely had a credit card. No, she was nowhere near done with him yet. And yes, it would be painful.

Angel felt a twinge of guilt for that. She hated the part when the cum got so backed up, it made its way up to their eyes, where it started to ooze and run down their cheeks as tears. That's the part that got to her. She always prayed that it didn't happen until the credit card maxed out. That was the only time she would relieve them, when the money was gone. And even then, only if they'd behaved themselves. For bald and chubby, only time would tell. He had a very long night ahead of him.

Chapter 29

Juan felt homesick, watching all the beautiful girls perform. It reminded him of his sister and her friends working the phone lines. He missed them and the attention they gave him. He wanted to make friends with these girls too.

He didn't have any money. He wouldn't be able to buy any dances. But Juan wasn't bald and chubby. He didn't need money for dances. Many of the girls weren't the hardcore businessmen Angel was. Some of the younger ones still thought of the whole thing as a party, a place to find cute guys and have some fun. And it didn't take long before they were competing for Juan's attention.

Ben observed the whole phenomenon from a distance, feeling more and more like a leper as he noticed the distinct lack of attention he'd been receiving. The girls all seemed to walk right past him as if he weren't there. When they looked in his direction, they seemed to look right through him. Juan was getting free dances. Ben wasn't sure he could *buy* a dance, even if he *did* have the money.

But that was Ben's life, always the observer looking in from the outside. While everyone else seemed to have parts in the play, the best Ben could do was buy a ticket and take his seat with the other spectators. That's how it had been his whole life, pretty much, that is until he let himself be kidnapped by his new friends, the criminally insane. For a while, he'd been allowed to participate. At times, he'd even had a speaking role. But as he grew more and more ill, he felt himself withdrawing, crawling back into the foxhole that was his existence, hiding from the explosions of life all around him.

As he watched the young girls in their underwear fluttering about Juan like butterflies, his mind drifted back to high school, to the only butterfly he'd ever known, to Jill Sterling. There she was, in her swimsuit, more of a firefly than a butterfly. And there was Ben. He was alive. He knew he was alive because he could feel it. He felt the texture of her blue and gold suit. He felt the wetness of her skin. He could smell her hair, taste her lips. He had a part in the play, a speaking role. He played the lead.

But that was then. And this was now. He'd been relegated to the audience for a long time now, so long his seat had become worn and uncomfortable. And since he'd learned of his AIDS diagnosis, he wasn't even in the theater anymore, as if security had escorted him to the door. How he longed to see Jill Sterling, perhaps one last time before he died.

Juan was in heaven. All he could see were pretty girls. Pretty girls in every direction. They flirted with him. They danced about him and giggled. They touched him and made his pants feel tight, just like at home with his sister and her friends. Juan loved this place.

"He's so cute," said one butterfly to another.

"I know," said the second. "And look how big he is," she added, grabbing the stiff pole in Juan's pants as nonchalantly as checking the freshness of a cucumber at the supermarket. Sure, they were young and silly, but they had no lack of experience. "I'd like to take this to the champagne room," she giggled.

Turning to Juan, "Hey, you have $500? You can take us both to the champagne room for $500."

"No, I don't have $500," replied Juan, grabbing the girl who was checking his vegetables and placing her on his lap.

"Do you have *any* money?" asked the other girl, circling behind Juan, beginning to massage his shoulders.

Juan had the girl on his lap by the hips and was moving her back and forth over his crotch.

"Hey," repeated the girl behind Juan in a sexy whisper, now pinching his nipples to get his attention, "do you have *any* money?"

"No," answered Juan, momentarily losing his rhythm, distracted by the tickling in his ear. "Angel didn't give me any money."

"Angel. Who's Angel?"

The girl in Juan's lap was beginning to sweat as she got into Juan's rhythm. "I don't care who Angel is," she started, through irregular breaths. "And I don't care if he's got any money. You've got to feel how big this thing is getting."

"Hey!" objected the girl behind Juan. "No fair, hogging him for yourself. What about me?" she added shoving the other girl off of Juan's lap.

"OK, OK," started the other, still a little weak in the knees. "No need to fight over him." And pointing at Juan's pants, "There's plenty to go around. Come on."

As if on cue, they each grabbed one of Juan's arms, stood him up, and headed toward the champagne room.

Watching them walk past, Ben couldn't help seeing it as a metaphor, a symbol of his very existence. Juan and his girlfriends represented all that was spontaneous, fun, and free of obligations, guilt, and second thoughts. They represented all that was life, or what life was supposed to be. And just as they floated past Ben's table on their endorphin high, so too was life passing him by. All his life, Ben concerned himself only with others' expectations, always trying to fill another's shoes, being what others wanted him to be. He was tired, tired of watching the game from all the way up in the cheap seats. He knew he was dying. While the other men in the club felt testosterone coursing through their veins, all Ben felt was AIDS virus. While the others lost their breath at the sight or touch of the beautiful women filling the room, Ben lost his most likely from Pneumocystis, the AIDS associated pneumonia. It was the bottom of the ninth for Ben, and he wanted to get in the game. He didn't have much time left. He could feel the life escaping him each time he exhaled.

It was then he decided he had to see Jill Sterling before he died. She wasn't too far away anyway, having moved to Miami. He hoped to achieve some closure, to tie up the loose ends of what little life he'd actually lived. No, not the time he'd spent with his nose buried in textbooks. That wasn't living. He meant the time when he still appreciated beauty, longed for it, hungered for love. He'd gaze upon her beauty one last time, tell her he was sorry, sorry for not appreciating her, for letting her slip away, for not taking her to the dance. How he'd dance today, given a second chance. He knew it was too late for that now. But he could still apologize, tell her what a fool he'd been. He'd wasted his life. And as he imagined Jill Sterling, to this day wondering what she'd done wrong that made him stand her up at the prom, he'd hoped to set the record straight. *He* was the fool. She hadn't done anything wrong. And if that fact could help her get on with her life, unfettered by any self-doubt, allow her to clear the cobwebs of the past and more freely experience the full and wonderful life she deserved, then she had to know. Benjamin Walker was sorry he'd hurt her. He was sorry he'd ruined her life. Just because he'd chosen to ruin his own life that night he decided studying for exams was more important than a high school prom, didn't mean he had the right to ruin hers. It takes two to dance. That never occurred to Ben before. He would look her in the eye and apologize for ruining her life. He would ask her for that dance now, better too late than never.

Angel was already in the champagne room. Prior to that, she'd been working the couch for quite some time when Bald and chubby seemed to become less responsive. He'd been well into his card's credit line when the semen backing up into his head seemed to cloud his senses. Like a crash victim with head trauma, he'd begun to experience altered consciousness. Angel would have to up the ante to hold the patient's attention. That's when she suggested he take her to the champagne room.

"W… why, w… what's in the champagne room?" asked the patient.

Angel had to keep dangling bigger and better carrots to keep her ride moving. "It's more private in the champagne room, more intimate."

Bald and Chubby wasn't sure what that meant. How much more intimate could it get? Separated only by two thin layers of material, his trousers and her thong panties, his sensory probe had already mapped out every hill and valley to be found in Angel's nether-region. What more could he experience? Unless… Unless… No, could it be? Could it be that the old expression, "Ain't no sex in the champagne room," was a lie? Maybe there *was* sex in the champagne room. Maybe that's what Angel was referring to. Maybe he, Bald and Chubby, would have sex in the champagne room. But the price of admission?

"How much?" he asked.

"It's only $300. And that includes the champagne."

He swallowed the bait.

And yet, after an hour in the champagne room, a bottle of champagne, and $500 in additional tips later, still no sex. The release he so desired continued to elude him, just out of reach. More intimate? If intimate meant sitting on a couch with his pants down around his ankles while the best pussy he'd ever seen continued to play his wad up and down his shaft like a yo-yo, never spilling a drop, well then this was more intimate. Even dulled by the champagne, the ache was all-consuming. Blue balls had progressed to blue body, and blue body to blue brain. He was against the ropes, not sure his legs had enough strength to escape the champagne room even if he could think with enough clarity to try.

Juan didn't waste any time. He'd had three orgasms before his two little friends had warmed up. But now he would last longer. Now they would get what they wanted.

Makesh Guptah wasn't just a rocket scientist. He was a man not of this world, a man, in fact, of other worlds. And the blonde space cadet with the silicone headlights, an ardent fan of astrology, could tell. It had started simply enough when she introduced herself and exchanged astrological signs with Makesh. It wasn't long, however, before she'd become enthralled by his tales of space travel and aliens. She'd soon pulled up a chair and huddled close, both she and Makesh unaware of her state of semi-undress. And like story time at the children's library, she kept wanting to hear another one. She'd forgotten why she was there and never even asked Makesh if he had any money. In fact, she'd turned away many potential suitors with cash to burn, trying to steal her away from Makesh, asking if she would visit the couches with them. No, she wasn't interested. She wasn't very good at her job. But she didn't care. She was with the Rocket Man and she couldn't get enough. They talked for hours, just passing the time. They talked about the mother ship and the little green men, or whatever color they were. They talked about the cure for cancer. Of course, she also asked if there was any sex on the ship, and if they were in search of any human females to mate with.

Unlike the others, Ben wasn't making any friends. Between his hacking cough and whining about love lost, he'd managed to drive off even the friendliest of the dancers. And as he wasn't occupied with any dances, the waitresses were quick to descend upon him, like vultures circling a wounded animal.

"Can I get you a drink?" they'd ask, one after another.

"No thank you," Ben would reply.

Noticing he had no empties in front of him, "This is a bar you know. You're supposed to drink in a bar."

"No thanks. I'm really not feeling very well."

"Then maybe you ought to go home. You can't just sit here watching the girls like some kind of pervert. You'll have to order a drink."

Ben saw she wasn't going to give in. That's when he made a strategic error. "But I don't have any money."

The waitress stepped back, hands on her hips, and looked at Ben as if catching a two-year-old with his hand in the cookie jar. "You don't have any money? How'd you get in here anyway?"

Ben hadn't yet seen his faux pas, and taking the waitress's hand, "Look, I don't mean to be any trouble. I'm just waiting—"

That's when Ben started coughing uncontrollably. It was a gurgling, windpipe-occluding cough. He doubled over, gasping for air, and held the waitress's hand to keep from falling to the floor.

The waitress tried pulling away from the deadbeat customer, but when a coughed up wad of projectile phlegm landed on her exposed arm, she'd had enough.

"Eeyoooo," she yelled in disgust, and started hitting Ben on the head with her empty tray.

Ben only held on tighter to keep from landing on the floor. He was rapidly running out of oxygen.

The waitress didn't care about that. Here was this freeloading, penniless, street person, grabbing her and getting drool on her arm. That wasn't part of the job. She wasn't going to put up with it. And that's when she knee'd him. Just like Daddy had taught her, fast and firm, she brought her knee up squarely between Ben's legs until both his feet left the ground.

If he'd had any breath in him, it would have been knocked out. Instead, Ben could simply concentrate on the pain. It just made it that much easier to focus all his attention on the jolt of lighting emanating from his battered testicles to all points of his being.

He wasn't sure if he'd actually passed out or not. All he knew was that by the time he was able to inhale, the bouncers had closed the door behind him and he found himself lying in the fetal position in the graveled parking lot.

Luckily for Bald and Chubby, it was near the end of the month and he'd already accumulated quite a balance on his credit card. It also helped that he wasn't the type to pay off his balance each month. So when the tab for Angel's services reached $5,000, the waitress informed him that the party was over.

It felt as though he'd been hard for days, like he'd overdosed on Viagra. He wasn't sure how long he'd been in the champagne room. But after the waitress had gone, he looked down at his throbbing member through bleary bloodshot eyes, and started to cry.

Angel hated that part. And judging from the angry purple color of his hard-on, she suspected there might have been some permanent damage. She couldn't leave him that way. True, she took all his money. After all, she needed it to get Juan home. But she wasn't heartless. She thought she might still be able to save the limb. Besides, what of her own needs? She hadn't even masturbated for the past several hours.

When she pulled the condom from her purse, she thought she recognized a faint glimmer of life in Bald and Chubby's eyes. From his perspective on the couch, in a state of paralysis, all he could make out was a shiny reflection of light bouncing off the foil condom wrapper. It must have been some basic survival instinct as the light registered in his brain, a brain barely able to stay afloat and keep from drowning in the ocean of semen that had backed up into his head. And from the darkness, all he could think was to head toward the light. Head toward the light.

Angel removed the condom from the wrapper and firmly grasped Bald and Chubby by the horn. She'd barely rolled the condom half way down his shaft when he erupted. The spasms continued for what seemed like hours to him. He was sure she must have changed condoms several times so as not to allow them to burst, catching gallon after gallon of semen. He felt his sinuses clearing first, then his lungs. Soon he had feeling in his legs again, and finally he thought he could sense some scrotal contractions, an impossibility only moments before due to the immense pressure and swelling. The orgasm itself was more pain than pleasure, yet strangely satisfying, something akin to lancing a boil. As his head cleared and the small champagne room came into focus, he saw he was still hard. He would soon learn that it would stay that way for a day or so, that is until he could depressurize it several more times. Even then, there was no guarantee that full function would return.

Angel had already left the room. The night was young and she was on a mission. After Bald and Chubby, the scene was repeated with Short and Skinny, then Old and Smelly. It wasn't until Tall, Dark, and Handsome that the script changed.

A crowd of young ladies was beginning to gather around Makesh, the fascinating space traveler, as word spread of his exploits. Juan's two young friends were equally fascinated by Juan's boundless endurance. And Angel, on a mission, tied up a champagne room for the entire night as if it were her own office. Ben was making new friends as well. It seemed Sapphire's own parking lot transvestite had taken a liking to Ben. Impeccable makeup, size-12 black leather pumps, spandex miniskirt, and feather boa, her modus operandi was to hang around the parking lot praying upon the club's clientele too drunk and horny to take note of a little facial hair or Adam's apple. That wasn't the case with Ben, however. She just felt sorry for the pathetic beaten figure lying face down in the gravel, a scene she herself was all too familiar with. There was something else she was familiar with. She'd seen too many good friends die from AIDS.

There was a hint of sunrise off to the east when Sapphire's neon sign went out. It was closing time and the parking lot was empty save for the green Roadrunner and mostly employees' cars. Ben was wheezing, his head propped up on his nursemaid's lap as he watched a dozen or so dancers accompany Makesh out the front door, each vying to stuff their phone numbers into his pockets. Juan had to help his two young friends to their car, as they were having some trouble walking after ten rounds with their Latin lover. Juan, on the other hand, had worked up an appetite, and was already into the box of Slim Jims the girls had bought for him at the bar on the way out.

They had to pry Angel off of her partner in the champagne room. They hadn't heard Tall, Dark, and Handsome pleading for help over the sound of the music. Only when the DJ went home did they hear the eerie cries of a man having the life sucked out of him. Angel hadn't planned on stopping until her itch had been scratched. Angel's was an itch, however, that could never be reached. And so, she too was escorted to the door, the ever-growing hum between her legs intact.

Chapter 30

When the others joined him on the steps to the parking lot, it was apparent Ben had been on the losing end of a fight. Between his waitress and the bouncers, he was pretty beat up. But those wounds would heal. His mysterious illness, however, would not. His transvestite friend could see it wasn't just bruises. Ben was ill, seriously ill. Earlier, when it was just the two of them, she'd asked Ben about it, and he'd complimented her diagnostic skills, confirming her suspicion that he had AIDS. Now, taking Ben's head from her lap and straightening out the wrinkles in her dress, she went over to Angel to discuss the situation. Then, sure that he'd been left in good hands, Ben's transvestite friend started walking home. She conveniently had a place nearby.

Ben looked about at his family reunited and began to say something, but started coughing instead, a seemingly endless hacking sound, punctuated by wheezing. Angel put her arm around his shoulders to steady him. He'd become ghostly pale. His skin was clammy. He looked terrible.

"Hey Hah-vud, we'd better take you to a doctor," Angel told him.

Finally able to get some words out, Ben brushed the suggestion aside. "Never mind that. How'd we do?"

Makesh answered first. "Very well, actually. I met some fascinating young ladies extremely interested in interplanetary travel and extraterrestrial life forms." Pulling the scraps of napkins from his pocket with a smile, "I have their numbers. See."

Juan echoed Makesh's sentiment. "I had fun," he stated simply through a toothy grin, holding his crotch with both hands.

Ben, losing his patience, turned to Angel. "I meant the money. How much did you get? Were you able to get a thousand dollars?"

When he saw Angel pull a fat wad of bills from her garter belt, he thought maybe she had. When she pulled out three more rolls, he was certain of it. When he realized they weren't just twenty-dollar bills, but included rather a good portion of fifties and hundreds, his eyes opened wide. And as Angel counted out the money into neat little piles, Ben could only marvel at her accomplishments. She was a force to reckon with that seemed able to overcome any obstacle, the perfect compliment of brains, looks, and boundless energy. If only he wasn't dying of AIDS and she weren't crazy, he might ask her to marry him.

"Ten thousand six hundred eighty dollars," Angel announced, proudly. "Not bad, huh?"

Juan had never seen so much money in one place before. "That's a lot of Slim Jims," he remarked, opening another stick of dried meat.

"No, Juan," said Angel. "That's home."

"Home?" asked Juan.

"Home," repeated Angel. "Isla de los Locos. This money is going to take you home."

Juan was speechless. He never dreamed he would see the farm or his grandmother again. But then something occurred to him, something sad.

"What about you guys?"

"What about us?" Angel replied.

"You're not coming, are you? You're sending me away."

"No, no. Of course we're coming. We have to make sure you get there OK," Angel assured him.

Juan had to make sure. He liked his new friends and didn't want to be lonely again. He turned to the others. "Are you coming?" to Makesh.

Remembering the alien-imposed deadline under which they were all working, Makesh offered a vaguely qualified reply. "As long as this earth continues to turn. As long as the sun rises in the east and sets in the west…"

A confused Juan turned to Angel. "Is Rocket coming?"

"Yes," laughed Angel.

He turned to Ben. "Dr. Ben. You too? Are you coming?"

Emulating Makesh's poetic response, Ben answered, "As long as there's air in my lungs." He then proceeded to expel all that air in a series of gurgling coughs which didn't subside until he started bringing up tinges of blood.

Again, Juan turned to Angel for a translation. "Is Dr. Ben coming too?"

Angel stared at the ghostly figure before her, noticing for the first time how much weight Ben had lost, and without breaking eye contact with Ben, answered Juan's question. "I don't know, Juan." And then, as if making sure Ben heard, "I don't know if Dr. Ben's going to make it. But he'll try." Finally looking at the others, "Why don't you two bring the car over while I get Dr. Ben ready. After the others had gone she turned back to Ben.

"How'd you get it? You're not exactly the poster child for HIV risk factors."

Realizing his transvestite friend had spilled the beans, he replied, "I don't know, but it seems like I caught it from a nun."

"From a nun?" asked Angel, less than convinced.

"Go figure," responded Ben. Then redirecting the conversation, "Angel, I'd like to do something before we take Juan home."

"What do you mean?"

"Well, I'm not sure how much time I have left, and there's something I need to fix while I still have the chance. It won't take long. Can you help me?"

"Sure I can. I'm at your service," answered Angel, taking Ben's hand.

"I'd like to see Jill Sterling," said Ben. "I want to make things right with her. I want to apologize for ruining her life."

Angel looked at her pathetic excuse for a psychiatrist. "You think you ruined her life by not taking her to a high school dance? Who's the crazy one now?"

"I'm serious. It won't take long. Is it so much to ask?"

"OK, OK," said Angel, giving in. "We'll go find this ghost from your past. But then we take you to a doctor. And after that, we take Juan home."

"It's a deal," agreed Ben.

Juan almost ran them over with the Roadrunner when he pulled up in a cloud of flying dust and gravel.

"Your chariot awaits," announced Angel, helping Ben up from the steps.

It was a simple matter of checking the Miami telephone directory to find Jill Sterling's address. The map they picked up at the gas station told them they were only an hour and a half away. Ben had an hour and a half to think of what he would say to her, an hour and a half to find the words to undo a wrong, an hour and a half to apologize and, by doing so, find some peace, peace he could take with him wherever he'd be going after this life.

Ben tried to picture the scene. Low rent housing in a seedy neighborhood. He'd ring the doorbell. After fumbling with several dead bolts and security chains, she'd open the door, her beauty somehow shining through the sadness permanently engraved in her features. She'd put on a few too many pounds spending her nights alone watching old romantic movies with a spoon and a carton of ice-cream. She'd recognize him instantly. After all, it had only been about ten years. She'd invite him into her sparse studio apartment, closing the door quickly so as not to let one of her many cats escape. She'd hang on his every word as he described his academic achievements and the rigors of medical school. Her job at the library wasn't quite so exotic. Marry? No, she never married. Oh yes, a couple of children would have been nice. But she had her books at the library, and her cats. He'd notice the picture taken of her in her prom dress, alone, apparently before admitting to herself that he wasn't going to make it. Picking it up, he'd sit next to her and apologize for that night, and for every night since, for every night of her shattered life. He'd beg her forgiveness and wait, wait for her to pass judgment on him.

There'd be a brief pause, ever so subtle, just long enough for Ben to wonder what the outcome was to be. Would she forgive him, release him from the guilt that blocked out the sunlight like a storm cloud over his life? Or would that be asking too much? Would the hurt she'd endured be too much to overlook, the wound too deep to heal? And then the sun would come out, a smile shattering the lines of sadness in her face. Tears too. There'd be tears along with the smile, tears of happiness, as she'd run to him, throwing her arms about his neck in an embrace held ten years in abeyance. She wouldn't be able to stop kissing him, wet tear-filled kisses. What was ten short years now that he'd come back to her? "I prayed you'd come," she would say. "And like a vision, you've come, my knight in shining armor, to whisk me away."

Ben was jolted awake when the Roadrunner hit a speed bump. The bump started him coughing, and the coughing hurt his chest. His fever made him dizzy and the sun hurt his eyes. He wished he could just die already.

"Oh good. You're awake," said Angel. Looking closer at Ben, "Can't say the rest did you much good. You look like shit."

Ben was trying to focus on her.

Angel pressed on. "Hellooo. Is anybody in there?"

Seeing Ben's blank expression, she continued. "It's a good thing we're just about there. Let's get this old girlfriend nonsense out of the way, then we can get you to a doctor. Rocket, how much further?"

"It should be on this block," answered the navigator.

Hearing how close they were helped bring Ben back to Earth.

Through watery eyes he was able to make out the tall manicured ficus hedges separating one mansion from the other. Circular stone driveways with fountains and covered entryways framed with columns reminded one that this was no trailer park. Another wave of dizziness was already coming over Ben when he heard Makesh announce, "Here! This is it! Stop the car!"

Makesh's excitement over finding their destination only served to make Ben even more lightheaded, to further constrict his already compromised airway.

"Wow," was all Juan could say, looking up at the mansion in which Jill Sterling lived.

"Not bad," added Angel.

"This is where Dr. Ben's girlfriend works?" asked Juan.

"No, Juan," answered Makesh. "She doesn't work here. She lives here. The phone book listed this as her address."

Angel looked about at the classic Miznerian architecture, a combination of cast stone and barrel-tiled roof. From the size of the arched windows, she estimated ceiling heights of 18 feet. A big Mercedes and a convertible Jaguar were already out front when a well-dressed gentleman came out of the mahogany front door turning back to say goodbye to those still inside. "Have a good day, everyone. See you tonight."

Ben heard a voice from inside shout back, "I love you." Ben couldn't claim to recognize the words, but the voice unmistakably belonged to Jill Sterling.

He watched the Armani suit enter the Mercedes and head down the driveway, stopping at the end just long enough to shout over to them, "Sorry, but you can't park there." Then he was gone.

Maybe it was the diesel fumes from the Mercedes, but Ben felt a coughing spell approaching to join his dizziness. Maybe it was just nerves, but, seeing the front door open again, he could feel the beads of cold sweat begin to run down his face.

Two children, aged two and five bolted out the front door and started climbing into the Jaguar. A large greyhound bolted out the front door after them, hoping to come for the ride.

"Mom, the dog got out!" shouted the eldest child, pushing the dog's paws off the top of the car door as it tried to get in.

Then a woman's voice from the house shouted, "Ben!"

Oh no. She'd seen him, thought Ben. He wasn't ready. What would he say? His heart raced as he involuntarily slouched down into the rear seat of the Roadrunner to hide.

"Ben!" called the voice a second time.

Ben felt faint. Then she appeared at the front door. A vision of beauty. Even Angel had to admit to herself that the woman was stunning. Dressed in a designer dress and heels, long hair elegantly trimmed, framing the impeccable makeup that only served to highlight a naturally angelic face, she flowed from the front door of the house like fine champagne.

"Ben! Come here!" she demanded. Her tone was so compelling, Ben found himself sitting up in the car and reaching for the door in order to comply with the woman's command.

"Wait," suggested Angel, grabbing Ben by the elbow. "Look."

She motioned up the driveway where the greyhound bolted directly at the woman, rearing up to place his paws on her shoulders and lick her face.

"Down!" she yelled at the slobbering beast. "Down Ben!"

Angel looked at Ben just in time to see his crushed expression at the realization that the dog's name was Ben. She was calling the dog. She'd named her dog Ben.

Ben slumped back into the seat of the car. Things weren't turning out the way Ben had expected. Beautiful home, kids, husband. She herself was a vision of beauty. And to top it all off, just to twist the knife a little, she'd named her dog Ben.

"Well, I guess I deserve it," muttered Ben to Angel. "After what I've done to her, it's only right that she thinks of me as a dog."

"Why do you always see the cup as half empty?" asked Angel. "She seems to love the dog."

Ben, the dog, was standing on his hind legs, paws on Jill Sterling's shoulders, licking her face. Jill Sterling laughed as she gently pushed the dog down and began to drag him into the house by the collar.

"The dog seems to love her too," noted Makesh.

"He's hugging her," added Juan with a giggle, noticing the dog was humping its master's leg as she pulled him through the front door.

"You'd better get up there now or she's going to get into her car and leave. You'll miss your big chance," urged Angel.

Ben started to get up, then hesitated. "What if she hates me? She's named her dog Ben, for Christ's sake."

"All the more reason for your apology," said Angel. "Isn't that why you're here? To make amends?"

Ben pulled himself out of the rear seat of the car with great reservation. As he stepped from the car onto the driveway, he almost couldn't stand. His legs were rubber. His vision was blurred through the beads of perspiration running down his forehead. He was dizzy from fever, and his heart was racing. His breathing was labored, accompanied by an audible wheeze. Ben looked toward the house. It was a long driveway, a very long driveway. Ben wasn't sure he could make it. He looked back at Angel.

Judging by Ben's condition, Angel wasn't sure he would make it either. But this was his decision, his cross to bear. She gave him a reassuring nod of her head and watched him start to make his way up the brick-paved driveway.

Ben had managed to drag himself halfway up the drive when Jill Sterling emerged from the front door, shutting it behind her. When she spied the stranger with the drunken gait staggering up her driveway, she instinctively shouted to her kids in the Mercedes to lock the doors.

"Can I help you?" she shouted to Ben.

Ben replied, but the words, almost inaudible through his constricted airway, only served to tickle his throat, setting off yet another coughing spell.

As the ominous stranger pressed on toward her, Jill Sterling looked about nervously, as if planning an escape route. She could easily run into the house, but she couldn't leave her children.

"Can I help you?" she repeated firmly, only the smallest trace of fear in her voice.

Ben was still 20 feet away when he was able to catch enough breath to respond again. "It's me. Ben." He looked to her for a sign of recognition.

Not even noticing the name was that of her dog, she shouted back, "I don't know any Ben. What do you want?"

Ben had to chuckle to himself. Sure, he must have looked a little different, what with his illness and all. And there was no denying it had been seven years. But the way she seemed to have repressed the memory of him was quite extraordinary from a psychological standpoint. "Jill, it's me. Ben. Ben Walker."

"Just stop right there, mister. And how do you know my name?" demanded Jill.

Ben continued to advance, "It's Ben Walker. We went to high school together." He was ten feet from Jill Sterling.

"Look. Whatever you're selling, I don't want it. Don't make me call the police," only shreds of calm lingering in her voice.

Ben started coughing again, unable to catch his breath. The momentum of his body doubling over in coughing spasms brought him within five feet of his high school girlfriend. "The prom," he choked. "I've come to apologize for not taking you to the high school prom."

The threatening stranger was too close. She'd never be able to phone the police in time. She'd unconsciously started to back away, but was soon up against her front door. "I don't remember any Ben Walker," panic finding its way into her voice. "I went to the prom with Jim Wright. He's my husband."

Ben had to think. Jim Wright? Who was Jim Wri… Jim Wright! Quarterback on the high school football team! That jerk? Ben became lightheaded. The woman and the house in front of him began to spin. "But I asked you to the prom. You were going with me." Small specks of light began floating across Ben's field of view.

Jill Sterling was about to scream. The stalker was within arms length. "Look. I don't remember any Ben Walker. If you think you had a date with me for the prom, fine. Apology accepted. Just please don't hurt us." She started to cry in fear.

It was finally getting through. She didn't even remember him. His high school sweetheart didn't even know who he was. All these years he thought he'd stood her up at the prom, she'd actually been going all along with the star of the football team. It was all too much. The house and the woman in front of him began to spin. He couldn't breath. He was blacking out. He was pathetic. He was falling. Just pathetic.

Chapter 31

At the same time her attacker lunged for her, Jill Sterling reached into her purse. Her husband was right. The pepper spray he'd given her saved her life.

There was just one problem. Pepper spray wasn't supposed to be lethal. Her assailant went down hard. He wasn't breathing, and he had no pulse. Benjamin Walker was dead...

Chapter 32

...for about a minute. It was a good thing Jill Sterling was a doctor. She'd gone to a six year combined undergraduate and medical school program, earning her medical degree two years ahead of Ben. It took her about a minute to shoo away the stranger's concerned friends, check for respirations and pulse, both absent, pound once on his chest, and finally, have the butler initiate CPR.

Apparently a good whack on the chest and a couple of blows down the old windpipe were sufficient to break up whatever muck was blocking things up.

At least that's how Ben's friends interpreted what the Chinese emergency room doctor had told them. The man's jet black hair was one big bed of cowlicks, pointing haphazardly in all directions at once. His accent was so thick they could only pick out a word here and there.

"Fliend need to rie down and lest. Vely tired. Need rots of fruid flom IV."

Ben was dehydrated. He hadn't been drinking enough to make up for all the fever and sweats he'd been having. While getting rehydrated, the doctor ordered a few tests including a chest x-ray. Angel told him everything Ben had said about catching HIV from a nun. It was like a game of charades trying to get the Chinese doctor to understand what a nun was, but a nurse immediately knew something was fishy. A rapid HIV test was ordered. And they waited.

None of them wanted to be there. They'd all had bad memories of hospitals and they all thought that at any moment security would surround them and whisk them off to the looney bin, just a matter of time before someone learned their story and sent them back where they'd come from. Angel thought of taking the others and going on without Ben. They had to get Juan home before they were caught. But Ben had become part of the team. And as pathetic as he was, she couldn't leave him alone to die. She'd actually grown fond of the jerk, emotionally handicapped little boy that he was. When it came to relationships, Ben Walker was crippled. When it came to love and sex, he was clueless. But like finding a little lost kitten, Angel couldn't just leave him there helpless. After all, love and sex were her specialties, though not necessarily in that order. She'd hoped to find that spark, that emotional seed she new lay somewhere deep inside her patient, Ben Walker. Unfortunately time was running out. She hadn't anticipated this AIDS thing.

When Ben's HIV test came back negative, the nurse got on the phone with the lab at Presbyterian Hospital back in New York. It didn't take long to get to the bottom of things. Presbyterian confirmed there'd been a mix-up. They'd been trying to find Dr. Walker ever since, but he seemed to have disappeared. They explained how they'd confirmed the mix-up by checking blood types. They'd had a known AIDS patient test negative the same day as Dr. Walker's test. The AIDS patient's blood type was O while Ben's was A. When they typed the blood from Mr. Love's and Dr. Walker's blood samples, sure enough, they were reversed.

"Oh, that kind of stuff happens all the time," said the Presbyterian lab supervisor. It's just a bit more problematic when it comes to HIV testing."

"Yeah, just a bit," confirmed the nurse.

After hanging up the phone, she immediately went to inform Ben's doctor. She found him in Radiology going over Ben's chest x-ray.

"Take a rook at your patient's fiwm," said doctor Foo when he saw her.

"Wow," was all she could say, looking up at the light box.

"Just rike in the textbooks, huh?" he added.

"I've never seen such a classic case," she agreed. "Will you be presenting it at grand rounds?"

"Oh no," he answered. "This much too easy. Even medical student get this one light. You take fiwm to patient's loom and tell his fliends I come talk at them."

When the nurse returned to the ER, Ben was awake again. He was still very weak, but a little bit of fluid had gone a long way. His fever had come down with a little Tylenol and he didn't look as ghostly pale as when he'd arrived. His cough, however, persisted.

"I've got some good news for you," announced the nurse to Ben, as she slapped his x-rays up on the light box.

Even from the gurney, Ben could make out something was wrong with the x-ray. Wanting to take a closer look, he managed to roll off the gurney and drag himself and his IV over to the chest films. Finally close enough to focus on the images of his lungs, he immediately saw something surprising.

"Hey," he began, "this isn't Pneumocytis pneumonia."

"Exactly," agreed the nurse. "Doctor Foo will be in with all the details, but I can tell you one thing, and you all better sit down for this."

They all found something to sit on, that is, all but Ben. Ben remained at the light box, studying the films. He saw a large complex mass in the apex of the right lung accompanied by innumerable tiny nodules scattered throughout both lungs. Ben knew of only one thing that presented a pattern such as that on chest x-ray.

The nurse continued with the good news. "The films don't show Pneumocystis, because Pneumocystis is an AIDS-related pneumonia. And you, Dr. Walker, do not have AIDS."

Angel almost fell off Ben's gurney.

Makesh turned to Angel. "But I thought you said…"

Juan continued chewing on a Slim Jim.

Ben hadn't moved from the light box, where he remained, going over his x-rays again and again. He didn't even turn around at hearing the good news.

The nurse continued, "It was all some kind of lab mix-up. You're HIV negative, Dr. Walker. Congratulations."

Angel jumped up in shock and threw her arms around Ben from behind, hugging him so hard he couldn't breathe. "Did you hear that!?" she shouted in ecstasy. "It was all a mistake!" Then, before noticing Ben's less than enthusiastic response, she turned back to the nurse and asked the obvious. "But if he doesn't have AIDS, then what's wrong with him?"

"I'll let the doctor explain that part. He'll be in shortly."

When the nurse left, Angel and Makesh looked at each other smiling, still numb from the good news. Ben, however, hadn't shown any reaction to the news.

Finally, Angel broke the silence. "Hey Hah-vud," she began, trying to elicit a reaction, "what's with you? Didn't you hear what the nurse said? You don't have AIDS. That's a good thing. Show a little excitement."

And finally, Ben responded, without turning from the light box. "No, I guess I don't have AIDS anymore. I can admit it. I had the wrong diagnosis all along. But, you know, there aren't a whole lot of things that can cause you to cough up blood."

"What are you saying?" asked Angel, moving to Ben's side.

"I should have known," responded Ben.

"Known what?" asked Angel.

"I should have noticed my illness was progressing way too fast for HIV. It normally takes years to progress from infection to symptoms. I may be stupid, but I'm not a hypochondriac. I may have had the wrong death sentence, but this is still a death sentence," he said, pointing at his x-rays.

"What do you mean?" responded Angel, taking his hand in concern.

"HIV could have taken years. But this? This is metastatic cancer. According to this chest x-ray, I've only got a few days left."

Angel dropped his hand in shock and had to steady herself against the wall. "What are you talking about?" she protested. "They can operate. They can take it out."

"Not this time," answered Ben. Pointing at the film, "It's spread to both lungs. It's inoperable."

Angel thought maybe she was being a bit ghoulish wondering what kind of cancer Ben had. Metastatic from where? But never mind all that. "There must be something they can do," offered Angel.

Turning from the light box, Ben yanked the IV out of his arm and headed for the door. "We'd better get Juan home. There's no magic pill for this."

They'd been gone from the emergency room only a couple of minutes when Dr. Foo walked in. "Dr. Walker, I have your magic…" He stopped when he saw no one was in the room. He was going to say "…pill."

Chapter 33

It wasn't as easy as they thought it would be to charter a boat to Cuba. Sure, they weren't exactly going to Cuba, but Isla de los Locos was so close that it didn't matter. They'd still have to enter waters controlled by Cuba. None of the boat captains wanted to risk having their boat seized by the Cuban military, even for $10,000. The four of them walked up and down the marina prepared to throw their money at anyone willing to take them to Isla de los Locos.

They were just about to give up, resigning themselves to coming up with a new plan, when they finally found a willing boat captain. His name, coincidentally noted by Makesh, was Captain Blackman. Perhaps it was the way Makesh couldn't see the man's eyes behind his dark sunglasses that disturbed him, but Captain Blackman made him somehow uneasy. His first mate, Mr. Smith, was unusually quiet, and obviously didn't know anything about boats, Captain Blackman pointing out for him that the bow line was at the *front* of the boat, not the back.

It was only a 32 foot boat with a small cabin, but it had plenty of power and was certainly capable of reaching their destination within a few hours.

Juan couldn't help humming the tune to Gilligan's Island as he boarded the boat, repeating over and over the lines, "…a three-hour tour, a three-hour tour." He didn't stop until he noticed something in the water off the side of the boat. It was big and brown. At first he thought it was a seal. But then he recognized what it was.

"Hey, look, guys. It's a manatee!" he shouted.

The others didn't believe him at first, but curiosity finally got the better of them as one by one they gathered at the side of the boat gawking at the huge sea cow.

"It's so cute," remarked Angel, watching the chubby creature rolling about. Makesh had to agree, marveling at the docile beast. Even Ben gathered the strength to stand up and peer over the side. As he did, the manatee came right over and stared at him.

"I think he's trying to tell you something," said Makesh.

"She," corrected Juan. "It's a she."

"How do you know it's a she?" asked Angel, staring and wondering to herself how big a male manatee's organ would be.

"That's Bessie," Juan replied with a smile. "She came all this way from New York."

"Who's Bessie?" asked Makesh.

"Oh, don't get him started," said Ben with a groan.

Angel filled him in. "She's that manatee that took a wrong turn and ended up in the Hudson River off Manhattan." Then, turning to Juan, "How do you know that's Bessie?"

"She told me so," he replied without hesitation.

"Now one of them speaks with animals," muttered Ben to no one, shaking his head as the boat pulled away from the dock. Then, addressing the others, "I guess he speaks Manateese," added Ben, in an awkward attempt at humor.

Neither Ben nor his three patients had ever spent any real time on the ocean. All four marveled at the deep blue color of the water, the refreshing salt air, and the marine wildlife. Flying fish, stingrays, and porpoises all came to greet the strangers. Juan stood at the bow railing right at the nose of the boat so as not to miss anything. He was the sentry, the first to point out any wildlife sightings. Makesh, despite the cold shoulder from Misters Blackman and Smith, couldn't get enough of the boat's gadgetry, constantly flipping switches and asking questions about how everything worked. The captain and his first mate were not particularly friendly to begin with, and Makesh's constant pestering only seemed to make things worse. Makesh was ultimately banned from the cockpit. Angel, of course, found the perfect spot for sunbathing above the hatch to the cabin. Her lack of a bathing suit wasn't a problem. Topless, in her thong underwear, she was sure to get an even tan. And just to divert some of the animosity building toward Makesh, she allowed Mr. Smith to apply the suntan lotion she'd purchased back at the marina. Besides, unsure how long the trip would take, Angel thought he might come in handy later.

They were all thoroughly enjoying their tropical cruise. All but Ben. Ben was seasick and couldn't understand how a chartered boat could head out to sea without a supply of Compazine. He stayed down below in the cabin to be close to the head, even though he suspected there couldn't be anything left in his stomach after his first two deposits.

It hadn't been an hour at sea when Juan spotted something at the horizon, which seemed to be growing in size. The others ignored Juan at first. He was probably just imagining a whale coming by to greet them. It wasn't too long, however, until Angel and Makesh joined Juan at the bow rail squinting to make something out of the approaching entity. Juan was the first to recognize the object as another boat. When the others realized how quickly it was approaching, Makesh went to speak to the captain, while Angel thought it wise to put some clothes on.

Blackman and Smith didn't seem too concerned, even when Makesh suggested they could be pirates.

"What do you think this is? Treasure island?" asked Mr. Smith, ridiculing Makesh's idea.

"It's not unheard of," countered Makesh. "We are, after all, on the open sea. Do you carry any firearms, Mr. Blackman?"

"Are we packing heat? You bet. Of course we're armed."

"If you don't believe in pirates, why do you arm yourselves?" asked Makesh.

By the look Mr. Blackman threw him, Makesh sensed it was time to leave the cockpit again. When he returned to the bow of the boat, he was startled to see how fast the other boat was approaching. Paranoid or not, it was headed right for them.

"I don't like this," said Angel, only reinforcing Makesh's fears. "Such a big ocean. Why must they be *here*?"

"Maybe they just want to say hi," offered Juan, ever the optimist.

Makesh had a different version. "Maybe they want to send us back to the loony bin. Or worse yet, maybe they're looking for plutonium."

"How would they have found us out here?" asked Angel skeptically.

"It's this cursed transmitter," complained Makesh, scratching behind his ear.

"I just can't believe someone would have chased us out here," countered Angel.

"OK. Have it your way," conceded Makesh. "They're not looking for us. They have no idea who we are. They simply want to kill us and steal our boat. I feel much better now. Thank you, Angel."

Angel ignored him. But when she looked back at Blackman and Smith in the cockpit, they almost seemed to be looking forward to the encounter, smiling and patting each other on the back. Angel began to sense this was more of a delivery than a chance encounter. And she and her friends were the package. Maybe Makesh was right.

Juan was already waving to the other boat in greeting when Makesh made out the black suits worn by two of the boat's passengers. He reflexively ran back to the cockpit. "Quick! We must get away! I know these men!"

The response from Blackman and Smith was swift and decisive. Makesh designed nuclear warheads for a living, yet he'd never get used to seeing guns. And certainly never so close to his nose. He didn't think he liked it.

"Get out of the cockpit," ordered Mr. Blackman in a no nonsense tone.

"No, no. You don't understand," began Makesh. "We must get away from these men. It's OK. I won't touch anything."

Pressing the gun to Makesh's forehead, Mr. Blackman tried to make himself clear. "You're going to be shark bait if you don't leave this cockpit at once."

Makesh raised his hands over his head, beginning to tremble. "But why are we stopping?"

"We have an appointment with these gentlemen."

Makesh felt as though he'd already been shot. "You mean, you know these men?"

"Only on a professional basis," assured Mr. Blackman. "You see, Mr. Rocket Scientist, my colleagues placed an order for merchandise and we're merely delivering it."

"What merchandise?" pressed Makesh, wondering at the same time how they knew he was a rocket scientist, "What do you have that they desire?"

"You, Mr. Guptah," he replied with a sneer. "We have you." And with that he forcibly shoved Makesh up onto the deck, following him with the gun. Mr. Smith shut down the engines and followed them up onto the deck.

The mysterious boat was already pulling up along side them when Angel and Juan saw Mr. Blackman shoving Makesh toward them with the barrel of his gun.

"What's going on?" demanded Angel.

"Can I play, too?" pleaded Juan, bounding toward Mr. Blackman.

The gun turned from Makesh to Juan. "Call off the retard!" Blackman shouted to Angel.

"Juan!" she shouted. "Leave Mr. Blackman alone. He doesn't want to play."

Juan stopped. But he knew what retard meant. "Just because he doesn't want to play with me doesn't mean he should call me names."

The two men in black were just a few feet away from Makesh, waiting impatiently in the boat along side them. He felt every hair on his body stand up as he flashed back to the various tortures they'd subjected him to while trying to find the missing plutonium, endless sessions of electroshock therapy running one into the next. He couldn't bear going through that again. He'd rather die, right then and there. In an instant, Makesh decided he wouldn't be taken alive.

Mr. Blackman sensed the situation unraveling. There was way too much movement, too much action, more than he felt comfortable with. These nut cakes were more than he'd bargained for. Distracted by Makesh running toward the rail of the boat to jump overboard, Mr. Blackman didn't see Juan approaching. But as the men in black intercepted Makesh, he saw Juan out of the corner of his eye coming at him.

"Say you're sorry," demanded Juan.

"What!?" shouted the startled gunman, turning toward him.

Juan pressed forward. "You were mean to me. Say you're sorry." he repeated.

Mr. Blackman turned the gun on the charging giant. And as Juan raised his hand to point an accusing finger at the name caller, Mr. Blackman, thinking Juan was reaching for his gun, pulled the trigger.

Angel cried out. "No!"

Chapter 34

A seasick Ben Walker pulled his head out of the toilet when he heard the gunshot. "What now?" he thought, annoyed by the disturbance. He'd finally found that if he sat on the floor and rested his head on the rim of the toilet at just the right angle, the nausea would subside to a tolerable level. He'd found a way to take his mind off the rocking of the boat. Akin to counting sheep, he envisioned the cancer cells in his lungs dividing. One became two, two became four, four eight, eight sixteen and so on, until both his lungs would become solid balls of tumor, until there was no room left for the air to go, until...

But now that peace had been disturbed. Like a small child crying for him in the middle of the night, his friends up on deck just couldn't seem to let him rest. It was always something. Why couldn't they just get Juan home? Then he could find a beautiful beach, swim out into the ocean until he couldn't swim anymore, until his arms and legs gave out, until the ocean sucked him in, and he could rest, finally rest. But that was later. For now, he was compelled to pull himself together to go up top and investigate.

He'd barely poked his nose out the cabin door when he noticed something was amiss. First of all, he saw there was a second boat. Since when had they joined an armada? People were shouting in anger. He instinctively held back, lingering at the cabin door, until he could assess the situation. Angel was frantic.

"You could have killed him, you fucking asshole!" she shouted, never one to mince words.

Mr. Blackman didn't take it personally. "If I'd wanted to kill him, I'd have done so. That was just a warning shot. Now if everyone has calmed down sufficiently," turning back to the men in black, "my well-dressed colleagues and I can get back to business. So that's $10,000 for Gandhi here," pointing the gun at Makesh. Combined with the $10,000 from his passengers, he had to admit that wasn't bad for a day's work. There remained some loose ends to tie up yet. "You sure you don't need any of the others? After all, we can't have any witnesses, now can we?"

"No thank you, gentlemen," replied one of the men in black. "All we need is Einstein here," pointing at Makesh.

"Can't we keep the girl?" pleaded Mr. Smith, walking over to Angel. "She's so fucking hot."

During the commotion, Angel's micro-dress had ridden up above her hip. She made no attempt to adjust it, hoping for any means of distracting Blackman and Smith from the job at hand.

Ben remained hidden, his mind racing for a plan, a plan to somehow seize control of the boat again. Then he saw Angel take matters into her own hands. In one smooth motion, Angel pulled her dress up over her head and off. Standing there, topless, in her thong, she served as quite a distraction. Mr. Smith was already approaching her. Angel licked her lips and smiled, encouraging Mr. Smith's advance. But when one of her hands began to fondle a breast while the other went between her legs, Smith forgot why he was there at all. The gun he held in his hands drooped as the one in his pants came to attention.

Blackman, on the other hand, was focused on Makesh. He started shoving him over to the boat rail, preparing to deliver his valuable cargo to the men that had ordered it.

Ben managed to find a fishing gaff. The pole with the sharp hook on the end represented a formidable weapon. As he worked his way around the other side of the cabin in hopes of blindsiding Mr. Blackman, things on deck began to escalate again. Smith had his butt to the boat rail as Angel squatted in front of him and worked his pants down around his ankles. The rod between his legs was being more than cooperative, pointing north.

Which was more than could be said for Makesh. The closer Blackman shoved him toward the other boat, the more combative he became. It was a primal instinctive thing, grabbing anything he could reach to prevent himself from being moved to the boat of his tormentors. And like trying to give a cat a bath, Mr. Blackman had his hands full, Makesh's arms and legs seemingly everywhere at once, wild-eyed, his unkempt long gray hair standing on end. If he'd had the ability to extend his nails as a cat does, he'd have done so. Makesh's shouts drowned out words of warning from the men in black on the other boat as they saw Ben with his gaff approaching Blackman from behind.

Smith's attention was elsewhere, eyes fixed downward, as he watched Angel's mouth prepare to dock with his own steal-hard gaff.

Ben's plan would have worked if only he'd chosen any other moment to start coughing. But that wasn't up to him. It was completely beyond his control. So as the coughing seized him and the phlegm lodged in his airway, Mr. Blackman momentarily let the wild Indian go to turn and see what was choking behind him. Seeing Ben brandishing his sharp-hooked weapon, Blackman concluded he was about to be ambushed. He'd had enough. He raised his gun toward Ben, preparing to put the sickly animal out of its misery.

The shot sounded before he could pull the trigger. There was a blaze of light. And then pain. Blackman fell backward against the boat rail from the impact. He'd been shot. But how? Had his gun backfired? All he knew was that he'd been hit in the chest and knocked off his feet.

"I win! I got you!" shouted Juan with glee. He'd seen the flair gun earlier, but hadn't thought of playing with it until Mr. Blackman started the game but wouldn't share with Juan.

Seeing Mr. Blackman on the ropes, Makesh wasted no time in lunging at him and sending him over the boat rail into the ocean between the two boats. Taking her cue from Makesh, it didn't take much of a shove from Angel to send Smith, pants around his ankles, over the rail as well. She then grabbed Ben's gaff and proceeded to jab the hands of either man trying to get back in their boat. Juan concluded his victory dance and started shooting flares at the occupants of the other boat, sending rainbows of color into the air.

Makesh wasted no time in taking the controls of the boat. His earlier observations paid off as he fired up the motor, punched the throttle forward, and took off. He'd even mastered the GPS and followed coordinates toward Cuba, and presumably Isla de los Locos, still a hundred miles away. It wasn't a spaceship, but it would have to do, as long as it put distance between himself and the men in black.

Angel had managed to throw her dress back on even amid the rough bouncing of the boat as it crashed through the waves, while Ben still lie on the deck floundering on his back, legs flailing the air, like a crab dropped from a fishing net. Juan was disappointed that the game was called so abruptly.

The other boat was soon out of sight. It wouldn't be long, however, until Blackman and Smith were hauled aboard and the chase resumed. Makesh had no choice other than to run for it. In fact, they'd actually put several miles between themselves and the other boat, when, sure enough, a speck soon appeared at the horizon behind them. Makesh began to panic again, unable to think of any means to significantly increase their speed. He'd already had his friends throw anything that wasn't nailed down overboard attempting to lighten the load. Angel insisted, however, in keeping the deflated life raft just in case. It didn't weigh much anyway.

But it was all to no avail. The speck behind them had grown to a dot, the dot to a thing, and the thing ultimately to a boat, apparently the faster of the two boats. There was no sight of land ahead, and the other boat was closing on them. It was just a matter of time. They surely would be intercepted before reaching land.

The time to rationally think of a way to escape his pursuers was over. The time, even to panic, had expired. Makesh was done with those things. It was different now. Now was the time to calmly, but fruitlessly, cast blame. And he blamed them. No, not the men in black. Not Blackman and Smith. Them. The little green men. The aliens. He'd gone out of his way to help them. Out of his way was quite the understatement. Since he'd acquired the plutonium for them, he'd lost his job and any money he'd had. He'd been mugged and had a transmitter surgically implanted in his head. He'd been committed to a psychiatric ward, then tortured by the mysterious men in black. No, out of his way just didn't seem adequate to characterize the situation. And where was the thanks? Where was an ounce of appreciation from those little monsters that would annihilate his beloved Earth just to replace it with an intergalactic McDonalds?

Makesh had never been a religious man. Always the man of science, in fact, he wasn't even sure which religion he was. At that moment, however, it didn't seem to matter. Makesh Guptah began to pray. He prayed that God wouldn't let them torture him. He prayed he and his friends wouldn't get caught. Oh yes, almost as an afterthought, he also prayed that God might see fit to save the Earth itself from destruction, although frankly that was not Makesh's immediate concern. He prayed for the hand of God to smite those that would harm them. He prayed for some all-powerful force to emanate from the heavens above. Divine intervention. A plague. A cataclysm. A bolt of lightning.

The men in black were clearly visible aboard the other boat now. Soon, even their weapons could be seen, then heard. Shots were being fired. And amid the ensuing confusion of ricocheting bullets whizzing past their heads, scrambling for cover, no one noticed the storm clouds begin to gather out of a clear blue sky. No one noticed the sun being blotted out, the wind picking up, the seas growing rough.

Already consumed by disease, Ben was further weakened from dehydration. Being seasick, any spare drop of fluid in his body had long ago been deposited in the toilet. It took all his strength amid the crashing of the boat against the waves merely to stay flat on his back on the deck clutching the through-bolted leg of a chair. But when the first of the growing waves came crashing over the bow of the boat, he didn't know how he managed to hold on. It hit him hard, cold and wet too, but mostly hard, a giant hand trying to brush a flake of dandruff off the shoulder of the boat. Perhaps it was the unexpected shock that woke up whatever strength remained. Of course, that was just the first one. As they began to grow in frequency and volume, Ben managed to pull himself up into a sitting position, hugging the leg of the chair like a child on his first carousel ride.

Juan, on the other hand, was enjoying the roller coaster ride. Still at the nose of the boat, he clutched the bow rail as the wind picked up and the boat dipped ever higher and lower between the growing white-capped waves. He wanted to raise his arms in the air as he'd seen people do on roller coasters, but even Juan knew that doing so would only assure his being washed overboard. So instead, he held onto the bucking bronco and shouted with joy every time a wall of water slapped him in the face.

Angel sat in the chair next to captain Makesh, somewhat protected from the elements by the boat's windshield. As if she wasn't concerned enough by the men hunting them, and the associated gunfire, Mother Nature was beginning to distract her. She looked out to sea like a meteorologist and didn't like what she saw. The waves had grown from eight feet in size, now easily ten to twelve. The wind, approaching 40 miles per hour continued to churn things up. But none of that concerned her as much as what she saw ahead. It was a wall of near blackness. They were headed into darkness, the sky blotted out by storm clouds. But as much as the occasional flash of lightning helped her see what was coming, the increasing frequency and proximity of the lightning bolts soon left her longing for the darkness.

The curtain of rain hit them almost as hard as the waves coming over the bow. In the fifty mile per hour winds, the raindrops pelted them like bullets, stinging their faces, their eyes more shut than open. Makesh kept looking back for the men in black, but couldn't see them anymore amid the waves, rain, and darkness. He pressed onward, nonetheless, possessed, hand on the boat's throttle like Ahab's on his harpoon. With each bolt of lightning, his half head of wild gray hair lit up like a torch.

The sky had become a thick blanket of swirling black clouds. The wind had reached hurricane velocity. And the waves towered over the now seemingly tiny boat. It was finally safe to say that the men in black were no longer anyone's concern. Only the storm. Only the storm concerned any of them at this point. How to keep from being washed overboard. How to keep the boat from capsizing. How to keep from being struck by lightning. Yet all those things seemed entirely out of their control. The storm was in control now. The storm had its own plan.

The rapid onset of the storm, seemingly coming from nowhere, caught them all by surprise. The resulting mayhem, however, left little time to contemplate the freak event. They were all more concerned with merely surviving at this point. Makesh, however, had his doubts that this was a natural phenomenon. And, in fact, at one point, looking skyward at the black clouds pressing down upon them, he thought he saw something. It was only for a moment. And no sooner had he focused on it, than it was instantly obscured by cloud cover. It only took a couple of seconds, but like processing the vague outlines of a Rorschach inkblot, his recognition of what the object represented came to him. Makesh was sure of it. He'd seen this thing before. It was them. The aliens. It was their spaceship. Just like when their car careened off the raised highway, yet miraculously landed unharmed on the pavement three stories below, the aliens had come to help. He'd prayed to God for some calamity to strike down those that would harm him, the men in black.

Now, Makesh didn't know what God looked like, but he'd seen this spaceship before. He wasn't sure why they were helping them. But they were. He was sure of it. And when the ship suddenly appeared again from behind the veil of clouds, Makesh motioned for the others to look up and see their saviors. But once again, like a magician making the Statue of Liberty disappear, the giant ship miraculously vanished without a trace, and no one else could see it. Why was it only Makesh that could see them? Never any of the others. A frustrated Makesh began to doubt himself. Was it just his imagination? Was it all something other than reality? Was he really nuts?

Angel had managed to find the life jackets below deck and made sure everyone wore them. They all huddled within the cockpit as Makesh attempted to keep the boat from being rolled. No longer running from the men in black, he was simply trying to point the boat into the oncoming waves. One hit from any one of the monster waves to the side of the boat would surely capsize the thing. Juan gripped Angel and Ben to help keep them from being washed overboard.

It wasn't bad enough that the lighting had fried their VHF radio so they couldn't radio for help. No, the lightning wasn't through with them yet. In fact, there was so much lighting, it seemed as if they had a second source of sunlight sprouting beneath the black cloud cover. So when the boat's engine took a direct lightning hit, it came as no surprise. In fact, no one even noticed, as they didn't seem to be moving anyway, and the wind and thunder had long ago blotted out any sound of engines.

On the other hand, they couldn't help but notice when the fire broke out. The heat at their backs felt good at first, but soon became unbearable. Angel was the first to turn around and see the flames. She'd smelled it singeing her hair. Alerting the others to the new turn of events, she urged them all to the front of the boat, as far from the flames as possible. It was only a matter of time before something exploded. Yes, despite the heavy rain and crashing waves, with gasoline to sustain it, the fire burned on, engulfing the stern of the boat.

The ensuing explosion sent most of the cabin enclosure flying past their heads. All except Makesh's head. He, instead, took a blow behind the ear from flying debris. He felt like passing out, but decided this wouldn't be an appropriate time. And as the flaming boat began to sink tail first into the ocean, its passengers clung to the bow rail, all too aware that in a matter of moments they would all be bobbing helplessly at sea.

Seeing they were about to be boatless, Makesh had but one thing to say. "I can't swim."

Angel pointed out to him that he was wearing a life jacket, so he really had no excuse not to float with the rest of them. But when she yelled over the howling wind and cracking thunder for them all to hold onto each other, to stay together, Ben couldn't really understand why. Surely, they wouldn't survive long in the middle of the ocean, in the middle of a hurricane. Why bother staying together? Nevertheless, he lacked the energy to argue about it with Angel. It was only as they watched the last of the boat submerge, on its way to the ocean floor, and they looked about, surrounded by vast walls of water, rolling amid the maelstrom of alternating darkness and lightning, did they notice Juan was already gone.

Chapter 35

Water everywhere. That's the first thing Angel noticed waking up. Then, looking at the two seemingly lifeless corpses clinging to her and each other, she assumed they were dead. But no, Ben was wheezing. And Makesh was mumbling under his breath, agitated, as if having a bad dream. Sheer exhaustion. That's the only explanation for it. It wouldn't have seemed possible to fall asleep in the middle of a hurricane, three life-jacketed friends, clinging to each other in the middle of the ocean. Yet there they were.

Apparently the storm had raged through the night, because, Angel could now make out the sun rising at the horizon. She assumed it was morning anyway, though technically, it could just as easily have been sunset, having no way of knowing east from west. Nevertheless, it only took a few moments to see the sun growing from, not shrinking into, the water.

Contrary to the previous night's events, the ocean was now as smooth as glass, a serene blue green, reflecting the warm glow of the rising sun. The water was warm and somehow soothing. It was hard to believe this was the same ocean that tried its best to kill them all the previous night.

Juan was gone. Angel awoke thinking he'd still be there, as someone might do waking up from surgery after having had a limb amputated. He'd become a part of her, of all of them. And now, as she looked about, she wondered how the strongest of them could have been the first to be taken. Looking across at the other two, she presumed Ben, being ill, would be the next to go. But Angel's musings over coffee and the morning newspaper were short-lived as the children began to stir.

They awoke almost simultaneously as the first movements of each woke the other. Ben started coughing almost immediately, attempting to expel that portion of the ocean that had lodged in his lungs during the storm. Makesh, on the other hand, awoke right where he'd left off.

"Where are they?" he shouted, whirling about.

"Who?" asked Angel in reply.

"The men in black! Where are they?"

"At the bottom of the ocean, I hope," answered Angel.

"Just a matter of time until we join them," Ben remarked, managing to control his coughing momentarily. "We're all going to die out here in the middle of nowhere."

The others knew he was right. No food. No water. No shelter. It wouldn't be long. Yet, always the ones to embrace the cup half full, over Ben's half empty one, they assured Ben that help would arrive. And sure enough, after only a couple of hours bobbing helplessly, three small needles amid a Midwest of haystacks, Makesh spotted something at the horizon. Ben, growing significantly weaker by the minute, couldn't summon the energy to focus in the direction Makesh was pointing.

"Who is it?" Ben began. "Your alien friends? Shouldn't they be up in the air?"

"You are correct, Dr. Walker," Makesh replied. "This appears to be in the water. And it approaches much too slowly."

Angel squinted in the direction Makesh was pointing, and, sure enough, she also saw something, just a speck, out in the water. "Could it be a ship? How can we flag it down? Should we swim for it?"

"Swim for it? It could be miles away from us," said Ben, finally able to see the distant speck himself.

"He's right," agreed Makesh. "We'll just have to wait and see." Then after a pause, "You don't think it could be the men in black, do you?"

"And what if it is?" Angel began. "As long as they're in a boat, I'll take my chances."

"And I," responded Makesh, "would rather take my chances here in the water."

As minutes turned to hours, the speck seemed no closer, and as the sun began to set on their first full day in the water, it was soon too dark to see it at all. They each eventually drifted off to sleep, gently nestled in the waterbed that went on forever, in every direction. They each had their own dreams of rescue, Makesh by friendly aliens come to save the Earth, Angel by the all male crew of a navy ship on maneuvers, and Ben by the only thing that could finally bring an end to his misery, death itself.

He dreamt he was no longer sick. The cancer, along with the rest of his body, had died. But his spirit was free, free of ills only the body could harbor, and free of the disappointments and failures only life could bring. He was in the clouds. He was walking toward the pearly gates. They would part as he reached them and he would enter heaven. At least that was the plan. But they didn't. Something was wrong. He bumped into the gates with his nose when they didn't open as he'd expected. He tried again. And again, he met resistance. He couldn't get through.

"Hey!" he shouted. "Anyone home?" He placed his face against the bars and peered inside. He thought he could see someone or something approaching. It was all white. "Hey!" he shouted again. "What's the deal? Look. I'm dead. Let me in."

The white figure approached, slowly taking shape. Soon Ben could make out that it was white because it was wearing a long white coat. A doctor's coat. And under that, white surgical scrubs. *God was a doctor?* wondered Ben. Then as the figure came closer, things went from strange to ominous. The doctor that came to the pearly gates wasn't just any doctor. It appeared that God was Ben's father.

"Dad? Is that you?"

"What's the matter?" his father replied. "You look surprised to see me here. Thought I would've gone the other way?" he asked, indicating a downward direction.

Ben began to stammer. "W… w… well, uh, I uh…"

"Hell? You thought I would've gone to hell?" his father asked again in disbelief. "Keep dreamin' Benjamin. No, not me. I'm not even dead yet. It's your dreams of becoming a surgeon that are dead. That's what I represent. I, on the other hand, am a respected surgeon. My life is a success. Hell is for failures. That sounds more like you. I guess that's why the gates won't let you in. You, my son, are a failure."

Ben was speechless for a moment, but then replied with indignation. "What do you mean, a failure? I didn't fail. I died. I would've been a surgeon. But I died. I got AIDS, no, I mean cancer. That wasn't my fault."

"AIDS. Cancer. Whatever. It's always something with you, isn't it Benjamin? Any excuse to take the easy way out."

"But that's not fair," Ben protested. "I didn't get a chance."

"Baloney. That's what they all say. You had your chance, Benjamin, and you blew it." Ben's father turned his back on him and started walking away. "Everyone wants a second chance."

"But I was sick!" Ben shouted, watching his father walk away. "I was sick!"

"You were sick?" his father replied, without turning around. "Should've called a doctor." And he was gone, white coat blending into the white clouds that were heaven.

Ben was alone again, clinging to the gates. But he wasn't alone for long. Almost instantly, another figure appeared out of the clouds, also clad in white, but not a coat. No. This one wore a bathing suit, a white one-piece bathing suit. It was the most beautiful woman Ben had ever seen. Wait. She looked familiar. Of course, it was Jill, Jill Sterling.

"Jill! What are you doing here? You're not dead," asked Ben through the bars of the gate.

"Of course I'm dead."

"But I just saw you. In Miami. The big house. The kids. You didn't remember me."

"Oh that," she answered with a giggle. "That was the real Jill Sterling. She's doing just fine. But that's not who I represent. I'm the Jill Sterling of your memory. The high school sweetheart you left behind, the one you thought you stood up at the prom."

"I don't understand. Why are you here?" asked Ben, confused.

"I told you. I'm dead. I died the day you decided those exams were more important than our relationship."

"But you didn't even know I stood you up. You were already going to the prom with Jim Wright, the quarterback. Remember? Shit, we didn't even *have* a relationship."

"True. But you didn't know that at the time. As far as you were concerned, you gave up the love of your life. That's who I represent. Love and romance. And you left me to die."

Ben felt a chill, standing stranded outside the gates of heaven. "So I can't get into heaven?"

Jill Sterling shook her head indignantly. "Heaven? Without love and romance? I should think not. Our competitor to the south, however, might have some room for the likes of you."

"Is love so important?" pleaded Ben.

Jill Sterling backed away from the gate, arms crossed. "You just don't get it, do you? You know, your creep of a father was right. You *are* a failure." With that she turned her back on him and walked away. Ben couldn't help but notice how beautiful her legs were as she walked off into the clouds beyond.

Ben felt a dull ache in his heart when she'd gone. He was about to give up and leave when yet another figure approached. "Oh, what now?" thought Ben, half expecting to see the ghost of Christmas future.

As it emerged from the mist, Ben could see it was a small person. No. A child. *Tiny Tim? Is that you?* he thought. No. It was a little girl. The little five-year-old girl from the hospital. The one whose mother was dying of cancer.

"Lucy? What are you doing here? Is your mother with you?"

The sad little girl came to the gate. Ben had to kneel to be at face level with her through the bars.

"No. It's just me," she answered. "Mommy's not here yet."

"But why you? You're not dead yet," asked Ben.

"You wouldn't understand," she answered.

"What do you mean, I wouldn't understand? You're only five. What could you know that I wouldn't understand?"

"Compassion," replied the little girl.

"Compassion?"

"That's right. The ability to identify with another's plight. To care."

"I don't get it."

"See. If you had just a drop of compassion, you'd know why I was here. I'm five years old. My father's dead. And my mother's dying right in front of me. I'll soon be an orphan. My body may still be down there. But that's all. My spirit's dead. That's me."

"Your spirit?"

"That's right. My spirit."

"You sound like you're blaming me," objected Ben. "What could I have done? The cancer was widely metastatic. I couldn't have saved your mother."

"Compassion. You could have shown some compassion. You could have taken more time to talk with me about it. Would that have been asking so much? Even a hug. That would have helped. You'd be surprised, the mileage a spirit can get out of a hug. But not you. Too messy, I suppose."

"I didn't know," said Ben apologetically.

"See. That's what I'm saying. No compassion. You claim to be a doctor. That's absurd. How can you be a doctor if you can't see pain?"

"But this isn't my fault," Ben protested. "I didn't give your mother cancer."

"I know," replied the five-year-old. "*I* did."

"You did?"

"I heard you say it. You said she would have been OK had she had the surgery to get all the cancer out instead of waiting until I was born. It was all my fault. I heard you say it."

"But I didn't mean—"

"It doesn't matter what you meant." She was growing angry. "I'm only five. You should have explained it better, in terms a five-year-old would understand. But not you. You've got the bedside manner of a mortician."

"You're right," admitted Ben. "I guess I screwed up."

"The committee was right. Your daddy said you failed as a doctor. Jill said you failed at love. They were all right. You're a failure. A failure as a human."

Ben knew when an interview was over. He slumped against the gait, defeated.

"And get your filthy hands off my gate, you asshole." With that, the little girl turned and skipped away into the marshmallow clouds of heaven.

"That's some mouth on that kid," muttered Ben. "What kind of place are they running up here?"

He didn't know what else to do. So he started banging on the gates. But they were like rubber, and his fists just bounced off. His frustration grew. So he pounded harder and harder, tortured still, even in his dreams.

Chapter 36

He thought maybe the storm had returned during the second night at sea. The pounding of the ocean woke him up. But when he opened his eyes, the ocean was still calm. It was morning. There was no storm. Yet, suddenly, there it was again, another pounding jolt. He turned with a start, and that's when he saw just what he'd dreamed for. It was Angel, Makesh, and Dr. Ben. And Dr. Ben, eyes still closed in sleep, was pounding Juan's rubber life raft with both hands like he was trying to break out of prison. Juan had found his friends after all.

During the storm, when Juan went below deck for the life raft he'd seen earlier in the day, he never imagined his friends would be gone by the time he returned. In fact, the whole boat was gone. Water flooded the cabin as the boat headed for the bottom of the ocean. Juan pushed his way through the cabin door, tugging the deflated raft behind him by a string. He was underwater, swimming for the surface, when the raft seemed to catch on something. Juan gave an extra hard yank, and to his surprise, the raft inflated and flew past him to the surface, dragging Juan with it.

The relative calm under the water was shattered by the storm raging at the surface as Juan emerged at the end of the raft's cord. Wind, waves, rain and lightning. It was everywhere. And his friends were nowhere. He was alone. He held fast to the raft's cord and eventually managed to get in. Juan was a good swimmer, but he thought the raft might come in useful later when he found his friends.

And now he'd found them, or they found him. Ben was pounding on the rubber raft. "Let me in! Let me in!" he shouted, still dreaming.

"OK. OK," said Juan, reaching down to yank Ben in by the seat of his pants.

Still half dreaming, Ben felt himself pulled over the pearly gates into heaven. Sure, it would have been nice to walk through the gates like everyone else. He never imagined having to go *over* the wall. But beggars couldn't be choosers. A win was a win, after all. He just wished God hadn't given him a wedgie in the process.

As he felt himself finally in God's embrace, he woke up to find Juan Martinez hugging him. "Juan, what are you doing here? Are you dead too?"

"Dead? Oh no, Doctor Ben. We are both alive." he replied with glee.

"We're alive?" asked Ben, sitting up to take in his surroundings. "Shit. I'm still alive," he confirmed in disappointment. Then seeing only water in every direction, "Alive and in the middle of nowhere. This is great. Just great."

"I know," agreed Juan, still grinning with the thought of finding his friends.

"We don't even have a paddle," noted Ben.

"Then this must be Shit Creek," announced Juan, proud of himself for determining their location. He didn't notice the dirty look from Ben as he reached over the side of the raft and pulled in Angel and Makesh, one with each hand.

They woke with a start, Makesh yanked from his place at the helm of an alien spaceship, Angel from an orgy aboard a navy ship.

"Juan!" they shouted in unison, hugging their savior. "You're alive!"

"Yes. We all are." answered Juan. "And we're up Shit Creek."

"You can say that again," Angel agreed, looking about.

"And we're up Shit Creek," repeated Juan.

"You can say that again," laughed Angel.

Another day at sea, and the Shit Creek joke had grown old. Everything had grown old. The endless ocean. The hot sun. All they'd had to eat in two days was one Slim Jim each, thanks again to Juan. Of course, that only made them thirst more for the drinking water they didn't have. They weren't completely alone, however. Over time, they'd seen some signs of ocean life. Some flying fish and even a few porpoises. But the thing that got their attention most was when Ben thought he saw a shark's dorsal fin a few feet away. They all came to attention when he pointed over the side of the raft and shouted, "Shark!"

They all huddled in fear at the opposite end of the flimsy rubber raft. All but Juan, of course, who leaned out to get a better look at the shark. When the fin finally cut through the surface of the water once more, Juan began to giggle. The others looked at each other, thinking it somewhat inappropriate, even for this crowd, for someone floating in the middle of the ocean in nothing but a rubber raft to be giggling about the presence of a shark.

"Juan," shouted Angel. "Come away from there. That's a shark." When Juan chuckled even harder, the others began to think maybe the sun and lack of water had taken its toll on Juan.

"She's just playing a joke on you. She's such a joker," said Juan with a smile.

"She?" asked Angel.

"Bessie," Juan replied.

"He's named the shark?" asked Ben to the others. "I knew you guys were a little off, but this—"

"Bessie's not a shark," protested Juan, dangling his last Slim Jim over the side of the raft to get the creatures attention. "She's just pretending. And she's fooled all of you," he added proudly.

"No!" shouted Makesh, lunging back toward Juan to snatch the Slim Jim from the water. "You'll attract it. Very dangerous."

"Don't be silly," said Juan, holding the Slim Jim from Makesh's reach. "Manatees aren't dangerous. They're vegetarians."

"Manatees?" asked Angel.

It all finally clicked in Ben's head. "Bessie, the Manatee?"

"That's right," confirmed Juan. "She followed us. I think she likes me."

And with that, the chubby sea cow poked its round head from the ocean, sniffed at the processed meat stick in Juan's outstretched hand, and politely rejected the offer with a gentle nudge of her nose back toward Juan. Makesh quickly confiscated the stick of shark bait and stuffed it in his pocket.

Angel stretched to get a closer look. "Oh, it is. It is a manatee. Look, Ben. She's so cute." Bessie then rolled onto her side, half submerged, with one flipper breaking the water's surface. "See. She *is* doing a shark impersonation." Angel then joined Juan in laughing at the ocean clown.

"You mean that creature came all the way down to Florida, and then out in the middle of the ocean, to end up here with us?" asked Ben incredulously.

"I told you," said Juan in reply. "She likes me."

"How do you know this one is Bessie?" asked Angel.

"Bessie," shouted Juan to the water. The pretend shark raised its head. "Come, Bessie. Come here." And, sure enough, the manatee swam to Juan, letting him pet her head. Juan turned back to the others with a big grin on his face. "See."

"Maybe she can go get us some help," remarked Ben. "Go on Lassie. Timmy's in trouble. Go get help."

The others actually looked to see what Bessie would do, but the big mammal just rolled slowly in the water, enjoying the feel of the warm sun on its belly.

"Humph," grunted Ben, turning away. "Man's best friend, huh?"

The brief episode of excitement over, they all lay back in the raft and returned their attention to the job at hand. Waiting. Waiting for land, rescue, or death, whichever came first. Angel made another round of applying sunscreen to everyone's backs. The bottle of lotion they'd found floating past the raft two days earlier represented the sole remains of the boat and their possessions. And with nothing else to do, Angel made sure no one would die sunburned. In fact, it was while applying lotion to Makesh's back, that she noticed the bruise behind his ear.

"Makesh, what's this?" she inquired, taking a closer look.

Makesh winced in pain when she touched it. He'd forgotten all about it. "Oh, something hit me in the back of the head during the storm."

"This is weird," said Angel, taking a closer look.

"What?" asked Makesh.

"It looks like whatever struck you, is still there, lodged partly under the skin. Ben, take a look at this."

Ben leaned over to take a look, and sure enough, he could make out a small metallic object half-embedded under the skin behind Makesh's ear.

"It's a piece of metal," he noted.

Then Makesh remembered. "Oh that. That's just the transmitter. Is it coming out?"

Ben couldn't believe it. "You mean there really is a transmitter in your head?" he said, taking a closer look, to validate the claim.

"Of course there is," replied Makesh, matter-of-factly. "Remember, you took my can opener away so that I couldn't remove it myself. Can you get it out now?"

It was really just barely hanging on anyway, so it didn't even hurt when Ben plucked it from behind Makesh's ear. It was a wonder it hadn't dislodged during the commotion of the storm. After studying it long enough to convince himself that it certainly could represent some sort of transmitter, Ben asked Makesh, "What should I do with it?"

"I will show you what to do with it," answered Makesh firmly. With that, he snatched the transmitter from Ben, stood up in the raft, and hurled it as far as he could out to sea. They all watched it plop into the ocean about a hundred feet away. "I only hope you men in black are already lying at the bottom waiting to catch your precious transmitter." Makesh flopped back down into the raft with relief, feeling as though a huge weight had been lifted off his shoulders. He was finally rid of that transmitter and the men in black. Even if he were to die at sea, at least he could do so peacefully, no longer a hunted man.

Of course, neither Makesh, nor any of the others could see what transpired ten feet under the water, one hundred feet off. They couldn't see the surprised look on Bessie's face, their manatee mascot, when she scooped up the shiny transmitter with her mouth, looking for a snack, and swallowed it whole.

Chapter 37

The next two days seemed more like two weeks. No food. No drinkable water. And without water, they would soon die.

For Ben, the thought of dying was nothing new. He'd already been counting his days since receiving his first fatal diagnosis. No matter the diagnosis had changed. It remained fatal, nevertheless. Between his now constant fever and sweats, dehydration had consumed him. He hadn't spoken in 24 hours, and was now more unconscious than conscious. He'd even stopped breathing from time to time for brief spells. Angel would notice whenever the familiar wheezing had stopped and would shake him until he started breathing again. It wouldn't be long now for Ben.

And it was a shame, thought Angel. Until the past week, you could hardly say he'd lived at all. What a waste. Sure, initially she toyed with him, made fun of him, made sure he was aware of the pathetic existence he'd led. But that was then. Over the last few days, he'd actually begun to grow on her. He'd saved the life of the diabetic man in the car accident. His Quixotic reunion with his high school girlfriend, or whatever she was. Even his bumbled attempt to save them all from Captain Blackman and the men in black. She'd begun to think there might be hope for the stuffed shirt after all. And now she'd never know. He was going to die right there in that raft.

Angel looked at his face. He seemed strangely at peace, even handsome. Peaceful, most likely because he was unconscious. But handsome? Snap out of it, she thought. She'd better get laid soon. She'd been off her medication for about a week. She was in heat. One of two things was going to happen. She was either going to run off with the first bull sperm whale she met (she didn't recall why they were called sperm whales, but it sounded like the appropriate solution to her problem), or she was going to start raping her fellow castaways. And that seemed too much like incest to be her first choice.

Juan dreamed of home, of Isla de los Locos. He dreamed of his grandmother, of the mango orchards, of his playmate Christina. He wondered when they would get there already. He was thirsty.

Makesh finally had the chance to calculate how many days left until Earth was to be destroyed by the aliens. Two. Two days left until the end of the Earth. Forty-eight hours. And here he was stranded in the middle of the ocean. He was helpless to stop it. Not that he had a clue yet how to do so. The deal was that he had to come up with a reason for the aliens to change their minds. What was unique to Earth that made it worth keeping? Unique in the eyes of the aliens anyway. Eyes, or eye. He didn't even remember how many eyes they had. No matter. He'd probably die at sea before the fireworks even began.

It was the morning of that next to last day on Earth when Juan, ever vigilant for signs of home, thought he saw something, just a speck really, off to the east. He was positive it was his island and would have had his belongings packed in no time if he'd had any. It wasn't for three more hours that they identified the speck as a small rowboat overflowing with people. It was heading west.

As they came within earshot, some of the passengers began shouting to them in Spanish. *"You're going the wrong way! Turn back!"*

"What are they saying," Makesh asked Juan.

"They are telling us to turn back."

"Turn back? Why?" asked Angel.

Juan conversed with them for a bit, then reported back to the others. "They are Cuban. They head for America." Juan turned back to them and explained that they were headed for Isla de los Locos.

The entire rowboat burst into laughter. *"Ah Locos,"* they nodded to each other in mutual understanding.

"Ask them for some water," suggested Angel.

"Please. Can you spare any water?" shouted Juan in Spanish.

The crew of the rowboat put their heads together to consider the request, only to turn back and shake their heads no. They themselves had a long trip ahead with nothing to spare for strangers, especially crazy ones.

Three more hours and they disappeared to the west. Over the next several hours, however, more Cuban refugees came and went. The first was a large raft made of wood. To imagine the desperation of people to head off across the ocean on a wooden raft. But there were others, soon practically an armada, representing all manner of floatation, a tribute to the ingenuity of people in desperation. There were large rubber inner tubes strapped together. The wooden raft began to seem rather seaworthy compared to the compressed Styrofoam egg cartons supporting a family of five. Two young men actually headed out to sea aboard a dozen basketballs. How the balls were bound to one another was unclear. But one thing was becoming very clear. Cuba could not be far off. It wasn't their first choice. But at this point, land was land.

The sun was beginning to set in the west when Angel thought she saw something again. Only this time it didn't appear to be more boat people. For a second, she even thought it might be land, but then, just as quickly, she convinced herself it was just the light playing tricks on the water. And as the sun finally dipped into the ocean once more, Angel nodded off with the rest of them, wondering if they'd make it through another night.

Angel's deep sleep was violently interrupted by blazing flashes of light. Flashes of light and deafening sounds! Not another hurricane, she thought in a moment of terror. As she tried to focus in the darkness, a blinding flash of light exploded in her face. She fell backward into the raft expecting the impact of an explosion. But there was none. No blast. No heat. No flame. No singed hair or burning flesh. Yet the blinding light persisted. Then the ear splitting sound again. Only this time, never more awake, she could recognize the sound. It was human. It was a man on a PA, hailing them, in Spanish.

"*Attention! Identify yourselves. You have entered Cuban waters without authorization. Identify yourselves.*"

"Juan! Juan!" shouted Angel. "What? What do they want?"

"They say we're in Cuba and we're not allowed to be here. They want to know who we are," he told her.

Apparently they'd been intercepted by a hundred plus foot Cuban military cruiser prowling the waters just off the shore of Cuba, a foreboding, nearly black mountain of steel armed to the teeth with all manner of firepower. The little yellow raft was dwarfed by the ship's shadow.

"Tell them we're sorry, but we're from America and our boat sank."

"*We're very sorry, sir, but our boat sank on our way from America,*" announced Juan into the blinding spotlight.

The ship's reaction wasn't quite what Angel had hoped for and something made her sense she'd made a poor choice of words. Perhaps it was the automatic gunfire that tipped her off. Warning shots.

"They're shooting machine guns at a rubber life raft," Angel shouted to Makesh.

"Maybe they don't like Americans," offered Makesh.

"*Does America come to invade Cuba?*" came the booming PA, followed by another round of gunfire into the water within a yard of the little raft.

"What? What?" Angel yelled to Juan.

"Makesh was right. He doesn't like Americans. He thinks we're invading Cuba," yelled Juan, frightened by the gunfire.

"Invading Cuba?" she asked, making sure she heard Juan correctly.

Then turning back toward the spotlight and standing defiantly, at least as defiantly as one can stand in the wobbly bottom of a small rubber raft at sea, she shouted angrily back into the night, fist raised, "In a rubber raft? Invading Cuba in a rubber raft? Look at us! You're right! It's the Bay of Pigs all over again! What are you a bunch of morons?" Then, giving them both middle fingers, "Fucking assholes!"

The PA spoke again, this time more subdued, less threatening. *"Make her stop. She sounds like my wife."*

Juan translated without prodding from Angel. "He wants you to stop. I think you're scaring him."

Then turning toward the light again, Juan responded on his own, from his heart. "Please, sir, I'm from Isla de los Locos! I want to go home!"

There was a pause, followed by hushed mumbling of debate barely overheard through the amplified PA. Angel, still standing, hands on her hips, was out of patience.

"Hey! Assholes! You gonna rescue us or kill us? Make up your minds."

Her outburst brought an end to the debate aboard the Cuban gunboat.

"OK. OK. We didn't know you were locos. We can take you home. Besides, the angry lady has nice melons."

Angel turned to Juan for translation. Juan was smiling ear to ear. "What?" she demanded.

Juan embraced Angel in a bear hug and lifted her in the air. "He's agreed to take us to my island."

Angel was smiling now too. "He said that? You're sure?"

"Well, he said some other things too."

"What? What else did he say?" laughed Angel.

Juan couldn't stop smiling. "Well, if you must know, he thinks you're crazy. But he likes your… uh… cassavas."

"My cassavas?"

"Your cassavas… uh… you know… melons."

"Oh, I see," nodded Angel, a wicked grin coming to her face. "Never fails."

An excited Juan put Angel down and turned to Makesh. "Makesh, did you hear? I'm going home."

Makesh smiled for Juan, from the bottom of his heart. No matter that the Earth would be destroyed by midnight the next day. For that was tomorrow. And today was today. Juan's day. He couldn't help but feel Juan's joy at going home. "Congratulations, my friend."

"Dr. Ben! Dr. Ben!" shouted Juan. "Did you hear? I'm finally going home to my Mama." He whirled about to see Ben's response, only to stop and stare, the smile fading from his face. "Dr. Ben?"

Ben Walker still lie at the bottom of the raft, pale and motionless. Even through all the commotion, the lights, and the gunfire. In fact no one had seen him move since they all drifted off to sleep earlier in the evening.

Makesh crawled over to Ben and shouted, "Dr. Walker. Wake up." But nothing from Ben. "Dr. Walker." Makesh was now shaking Ben by the shoulders, to no avail. He stopped and looked up at Angel.

Afraid of what she might learn, Angel was hesitant to come closer.

"Angel. Please," pleaded Juan.

Angel knelt down beside Ben and touched his cheek. His skin was cold. She put her ear to his mouth and placed one hand on his belly. She couldn't detect any breathing. She looked up at the others, saw their expectant stares, and then slowly put her ear to his chest. She shut her eyes in concentration. Nothing. The only heartbeat she could make out was her own, pounding between her ears. They were too late. He'd been in no condition to survive an ordeal such as they'd just been through. Come to think of it, he'd been ill equipped to handle life in general. It was almost as if he'd never actually lived at all. Oh, he'd gone through the motions, alright. But he'd never really felt the pain of his patients, and never experienced true love. Angel had taken on quite a project the day she met Benjamin Walker, medical student. She'd had high hopes for him, hopes for better things, for tasting all of life's diverse flavors. Joy, despair, compassion, desire. Things Benjamin Walker had never experienced. She'd have succeeded, too, sooner or later. It was just a matter of time. But time was in short supply for Ben Walker. And now it was gone. Tears welled up in her eyes as she sat back against the raft in defeat. Juan and Makesh soon matched her tear for tear.

The gunboat's spotlight was extinguished as Cuban sailors reached the raft in their own motorized dinghy.

Chapter 38

It was just as Juan had remembered, just as he'd dreamed each night since he was unexpectedly packed off for New York. Isla de los Locos. Paradise. Home. From the white sandy beaches and aqua surf to the majestic palms waving a warm welcome in the tropical breeze. He'd never learned his way around the island of Manhattan, but as soon as he stepped off the Cuban gunboat at the Locos marina, Juan knew exactly how to get home.

Rejuvenated by the food and water kindly provided by his Cuban saviors, he set off, almost skipping with joy, down the path toward his grandmother's hut. He could smell the sweetness of the ripening mangos as he passed through the orchards where he'd played hide and seek, years before, with his friend, Christina. He practically floated past the neighbors' huts in a state of euphoria.

They stopped and stared when they spied the tall, familiar young man, striding past their homes as if he knew where he was going, as if he were on a mission. And so he was. He was going home. Home to Mama, the woman that had raised him as her own when his mother had abandoned him as a young child. He couldn't help but break into a run the final half a mile.

By then, the word had spread. Young Juan was back. He'd come home, something they'd never before seen. Very few, in fact, ever left Isla de los Locos. But those that did, certainly never came back. Yet there was no mistaking it. Juan Martinez had returned. He ran up the path to the family hut, out of breath, bursting with excitement.

Nothing had changed. A simple thatched hut, yet always impeccably maintained. Mama always took pride in keeping a clean and orderly hut. He wasn't through the door yet when he began calling out.

"Mama! I'm home!"

No reply. He searched the entire hut, both rooms. No Mama. Something was wrong. Everything looked unchanged, yet something was different. Then Juan figured out what it was. The smell, or more exactly, the lack of smell. Where was the Mama cooking smell? Where was the comforting aroma of a freshly prepared meal, ever ready for family or visitor alike? Something was very wrong.

By that time, a small crowd of neighbors had gathered before the hut. As Juan emerged, still calling for his grandmother, he met their somber stares. Juan was happy to see the familiar faces, yet he read their sorrow.

"What is it?" he called out. "Where is Mama?"

They looked at one another, each hoping the other would be brave enough to relay the news, the bad news. Finally, the eldest among them stepped forward, an old woman, old enough such that life was too short to mince words.

"She's dead." Simple. Direct.

Juan's knees felt weak. First Dr. Ben. Now this. "What do you mean, dead?"

"Dead. What's not to understand?"

"But how? Why?"

"She was an old woman. And when they took you from her, she had no reason to go on."

Juan's legs gave out. He sat upon the sand, hugged his knees to his chest, and unconsciously began rocking. He was alone. He'd dreamed of this day, of returning to his beloved island, to his home. He'd escaped the hospital and a possible death sentence, traveled all this way, survived a hurricane at sea, only to find his home was gone. Without Mama, this was no home. He was too late. He lowered his head to his knees and began to weep.

There was a murmur among the crowd of neighbors as one of their own, just arrived, came forward and sat down next to Juan. It was a young woman. A very beautiful young woman. She put her arm about Juan's shoulders to comfort him. He looked up at her and was mesmerized by her beauty. Bright green eyes framed by long dark hair. She smiled at him, a perfect smile, and he thought he'd gone to heaven. And then she spoke, the voice of a goddess.

"Juan. It's me."

Even if he could get his mouth to function in her presence, Juan didn't know what to say. "I… uh…"

The vision giggled. "It's me, silly. Christina."

Juan sat with his head cocked to one side like a confused Irish Setter. He recalled a childhood friend named Christina, but she was just a little girl when… His eyes opened wide. "Christina? Is that you?"

"Of course it's me," she laughed, wrapping her arms around Juan in a warm, soft hug. So much for Mama, as he felt Christina's breasts press against his chest. "I missed you so much. I can't believe you're back," she added.

Juan had grown quite attached during their short embrace and Christina had to pry him off as the other neighbors approached in turn to offer their own words of welcome. But when she noticed the effect she'd had on the front of Juan's trousers, she pulled him close again and whispered in his ear, "I've learned some new games to teach you. We can play them later."

Yes, life on the island looked promising for Juan.

And that was just the beginning. As the neighbors each greeted him in turn, they wanted to know all about America and New York. Did they really have indoor plumbing? Was the air really so dirty that they needed these things called skyscrapers? After all, none of them had ever even left Isla de los Locos. Juan, on the other hand, had become well-traveled. He'd learned English. He'd seen the world.

The neighbors began to talk among themselves. "He'd always been such a bright boy."

"I knew he'd be somebody one day. Hey, maybe he could be our head of tourism."

"Head of tourism for one so bright? I think not. President. We should elect him our new President."

"But *I'm* the President."

"And *you* are an idiot. I say we vote."

And sure enough, within the hour, the votes were counted (it was a small island) and the vote was unanimous. Juan Martinez had become President of Isla de los Locos.

At the inauguration later that day, Christina herself crowned Juan with the ceremonial wreath of mangos, a traditional offering, stemming from the island legend of Muchas Frutas, God of Fruits, to those returning to Isla de los Locos after a prolonged absence. Yes. Life on the island looked promising for Juan.

But Juan wasn't quite ready to celebrate. He hadn't seen his friends from America since disembarking from the Cuban gunboat. He was beginning to worry about them. After all, they'd taken such good care of him back in America and risked their lives to get him home, not to mention Ben Walker's sacrifice. He felt an obligation to return the favor. And even at his inaugural celebration, Juan was distracted by concern for his friends. He didn't know why, but every fiber in his body screamed out to him that something was dreadfully wrong. President Martinez had to find his friends.

Chapter 39

Like a tourist receiving a Hawaiian lei, Makesh Guptah had also been bestowed with a ceremonial wreath of mangos. Makesh, however, did not have the luxury of time to play tourist. He'd escaped the Psychiatric Institute, fled across the country, ditched the men in black, survived a hurricane, and brought Juan safely home. But that was all just a preamble to what was now to come. Tomorrow, aliens would destroy the Earth and everyone on it. Makesh Guptah was on a mission. Makesh Guptah had to save the world.

But how? Where to begin? He needed to think. There were too many disturbances in town. What between the natives unending questions concerning life outside the island to the village idiots singing in the town square, it was impossible to concentrate. He'd never be able to save the world under such conditions. He needed to be alone with his thoughts. He needed seclusion, a quiet place in which to ponder the future of mankind.

Makesh was directed to a beautiful place just outside of town. It was a lush tropical landscape boasting a narrow hundred-foot waterfall gently cascading into a small, but deep, body of water surrounded by thick green foliage and vibrant flowering orchids. It was a holy place, the very place where Muchas Frutas first descended to the island from the heavens above.

If anything were to inspire one to save the Earth, this place was it. Makesh was smitten by its unspoiled beauty, a virtual Garden of Eden. He sat upon a moss-covered boulder, gazing out across the small pool of water to the waterfall beyond. What was he to do? What could convince the aliens to spare Earth and all its inhabitants? What treasure unique to the third planet from the sun could turn their heads and make them say hey, this is better than fast food?

The whole idea was so surreal, Makesh began to wonder if it was all a dream. Any moment now, he would wake up in his familiar work cubicle at the Lawrence Livermore laboratories, refreshed from his little daydream, better prepared to resume his work at designing nuclear warheads. *Please, somebody pinch me*, he thought. On the other hand, maybe it wasn't a dream after all. Maybe he was just crazy, as everyone presumed. Maybe he really had gone nuts. But what about the transmitter? No one believed him about that either. Yet there it was. They all saw it back on the raft. Didn't that count for something? Probably not. They might believe the FBI were after him. After all, that's what happens when you steal plutonium. It's to be expected. But aliens? Little green men? That was another story.

No matter. This was no poker game for Makesh to guess whether his brain was bluffing or not. The stakes were too high. Time was running out and he didn't even hold a pair of deuces. He had nothing, not a clue as to what these aliens might want. What could possibly change their minds, make them see Earth as something of value, not just a pebble to be cleared from the roadway?

Makesh sat on his perch through the night, racking his brain for the solution. He saw the sun set. The birds ceased chirping and the crickets began. The stars came out, and Makesh looked beseechingly out upon them as if some constellation might spell out the answer. But no such sign came.

And sooner than he imagined possible, as if by time-lapse photography, the sun began to rise. Despite whatever was responsible for the sudden storm at sea Makesh had prayed for, he didn't believe in God, certainly not since his young daughter was taken from him. And yet, here he was, back to the wall, about to pray for the second time in a matter of days. Were it just for himself, he would have passed on the idea. But this was different. This wasn't about Makesh Guptah. This was for all mankind. It was the final seconds of the game, no timeouts remaining. And in a clutch situation such as this, you don't leave God sitting the bench. It was time to put the big guy in the game. So Makesh prayed. He got on his knees, put his hands together, closed his eyes, and prayed.

His eyes were still closed in prayer when he first heard his name.

"Makesh," a voice called.

Thinking he was alone, Makesh opened his eyes in surprise. But there was no one there. He thought it must be his imagination, the stress and all. So he closed his eyes once more to continue beseeching the Lord's intervention, only to be interrupted once more.

"Makesh Guptah," called the voice a second time.

Makesh opened his eyes and jumped to his feet. "Who's there?" he shouted, trying to hide the fear in his voice.

"It is I," came the voice in reply.

Makesh frantically whirled in every direction straining to localize the source of the voice that tormented him. It wasn't a particularly threatening voice. In fact, it was rather meek. "Where are you?" Makesh shouted. "Show yourself."

"I'm over here."

Makesh strained his eyes, examining the dense tropical surroundings for signs of life. Unfortunately, life seemed to be everywhere. Makesh's attention was caught by innumerable birds flitting about the trees. He saw the motion of fish, all sizes and colors, darting through the body of water between himself and the waterfall. He even saw a small white rabbit peering at him, a mere three yards from the boulder where he knelt.

"I don't see you," complained Makesh.

"You're looking right at me," insisted the voice.

His eyes were drawn back to the vicinity of the rabbit. That was odd. He didn't think he'd ever seen a rabbit in the tropics before. Maybe it was someone's escaped pet, he thought, as he was about to turn away and resume his search for the mysterious presence.

"That's right. Down here."

Makesh did a double take. He could have sworn he'd seen the rabbit's lips move. No, not like it was chewing a carrot, but like it was mouthing the words. "No," was all Makesh could say, in disbelief.

"Why not?" said the little white rabbit, sitting up and placing its front paws on its hips in indignation.

Makesh froze. Could it be, thought Makesh? Could this rabbit truly be the answer to his prayers? God, himself? Trembling in anticipation, Makesh dared call out, "Is that really you?"

The squeaky little voice replied, "It is."

Makesh felt a weight lifted from his shoulders. The cavalry, be it in the form of a little white bunny, had arrived. In a flood of words, Makesh began rambling to God about all that had transpired and how now he needed his help to save the world.

"Makesh," came the little voice again, "why do you tell me this?"

At first Makesh was confused, but then understood the meaning of the question. "Oh, I'm sorry," he offered apologetically. "That's right. I'm sure you already know all about it. I didn't mean to imply—"

"Of course I know all about it," interrupted the voice. "But why do you think I would want to save the Earth?"

The question caught Makesh off guard. "Why wouldn't God want to save the Earth? What do you mean, o' Lord?"

"I mean, what's so great about Earth? And who's God, and this o' Lord guy?"

Makesh's relief at hearing God answer his prayers was rapidly fading. Something was wrong. This wasn't going as he'd imagined it would. Then a shocking thought occurred to him. "You're not God, are you?" he asked, at the same time wishing he hadn't, for fear of the answer he might receive.

"You must have the wrong number," the rabbit replied. Then, grabbing his own hide, and stretching it out to either side, "No God in here."

Makesh felt his heart fall. His exuberance at hearing the voice of the Messiah quickly turned to despair, as reality, at least as Makesh knew it, set in. "You're them, aren't you? The aliens?"

"Bingo," the rabbit replied, pointing both paws at Makesh.

Makesh stared at the smart aleck in disbelief, and then, with a frown, "You look ridiculous, you know. Why a rabbit?"

"We don't like to cause a commotion when we reveal ourselves. Bad form, you know. I thought a meek little bunny rabbit was a damn good idea. Imagine the ruckus if I'd shown up as some giant slithery reptilian?"

"I'm sorry," offered Makesh, seeing his point. "It's just, well, you look so silly in those floppy ears."

"Oh, these?" said the alien, flipping the large pair of ears out of his eyes. "Yeah, well, they're necessary to hide the antennae. Besides, you shouldn't talk about silly with your one-sided Mohawk hairdo."

Makesh lowered his eyes in despair as he sat down again on the boulder.

"What's wrong?" asked the extraterrestrial rabbit, hopping up to Makesh. "You look disappointed to see me."

Makesh looked down at the furry visitor. "Oh, it's just, well, I was expecting someone else."

"It has been three months hasn't it? Who were you expecting? Our competitors?"

"You have competitors?"

"Of course. This is prime real estate. Any number of alien races would give their right antennae for this spot. But we found it first. Early bird gets the worm, you know."

"Well, you weren't exactly first," noted Makesh. "But if this is such prime real estate, why are you destroying it?"

"Oh, my naive friend. I told you before. Location. Location. Location. It's not the planet itself. It's the location. This place wouldn't even qualify as a fixer upper. Good money after bad. Teardown if ever I saw one," added the rabbit, looking about. Then, scratching behind his ear with his hind leg, "You know you've got bugs here?"

Makesh placed his head in his hands in despair.

The rabbit hopped up to him twitching its cute little nose and whiskers. "What's the matter?"

"What do you mean, what's the matter?" demanded Makesh. "You're about to destroy my planet? Something like that doesn't exactly happen every day, you know."

"Oh," acknowledged the rabbit sympathetically. Then almost as an after thought, "Well, I did give you an escape clause. Remember? All you had to do was give me a reason, one good reason to keep this flea-infested ball of mud, and the deal's off."

Makesh knew he had nothing to offer, but with nothing to lose, he straightened up and decided to throw out a few ideas. He looked about at the beautiful tropical garden and pointed for the benefit of the judge, "Look at this place. Look how beautiful it is." The rabbit looked about. "Isn't this worth saving?"

After a quick survey of the area, the rabbit turned back to Makesh. "Frankly, I find it a bit primitive. A little claustrophobic too. The open look is in now, you know."

Makesh persisted. "We've got open too. There's the Grand Canyon. The Sahara Desert."

"No. No. I meant the whole place," the rabbit countered. "The total square footage. A planet so small just doesn't give you much to work with. No. It really wouldn't do at all."

Strike one for Makesh. But he wasn't ready to give up yet. "But Earth is unique to this solar system. It's teaming with life. What about all the plants and animals?"

"In a word," the rabbit replied, "allergies. That's a world of pollen and dander you're talking about. Not to mention the dust mites."

"What about the people? All the children? Are you allergic to them too?"

The rabbit crossed his arms and threw Makesh a frown. "No. We're not allergic to children. Don't be ridiculous. Guilt, however, is a distinctly human trait, wasted on me and my race. Nice try, though."

Makesh's mind raced for something else. Another uniquely earthly trait that might dissuade the alien from his planned course of action, annihilation. Anything. Maybe he could just stay there, guess after guess, forever. Were there no time limits?

But then, as if reading his mind, the rabbit spoke. "We really don't have all day, you know. This isn't some governmental project that can be dragged out infinitum. We must keep on schedule," he added, tapping his wrist as if he wore a watch. "Demolition must commence today."

One more possibility occurred to Makesh, almost as if he'd intentionally saved the best for last. This would, however, apparently be his last shot. The future of all mankind would hang in the balance. If this couldn't save the world, nothing could. Makesh steadied himself to deliver his final solution, Earth's last chance. And then, with a tone of finality, Makesh spoke.

"Love."

At first the rabbit didn't react, almost as if he hadn't heard Makesh.

"Excuse me," he said.

Makesh repeated the word. "Love."

The rabbit looked perplexed. "Love?"

Praying the rabbit's confusion was a good thing, "You do know what love is, don't you?" asked Makesh.

"Love. We are all too familiar with this love of yours and all its trappings. The emptiness of unrequited love. The pain of love lost. Heartache and misery. Caused by a virus, you know. Infects the brain. It took our civilization forever to eradicate it. And now you threaten to reintroduce it. You're joking, right? Is that it? Is that all you've got?"

Makesh sighed. That was his last shot. He was out of ideas. Besides, he had the distinct impression that the rabbit was just humoring him with this escape clause and really had no intention of sparing Earth. And so Makesh hopped down from his perch on the boulder. As he did, one of Juan's Slim Jims fell from his pocket. Makesh scooped it up and approached the rabbit. "Slim Jim?" he offered.

"Oh, no thank you," replied the rabbit. "Processed meat by-products. Bad for the cholesterol, you know," he added, patting his belly.

The thought briefly occurred to Makesh that he might just step on the rabbit and crush its alien skull, but he knew that was futile. There were plenty more where that one came from. So instead, his mind made up, he tossed the Slim Jim back on the ground, shook the rabbit's paw, and starting walking toward the edge of the deep pool at the foot of the waterfall. Makesh didn't know how to swim. And this time, unlike when the boat went down in the hurricane, he had no life jacket.

Frankly, he still wasn't completely sure this whole thing wasn't just a delusion of some sort. Alien rabbits come to destroy Earth. It sounded more like an old B movie. Nevertheless, it didn't really matter anymore. If he was only crazy, he didn't want to continue living this way anyhow. And if the Earth really was to be destroyed, he certainly didn't want to stick around to see it happen. There was no way around it. It was definitely time to check out.

He began to walk into the natural pool, and the water had risen to his knees, when he stopped once more. He was still wearing the ceremonial wreath of mangos Juan's people had bestowed upon him, and it just didn't seem right to take it where he was going. So he removed the wreath, left the water again, and approached the rabbit, who remained sitting, silently, up the bank from the water, calmly observing Makesh.

Makesh laid the mangos on the ground near the rabbit and said, "Los Locos say a wreath of mangos shall be bestowed upon those returning to the Island after a prolonged absence." And with a sweeping bow to the rabbit as he backed toward the water's edge, "We welcome you on your long-awaited return to our home… albeit short lived."

The water was surprisingly soothing for one who entered it unable to swim. And as Makesh's feet soon parted with the bottom, necessitated by the depth of the water, his head went under and he calmly held his breath, soon to see his beloved daughter's face again.

As for the rabbit, it quietly hopped over to sniff at the Slim Jim left behind by Makesh. Its head shook in distaste and it proceeded to urinate on the objectionable material, then bury it with its powerful hind legs. It then moved on to the mangos. Again a sniff with its little nose. Only this time, a different reaction. The rabbit ventured a small bite of the ripe tropical fruit. Lifting its head up to chew, its ears immediately stood straight up. And as the sweet juice of the mango dripped from the corner of its mouth, one eyebrow unconsciously rose in wonderment.

Chapter 40

Shrunken heads. They were hanging all about the primitive thatched hut. The crisp sound of a rattle shaking and guttural chanting filled the air. The heads were soon blocked out of view by a larger head, this one, alive. It was the fierce war-painted face of a black native, framed in dreadlocks, complete with the mandatory chicken bone through the nose. It was a witch doctor. It spoke.

"Ah. You're awake. Welcome. You're just in time for dinner."

He'd dreamed about not being allowed through the gates of heaven, but Ben Walker had never imagined he'd go to hell. And yet there he was, about to be served for dinner to a tribe of head shrinking cannibals. He tried to move his arms, but they were apparently tied down.

"Wh... where am I?" he managed from his parched throat.

"You are back. Back from the dead," answered the witch doctor, looming over Ben with wild eyes.

Ben struggled against his restraints.

"Stop that. You'll pull out your IVs," the savage argued.

"IVs?" muttered Ben, looking down at his arms. "Who are you?"

The cannibal leaned over Ben again. "They call me Needles."

"Needles," repeated Ben, tugging once more at his restraints. "Not a common name. Why do they call you Needles?" he asked, wracking his brain for an answer that wouldn't compound his already mounting anxiety.

"Some would say that it comes from this," began the savage, producing a misshapen voodoo doll and waving it in Ben's face. He proceeded to pull a small needle from the doll's neck.

Ben felt perspiration beading on his forehead. "You said some. And others? What would others say?"

"Others would say it comes from this." The wild man held a small syringe and needle under Ben's nose.

Ben preferred the voodoo doll.

"It is the children. A little nickname they've come up with. They hate getting their vaccinations. But we are both doctors, you and I. We know how necessary they are."

Ben grew more and more confused. "You're a real doctor?"

"Columbia College of Physicians & Surgeons. Class of '60. That's your school as well, so I've been told. In fact, I knew your father. Small world, hmm?"

"Wait. You graduated from Columbia medical school?"

"Not only that. I practiced internal medicine in Manhattan for 20 years."

"Then why are you here?"

"Oh, this is much more fun. I was burnt out, fed up with the rat race, you know. So I took a cruise to unwind. As fate would have it, the ship had to make an emergency stop here for some repairs. Needless to say, like everything else on Isla de los Locos, the repairs took a little longer than expected. So I got to know the place. To know Locos is to love Locos. I never got back on that ship. That was five years ago. I've lived here happily ever after."

"And the witch doctor getup?"

"As they say, when in Rome…"

Ben didn't know what to ask first. Did this witch doctor actually graduate from Columbia medical school? What was Ben's father like back then? Who did the voodoo doll represent? But all that could come later. First things first.

"I'm not dead?"

"Dead?" replied the witch doctor. "Almost. But no Cuban cigar, I'm afraid. You were so dehydrated, even the medic aboard the Cuban gunboat couldn't detect a pulse. Your lungs were in such bad shape, they couldn't find breath sounds even with a stethoscope. But they did hear a heartbeat. Your friends were already off the ship by the time the crew discovered you'd somehow survived your voyage."

Ben seemed disappointed by the news. He was like the monster in all those cheesy horror movies. Just when you were sure it was finally dead, it kept popping up again and again. Ben began to wonder what it would take to put him out of his misery. A silver bullet or a golden stake through the heart perhaps. Ben closed his weary eyes.

"Just leave me alone. Let me die."

"Let you die? Oh no. That would be in violation of my Hippocratic oath."

"But there's no magic potion to cure what I have. The Hippocratic oath doesn't call for you to needlessly prolong suffering. I'm terminal. But I guess you didn't know that."

"No, I didn't know that. I didn't know that because it's not true."

"What's that supposed to mean?"

"I checked your records at Presbyterian. I know all about the lab mix-up and your HIV scare."

"Well, for your information, Sherlock, I'm not dying of AIDS. I've got cancer."

"Ah, so that's your diagnosis, is it, Dr. Watson?" chuckled the island doctor.

"Widely metastatic. Both lungs involved. I saw the chest x-ray myself. Classic case," added Ben.

"Well, Presbyterian directed me to a Dr. Foo in Miami. We discussed your films. You were right about one thing. It is, indeed, a classic case."

"I told you so," replied Ben, triumphantly.

"Classic, yes. Cancer, no."

"What?"

"It takes a medical student to bump into a horse and see a zebra."

"What are you saying?"

"Why must the students always presume a rare diagnosis when confronted with a common one?"

Ben was confused. "Go on."

The medicine man resumed teaching rounds. "You're what, 23 years old?"

Ben nodded.

"Cancer is pretty rare in 23-year-olds, is it not?"

"Well yeah, but—"

"OK, you're right. Twenty-three-year-olds can rarely get cancer. Have you, Dr. Walker, been previously diagnosed with cancer?"

"Well no, but—"

"Wouldn't you expect someone to present with an initial primary tumor before it metastasized?"

"Usually, I guess."

"So, in summary, you're a perfectly healthy 23-year-old, an unlikely candidate for cancer to begin with. You've never had an initial diagnosis of cancer. And yet, when confronted with an admittedly highly abnormal x-ray, you presume you have metastatic cancer. Like I said, young Dr. Walker, you live on a farm, yet you see zebras."

"But the x-ray," protested Ben, not ready to give in. "What about the x-ray?"

"Well, let's see. We've already discussed the zebra. How about the horse?"

"OK, Dr. Needles, tell me about the horse." Ben was growing impatient with this game.

"You work at an inner city hospital, correct?"

"I'll say," agreed Ben.

"You deal with all sorts of immigrants who bring with them diseases common to their countries of origin. These diseases are commonly infectious ones. Right?"

"OK."

"You deal with another population common to inner city hospitals."

"Which population is that?" asked Ben.

Needles chuckled. "Why, the very population you thought you'd joined. AIDS. Immunocomprimised AIDS patients."

"So?"

"So what do you get when you mix third world infectious diseases with immunocomprimised AIDS patients?"

"AIDS patients with third world infections? What's all this got to do with me?"

"You're a medical student," pointed out the elder physician, leading Ben by the nose. "What do you get when you mix medical students with AIDS patients carrying third world acquired respiratory infections?"

"I don't know. But it's giving me a headache?" Ben still didn't get it.

"You weren't at the top of your class, were you?" the frustrated Needles inquired. "Tuberculosis! You get medical students with tuberculosis! Completely curable with the proper medication, I might add."

Ben narrowed his eyes in disbelief. "TB? You think I have TB?"

"I know you do. According to Dr. Foo, your chest x-ray was, as you said, classic. But not for cancer. For TB. Ain't no striped horses on the farm."

Ben was silent. It was a lot to absorb.

Needles broke the silence. "Yes, I'm afraid you'll live. And now for your cure." He turned, went across the room, and came back carrying a couple of pills and a glass of water.

"That's it, huh?" Ben began. "The magic cure?"

"That's right. You put de lime in de coconut, you drink it all up," sang Needles in his best Jamaican accent, holding the medication out for Ben.

Ben looked away.

"You seem disappointed." The older man sat down next to Ben. "You know these pills will cure tuberculosis. That's usually a disease of the lungs. You, on the other hand, appear to be suffering from an additional malady, one for which there are no pills. What's wrong?"

Ben looked at the man and sighed. "You know, dying was easy. All the pressure was off. It was actually the time of my life, in a pitiful sort of way. But now, you tell me I'm going to live after all. Living is much harder. Now what do I do?"

"It is no different, Benjamin. From what I hear of your adventures, this little detour from school did you some good. You keep doing what you've been doing. Continue to live as if you were dying, Ben Walker. You've found your heart. Now follow it."

"But where? Back to school? You've seen my skills as a diagnostician. I'm an idiot. I'll never be a good doctor."

Needles leaned forward in his chair. "Oh, I don't know about that. Nothing a little experience can't overcome. As long as you've got the heart. And from what my good friend President Martinez tells me, you're going to make a great doctor. He's an excellent judge of character. Perhaps when you complete your training, you might take over my practice here. I am getting on in years, you know."

Strangely enough, the idea was not exactly unappealing to Ben. But then, something Needles said caught his attention. "President Martinez?" asked Ben, getting up on one elbow.

"That's right. Juan Martinez, newly elected president of our humble island. It's a long story. But he's been camped out in the waiting room for two days now. Since he heard you were alive. He'd love to see you."

Ben had to smile. He hadn't had time to think of his friends. "Well, what are you waiting for? Bring him in."

When Juan entered the room and saw Ben, he couldn't contain his joy. He practically jumped onto the bed, attempting to pull his restrained friend into a bear hug.

"Easy. Easy," interrupted Ben's doctor.

"Oh. I'm sorry, Dr. Needles," Juan apologized. "I'm just so happy to see him. You look great, Dr. Ben."

After escaping Juan's grasp and catching his breath again, Ben returned the compliment. "You certainly seem fit, Juan. I guess we made it after all. So, Mr. President, where are the others?" asked

Ben, straining to look around Juan's bulk to see if Angel and Makesh were also outside the door.

Juan's smile quickly disappeared. "Well, that's partly why I've been sitting here waiting for you to wake up. Something's wrong."

Ben's smile also faded to a look of concern. "What do you mean, something's wrong?"

"They're gone."

"They're gone? How big is this island? Where could they be?"

Juan had to concentrate. "Well, Rocket said he only had one day left to think of a way to save the world, so he went to the waterfall to be alone and think. That was three days ago."

Ben had to chuckle, shaking his head. "Well I guess that means he must have saved the world then, didn't he?"

This seemed to cheer Juan a bit. "Hey, that's right, Dr. Ben." Then, almost as an afterthought, more serious again, "But there's water there. Rocket can't swim."

After an uncomfortable silence, "And Angel? What about Angel?" asked Ben.

"She was very sad when we all thought you were dead."

"And then…" added Ben, pulling the story from Juan.

"Well, then she went to play with the Cuban sailors. She liked a couple of them. But then they all wanted to play. They weren't being very nice to her though."

"She went to play with the sailors?" Same old Angel. Ben couldn't believe it. "Where is she?"

"I don't know," answered Juan.

Ben thought of where Angel would have gone with a bunch of sailors. Then he turned to Needles. "Any sleazy bars on this island paradise?"

"There's only one place on the island that fits that description," answered Needles.

"And what's it called?" asked Ben.

"The Sleazy Bar."

"Yeah. What's it called?" repeated Ben.

"But that *is* what it's called, at least by the locals. The Sleazy Bar. It's owned by islanders, but the clientele represent an unusual mix of Cuban and American sailors living a peaceful cold war coexistence between assignments. An international watering hole of sorts."

Feeling energized, Ben yanked his arms from their restraints and sat up. Then, pulling the IV from his arm, he hopped off the bed. "Let's go, Juan. Let's find Angel."

Juan had to catch Ben to keep him from collapsing. "Are you OK, Dr. Ben?"

"Whoa. Legs still a little rubbery I guess," admitted Ben. "I'll be alright." Ben headed for the door with Juan at his side, but then turned and came back to the bedside table where he threw the two pills he'd turned down earlier to the back of his throat and chased them down with the glass of water. Then with a wink and a nod to the witch doctor, he and Juan bolted from the room on a mission.

Chapter 41

The Cuban sailors had seen many things. They'd never seen anything like Angel McGovern. Two weeks off her medication, four days adrift in a life raft, and then Ben's death. Each by themselves would have been enough to send many people over the edge, but together the reaction was synergistic. Angel had lost her grip. She was in free fall.

At first glance, one could have thought it was just Angel being... well... Angel, taking her usual spot, center stage, half naked, amid a room full of horny young men. Only this was different. Those that knew her would not have been so easily fooled. Her makeup had crossed that fine line between sexy and gaudy, her hair looked as though it hadn't been brushed, or washed for that matter, in days, and her usually confident and graceful movements now appeared unsure and borderline clumsy. Seeing Angel now, those that knew her when would have seen a finely tuned high precision automobile rattling so badly it was about to throw a rod.

Most of the men watching her now, though, probably assumed she was just another drunken hooker. Even then, she remained unique. She'd become more than just something to look at. Her mania had added an element of audio to her performance repertoire. In pressured run-on sentences, she was reciting lines from Hamlet and King Lear. Even had they understood English, however, her Shakespearian diatribe would have been lost on this crowd. A PhD in literature really wasn't much of an asset for a stripper amid a sleazy bar full of drunken sailors.

Standing astride a pool table, Angel did the best she could to please the crowd. Many threw money at her feet, but this time it wasn't about money. This wasn't about anything. This was just crazy. During previous manic orgies, Angel would have had the sailors lined up around the pool table, each waiting their turn to get to know her better, stretched out over the cool felt covered slate. Not that that wasn't her plan. She'd accompanied a couple of cute ones to the bar with just that in mind. But as things began to spin out of control, what was in her mind and what actually happened became more and more divergent. Each time one of the sailors would make what they saw as an invited advance, Angel would uncontrollably dance out of reach, spewing lines of Shakespeare as she went. Oh, she wanted them. She wanted every one of them. She just couldn't stop moving. She couldn't stop talking. She couldn't stop.

That's when they started hitting her. First it was a slap to get her attention. But she was beyond paying attention. She'd begun to babble incoherently. Her rendition of Richard III would have been unintelligible even to the most experienced of British stage veterans. Then it was a shove to get her to lie down. She wanted to comply, but she couldn't stay down. She'd involuntarily bounce back up and they'd shove her down again. They were trying to remove her clothes, as was she, yet her perpetual motion only impeded any advances toward that goal. They'd managed to rip the top of her dress open, but things were going frustratingly slow for the impatient crowd. It wasn't long before they were beating her, as if they could win her cooperation through force. Blood from her busted lip.

That's when Ben and Juan burst in. They weren't prepared to find anything like what greeted them, Angel trying to stand atop a pool table, half naked and bleeding, speaking in tongues, while a dozen men took turns striking her. Juan was in shock. As big a man as he was, he remained a child at heart, frozen with fright.

Not exactly a longshoreman himself, Ben had to steady himself with a barstool as he felt his knees turn to jelly. As his eyes strayed from the pool table, he saw there was another dozen sailors at the bar. They were observing, but not participating in, the melee. They were Americans. The Sleazy Bar on Isla de los Locos was indeed a microcosm of the Cuban American cold war. Ben quickly turned to his idle countrymen and shouted over the music. "Aren't you going to do something?"

One American, apparently an officer, took another swig from his Budweiser long neck, and without turning to acknowledge Ben, calmly said, "Nope."

"Nope?" Ben shouted back.

"Nope," repeated the officer, turning toward Ben. "These are international waters and we have no jurisdiction on this island. We're under strict orders not to intervene in local skirmishes." He went back to his beer.

Ben couldn't believe his ears. "You would sit here and watch an incapacitated woman beaten and gang-raped right in front of your eyes?"

"Just looks like a messed up hooker in over her head to me. Came in asking for trouble," the officer responded. "Strictly a local affair."

Ben couldn't find the words. They had to do something. Then, in one last shot at diplomacy, "She's an American, you know."

A brief flash of concern passed over the officer's face, only to be swallowed by the upturned beer bottle once more. With the Budweiser back on the bar, he replied. "You think I would start an international crisis over some skanky whore? She shouldn't have come here. There's nothing I can do."

Ben was out of his mind. He could no longer sit idly by and watch Angel being hurt. All his life he'd stood on the sidelines, unwilling to dirty his hands. It was so easy watching the world go by from the other side of the glass. Getting involved always seemed so messy, whether it was caring for the sick, or simply going to the prom. But things were different now. Ben was different. Since the day he'd hit the road with his fellow escapees, he'd been thrown headfirst into the pool of life, and it certainly was messy. He'd saved lives, made friends, been thrown out of bars. Life was no antiseptic spa, he'd learned. It was sloppy with mud, and Ben had learned to wallow in it with the rest of the swine. Angel was the one that pulled him kicking and screaming toward the light. She held enough life in her for ten people. Now Ben saw Angel, that rare and magical creature, hunted down like a unicorn, pummeled until her blonde mane was bloodied.

The fierceness of Ben's attack surprised himself as much as anyone. For one recently unconscious, life dripping back into him through an IV, it was a sight to behold. Throwing himself at the angry mob ringing the pool table, he'd actually knocked three or four to the ground before they knew what hit them. Unfortunately for Ben, once they saw what hit them, they started hitting back. It was like something out of the World Wrestling Federation, replete with chokeholds and body slams, all directed at Ben. Even when healthy, Ben was no match for a dozen sailors.

From the wrong end of a full nelson, he beckoned for Juan to join in. Juan's massive size was impressive, but he stood his ground, frozen with fear. He was afraid for Angel. He was afraid for Ben. He was afraid he might hurt someone again.

Eventually the crowd tossed Ben aside, as a cat would a dead mouse with which it had grown tired of playing. Juan ran to help him up as the sailors went back to the favored live prey. Ben was cut and bruised himself now. He turned to Juan and implored him to help.

"Juan, you're a big guy. You've got to help. They're hurting Angel."

"I c… can't," Juan replied.

"But why?"

"Fighting is bad."

"Are you afraid you'll get hurt?"

"No."

"What is it then?"

"I'm afraid someone else might get hurt, and then I'll get into trouble again."

Ben grabbed Juan by the shoulders. "Juan, they're going to kill her if we don't do something. Don't let the nice guys finish last."

"But I—"

Ben knew there wasn't any time for debate. "Juan!" he shouted. "Grow up!"

Juan stared at Ben for a moment, then wiping a tear from his eye, he turned toward the carnage at the pool table. Angel's clothes were in shreds as the men held her down preparing to take things to a new low. Juan knew what they were doing. Ben was right. He had to be a grown-up. Even if that meant being not so nice.

Juan tentatively walked up to the out of control mob and tapped one man on the shoulder. The sailor was preoccupied and didn't notice. Juan tried again, but still no reply. He didn't know what else to do as he saw one of them crawl onto the pool table between Angel's legs. But when Angel managed to control her incoherent flailing just long enough to make eye contact with Juan and mouth his name, it all became clear.

A man on a mission, no longer the gentle giant, Juan began grabbing them, one at a time, by the collar and seat of the pants, and tossing them across the room. After the third one, he'd reached the table. He jumped up, ripped the perpetrator from his beloved Angel, spun around twice, then threw him as far as he could. The American sailors just managed to pull their beers to safety before the half-naked Cuban landed on top of the bar.

Juan's triumph, however, was short lived. With the element of surprise spent, the eight remaining sailors chopped Juan down at the legs and pulled him from the pool table. He was big. But even after Ben jumped back into the fray, they were badly outnumbered.

There were three los Locos locals employed at the Sleazy Bar. There was a bartender, a janitor, and a third man whose roll was unclear other than the fact that he could read. It was that man that recognized the big man on the bottom of the pile as Juan Martinez, newly elected president of Isla de los Locos. He turned and said as much to the bartender, who then called the janitor over and passed the word on.

In a matter of moments, the three locals jumped in with such patriotic fervor that the tables were soon turned once more and the fight began to swing back in the other direction. The fight had now escalated to fill most of the room.

Despite the ever-expanding boundaries of the brawl, the American sailors, to that point, had remained on the sidelines, true to their directive concerning rules of engagement. They even began wagering on the fight's outcome as the odds remained three to one in favor of the Cuban sailors. It was only a matter of time, however, until the action began to spill onto the bar in the form of broken bottles and flying bodies. And as they saw their beloved Sleazy Bar, the only source of alcohol between Florida and Portugal, being destroyed in front of their eyes, they knew the time had come to act.

The original combatants were already pretty much spent when the dozen American sailors joined the fray and quickly diffused the situation. The Cubans weren't looking for a fight to begin with, and by this point, frankly, they were so tired they'd lost interest in the crazy hooker. Ben, who'd already taken a few too many blows to the head, was now sleeping it off under the bar.

Juan, however, seemed untouched. As soon as he realized he no longer had five or six Cubans on his back, he ran over to check on Angel. Her still and bloodied body lay where they'd left it, on top of the pool table. She was no longer babbling, or making sounds of any kind, for that matter. She lay motionless, unnaturally sprawled atop the green felt. Juan was afraid to touch her at first, afraid she might fall apart, like a small child's favorite stuffed toy whose stitches could barely contain it after years of too many hugs. But he couldn't not touch her either, and he soon crawled onto the pool table with her, raising her head and shoulders to cradle her limp body in his arms, rocking back and forth.

Seeing the big man hugging the unconscious woman, the American officer, misinterpreting Juan's intentions, ordered him to put her down and get off the table.

"That'll be enough of that, now. Leave the whore alone."

"She's not a whore," Juan stated for the record as he got down from the pool table. He knew what a whore was.

"Well, whatever she is then. Let's have no more thoughts of rape and murder tonight."

Juan recognized those words too. "Rape and murder?" he said. "That's what they said I did back in America. I think that's why they were after me."

The officer looked at the big man suspiciously. "So you're wanted for rape and murder back in the States, huh?"

"I think so," nodded Juan in agreement.

"Why don't you come along with us then, big fella?" The officer, backed by five of his crew, then gently took Juan by the elbow and escorted him from the bar.

Ben, meanwhile, had regained consciousness and managed to crawl over to the pool table where he found Angel's seemingly lifeless body. As he looked down at what remained of his patient, his friend, he flashed back to all the patients for whom he'd lacked compassion, to the close friends he'd never had, to all the times he'd walked away. This time, though, something was different. He knew instinctively what he had to do. Dr. Benjamin Walker initiated CPR.

Chapter 42

Things were pretty much unchanged at New York's Presbyterian Hospital. Buck the Preacher continued his fight with Satan, as subterranean life forms continued to crawl from the soot-filled subway station. Yet another automobile stood ablaze in the no parking zone across from the ER. The hospital's familiar coat of construction scaffolding persisted. And while, on the surface, it might appear as if nothing ever changed beneath the intricate web of rusted scaffolding, one could also see the never-ending work in progress as a metaphor for life itself.

The player's roster at the Psychiatric Institute remained stable with only cosmetic changes. Erika Robinson, the gender confused young man known as the ward's den mother, was calling himself Erik this week and dressing as a man. He'd decided that dressed as a woman he was only attracting straight men and, as a result, his social life had suffered intolerably.

The recently-escaped Anastasia, long lost daughter of Russian Czar Nicholas II, had only managed to reach Des Moines when she was rounded up again and shipped back to the Institute. She'd found enough time, however, to trade her old fur coat for a modern winter parka. She'd replaced the down insulation with hundred-dollar bills, of course.

Dr. Brunning, returned from his brief but prestigious position as visiting professor of Neurosurgery, strutted about the ward announcing the commencement of morning rounds.

The chief resident, Dr. Gelner, was already relaying to the interns and students the sordid details surrounding the saga of Dr. Benjamin Walker. He took great pleasure in poking fun at Ben's diagnostic blunders. Only a Hah-vud graduate would believe he contracted HIV from a nun. And then there was the chest x-ray which the doctors from Miami were kind enough to send up north. It was permanently mounted in the Presbyterian radiology department as a classic example of Tuberculosis so that all the students and interns passing through the department might never mistake it for anything incurable.

It was to be Ben's first day back on rounds and he was already late, a fact well appreciated by Gelner, as Ben burst into the room out of breath.

"Ah, look who's decided to join us. It's our traveling Dr. Hah-vud, returned to civilization. Did you enjoy your vacation to Club Med Locos?"

Ben scrambled to take his seat, trying to minimize any disruption.

"Sorry I'm late. I was registering to volunteer at the AIDS clinic and they had a lot of questions about my Tuberculosis."

"Volunteer work with terminal patients? I see you've picked up some nasty habits along the road," chided Gelner. "And what *about* your Tuberculosis? Is it safe for you to be walking among the living? Shouldn't you be quarantined or something?"

"No need to worry," Ben assured him. "I've been taking my TB medication long enough that I'm no longer a threat to society. And as for the volunteer work, they said they're always looking for compassionate individuals with a sense of altruism. I gave them your name and number as well. I hope you don't mind."

"Touché," replied Gelner. Then, without missing a beat, "Remind me to change my number."

He then turned to the stack of patient charts at his side.

"Shall we get to work then? Let's see, now, Dr. Walker will be needing some new patients as his, shall we say, somewhat unorthodox method of case management and patient disposition have left his schedule wide open."

Ben had had some time off back in New York during his initial treatment for Tuberculosis to digest all that had occurred over the days prior, from his own personal growth to the loss of his dear newfound friends. It was only this small buffer of healing time that allowed him to ignore Gelner's remarks and keep from grabbing the pompous shit by the throat.

"Ah, here's one," Gelner resumed. "We don't even have her name yet, but she appears to be right up your alley. It's the story of a young lady who's taken many wrong turns along the road of life, turns that have alienated her from her parents, leaving many burned bridges in her path, bridges she hopes to mend. Unfortunately she suffers from a chemical imbalance of sorts. And that's where you come in Dr. Walker. I believe this young lady is not too dissimilar from one of your previous treatment failures."

Ben was barely holding it together.

"Oh, but Dr. Walker," added Gelner with a final twist of the knife, "if it wouldn't cramp your treatment style too much, let's at least try to keep this one in the country."

Ben grabbed the chart marked Jane Doe and left the room before doing something he might not terribly regret. He walked past the old familiar ward recreation room where a crowd of assorted characters sat gathered around the television set embroiled in debate over the relative strengths of various cartoon superheroes. He walked past the various treatment rooms, each a reminder of one of Ben's previous encounters with Makesh Guptah, Juan Martinez, and Angel McGovern.

He'd become rather choked up by the time he reached the room where he was to meet Jane Doe. It took all he had just to turn the knob and enter the small dimly lit room.

To Ben's surprise, the room was empty. Just as well, he thought. It would give him a few moments to collect himself, to be focused for the new patient. Ben was startled when his watch alarm started beeping. His pills. He'd forgotten to take his TB medication. He took two pills from the vial in his backpack but then realized he had no water. Leaving the two pills with his backpack on the small table holding a lamp, Ben stepped out briefly into the hallway to get a cup of water from the nursing station.

He quickly returned and, scooping the pills off the table where he'd left them, raised them to his mouth. At the last second, he stopped. Something was wrong. He looked down at his hand and saw *three* pills where there should have been only two. Had he taken an extra one out of the vial? No, the third one was a different color all together. He raised it to his eyes to get a better look. Lithium? How did that—?"

"I've had to take TB meds since you gave me CPR," came a voice from behind him. "It's only fair that you take some of my lithium pills."

"Angel!?" said Ben whirling about at the familiar voice. "Is it really you? You're OK?" he blurted out, grabbing her by the shoulders, touching her face. "I couldn't find out anything since they pulled me off of you back in los Locos. I didn't know if you were dead or alive." He pulled her to him and hugged her until he stopped shaking.

Angel had badly missed Ben as well. So Ben wasn't particularly surprised when she saw his hug and raised with a kiss. It was only when her tongue forced his lips apart reaching for the back of his throat while her hand groped his crotch that Ben pulled away. Staggering backward in surprise, Ben realized, "You're Jane Doe, aren't you?"

Angel stood in front of him, seductively sucking one finger, the other hand buried down the front of her jeans, and nodded. Ben had to smile. Just like old times. But was it?

"I understand you want to make up with your folks," he asked.

Angel nodded again.

Ben took the stray lithium pill from his hand and held it out to Angel. "Then you'll be needing this." Angel took the pill from his hand and swallowed it with some of Ben's water. He smiled at her, and taking her by the arm, walked out of the room. "I think that'll do for our first session. We need to let those pills kick in before we're going to get anywhere."

As they took a stroll down the hall, old friends reunited, Angel put her arm around Ben and grabbed a piece of his ass. There was no putting out her fire.

Ben was still playfully fending off Angel's advances when her ward mates Erik and Anastasia came running up to them shouting, "Hurry! They're on the news. You won't believe it."

"Who?" she and Ben asked in unison.

"Just hurry!"

They all hustled into the rec. room just in time to see one of their local newscasters thanking her producer for sending her to a tropical paradise just to follow up on a little fluff story she'd reported on months ago. She stood wrapped in a sarong at the end of a dock jutting out from a white sandy beach, tropical umbrella drink in one hand, microphone in the other.

"I'm reporting on location here from Isla de los Locos, a charming little island off the coast of Cuba, an assignment no New Yorker could pass up as the weather turns cold back home. Apparently you and I are not the only ones that feel that way. You may recall a recent visitor to the Big Apple I introduced you to a little while back."

The camera panned back to include a bulbous brown object bobbing in the water just off the dock.

"That's right, ladies and gentlemen. Bessie the Manatee is back in the news. It appears that Bessie has finally found a home here at Isla de los Locos. How do we know this particular manatee is our Bessie? Well the president of Isla de los Locos personally assures us it is. And here's some earlier footage of President Martinez making his point."

"Hey, that's Juan," came shouts from the psychiatric recreation room. "Yay, Juan. Look at him. President Juan." Juan was seen waving to the camera, calling Bessie by name and having her perform tricks for the camera like a trained porpoise.

Angel was smiling ear to ear, and Ben couldn't believe his eyes. He had assumed Juan had been brought back to the U.S. by the American sailors to face criminal charges of rape and murder.

The announcer continued. "You'll be happy to know that New York, and America in general, are not the only sources of corrupt politicians. The very same President Martinez you just saw playing with Bessie is apparently the same Juan Martinez wanted back in New York in connection with a notorious rape/murder case. Being the president of an island so strategically located for purposes of national security, however, he's been granted diplomatic immunity. This information comes directly from the island's newly appointed attorney general, Christina Carballo. Ms. Carballo, we're told, just happens to be the president's girlfriend."

Ben and Angel looked at each other, beaming with joy. Their Juan was going to be OK.

"As amazing as this all may sound," continued the announcer, "the story doesn't end there. That's right. There's more. President Martinez, through his attorney general, has just had two American FBI agents deported to the states where they face charges of jeopardizing an endangered species. You guessed it. Our Bessie." A grainy picture of two men dressed in black suits, hats, and sunglasses was briefly shown. "It seems the agents have been tracking Bessie for weeks with some crazy story about transmitters and missing plutonium. Yes, it just keeps getting better folks. This is Jamie Johnson, with our very own radioactive manatee, Bessie, signing out, from beautiful Isla de los Locos."

The crowd in the rec room cheered as Bessie waved goodbye to the camera with her flipper. They began to disperse with high fives all around as the news ended.

Ben and Angel were turning to leave as well when they saw the little five-year-old girl whose mother had been dying of cancer. She was giggling about the manatee as she stood with the little backpack holding her stuffed bear next to a striking young woman with an overnight bag. Ben and Angel's joy over Juan was short-lived as they approached the little girl.

Ben bent down on one knee and asked, "Where are you going, Lucy?"

"I'm going home," she sang with a smile.

Ben looked up at Angel with concern. Then looking back at the little girl. "You're going with this nice lady from the government? I'm sorry, Lucy. Did your mother… uh…?"

"This *is* my mother, silly," she giggled, saving Ben from having to say the word.

Ben looked at Angel again, confused. Then to the little girl again, "But that can't be your mother. Your mother was very sick, Lucy."

"No she's not, Dr. Walker. She's all better. See for yourself." Lucy looked up at the woman next to her smiling.

The woman reached out to shake hands with Ben. "It's a pleasure meeting you, Dr. Walker."

"And that's my friend, Angel," added Lucy cheerfully.

The smiling woman shook Angel's hand warmly. "My daughter's told me so much about you."

Ben was speechless. He just stood there, mouth gaping, staring at the very woman who stood at death's door only weeks before. Sure, Ben's illness was a case of self-inflicted misdiagnosis. But hers was not. Her cancer was biopsy proven, its metastatic spread documented, no longer responsive to chemotherapy. She was even listed as DNR. (Do Not Resuscitate). Not yet dead? Possible. Fully recovered? Impossible.

"But how could you…?"

Lucy's mom, the picture of health, responded. "I have no idea, Dr. Walker. I just know I woke up like this a couple of days ago, my old self again. They've just finished running all of their tests and I'm completely cured. It's a miracle, I know."

Then turning to her daughter, she bent down and picked her up. "But Lucy has her own ideas."

Angel couldn't resist. "What ideas? What do you think happened Lucy?"

All eyes were on Lucy as she placed the index and middle fingers of each hand on her temples, shook her head no with a frown, then yes with a smile. "Good as new," she chirped, bouncing with joy.

"Who taught you that, Lucy?" asked Angel.

"It was the little green men," she answered matter-of-factly.

Her mother politely smiled and shook her head in embarrassment. "I'm sorry. I told you she had her own ideas."

Then Lucy remembered something. "Oh, I almost forgot. They said to thank everyone for the mangos. They said they're much better than fast food."

The three grown-ups looked at each other mutually confused.

Then Ben knelt down by the little girl and spoke. "You know, Angel and I used to have a friend that talked about little green men all the time before he died."

Lucy was saddened to hear their friend had died. "How did he die?" she asked.

Ben answered. "Well, I guess he never took swimming lessons. And a couple of weeks ago he fell in some water and he drowned." Ben looked up at Angel who had started to cry. "So you'd better take swimming lessons so *you* don't drown like our friend, Rocket."

Lucy looked confused. "Rocket? I know Mr. Rocket."

"I forgot. That's right," nodded Ben, taking her hand. "You probably met him when he was a patient here."

"I did," she confirmed. Then, almost as an afterthought, "But Rocket isn't dead."

"What do you mean?" asked Ben.

Lucy smiled. "I just saw him the other night."

"The other night?" asked Angel, looking at Ben as she quickly knelt down next to Lucy.

"He was with the little green men. I was scared. But he told me they were friendly."

Angel began to smile and cry at the same time as she turned to hug Ben.

"He said they were friendly, huh?" asked Ben, not sure whether to believe or not.

"Yep," said Lucy, with a smile. "They're even letting him steer the ship."

ALSO BY DAVID ABIS

LAST GIRL STANDING

In this bittersweet ill-fated teenage romance, Audrey Spencer thought the world a safe place, until she's forced to move to a sketchy trailer park at the outskirts of a West Virginia coal town. There she befriends Zachary Ledbetter, simultaneously fascinating, dangerous, and anything but normal, that missing link between impetuous young boy and psychopath. Coming of age together while confronting obsession, rage, and survival, soon even the line between love and stalking becomes blurred, until things literally blow up at prom when shots are fired.

CALAMITY IN SWEETSPOT: A POLITICALLY UNCORRECT WHIRLWIND REDNECK ROMANCE

All they needed was a natural disaster and they'd all be living on easy street. As mayor of Sweet Spot, Mississippi, a pathetic collection of dilapidated shacks and underachievers situated smack-dab on the very buckle of the tornado belt, Buck Jones believes it's his civic duty on behalf of his little town of antigovernment moonshiners, gun-toting preppers, and born-again meth addicts, to score some of that sweet federal aid being thrown around so freely. Well, Buck Jones may be a man of vision, but the last thing he envisions is falling madly in lust with Jennifer Steele, that spitfire journalist from CNN who arrives when Buck's prayers are answered by a crew of naive Yankee reporters assigned to cover tornado victims in the rural South. Fireworks abound between the redneck flimflam man and the bleeding-heart city girl as the scheme to defraud the government threatens to blow up in their faces and the town's very existence is imperiled by a thoroughly peeved Mother Nature who finally sends Sweet Spot's chickens home to roost. In the end, it may be up to small town U.S.A. to save the day, but it's up to Buck to get the girl.

THOUGH I WALK THROUGH THE VALLEY

Her daddy was just a small-town preacher. But that was before. He ain't nothin' now... except dead. What truly happened between 19-year-old Jaime Jo Tremper, Tommy Harris, and her daddy would be the subject of conjecture for years to come. Yet secrets always trump gossip in a small town, and only those involved, and their maker, can ever really know the truth. Jaime Jo and Tommy have a history together, and the scars to bear for it, both mental and physical. No one ever expected to hear from Tommy again after being packed off to war. Yet two years later, resilient as a cockroach, the Special Forces psychopath comes home to the mountains of North Carolina to claim his girl. The overwhelmed local sheriff does his best to separate the two, but love can be a powerful thing, not everything is as it seems, and only Jaime Jo and Tommy know the truth. As a desperate young woman places her fate in the hands of her Lord, a vengeful Vietnam vet takes matters into his own, coming home to save his girl and finally end the nightmare that began the day Tommy Harris met Jaime Jo Tremper.

PURE CANE

Coming of age on a sugarcane plantation during the 1986 Philippine revolution, young Lisa Salonga, pampered niece of the wealthy Delgado family, lives only for hacienda socials amid the sweet scent of the cane harvest, that is until her idyllic childhood ends when she falls hard for a mere cane worker from the other side of the tracks who turns her carefree world upside down. Even though her relationship with Johnny appears doomed from the start by a class-conscious society, Lisa remains determined to unravel his mysterious past in America and the unspoken taboo surrounding his family ties to the plantation. Their fledgling romance only grows as Lisa and Johnny play pivotal roles in the church-led people's revolution overthrowing the corrupt Marcos regime, but soon, amid a growing communist insurgency, the lovers are caught in the crossfire and Lisa begins to wonder which side her Johnny is really on. It's only when a deadly typhoon threatens to destroy them all that she discovers just who her Johnny really is and what he represents for the future, both the plantation's and hers.

VOICES IN MY HEAD

Wouldn't it be fantastic if everyone could simply access social media directly with their minds? It's the year 2050, and sixteen-year-old Grace Malone is finally old enough for Voices, a tiny computer chip painlessly implanted directly into the brain to replace all those old-fashioned cellphones and computers. But when her head is suddenly inundated by a world full of political unrest and social justice warriors, Grace is having second thoughts. That's when she meets a boy named Max, a techie geek from the other side of the tracks who refuses to be chipped, and she begins to question all the social media groupthink, cancel culture, and internet bullying bouncing around her brain. Inevitably, when packs of marauding violent mobs take things too far, infiltrating the government and law enforcement, even threatening her family, Grace and Max are ultimately drawn into the battle between right, left, anarchists, police, and the military. But will they be able to stop a world gone mad with just an antique Android phone, a glitchy portable Nintendo game console, and the best of intentions? Oh, and did I mention the ballistic missile?

www.ingramcontent.com/pod-product-compliance
Lightning Source LLC
Chambersburg PA
CBHW071108250626
47159CB00002B/644